Books by Niki Livingston

Theia's Moons Series

Eyes Wide Shut

Enyo's Warrior

Protectors of the Stars

Guardian

The Chaos Awakened Saga

Marked Chaos

Expanded Chaos

Transformed Chaos

Novels

Be My Leprechaun

Novellas

Wrong Side of the Mirror

Novelettes

A Web Through Time

Wicked Heart

Wicked Soul

Jolly Old Monster

Unable to Wake

THEIA'S MOONS

Guardian

NIKI LIVINGSTON

Guardian

Copyright © 2018 Niki Livingston

Publisher: Unbound Wonders Press

Editor: Erin Sandlin

Cover art © Niki Ellis Designs

nikiellisdesigns.com

ISBN-13: 978-0-9976644-6-1

To connect: www.NikiLivingston.com

This book is dedicated to my childhood. Long, summer nights, lying on the trampoline or camping on the edges of darkness (thank you, Dad), staring up into the stars and wishing I was up there.

"Sometimes you don't realize your
own strength until you come face to face
with your greatest weakness."

-Susan Gale

ONE
The Pale Elven

"*I DON'T WANT to see her*," Esta shrieked at Mataya. Her fingers clung protectively to her blanket as she hovered in the corner on the bed. Pressing her back firmly against the stone wall, she averted her eyes from Malkia, sniffing in response.

Mataya glanced over at Malkia, her weary eyes filled with grief, and shook her head. Stepping away from Esta's doorway, Malkia sagged against the wall behind her, dejection shattering her heart.

"Esta?" she heard Mataya speak to her daughter. "Look at me, please."

"*He just left me*," Esta sobbed. Malkia could hear the despair in her voice and it tore her insides into shreds, knowing her daughter was aching to be back with her papa. "He didn't say a word to me." The young girl hiccupped and Malkia slid to the floor, covering her face with her hands, listening to her daughter's voice quiver. "Just shoved me out of that ship and left me standing there, all alone."

Her words were met with silence and Malkia peeked out from behind her fingers, worried Esta caught her eavesdropping in the hallway. But the doorway remained empty and Esta's muffled sobs swirled around her ears, invading her numb thoughts. A few moments passed and the creak of the bed was the only other sound she heard, before Esta spoke again.

"I don't even know her," she whispered. Her words sliced right through Malkia's heart. "I thought I would be happy to see her, but all I can think about are the awful things she has done to hurt my papa."

From her viewpoint, Malkia noticed Mataya shift on the bed and move closer to Esta and out of sight completely. "Your mother loves you, Esta," her sister replied, her own voice shaking. "Everything she's done, has been to find you and bring you home."

"I was already home," Esta snapped. "My papa was my whole world."

Malkia's body stiffened from her daughter's harsh words and she pressed herself off the ground, creeping away from the room. The anguish was spreading and she was terrified by the pain writhing in her gut. Her daughter despised her. *My father has won*, she thought. Heat stained her cheek as she raced down the stairs of the cottage, yanking open the door and sprinting across the vegetation, ignoring the pounding of her pulse inside her skull. If she ran, she might be able to clear away the madness suffocating her.

Damon was down the trail, speaking to one of the Fallen Angels. A scowl melted down his face as he lifted his eyes and locked onto her own. Shaking her head, she twisted away and pushed the soles of her feet hard against the terrain, focusing on placing one foot in front of the other and moving away from her chaotic life.

"Malkia," Damon yelled behind her. "Something has happened. *Stop*."

She ignored his demands, sprinting faster, racing into the safety of the trees and away from the Fallen Angel city. Just as she thought she was in the clear, a hand clutched her shoulder and pulled her to dead stop. Panting, she whirled around, balling her hands up in fists to punch them in face.

Damon stood a few feet away, holding his hands up in defeat. "Why didn't you stop?" A line etched in between his brows, as he took a few deep breaths.

"I have my reasons. Why did you insist on following me?" she snapped, her expression hardened as the tension pulsated in the air between them.

"Malkia," he replied, stepping toward her. "It's only been three days since our battle with your father. Give the child some time to sort out this mess in her head."

She clenched her jaw, tears swimming in her eyes as she glared at him. "She hates me. My daughter thinks the worst of me and all because of my father's lies," she screamed the last few words. A deep ache twisted inside her gut and instinctively she covered her hands over her abdomen, afraid Damon would realize her faintness. "He has poisoned her mind against me. *Time won't take that away.*"

He nodded, taking another step closer. "What has happened by your father's hands is unforgivable. I understand, all too well—."

"How would you ever understand?" Her words tasted like acid on her lips, but they tumbled out before she had the chance to think of their impact.

Sorrow clouded his features as the color drained from his cheeks. "I had three children. Remember?" he whispered the question and she hung her head in regret.

"I do remember." She nudged a rock with her foot, inwardly cursing herself for being so cruel. "I meant, what does that have to do with my father? He didn't take their lives."

Damon groaned. "But he did," he muttered, flashing her a frosty glare. "Are you that naïve, Malkia?"

"What?" she questioned, her eyes boring into him. "Your children were murdered three years before we met."

"Who do you think sent Dario and the mutts to Esaki?" he snapped, throwing his hands up in the air. "Seriously, Malkia. Do you still think this is just about you? Everything that happened to bring us together, was orchestrated by your father." He paused, watching the terror melt down her face. "Yes, your father gave the orders to have my children slaughtered."

Her breath came in short. Sinking to her knees, the realization washed over her like ice cold water. "No, he wouldn't," she cried, grasping onto a fist full of dirt and squeezing it.

"This wasn't the point of stopping you," Damon spoke loudly, interrupting her fit of rage. "The Angels have found a body just outside the boundaries of their city. They believe it's a message from your father and the Elven leader."

Malkia closed her eyes and inhaled sharply, before refocusing on Damon's dark eyes. Rising and straightening her posture, she swallowed the grief and guilt. "Lead the way," she muttered, waving her hand for Damon to show her where to go.

He shook his head and swiveled around, stomping away from her. Taking one more deep breath, she wiped away the tears in her eyes and stepped forward, following after the man she loved and the father of her unborn child. Running her hands over her core, she sensed the energy bubbling within. She should feel elated by the tiny human growing inside her, but instead her blood ran cold, petrified by the thought of protecting him from her father.

Jogging to catch up to Damon, she entwined her fingers with his and leaned against his arm. He squeezed her hand, giving her a fraction of reassurance.

Malkia noticed Ti before Damon spoke. His head had fallen toward his right shoulder, sweeping his white hair over a large portion of his face. A gasp swept across her lips and she quickly shielded her mouth with her hands.

A sword had been plowed through his torso and into the tree trunk behind him. His decaying and animal-bitten feet dangled about a foot off the ground, with a pool of blood underneath him. A milky film clouded his pale rose irises, and the skin on his face clung to the bones. He had been there for at least a day, if not more. Wild animals had begun to feast on his lower legs and feet, leaving the rotting remains of which hung in tatters from his bones.

Chantum stood near Ti's body, peering up at his face. Taking a few more steps, Malkia stopped beside him. "Is there a message from my father or was this done by the hands of others?"

The dark godlike angel twisted to see her and nodded his head. "I believe it's your father's doing. We did find a note, clutched within this elven's fist. It's possible he died to ensure its concealment."

"What does it say?" she asked, holding her arm over her nose, blocking the stench that was permeating the air around the corpse.

He opened his hand, revealing the small, crumbled piece of parchment. She grasped it, unraveling it frantically and nearly dropped it when she read the words.

He knows there's another child.

"What does it mean?" Her voice shook as she took a few steps back and fell into Damon's arms. She handed him the note.

Chantum's eyes bored into her, and she already knew his answer. "The child in your womb. Your father is already aware of his existence and will stop at nothing until he possesses him." The angel slid past her and Damon, eyeing her with freezing disdain.

"He knows, Damon," she whispered, fear paralyzing her against his chest. "I don't know how to stop him. He's always one step ahead of us."

Damon gripped her shoulders and turned her to face him. "We'll find a way. But first, we must abandon this quest here on Thalia."

She sighed. "You can't ask that of me." She backed away, shaking her head. "I'm supposed to end this war and we both know I *cannot* stop until it's done."

He closed his eyes as he clenched his fists. "He's my child, as well," he growled, breathing several deep breaths before opening his eyes and glaring at her.

She swallowed hard, nodding her head in agreement. "Taking the fight to my father is the only way," she pleaded, biting down on her lip and surveying their surroundings. "If we stop now, he'll have too much time to recoup and bring more fire to the battle. Please allow me to be the leader I was asked to be, and finish this war once and for all."

Damon threw his arms in the air, huffing out in defeat. "You know I couldn't stop you, even if I tried."

She twisted to look back at Ti, remembering him from Enyo as one of Errandor's servants. "Why do you think he was here, and why would he sacrifice himself to warn me?"

"We could use the ship to speak with Errandor," he replied, pulling her away as the Angels cocooned Ti's body within a sparkling sheet of silk.

6

They watched the Angels use their powers to wrap the Elven tightly and float him above the ground, as they all followed behind. Malkia grasped unto Chantum's arm. "Where are you taking him?"

"We have to know his last thoughts," the angel replied, shaking off her grip. "You may join us in our laboratory and see for yourself."

She glanced back at Damon, clutching onto his hand and dragging him with her as she followed Chantum and the other angels. There was no way she'd miss this opportunity.

TWO
Last Thoughts

THEY PRESSED FORWARD silently. When Chantum discovered the number of Angels slaughtered in the fight with her father, his fury had echoed against the broken walls of their city. She understood his anger, and just like him, she blamed herself for the massacre.

Her own rage had subsided when she retrieved Esta, but even though her only desire was to flee, she knew the battle was far from over. The Aletheians had placed all their faith in her and now the Fallen Angels, along with the rest of the civilizations of Theia were depending on her to end his dominance.

"When we finish with this, let's return to the ship and reach out to Errandor," she said to Damon, squeezing his hand as they walked a few steps behind the others. "Or Tarance. One of them has more answers then they have been willing to disclose."

The Fallen Angel's laboratory was situated in one of the buildings far from where the bulk of the fighting took place. Malkia had the feeling they had intentionally kept this area protected and concealed. It was filled with machines and pods she had never seen before, along with a massive white screen on the far end of the room.

They slipped Ti's body within a pod and closed a half-moon, glass lid over the top of him. Within seconds a light flickered on the white screen, grabbing Malkia's attention. Then he was there. Her father. He was speaking to a tall elven, but what they were saying was difficult to hear.

"But she was always under my control to her very last breath," were the only words she could understand.

Ti stepped away and her father's face disappeared behind the branches of the trees. He was rushing through the vegetation for quite some time, when he ran into a clearing and standing in front of him was her father, with a dozen Elvens. A small ship was behind them, with the gangway facing toward Ti. He gasped and stepped back, but was quickly seized by two other Elvens.

Malkia watched in horror as they forced him down to his knees and whipped him several times. He screamed in pain, but remained as still as possible.

Her father stepped up to Ti. "What did you hear and who sent you?"

Ti shook his head and remained quiet, even after Thane struck him with his fist several times. His memories blurred and when he focused again, he was lying on the cold floor inside the Elven ship. Thane stood over him, ordering them to deliver Ti to the Angels as a message to her.

Malkia groaned. Her father was a tyrant. Ti waited until they all turned their backs to him and then pressed himself against the wall of the ship, slipping a piece of parchment from his pocket. Just when he was going to start writing, he lifted his eyes and focused in on a child sitting quietly on one of the seats. His dark hair and amber irises stood out from the Elvens, and Damon suddenly gripped Malkia's shoulder.

"Wait, stop," he yelled, holding his hand out toward the screen. "Go back."

Ti's eyes had already returned to the parchment, but he quickly glanced back up as if the child was now of an interest to him. The small boy, maybe seven or eight, was watching Ti with tears in his eyes. He was terrified.

"That's my boy," Damon cried, rushing forward and moving as close to the screen as he could. "That's Landon, my son!"

"Wait, what?" Malkia said, curling her fingers around Damon's elbow. "I thought all your children were executed."

Damon whirled around to stare at her, his eyes twitching as if he hadn't heard her. "I never found Landon's body. Genevieve told me the sky people abducted him, after they knocked her out. But Oridian told me she saw them discard pieces of his body over the land." He shook his head, pushing the heels of his hands into his eyes. "This isn't possible. *Three years*," he screamed, throwing his hands in the air. "Your father has had my boy for three years!"

Without another word, Damon plowed past her and through the group of Angels, slamming the door as he left. Malkia stood petrified, shock spreading numbly through her body.

"Can we finish watching his final thoughts?" Chantum asked, interrupting her murderous ploys against her father.

She focused back on the group and nodded her head as she turned back to face the screen. Ti examined the boy for a few seconds, then scribbled on the parchment. *He knows there's another child.*

Now, Malkia was confused. She looked over at Chantum. "Do you think he means my unborn child or Landon?"

"Your unborn child seems to be the clue," Chantum replied, not taking his eyes off the screen. "I wouldn't lower your guard, but it's possible it could mean something about Damon's child."

Malkia's throat constricted and she had difficulty swallowing as her palms covered her chest. Her heart was galloping inside her chest and no amount of deep breaths were easing the panic clawing through her nervous system. Turning back to the screen, Ti was being forced off the vessel and gagged. The next few moments, Malkia glanced away several times, not eager to witness the slaughter of the innocent hybrid.

After witnessing his brutal execution, she left the room and walked absentmindedly toward their ship. Their mission had just been thrown in an entirely different direction. They now knew Landon was alive and was possibly being used by her father. This meant they had to rescue him before her father left Thalia or any battles between their people ensued.

As she stepped onto the bridge of the vessel, she could see Errandor and Tarance on the screen speaking to Damon. A crimson tint was covering his face and neck, with the tendons in his necks protruding as he clenched his jaw.

"Damon we didn't know anything about your child," Tarance was saying. His complexion had paled and Errandor's face had a green hue crawling up it and tears streaming down his cheeks.

"Ti knew something," Damon snapped, ramming his fist into the console next to him. "Someone has to know why Thane abducted my child and kept him secret from all of us, for so long. It doesn't make sense."

Tarance sighed, catching sight of Malkia as she slid next to Damon. "We are devastated to hear that Ti was executed. He was one of our most resourceful comrades. Being half elven, he had the ability to go undercover for us inside their cities." He curled his arm around Errandor as she did the same to Damon. "Your friend, Ustarum, arrived yesterday and has been berating us for hours and now this. We need a moment to mourn our friend."

"Why did you send Ti to spy on my father?" Malkia asked, ignoring Tarance's request.

"We already divulged our reasons to Damon," Errandor muttered, hanging his head in defeat. "After I discovered your treachery, I knew I had to intervene in any way that I could. Unfortunately, Ti didn't arrive until after your battle with your father and so gathering information was difficult. The last correspondence we had with him, your father had just returned to the Elven city, Xenor, and he believed he would have the chance to eavesdrop on a few of the conversations."

"He was obviously not as well hidden as he believed," Tarance interrupted, throwing them a pointed stare. "I'll let Ustarum know he is able to contact you on this frequency. When we have had enough time alone, we will reach out to you." He tugged Errandor away. "Farewell, my friends."

The connection ended and Damon twisted around to stare at Malkia. "I'm at my wits end," he cried, rubbing his hands over his face. "Why did Oridian tell me that Landon was murdered?"

"Did you know her prior to his abduction?" Malkia asked, sinking into a nearby seat and leaning her elbow against one of the armrests.

Damon shook his head as his eyes closed. "She found me while I was searching for Landon and told me that she already knew who I was." A growl rumbled up his throat. "How could I be so senseless? She was playing me from the beginning."

"Take a deep breath," Malkia coaxed, leaning forward in her chair and rubbing her tired eyes with her fists. "We don't know who she was or what her motives were. Give Ustarum a moment to—."

"Give me a moment to what?" Ustarum asked, his voice boomed

through the speaker, followed by his face popping up on the screen.

Malkia bounded up from her seat and stepped forward, gripping Damon's elbow. "It's good to see you again, Ustarum." She shot him a wary smile, nodding at Damon. "We've had more than one problem since we last saw you, but our most immediate one is that my father is holding Damon's son as a prisoner."

Ustarum pressed his lips together, slightly nodding his head as he glanced back and forth between the two of them. "Where's Mataya?" he asked, running his hand over his beard.

"Back at our cottage with my daughter," she replied, bouncing lightly on her toes. "Why do you ask?"

"I have so much to talk to all of you about. No, I didn't know about Damon's son being with your father, but I do believe if they're still on Thalia, you need to strike soon." He paused, stepping backward and clasping a thick robe hanging on a hook behind him. "I need to speak with Mataya, but I also have a plan to meet up with all of you. I hear the Nesoi have made contact."

Malkia and Damon glanced at one another and then back at Ustarum. "How did you know about that?" Damon questioned, yanking his arm away from Malkia and moving toward the screen.

"Mataya and I have a connection." Ustarum shook his head and waved his hand. "I'll tell you everything when we meet up. But first, make your move against Thane soon. If he has your son, you must retrieve the child before he escapes Thalia. You'll also need to finish gathering all the information from the rest of the pyramids, so I'll plan on meeting you on Thallassa. The Nesoi and Mataya have the ability to create the wormhole without the extra worry and risk that you experienced when traveling to Eris. Ask her about it. She'll know the answer." He flung the dark robe around his shoulders and flipped the hood over his head, giving them one last glance. "Contact me again, once you have finished these two tasks. As soon as I'm able, I will depart Enyo." Without another word, he left their line of sight, leaving them staring at his empty room.

Damon pressed on the screen to end the connection, exhaling with a huff. "That man is a lunatic."

"No, he's not," Malkia snapped, her eyes narrowing. "He's wanting to help. I'm going to find Mataya. If Ustarum says we need to go after my father today, then that is exactly what we'll do." She pivoted on her heel and stomped off the bridge, leaving Damon to chew on her words.

THREE

Her Inner Anguish

HER FRUSTRATION FROM the entire beginning of her day was sliding through every cell of her body and the tightness of her muscles was causing her head to pound. Leaving the ship, she sprinted toward her house, eager to discuss what she had learned with her family and friends.

As she turned onto the pathway to the front door, she came to an abrupt halt, seeing Esta sitting on the steps, wrapped in a blanket and sobbing. "Esta!" Malkia exclaimed, racing toward her daughter and drawing her close. Her arms encircled the child's trembling body. "Why are you crying?"

Esta didn't resist but wept harder into the crook of Malkia's neck. "Something's wrong," she stuttered through the tears. "Papa said he would always take care of me, but he also promised to never abandon me. Was everything he told me a lie?"

Malkia felt the heat of anger and sorrow staining her cheeks as she hoisted Esta up into her arms and held her tight against her chest. Stepping into their home, she settled onto the nearest couch, setting her daughter on her lap.

"I don't know," she finally replied, whispering in Esta's ear. "He's my father and he abandoned me, too."

Esta's sobs quieted as if she was contemplating her mother's words. Giving her daughter the silence she needed, Malkia inhaled deeply, tightening her hold on her child and waiting for her to work through the confusion within her mind.

After several long minutes, Esta sighed and wiggled off her mother's lap. Holding her breath, Malkia waited for her daughter to stomp off again, leaving her with another shattered heart. Instead, Esta settled in next to her and leaned her head against Malkia's shoulder.

"I never thought of it that way," Esta whispered, entwining her fingers together and biting on the edges of her thumbs. "He told me that Mamu was the reason you were taken away at such a young age and her friends poisoned your mind against him."

A trembling breath passed over Malkia's lips and she twisted to see Esta's young, obsidian irises. "That's exactly what he was doing to you. Poisoning your mind against me." A tear slid down Malkia's cheek and she quickly brushed it away. "He stole you from me, then cut me off from ever discovering that you lived and proceeded to raise you with a mindset that I was the enemy. Your Mamu was not a monster, and neither am I. If I had known you'd survived the blast on our home, I would have moved heaven and Theia to find you."

Esta nibbled on her bottom lip, her eyes straying to her hands. "He was so wonderful to me," she muttered, her chin trembling as fresh tears tumbled from her eyelids. "But he wouldn't allow me to have much contact with Mamu and he warned me about the day we would finally make contact with you. If you chose to disobey him, then it meant you despised me and had freely given up your rights to be my mother." She exhaled a long breath. "And I believed him," she whispered the last few words. "You crushed my heart that day."

Malkia's arms wrapped around Esta, squeezing her tight. "I know I did." She paused, swallowing the knot that was rising up her throat. "And I'm so sorry for the pain you had to endure. Is there any way for you and me to start over?"

She felt Esta's hands press against her. Easing up on her grip and leaning back, her face fell when she saw the anger behind her child's eyes. But then Esta blinked and as a fountain of tears escaped down her cheeks, the anger within her eyes vanishing.

"I'm scared," Esta murmured and gulped down another sob. "I don't know you. He left me in the hands of strangers." Malkia froze against the cushion, watching her daughter stare down at her lap, trembling with grief. "But I want to know you. I want all this sadness in my heart to go away."

Malkia nodded, pressing her lips together and giving Esta the space to think this through. In the corner of her eye, she noticed Damon walking along the pathway, toward the front door and she closed her eyes, hoping he would be considerate of their privacy. If only he could read her mind.

Mom? Malkia heard Esta speak inside her mind. Her eyes flew over to her daughter's face, her heart nearly stopping.

"You have telepathy?" Malkia questioned. Her hand gripped the pillow beside her.

Esta nodded. "Papa warned me to block you, so you wouldn't have the ability to manipulate my mind." Clearing her throat, the young child rose from her seat and turned away from Malkia, just as Damon stepped into the house, slamming the door behind him. Esta jumped and twisted back around, the color draining from her face.

Malkia glanced over at the front entry way and watched Damon's receding back as he climbed the stairs on the other side, never looking their way. Turning back around, she jumped up from her seat and lightly touched Esta's elbow. "You look like you've seen a ghost. Are you okay?" she asked, her brow furrowed with concern.

Taking in a deep breath, the color in Esta's cheeks returned and she peered up at her mother. "The door just scared me." She turned away and walked over to the stone fireplace, settling down on the rock bench in front of it. "I was afraid to tell you that I had telepathy. I've been petrified since the moment Papa forced my Mamu into her locked prison and wouldn't explain to me why I couldn't speak to her. I'm frightened and hateful, and I don't understand why all of this is happening." Her gaze met Malkia's. "I want to blame it all on you, but my heart is telling me that this is Papa's fault."

"What would you like me to do?" Malkia asked, kneeling a few feet away from Esta.

Esta drew in a raspy breath, as she squeezed her eyes shut. "I don't know," her voice trembled, and she opened her eyes, focusing on the window behind her. "I want to scream. I want to tell Papa how much he hurt me. I want to yell at you. I want my Mamu to hold me."

Malkia nodded, listening to her daughter and fighting the urge to gather her up in her arms again. The child fell silent, her gaze still glued on the outside world.

"Can I be alone?" Esta asked, finally looking at Malkia again.

"Of course." Malkia rose off the ground and leaned over, kissing her child on the forehead. "I'll be in my room, if you would like to talk more."

Walking out of the open room and up the stairs, Malkia dreaded facing Damon, but knew they had to come to a decision soon. Easing open their bedroom door, her eyes fell on him. His body was stretched across the bed with his eyes closed. Shutting the door, she moved toward him, settling down on the bed beside him.

"I know you want answers," she began, giving him a sideways glance, "but if we wait too long, my father could possibly disappear again, if he hasn't already. We must go retrieve Landon and kill my father, before it's too late."

"What about Esta?" he asked, not budging from his position.

"What about her?" She twisted all the way around, sitting with her legs crossed in front of her.

"Where will she hide, while we're off battling your father?" He peeked out under his eyelashes and then closed his eyes again.

"She will stay with the children of the Angels, inside the caves." Malkia's jaw tightened and her temples throbbed with fury. "Why are you asking?"

He sat up suddenly, jumping up from the bed, his face turning scarlet. "*You have your daughter.* Maybe if we hadn't been in such a hurry, we could have saved Landon as well."

"Stop it," Malkia muttered, biting back the bitter words she wanted to toss at him. "We didn't even know Landon was alive, let alone that my father had him. Don't you dare bring Esta into this. She has been through enough already." She clenched her fists, drawing in a deep breath. "And why are you really so angry with me?"

Damon slammed his fist into the wall behind him, splintering the wood behind it and leaving a gaping hole in its place. "*I'm more than angry*," he shouted, the muscles in his jaw twitching and perspiration glistening on his brow. "For three years I believed he was dead. And now I'm faced with my past—" He waved his hand to the window.

"And my future." He pointed at her, gritting his teeth as he wiped the back of his arm across his forehead. "I have to protect you and your daughter, but I must retrieve Landon."

A soft knock startled them both and they stared at the door as if a monstrous demon was going to barge in. Malkia shook her head and tugged the door open. Esta stood on the other side, but she backed up a step as her gaze fell on Damon.

"I know Landon," she whispered, dread washed across her face as she hugged her chest.

Malkia stooped down and felt the heat of Damon's presence right behind her. "Tell us more," she coaxed the child, blocking Damon from drawing closer.

"He was my only friend," Esta replied, her eyes darting between the two adults. "Papa told me that we had a connection to one another and that he needed us both to clear away all the bad people."

Malkia closed her eyes. It all made sense now. Her eyes flew open, when Esta's fingers grazed across her cheek. "Esta, did he ever ask you and Landon to perform any strange ritual or force you into any sort of seclusion with one another?"

"No," Esta replied, shaking her head as her fingers played with a strand of her mother's hair. "But he talked about a moment where Landon and I would have to be united together. Whatever that means." Her weary eyes met Malkia's, confusion and questions dancing in her inky irises.

Damon's hand pressed on Malkia's shoulder, and she glanced up to meet his gaze. "You're right," he said, gritting his teeth. "There's no time to waste. I'll ask the Angels to have their forces pulled together if you'll gather our people."

She nodded, watching him trot down the hallway and out of sight. "Esta, my love, I'll need you to stay with the other children in the safety of the mountain walls, until I return. Can you do that for me?" A tired smile spread on her closed lips, eyeing Esta with caution.

The young girl nodded. Malkia rose, gripping her daughter's hand just as Mataya waltzed around the corner.

"I've been searching for you," she said, her eyes darting between Esta and Malkia. "I ran into Damon, and he muttered something about his son and that we are preparing for another battle with your father." She bounced up and down on her tiptoes.

Malkia tugged Esta in front of her, giving Mataya a pointed look. "Damon's youngest son lives and is my father's prisoner. I'm leaving Esta with the other children in the mountain passage, while I deal with this problem."

"I'd be happy to take her." Mataya reached out her hand to Esta, smiling sweetly at the child. "Let's go seek safe refuge and we can chat more about your Mamu."

Esta's head tilted upward, her eyes meeting Malkia's. Nodding her head with a smile, the child stepped toward Mataya and the two of them departed the house moments later.

An ache tugged at Malkia's heart, and she fought the urge to race after Esta. Instead, she twisted around, gathered her scabbards, along with her bow and arrows. Within the hour she had her group gathered and waiting in the center of town, with the four dragons. The Nesoi had receded into the mountain terrain, only emerging once in the past week. Their eagerness to be of assistance seemed to be placed on hold for the time being, and Malkia wasn't counting on their help.

Her gaze fell on Damon's distraught expression as him and the

Fallen Angels approached. Apollo stepped up beside her, his massive hand resting on her shoulder.

"I believe this decision is a wise one," he said, glancing down at her and then back at the group of angels moving toward them. "A choice like this will be met with resistance and possibly resentment, but you've been tasked to end your father and the Elven's ploy to find the Creators. You must stand your ground and give them a leader they know won't abandon the cause."

Malkia nodded, examining the blackened and crumbling buildings surrounding them and swallowed the ball of sorrow that was rising in her throat. The memories were burned into her mind. Misty, Palma, and Skye, along with Adelina had all perished in this place. Her heart would forever be broken from that battle.

Chantum was ahead of the group and reached her first. "Malkia, if we're to rush back into this fight, we must have one day to prepare." His crystal blue eyes sparkled from the suns rays, and she softly smiled at the memory of the first time she saw this dark Angel. So many lives had been lost since that moment.

"We don't have a day," she replied, tilting to the side to see Damon halt behind the Angel. "The attack needs to take place before the end of this day."

Chantum's jaw clenched, and his eyes swept across the group behind her. "How do you expect to win? We've lost nearly half of our warriors and your group has dwindled as well. Without the Nesoi, we will be setting ourselves up for another failure."

"You're right," Damon spoke up, sliding up beside Apollo and eyeing Chantum. "We can't go up against the Elvens again without a proper plan. This time, we need to take them by surprise, instead of the other way around."

"And what do you propose?" Chantum asked, his arms folding across his chest.

A smirk spread across Damon's face. "I have an idea, but some of you won't like it."

FOUR
Rescuing Landon

"I'M RISKING MY people, for *your* cause," Chantum barked at Damon, his piercing eyes falling on Malkia. "You want me to send in my best warriors, again, while your people stay out of harm's way. How is that even fair?"

"Wait," Malkia spoke up for the first time since Damon had revealed his plan. Holding up her hand and stepping up to the angel, her eyes narrowed, shooting him a look of disgust. "We sacrificed so many of our own people to wage a war you claimed you were prepared to fight. How is this not fair? You already know these warriors are indestructible, so why don't we use that advantage?"

"Because if they're able to capture one of my newly Fallen Angels, they would be able to draw out their powers and use them against us. How do you think the Elvens created the magic behind Misty's abilities?" His hands had balled up into fists and the burning fury from his expression, seared Malkia.

Her hands flew to her chest, resting over her heart. "What?" she whispered, her breath catching in her throat, staring wide-eyed at Chantum. "That's how they created the darkness within her soul?"

"Yes." Chantum sagged into the chair behind him and rested his face in his hands. "I didn't want to tell you, but you've given me no choice."

"What about when we sent them into the fight to defend your city?" her voice rose an octave, fear sliding over every inch of her body.

He inhaled deeply and peered up at Malkia's frightened eyes. "Your father didn't know there were more, but now he does. We used that advantage and now they cannot be used in battle, until they have completed their fall. If he has the chance to take another one captive and use their essence, we'll not only lose another one of our own, but he'll have the ability to create another demon."

She nodded slowly, twisting to see Damon and biting on her bottom lip. "We should stop talking about this. I was mistaken." Her chin quivered with her exhausted exhale. "We need to ambush the Elvens. Damon, you and I will go in, with a few hand-picked warriors and find Landon, before my father disappears again."

"That's out of the question," Chantum shouted, bounding up from his seat and forcing the humans and Apollo to cover their ears from his authoritative voice. "You're with child and from what I'm understanding, a powerful one at that. You would be a fool to put yourself in harm's way, especially now that your daughter has returned."

"I'm doing this," she snapped, glaring at the angel and grasping Damon's hand. "With or without your help, we will advance on the Elven city tonight."

Chantum growled, turning to face Damon. "Is she always this stubborn?"

"Yes," Damon whispered, tugging her into his arms. "Yes, she is."

"Fine," Chantum barked. "I'll go as well, along with ten of our finest, completely fallen warriors. But it must be a stealth mission. We go in, fetch the child, and then we leave. No other tasks or distractions, even if you see your father and believe you can slaughter him without recourse. Do we have a deal?"

"Yes, we do," Malkia replied. She clutched Chantum's wrist in a united agreement.

Malkia's legs were shaking as they neared the Elven city that sheltered her father. The dragons had stayed behind, much to Tantiana's disappointment, but she couldn't take the chance that they would be seen. Apollo was positioned a few yards to her right and Damon stood poised for battle, just a few feet to her left. They both held the laser weapons of the Artemisians, while she clasped tightly onto her bow.

She could see Chantum and his warriors spread out around them, crouching in watch as the final sun made its descent on the horizon. They had sent a spy to find out where her father was staying, hoping that he would keep Landon close. The spy had returned with both their whereabouts. The road outside the home crawled with guards, but the field in the back only had three posted near the backdoor. It was their best shot.

Resting her free hand on her abdomen, she could feel the power growing within her, but it wasn't for her any more. The nausea had risen quickly over the past few days and her light had failed to appear on several occasions since the battle in the city of the Angels. *Please allow me to keep myself and these warriors safe,* she whispered silently, hoping the tiny fetus wouldn't continue to steal all her abilities.

The sound of a bird whistle filled the air and her focus returned to the men and women around her. Chantum waved for them to move in. Following behind Apollo, she flew just above the brush, careful to keep her feet off the ground.

Moments later, they were slipping into the large home and moving in their pre-coordinated directions. Malkia stayed with Damon and Thora, just like they had requested. They were to search the upper west wings. The trio tiptoed quietly up the marbled stairs and she paused when she saw the painting of the Blue Planet hanging in the hallway at the top. Damon nudged her along, bringing her focus back to the mission.

One by one, they searched each room, coming up empty handed. Damon's expression was hard to read, but he kept going and ignored Malkia's concerned looks. Just as they were finishing up the last room in their area, a young voice caught their attention.

"Papa, why do we have to leave again?" the voice asked.

"I told you to stay quiet," her father's voice snapped.

Malkia raced across the hall, flinging open the door and coming face to face with Thane. Her father jumped from the intrusion, but collected himself quickly, grasping Landon's shoulder and forcing the boy in between him and her group.

"I will execute my guards," he hissed, eyeing her with freezing disdain.

Damon stepped around Malkia and pointed his weapon at Thane's forehead. "Release my boy now or I'll blow your head off your body."

"You wouldn't dare put your own child at risk. What if you miss and hit him instead?" Her father's eyes darkened as a devilish grin twitched on his lips.

"You're a monster," Malkia cried, taking another step toward the duo.

"Papa," Landon's voice shook as his gaze darted between Malkia and Damon. "Why are you doing this?"

"Don't worry," Thane leaned down and whispered in the boy's ear. "They won't hurt either one of us, as long as you stay strong and protect us both."

"I'll always protect you, Papa," Landon assured him, staring hard at Damon. "But why did you say this man wouldn't hurt his own child?"

"Because I'm your father," Damon replied, not allowing Thane to speak as he took another step forward. "This man is not your papa. He kidnapped you three years ago. Don't you remember me?" He lowered his weapon and kneeled so he was eye level with his son. "My little man, please remember me."

Landon's eyes widened, but then narrowed quickly. "My father died. Papa told me so and he's never lied to me."

"He's not your papa," Damon reached out to Landon as Thane tugged him back to the far wall.

"I hate to make this visit so short." Thane chuckled, his grasp tightening around Landon's bicep as he placed his hand on a scanner on the wall. A door slid open, revealing an escape pod on the other end.

"*No*," Damon screamed, jumping up from the ground.

"Don't worry, I no longer need your imbecile child." Thane threw a smirk toward Malkia and shoved Landon at them, stepping back into the pod and shooting off before they had a chance to react.

Landon stood petrified in his spot, staring at the hole that once held his Papa. Malkia looked over at Damon, who was glued to his position as well, his focus remaining on his long lost son.

"Go to him," she coaxed, touching his forearm. "It won't be long until the Elvens show up to find out what happened."

Damon didn't hesitate. He swooped his child up into his arms and barged out of the room, followed by Thora and Malkia. Just as they reached the marbled steps, she sensed a presence behind her, but before she could turn, a hand muffled her screams, yanking her away from the others. The end of a sharp blade was pressed against the small of her back, ending her resistance as she was dragged inside a dark bedroom.

"Did you really think it would be that easy?" Ginny's voice whispered in her ear.

Malkia gasped, her pulse beating ferociously in her ears. "*You were dead*," she stuttered, remaining as still as possible, her protective light failing to emerge.

"I thought your mother told you what powers I possess." A laugh echoed against the walls and Malkia cringed from her own stupidity. "I made you believe you killed Kelsey and me, but we left Enyo shortly after you. And now, here we are again, like old friends."

"What do you want?" Malkia hissed between clenched teeth. She frantically searched her mind for any bubble of her powers, but came up empty. Her child was taking every fraction of her abilities.

Ginny shoved her to the ground, chuckling when Malkia's forehead struck the ground. "What do *I* want, you ask? Silly girl." The older woman shot her a wicked grin as a groan spilled from Malkia's mouth. "I want you dead. And more importantly, I want that child within your womb, destroyed."

Malkia's eyes widened and she scooted away from the insane

woman, stumbling to rise from the ground. But Ginny grasped her hair, yanking her backward, before she had a chance to right herself.

"It's over," Ginny growled, bringing her dagger down and driving it inside Malkia's stomach.

A scream tore from Malkia's lips as she fell back to the floor and grasped her bleeding stomach, just as Ginny stabbed her again, right below her hands, followed with another and another. Tears sprang from her eyes, as her trembling and bloody hands shoved Ginny away. Using the last bit of energy in her body, she pulled back her leg and kicked the woman in the nose.

Ginny stumbled back and laughed, smearing the blood from her nose with the back of her hand. "Good riddance. This home will be your tomb." She reached over Malkia's bloody hands and yanked her pendant from its clasp. "And you won't be needing this anymore." Whirling around, she stepped out of the room, shutting the door tight behind her.

Malkia peered down at her stomach, watching the red blood oozing from her wounds as the copper stench filled her nostrils. "*Damon*," she cried out, using elbows to crawl toward the door. But then another smell swept across her nose. Smoke.

"*Please, no,*" she screamed. "*Thora. Damon. Please help me.*"

She pulled herself to the door, reaching up to the door handle, but fell back against the plush carpet. Her hands pushed on the floor, but the blackness seeped into her sight, and she tumbled to the side again, striking the side of her head against a wooden chair and losing consciousness.

"*Malkia*," she heard Apollo's voice, but it was so far away.

"*Apollo, let's go*," Thora was screaming, and Malkia moaned from the agony pulsating in her head.

Her eyes fluttered open. She was bouncing up and down, while peering upward at the ceiling. Or was it downward at the floor? Then she saw Apollo's face. He was looking over her, and then his head whirled to the side as the bouncing halted.

"This way," Thora's voice again, but it was barely a whisper.

The blackness swallowed Malkia's mind, just as the bouncing started again.

FIVE

Return to Esaki

"THE CHILD SURVIVED," a melodic voice reverberated within a misty fog, pulling at Malkia's mind. "He's siphoning all his mother's powers, which is why she's struggling to return."

Prying open one of her eyes, Malkia focused on the pixie she had spoken with on Esaki. Her brilliant light was overwhelming, and Malkia quickly squeezed her eye shut and groaned, rolling onto her side, allowing the tug of sleep to yank her back in.

"She needs to rest," the pixie whispered from a far off place. "We've given her enough magic to heal her wounds completely, but it will take time for her energy to move it through her body."

"Can we leave Thalia?" Damon's voice swam through her thoughts, just as the blackness devoured her once again.

Her first instinct was to lie still, until she could figure out where she was, but her head was pounding and the whispering from her unknown visitors grated on her nerves. Groaning, Malkia reached up and rubbed her temples with the palms of her hands, peeking through her eyelashes at the darkened room. Two figures rose from nearby chairs. Seeing their blurred faces, her eyelids flew open the rest of the way.

"Ustarum," she moaned, supporting her weight on her elbows. "When did you arrive?"

"I hitched a ride back from Thallassa," Ustarum replied, sinking down on the bed next to her. "How are you feeling?"

"Like I've been turned inside out. Why am I in so much pain?" she asked, lying back on the cushion just as Alyssa sat on the foot of the bed.

"You're baby required more healing then even you could provide. Whoever left you for dead, was wanting your child slaughtered alongside you," he replied, placing his hand on her forehead. Instantly, relief washed over her as the ache pounding in her skull subsided.

She sighed and relaxed her shoulders against the cushion. "It was Ginny," she muttered, closing her eyes.

"We executed Ginny back on Enyo," Alyssa stammered.

Malkia opened her eyes, focusing on her Esaki mother. "It was one of her illusions. She and Kelsey survived." Her eyes darted to Ustarum. "And yes, she wanted my child dead. Is he really siphoning all my powers?"

"Yes," he responded, running his hand over his beard. "I'm surprised you had any powers the few weeks before Ginny's attack."

Looking at the door on the other side of the room, she eased herself into a sitting position, reaching for the pendant that was no longer around her neck. "I didn't." She patted her chest. "What little I had was gifted through the pendant. But my powers faltering only began a few days before the attack from Ginny. They came and went, but on that day, I couldn't evoke more than a fraction of my powers."

"Why didn't you warn us?" Alyssa questioned, her brow furrowing as she shook her head.

"It didn't seem necessary. I'm still an excellent fighter." She held out her hand for Ustarum to help her up and rose to face everything she had missed.

"Not excellent enough," Alyssa muttered under her breath.

"What have I missed?" Malkia asked, ignoring her mother's words as she held onto the back of a chair to steady her shaky legs. "Are we still on Thallassa? Were the others able to penetrate the pyramids magic and find the map?"

"No, we aren't on Thallassa, but yes the map from Thalia and Thallassa have been recovered." Ustarum wrapped a shawl around her shoulders and gave her a sideways hug. "The pixies told Damon that your body's healing could take weeks, which it did. You've been unconscious for nearly three weeks."

"In fact," Alyssa joined the conversation. "We will be landing on Esaki soon. Damon had just announced our imminent descent, right before you woke." Her eyes glazed over for a moment, staring off at the far wall, before focusing back on Malkia. "Home sweet home."

"Don't sound so disappointed," Malkia replied, shaking her head and walking toward the door. "We won't be here long anyway. Where's Esta and Damon?"

"Damon's on the bridge, and Esta could be anywhere." Ustarum strolled next to her as they made their way down the corridor. "She tends to keep to herself, but she loves Mataya and Landon. And Koleton has kept them giggling for the duration of the voyage."

"That's good to hear. Have Damon and Landon worked through their issues?" she asked, glancing over at Ustarum.

"Yes and no," Alyssa replied from behind them.

Malkia halted in her tracks and turned to face her mother. "What do you mean?"

"Landon is convinced that your father is his Papa and that Esta is his sister." For the first time since Malkia woke, she noticed the weariness in her mother's eyes.

"Mom, are you okay?" she asked, gripping Alyssa's forearm. "You look exhausted."

"She rarely left your side since your return from the Elven city," Ustarum explained, curling his arm around Alyssa's shoulders. "You've been her primary concern, and she gave all her powers and energy to heal you and your baby."

Malkia pushed Ustarum's arm away and folded her own arms around her mother's neck, embracing her tightly. "I'm so sorry, mom. Thank you for your love and strength."

"Don't make a fuss over me," Alyssa mumbled, hugging her back and then leaning away. "We have you back and now we have a mountain of decisions to make."

"Alright, let's go find the rest of the group," she replied, stepping back down the corridor toward the bridge.

A few minutes later, the door to the bridge slid open and she gazed in with a smile. Damon stood over to one side, speaking quietly with Justin and Apollo, while Koleton sat at the helm, his eyes closed and his head resting to the side.

"No sleeping on the job," she barked the command, grinning wide when Koleton jumped up in a frenzy and the other three whirled around to face her.

"Yeehaw!" Koleton yelled, hurtling toward her. Gripping her sides, he swung her up in the air. Seconds later, she was swallowed into his arms, laughing hysterically as she attempted to wiggle away.

"I wasn't gone that long," she muttered, her cheek pressed firmly against her friend's chest.

Koleton released her, only to have another set of arms tug her into an embrace. "Way too long," Damon whispered into her ear as she inhaled his musky scent. "You have no idea how much I've missed your smiling face and how worried I was about you and our child."

"I can imagine," she murmured. Rising on her tiptoes, she pressed her lips against his, ignoring the stares from the others.

"We have a lot to speak about," Ustarum spoke up, interrupting her moment with Damon.

Her heels connected with the floor as she pivoted to face her friends but stopped mid-turn when her eyes fell on Esta standing in the doorway. "Baby girl," she whispered, warmth filling her chest as she stepped toward her daughter. Without another word, she gathered Esta into her arms and hugged her tight. Her fingers ran through the child's long, blonde hair, and she planted a kiss on her cheek.

"Mama." Esta tightened her grip around her, and Malkia heard a long sigh sweep across the child's lips. "I missed you, so much."

Malkia's heart danced with joy and a single tear slid down her cheek. "I won't leave you, ever again. I promise."

"You can't promise that," Esta whispered and loosened her grip. "What if you have to leave me?"

"I'll do everything in my power, never to leave you again." Malkia's hand gripped Esta's chin, pulling her eyes over to hers. "That I can promise."

Rising from her knees, she turned to face the group, her fingers closed protectively around Esta's dainty hand. "What happened after you found me in my father's estate?"

"Let's strap in," Koleton interjected. "Then, you're free to chat about anything you desire."

Damon motioned for Malkia to follow him to a seat. She and Esta took the first two seats, strapping in for their descent to Esaki and everyone sank into their own, watching Koleton prepare the vessel.

"Apollo and Thora found you in a pool of your own blood, inside the library of your father's home," Damon explained, reaching over and grasping Malkia's hand. "I had already exited with Landon, when Thora announced you were no longer behind us."

"I came around the corner and heard their discussion," Apollo interrupted, his long fingers tapping on his armrest. "Damon had his hands full with his son, so Thora and I raced back inside and searched room after room, avoiding the fire that was spreading, until we found you. When we returned to the Angel's city, they did an examination and discovered that your baby was absorbing all your healing powers, and was thankfully alive and still thriving."

"But," Alyssa jumped in, "you were fading and without his mother, the child would perish. Asha, Bella, and I began every healing spell we could find, but when Mataya arrived from the caves, she dove right in with powers we didn't even know existed." Alyssa's hands curled around the armrest as she leaned against the restraints. "But what Esta brought to the mix, even shocked Mataya."

Malkia's brows furrowed and she twisted to stare at Esta. "What does she mean?"

Esta sank farther into her chair, giving Malkia the stink eye for the unwanted attention. "I don't know how it happened. When I saw you lying there, my body shook and words I don't understand poured from my own mouth. The pixies arrived from nowhere, and assisted in whatever incantations I was speaking." She paused, grumbling something under her breath, before continuing, "Alyssa understands it, not me." The child pouted, heat suffusing her cheeks as she averted her face.

Malkia squeezed Esta's hand, her eyes darting over the faces in the group and spotting the lands of Esaki through the window. The ship groaned from the pressure outside as they drew closer to the ground. "Maybe this part of the tale should be more private. What I really want to know is, how did you find the Thalia pyramids and penetrate the magic? It had to be the most protected, considering it was in the Elvens' realm."

"Same way we began your healing," Damon replied, rubbing his thumb over Malkia's hand. "Mataya did most of the work. Your daughter and the pixies were tending to you, so we were able to focus on the pyramids while you healed. It did take more time than the others, once we discovered where they were hidden, but your sister was the key to breaking in." He paused, his eyes resting on the nearing fortress of Domesca and he smiled. "They're rebuilding." He pointed at the window and everyone turned to see.

"This is the best sight I've seen, since I saw Esta's face again," Malkia exclaimed, a smile stretching across her face. She leaned over and kissed her daughter's head. "I'm sorry for embarrassing you. Let's talk about this later, just you and me, and probably Mataya."

"And Alyssa," Esta whispered, sitting up straight to see the approaching landscape. "Can I call her Mamu?"

"I think she would love that," Malkia replied, winking at her.

"This is where I was born?" Esta asked, her eyes glued to the outside world.

Malkia nodded as she ran her hand over Esta's hair. "Yes, this is home. Your father is buried here, along with your Papa."

"It seems strange," the young girl muttered, nibbling on her bottom lip.

"What seems strange?" Malkia's hand paused in mid-air.

Esta's eyes met her mother's, stretching her legs out in front of her. "This different life that I don't remember, but could have been mine if Papa hadn't taken me away from you."

"We will make up for lost time." A weight settled onto Malkia's heart. She realized her relationship with Esta would have to take second place to the mission. In that moment, she vowed to herself that when it was complete, she would disappear to the farthest stretch of land she could find and raise her children in peace.

It didn't take long to settle into the clearing near the crumbling boulders from the fortress. As they exited the vessel, they could see several sections of Jasper's broken home being built up again. The most surprising sight was the Artemisians working hand in hand with her people.

She turned to face Apollo. "What else did I miss?"

He halted midstride, twisting his head to face her. "I've been in contact over the past couple of weeks with my people. After many explanations, and with the help of Chantum and then Ustarum, I finally was able to convince them of your innocence." He pursed his lips in thought. "Aside from my home moons destruction, that is."

"Thanks for the reminder," she mumbled, gripping Esta's hand and watching Damon and Landon stroll down the gangway together. "I'm looking forward to hearing everything. Three weeks without being in the know, and it feels like the entire universe shifted."

Apollo chuckled as he walked away. Two arms circled around her waist and her sister's familiar aroma strayed across her nose.

"I was sleeping when you woke," she whispered, squeezing Malkia tight as a yawn overspread her lips. "I missed you so much."

Malkia leaned back into the hug, patting Mataya's arm with her free hand. "We need some time to catch up. You, Esta, mom, and me."

"Tonight," Mataya suggested, releasing her sister from her grip and waltzing around her. "A few days on Esaki would be therapeutic."

"I don't know if we have a few days, but we could spare a day, maybe two." She closed her eyes, pressing her lips together as she inhaled the fresh air. "I need to connect. Not only to the spirit of Esaki, but to my family." Her eyes flew open and fell on Mataya. "We will make the time. By the way, where are the dragons?"

Mataya grinned, grasping Malkia's hand and towing her and Esta toward the fortress. "They should've already arrived with about a dozen of the Nesoi. We discovered that the Nesoi have the ability to create those wormholes all on their own, just like I can step through your visions. That's how they met us on Thalia." She pointed past the people and Artemisians and Malkia could see one of the hatchlings. "Most of the Nesoi returned to Hemera, along with Sirath. The young ones remained with Tantiana, coming here to meet us."

"That's amazing," Malkia responded, seeing Parowan galloping toward her. "And here is another beautiful sight." A grin exploded across her face, tugging Esta in close. "You're about to meet one of my dearest and closest friends."

Esta's eyes were dancing with joy, watching the winged horse race toward them. "She's yours?"

"She belongs to no one," Malkia corrected, grinning down at her daughter. "On Esaki, the creatures are our comrades. Although we might refer to them in a possessive way at times, they're definitely free to come and go as they please."

Parowan skidded to a halt in front of the trio, nuzzling Malkia with her snout and stamping her hooves. Malkia combed her fingers through her mane and kissed the beasts neck, before whispering in her ear. "I found my daughter. Would you like to meet her?"

She stamped her hooves more, nodding her head with wild and happy eyes. Malkia sank to her knees, followed by Parowan who folded her wings around her body and stared at Esta. "Esta, this is Parowan. She has been one of my closest friends for more years than I can count. Parowan, this is Esta, my daughter."

Parowan eased her face forward, nuzzling Esta's hand and Malkia smiled when Esta ran her hand down the beast's nose. "Hi, Parowan. I'm delighted to meet you. May I sit on your back?"

Rising from her perch, Parowan nodded again, bowing so Esta could climb on her back. With the help of Malkia, Esta sat proudly on top of the pegasus, smiling from ear to ear. The four of them continued toward the others, joining the group who were working on rebuilding the structure.

SIX

Alyssa's Demons

THE EVENING BLEW in quickly and Malkia found herself being towed by Esta toward a small fire pit, where Mataya and Alyssa were waiting. The shadows of a few Nesoi quivered near the forest edge, followed by the young dragons swooping down to meet them and Tantiana. A soft smile played on Malkia's lips, and, for the first time in so long, hope fluttered within her.

Esta tugged her down onto a log stump and cuddled up next to her as soon as she was seated. Breathing in the fresh air, her eyes danced across the horizon, grateful to be on Esaki once more.

"It feels surreal to be here again," Mataya broke the silence, leaning forward. "The last time was so brief, we barely had a moment to breath. Now our home is bustling with life again."

Malkia nodded and smiled, turning to peer at her Esaki mother. "How are you feeling?"

"Regretful." Alyssa dabbed at her eyes and wiped away a tear. "There are many things I would do differently, if I had a chance. Starting with returning here and abducting Mataya from her home. My paranoia with the way I envisioned this war heading, erased all rational thought."

"Let's forget the past, mom," Mataya replied, reaching over and patting Alyssa's hand. "You thought you were keeping me safe, by teaching me the ways of our ancestors. I understand."

"There's so much more," Alyssa muttered, sitting up straight and looking past Malkia at the rest of their group. "Ustarum." She paused and closed her eyes, biting down on her lip as her chin quivered.

"What about Ustarum?" Malkia asked, running her fingers through Esta's hair.

"He should be here for this." Alyssa suddenly rose, holding out her hand and signaling for them to wait as she hurried away.

Malkia's gaze locked with Mataya's. Her sister shook her head as she watched their mother's receding back. "What's going on with her?" Mataya asked, rubbing her hands together.

"Ustarum and she have some kind of history," Malkia mused. She squeezed Esta as she laid her head in Malkia's lap and closed her eyes. "I noticed their bizarre behavior toward one another back on Eris."

"Strange," Mataya whispered, rising from her seat and spreading a blanket out in front of it. She sank down on top of it, leaning back against the log.

Malkia's eyes wandered around the tree line behind Mataya, a sense of peace wrapping its warmth around her as she stared over at Theia. She was anxious to speak with the Aletheians again, but was also content to remain on Esaki for an extended period of time. It seemed as if there was so much to learn, right here on her home moon and she dreaded the day they would have to depart.

"Mom and Ustarum are headed this way," Mataya interrupted her thoughts.

Twisting around, she watched as the duo traipsed toward them, a frown creasing the lines around Alyssa's eyes. "Mom's worried about something, that's for sure." She turned back to face Mataya. "And I'm afraid it's about to turn your life upside down."

"Me too." Mataya inhaled a deep breath, wringing her hands together, and watching her mom and Ustarum approach.

"Good evening, ladies," Ustarum greeted, flashing them both one of his brilliant smiles, making his amber eyes sparkle.

"Hello, Ustarum," Mataya replied. Her gaze darted around the group and came to rest on her mother's face. "Mom, what's going on?"

Alyssa sank onto her seat, rubbing her hands down her legs as she waited for Ustarum to find his own seat. "I have a confession. One that I've held onto for your entire life and then some." She paused, swallowing with difficulty. "Mataya, you knew you had an instant connection with Ustarum, but the reason isn't because you both possess such powerful sorcery."

"What do you mean?" Mataya asked, sitting up straight.

Malkia could see the terror sliding across her sister's face and she eased herself out from underneath her sleeping child, lying her on the blanket at their feet and stepped over to Mataya. Slipping next to her sister, she wrapped her arm around her waist. "I'm here, little sister," she whispered.

Mataya didn't react, her body tensing as she continued to stare at their mother. "Mom?"

"Ustarum is your biological father, Mataya." The words rushed from Alyssa's mouth. Her eyes darted over to Ustarum as her fingers flitted up to her quivering chin.

"What?" Mataya and Malkia shouted in unison. Tightening her grip on her sister, her eyes narrowed as her gaze locked onto Ustarum. "Did you know this?" Malkia barked at her mentor.

He nodded, raising his eyebrows and shrugging his shoulders. "I wasn't allowed near her or speak of it to anyone."

"Since when do you take orders from others?" Malkia asked, her voice rising an octave, holding onto her shaking sister.

Ustarum threw her a lopsided smile, unfazed by her snappish tone. "Since I fell in love with this woman and knew if I interfered, her family would ruin any chance of me seeing my daughter in the future."

"What about Dad?" Mataya whispered, slowly returning from her shocked state and refocusing on her mother.

Alyssa raked her hands through her hair. "He never knew," she replied, clenching her jaw as a tear swam down her cheek. "I believe he suspected I was up to something, as I returned to Eris several times over a period of a year. But my story was always that my sister needed me."

"What does Asha say about all of this?" Malkia asked, frozen from the realization spiraling through her thoughts.

"She doesn't know." Alyssa's head sank into her lap. "But she has been accusing me of hiding something from her," her muffled voice shook with regret and heartache. "She's wondered what happened since the moment she found out I snuck away to see him." She peered over at Mataya. "I never meant to hurt you, but I knew you deserved to know the truth. Ustarum is a good man, but our families have feuded for hundreds of years and if anyone had found out our betrayal, we would have been executed by our own families."

"That seems a bit harsh," Malkia muttered, throwing her mom a sharp look.

"You wouldn't understand. Neither of you would," Ustarum interrupted. He leaned forward, running his fingers through his beard.

"You were both sheltered here on Esaki, away from the judgements of our families and the Eris people. Magic wasn't spoken about while you were being raised and you know nothing about the persecution, the heated grudge, or the heartache your mother has held within herself for far too long." His eyes shifted around the group, finally settling on Mataya. "My dear, sweet child, take some time to cool down and digest this new information. You and I can be friends and I'll teach you everything I know, expanding your abilities and showing you why you're so intuitive. But for now, sleep on it and let's speak again tomorrow."

Malkia kissed her sister's head. "Esta and I will stay with you tonight, if you would like."

"No." Mataya shook her head. "Thank you for the offer, but I need to be alone. Please tell Justin that I'll explain it all to him tomorrow, but that I won't be joining him tonight."

"I can do that," Malkia replied, squeezing her sister tight before rising and scooping Esta up into her arms. "We all make mistakes, Mataya, but your life isn't one of them. Remember that. And know that I'll always be here for you."

Malkia looked over at her mother, closing her eyes briefly with a deep sigh, before focusing on those weary eyes again. "I love you, Mom. I hope you find peace in this confession."

Alyssa nodded as tears over brimmed her lower lashes. She wiped them away and watched as Mataya stood, leaving them all to their own thoughts. Malkia stepped toward the crowd at the other end of the fortress, searching for Justin.

SEVEN
Keeping the Peace

"GOOD MORNING, ASHA." Malkia strode toward the small gathering under the makeshift eating hall. Esta was glued to her side, holding tightly onto her hand and eyeing the Artemisians in the company of Asha.

Asha nodded and threw her a tired smile. "I take it that my sister spoke to all of you last night?" she asked, curling her thin fingers around her cup and raising it to her lips.

"She did," Malkia responded, helping Esta fill up a plate of food. "She must have spoken to you afterward?"

"Yes." Asha nodded and leaned back in her chair. The Artemisians said their goodbyes and left the three of them alone. "She's distraught and blames herself for everything bad you and Mataya have experienced in your lives."

Malkia sighed, filling her own plate and sinking into a chair across from Asha. "That's ridiculous." Picking up the meat, she gnawed off a piece with her teeth and chewed as she watched Esta do the same. "She and Mataya will work it out and having Ustarum as a father isn't the worst thing that could happen to that girl."

"I can't entirely agree with you, on that," Asha mumbled, sipping from her cup and rustling Esta's hair with her other hand. "Ustarum's family is our enemy."

"Please stop," Malkia groaned, holding up her hand. "I know Ustarum, and he's never even mentioned a family before. If there is some ancient feud that keeps you from forgiving him, then I believe the problem is with you, not with him."

"You don't know what they've—"

"Did Ustarum do something to hurt you or anyone you love?" Malkia interjected, gripping the end of the table and stared pointedly at Asha.

Asha paused, blinking a few times before taking a deep breath. "No, he hasn't ever done anything against our family."

"Then drop it," Malkia muttered, picking up her food and resumed eating.

The fowls' song and chatter from the nearby wildlife was all that was heard for several minutes. Malkia ate her food and took a long drink of the juice, tapping her fingers on her glass as she sank into deep thought. The warmth of the morning sun was spreading across her legs, and she grinned to herself as she listened to Asha and Esta quietly talk.

From afar she noticed another group of people heading their way and sat up straight when she saw the person walking in the midst of the excitement. It was Alexa. Rising from her chair, she hurried toward the woman, waving as she neared.

A smile stretched across Alexa's face as they grew closer to one another. "*Malkia*," she exclaimed, trotting toward her and throwing her arms around Malkia's neck. "It's so good to see you again. I'm glad you and Damon were able to work through your disagreements."

Leaning away from the woman, Malkia's gaze swept up and down Alexa's face before speaking. "Where have you been?"

"While Damon and you were fighting at the castle, my kids and I slipped away and traveled south for a few days. We've been living in a small village, hidden in the forest, ever since." Alexa turned to the group behind them and waved. Two children stepped out and walked over to them. "These are my kids, Zoe and Branston."

Malkia held out her hand and grasped each of their wrists, smiling warmly at them both. "It's great to finally meet you two."

"We've heard a lot about you," Zoe gushed, grinning up at her with sparkling pale lavender irises and then looked over to Esta. "Is that your daughter?"

Glancing over at Esta, she smiled and waved for her to join them. "Yes, this is Esta. Esta, this is Zoe and Branston."

Esta hid halfway behind Malkia, but smiled at Zoe. Leaning toward Esta, Zoe flashed her a huge smile and waved her fingers. "We're about the same age. Maybe?" Zoe asked, peering up at Malkia.

"Yes, I believe so," Alexa agreed. "Why don't you three go find some mischief and let Malkia and I speak for a moment?"

Esta giggled and raced after Zoe, followed by a more bashful Branston. The women watched as they ran toward Tantiana and the hatchlings, before turning back to face one another.

"I was worried about you," Malkia fretted, shaking her head and setting her hands on her hips. "You left without a word and no one had a clue to your whereabouts. I was terrified the wolfmen took their anger out on you, before they confronted me."

"I had to leave," Alexa responded, linking her arm with Malkia and making her step with her as they walked away from Asha and the rest of her welcoming group. "I always planned on escaping, but I needed a moment where the focus would be shifted for a long period of time.

Once we set up camp near the fortress and most of the warriors and the last two wolfmen had followed Damon to confront you, I didn't hesitate." She paused, sighing heavily. "It wouldn't be the first time that I've planned an escape."

"I'm just grateful that all three of you are safe." Pausing midstride, Malkia twisted to face Alexa. "We're in the middle of hunting down my father and I've lost so many loved ones, along with returning here and discovering the onslaught that occurred in my absence. It's been an awful few months and I'm overjoyed to find out you're alive and well. We never had the chance to spend more time with one another, but I hope before I leave again, we will become great friends."

"Me too." Alexa grinned, elation sparkling in her eyes. "When we met in Damon's camp, I knew you and I would connect again."

"You did?" she asked, her brows furrowing.

Alexa laughed at Malkia's confused expression. "I can do more than find people with powerful abilities, but I never divulged that to Damon. I believe I'm some kind of witch, but I'm not entirely sure. I heard your sister is a warlock and I would love some time with her to see if she can help me understand my powers."

"We'll be traveling to another area of Esaki today, but when we return this evening, I'm sure she would be delighted to spend some time with you," Malkia replied, noticing Damon and Apollo standing near their ship, both of their faces crimson as their voices began to rise in volume. "If you'll excuse me, will you let Esta know I'm headed to the ship if she needs me?"

"Yes, of course." Alexa leaned in and gave her a squeeze, before hurrying in the direction of the children.

Malkia trotted over to Damon, growing anxious as Apollo threw his hands up in the air and released a deep growl. She slid up next to them. "What's the problem?" she asked, folding her arms over her chest.

"Apollo wants to join us today and I've told him that it's not possible." A deeper flush had risen in Damon's face and a muscle in his jaw twitched as he glared at Apollo. "He wants to know why, and I've told him it's none of his business."

Apollo's lips drew back in a snarl and his crimson skin simmered with heat. "I'm just as much a part of this crew as you are and I demand to be treated as an equal," he shouted, sneering at Damon as he leaned toward him.

"*Stop it,*" Malkia yelled, stepping in between them. "Damon, you're not the commander of this mission and Apollo has every right to understand what we are doing and why." She turned to Apollo. "You need to go take a breather. We're departing soon, so if you want any information, I expect you to calm down."

Apollo spat to the side as he stomped off toward the broken fortress. Malkia released a tense sigh as she pivoted around to face Damon. "Why did you do that?"

Damon shook his head and pointed at Apollo's receding back. "He's a barbarian. Always throwing in his nonsense way of doing things and never giving anyone the benefit of the doubt. I don't need him accompanying us, especially since we agreed this was to be kept between the three of us."

"Don't forget, *you* were a barbarian," Malkia snapped at him, her hands settling on her hips as she squared her shoulders toward him. "Stop acting like you're above him. All of you men want to be in charge and for some reason have forgotten that our enemy is still running free out there somewhere." She jabbed her finger up at the sky. "I'm exhausted. My powers aren't working, and I'm nauseated every single moment, of every day. Please stop bickering with everyone. We're *all* frustrated with the lies and the secrets and the sudden reappearance of our children in our lives. Stop taking it out on me and everyone else around you or you'll run out of friends quickly."

Pivoting on her heel, she stomped away from him, walking up the gangway of their ship and made her way to her room. The day was already becoming a hot mess.

Locking her door, she curled into a ball on top of the bed covers. Shaking from head to toe, she sobbed into her hands, thinking of her mother's and Skye's deaths and everything that had transpired since she had landed on Thalia. The harder she worked to finish this battle with her father, the more heartache entered her life. It was tempting to take her family and run as far away as she could, escaping the bloodshed that was promised in her future. It lacerated her psyche, thinking of all they had lost. And it wasn't over yet.

After several minutes, her body calmed, and the sobs subsided. Her mind relaxed and she closed her eyes, allowing the numbness of peace to infuse within her body. Just as she was slipping into a meditation, a knock on her door brought her flying back to reality.

Sitting on the edge of her bed, she wiped away the semi-dried tears with the sleeve of her shirt. "Who is it?" she called out, not wanting to check the monitor.

"It's me and Esta," Mataya's muffled voice filtered through the panel.

Inhaling a deep breath, she rose from the bed and opened the door. Stepping aside and waving them in, she waited until they were both sitting at her table, before joining them.

"Are you okay?" Mataya asked, running her hand down Malkia's arm.

Giving her a sister's hand a squeeze, she nodded. "I'm tired. This baby is sucking out all of my powers and energy." Her weary eyes locked onto Esta's. "I'm sorry, little lady. I wish I had the motivation to run and play with you."

"It's okay, Mama." Esta's obsidian eyes dropped to the ground. "I don't want to stay here with Asha today. May I please come with you?"

"This is something Mataya and I have to do together," Malkia responded, reaching across the table and covering her daughter's hands with hers. "This will be a great time to bond with Tantiana and Parowan, while hanging out with your favorite friend, Koleton. I need someone to stay back and keep an eye on him anyway. Do you think you can keep him on the straight and narrow?"

Esta giggled and nodded. "What's the straight and narrow?"

"Keeping him in line. Don't let him go off and do anything crazy and foolish." Malkia ruffled her daughter's hair, throwing her a wide grin. "If anyone has the ability to keep his feet on the ground, it would be you."

"I can do that." Esta rose from her seat and walked around the table, embracing her mother. "I'll see you soon, right?"

"In the evening," she responded, reaching up and kissing Esta on the forehead.

Esta smiled, before hugging Mataya and leaving the room. Malkia turned to her sister. "Where did you go last night?"

"For a long walk," Mataya responded, her dainty nose crinkling. "I stopped by a creek and napped against a rock. Not my best idea." She shot Malkia a lopsided smile. "I woke up smelling like rodent droppings and a giant ritter was across the stream, eyeing me for breakfast. It's a good thing I've learned a few spells to keep me from being eaten."

Malkia's laugh echoed through the room and she almost started sobbing again. "I need to breathe," she finally replied. "Mom, Ustarum, this child, Esta, Landon, they're all draining me of what little energy I have left and we still have so far to go. Any advice, sister?"

"Let's leave for the day like we planned." Mataya rose from her chair, tugging Malkia up next to her. "The pyramid and scrolls have answers that we need."

"I think we should bring Ustarum," Malkia suggested, giving her sister a sideways glance.

Mataya shuddered, shaking her head rapidly. "No, I can't do that right now. I need to breathe, as well."

"Alright." Malkia gripped Mataya's hand and together they walked outside.

Malkia could see Esta playing with Zoe, and Apollo was standing with Koleton and Justin. Damon must have gone up to the bridge, to prepare the ship.

"I need to speak with them." Malkia pointed her thumb toward Apollo and his companions. "Could you let Asha and Alyssa know we are leaving, and they'll need to keep an eye on Esta and Landon for me?"

Mataya nodded, skipping away from Malkia. She twisted around and strolled over to the trio near the tree line. "Hey," she called out as she grew closer.

They turned to face her, pausing in their discussion. "Are you leaving soon?" Koleton asked, looking beyond her toward the children.

"Yes, but first I wanted to give you an idea of what we're doing and why it will only be the three of us leaving," she said, staring pointedly at Apollo. "We had to conceal the scrolls in a place that my father couldn't enter. The pyramid on Esaki seemed like the most appropriate spot, as the magical ward surrounding it is difficult to shatter." She sighed, exhaustion seeping into every muscle of her body. "I'm weary and have no idea how I'll defeat my father while I'm carrying this child. The thought of attempting to use my powers today, makes me sick to my stomach and I'm afraid we will fail. We might return early, as Mataya doesn't want Ustarum to join us and she isn't speaking with Alyssa right now. That being said, I also need you to know where we're keeping the scrolls and what our destination is, in case something happens to us. You'll need to come find us, or send Tantiana our way."

Koleton curled his arm around Malkia's shoulders and kissed the top of her head. "You're taking on too much worry," he whispered, his red beard glistening in the sunlight. "Thank you for the information, but I believe you'll be just fine. If you don't return before the second sun sets, I'll come looking for you, I promise."

Malkia's chin quivered and she brushed away a tear as she peered up at her friends. "Waking from that sleep and finding out so much has changed, along with the contention I'm noticing between many of my family and friends, I'm beginning to feel overwhelmed. Relying on my powers to end this war has made me weak without them."

"You're not weak," Apollo said, wagging his long finger at her. "You can still do this, but it will take some shifting on your part." His mouth curved into a smile. "I believe in you."

"Thank you," She licked her lips and tucked strands of hair behind her ears, before hugging each of them, ending with Justin. "Mataya will need your support when we return. She has had her own surprises and deceit to endure," she whispered in his ear, feeling his shoulders tense for a split moment.

"I'll be here waiting," he replied, quickly stepping back and patting Malkia's shoulder, and appearing relaxed and unworried.

My paranoia's getting the best of me. Waving goodbye to each of them, she strode back to the ship, with one last glance at the children. Mataya was waiting at the top of the gangway, closing the door as Malkia passed her by.

EIGHT
The Aletheian's Warning

MALKIA'S BODY HEAVED as more bile rose up her throat and splashed into the lake water, settling against the rocks below. Fresh tears stained her cheeks, and she could feel the stares of Damon and Mataya from afar. She'd told them to leave her alone, but they were always closer than she wished.

She washed out her mouth with the water from her bottle and spit out the last of the bile, wiping away the beads of sweat from her forehead with the back of her sleeve. She adjusted her hair into a high bun on top of her head and tucked the wisps behind her ears, before turning to face her companions.

Climbing up the sandy hill, she swallowed back anything else threatening to travel up her throat. She waved away Mataya's and Damon's concerned expressions, stomping past them and hurrying to the entrance of the pyramid.

Standing in front of it, she closed her eyes, searching for the magic surrounding the building. She felt Mataya's fingers entwine with her own and a sudden strength swept over her. Snapping her eyes open, she glanced at her sister and noticed that her eyes were closed, but a smile was teasing the edges of her lips.

Why am I so stubborn? She asked herself, realizing her sister always had the gift to help her through this, just like Ustarum. They were more alike than Mataya wanted to admit.

Shutting her eyes again, she focused on the energy cocooned around the pyramid and began to chant the spell to open the hidden door. Esaki's light enveloped her and for the first time since she woke, she felt the connection with her powers once more. She inhaled the sweet scent of the budding flowers surrounding them as her own lips rose into a much needed smile. A tingle of joy swept over her body and pulsated with the magic in the air.

Moments later, Damon cleared his throat and she opened her eyes to see that the door was open and the nausea had finally dissipated. "This is exactly what I needed," she whispered, peering over at her sister as she tugged her inside the open doors.

The trio paused at the base of the greeting statues, admiring the work of their ancestors. The winged female's tresses cascaded over their shoulders and fell to their hips, curling against the gowns that flowed to their ankles. Sparkling purple and auburn jewels were embedded in the corners of their closed eyelids and a flowered crown adorned each of their heads.

"I didn't notice the jewels last time." Damon broke the silence, rising on his toes to see them better.

"Whoever created these statues, along with all the smaller ones, had a message for others." Malkia ran her fingers across the dress of one of the statues. "I just wish I knew what it was."

"Maybe they left these here for themselves," Mataya responded, wiping away the dust on the base of the statue nearest to her. "Have you ever wondered why the Creators have never returned? Or maybe they have and these statues and pyramids are their connection to our moons."

Malkia stepped back and gazed up at the statues once more, shaking her head. "You could be onto something. If these are a way for the Creators to travel back and forth to our moons, we should find a way to understand it. Even if it means we have the knowledge, in order to destroy it."

"Why would we destroy it?" Damon asked, twisting to look at her, his eyes narrowing.

"I don't trust them." Malkia stepped around the statues and moved down the corridor. "The Aletheians don't want them to return and my grandfather had a reason for not wanting them to know he had ventured here. And Jacob warned me that if the Creators returned, no matter who was here, they would most likely end all life after seeing what their creations have done with this star system." She halted and turned back to face Damon and Mataya. "I don't know why my father and the Elvens are determined to find the Creators, aside from gaining the gift of eternal life, but if they succeed, it's possible a war we can never win will engulf us."

Mataya clapped her hands together. "Let's get this show on the road. I have no desire to meet the Creators. We have enough problems without inviting them into our conflict." She scooted past Malkia and stepped around the corner, disappearing into the moss filled room and leaving them to hurry after her.

The crates of scrolls were exactly where they left them, safely tucked away in the pyramid. Malkia began picking up each of them, scanning over them as she searched for the crate that held the spells created by Elvens to eliminate their own people. They hadn't wanted to take it this far, as there would be Elven children and elderly in harm's way. But if her father forced their hand, they would have no other choice.

It didn't take them long to find the crate. They set it to the side to take on their way out of the pyramid. Malkia rummaged through a few more crates, searching for the maps of their star system, particularly anything to do with Hemera, as that was their last moon to explore. Digging her way through each of the containers and finally finding everything she needed, she placed those with the others, turning to face Damon and Mataya.

"I want to see the planet again," she said, pointing her finger upward, a growing excitement racing through her.

Mataya glanced over at Damon, who seemed to be in deep thought. "I want to examine the small statues in the other room before we leave." Her eyes trailed back to Malkia, the corner of her mouths quirking up.

"Are those really reasons why we should stay longer?" Damon asked, a haunted look spreading across his eyes. "I don't want to be a party pooper, but I also don't want to be away from Landon too long."

"We understand," Malkia replied. She curled her fingers around his forearm. "I won't be long, and I do agree with Mataya. We need to understand those statues. Why don't you two work on them and I'll spend a few minutes studying that planet?"

Damon's eyes narrowed. "I don't think it's wise to separate."

"I'll be fine," Malkia grumbled, turning to leave without another word. She heard him growl, but he didn't say anything more and neither of them stopped her. Finding the narrow entrance to the corridor, she gave them one last glance before disappearing behind the stone wall.

Climbing the stairs, she illuminated her light and stretched it upward. Reaching the top, she waited for her eyes to adjust, as she pressed her light even farther out, stopping when it reached the planet. It was still there. Floating a foot off the ground and rotating slowly. She stepped toward the control panel, wiping away the film that had settled over it since they had last been there.

She pressed a few of the buttons, watching areas of the planet light up and speculating the importance of these places. Turning her attention back to the control panel, she searched for instructions or any kind of explanation, stopping at a bright yellow button that was set at the top of the panel.

Her eyes swept to either side of it, noticing it was the only one with no writing underneath it. Trembling, her fingers hovered over it, a mixture of dread and excitement permeating every cell in her body. Inhaling a quick breath, she depressed the button firmly and jumped when the entire room brightened with a light so white, it burned her eyes.

Falling to her knees, she shielded her eyes with her hands, hearing a familiar whirl from the moments she was tossed into the wormhole that took her to the Light Beings. But this was different. She removed her hands and bounded to her feet when she saw the Aletheians standing in the room with her.

"What just happened?" she asked, trembling from head to toe.

A shorter Aletheian, about eight feet tall, moved forward. It was the first time Malkia noticed physical attributes of each of the Beings. This one had dark, almost ebony hair that stood vibrant against her brilliant light, hanging down past her torso, just like the winged statues in the pyramids entrance.

"This place was designed to draw us near, when needed," she spoke, her voice reverberating against the stone walls.

Malkia's hands shot up to her ears, drowning out the echo that caused her heart to quaver. "It's a way to summon you?" she asked, keeping her ears covered.

"Yes and no." The Aletheian pointed at the planet. "When the Creators arrived to this particular planet, they needed a way to communicate with us and to know when it's time to return to the moons that surround Theia. This place is guarded by the most intense magic, and only the Chosen Heir would be able to enter. When she did, they would know." The Being swept her hair over her shoulder. "You've begun the merge of your worlds."

"What?" Malkia cried, pressing her hands against her head, wishing she never came up those stairs. "What do you mean?"

"They're coming," the Aletheian replied, stepping back into the group.

"Why would they come here?" she asked, fear clawing through her stomach as her eyes darted from one Aletheian to the next.

A taller, more robust Aletheian stepped forward, the muscles of his bare chest quivering with each step. "This star system is their first beginning of life. All the species that survived their experiments are the results that span over the moons of Theia. If the button in their pyramid has been pressed, then they know the next prophecy has come about." He leaned down toward her, his words like a flame to her heart. "It's possible they won't allow you to live. Or anyone else for that matter."

"Why didn't you warn me?" she screamed up at him, a sudden fury thundering through her veins.

"We didn't believe you would be foolish enough to push an unmarked button," he replied, stepping back and quieting his voice.

"You're supposed to be All-Knowing!" she cried, covering her face with her hands. "How do I stop their invasion?"

"Close up the pyramid and leave," the male Aletheian ordered her. "It's too late to stop them from coming, but it's possible to save yourselves or convince them to halt their invasion."

"How?" she asked, her whisper barely audible.

"Eliminate your father and stop the Elvens pursuance for the Blue Planet." The Aletheian moved back into the collective, reabsorbing into their energy. "Then, find the All-Seeing Eye on Theia and destroy it."

Their light faded and Malkia rose to her shaking legs. She brushed herself off, wiping her face with both hands and watching as they disappeared completely. *They didn't tell me how much time I had*, she thought, flinging a small pebble in their direction and hearing it ricochet across the room.

She raced down the stairs, two at a time, nearly slamming into the rock wall at the bottom. Running down the corridor, she shot into the room filled with the moss and scrolls. She shoved the few crates they had already planned on taking with them out into the corridor, before rushing back in and snatching up any other scrolls she felt would be needed. Tossing them into the pile, she rushed into the other room across the hall and focused in on Damon and Mataya at the other end.

"We need to leave now," she ordered, beckoning for them to follow her.

Damon rose from his position and stared over at her, while Mataya ignored her, brushing the dust from one of the statues.

"Why are we rushing now?" Damon asked, sighing in exasperation.

"The Aletheians just appeared to me," she replied, clutching one of the scrolls, staring wild-eyed at Damon and Mataya.

Mataya pressed up from the ground and whirled around to face her sister. "What did they say?"

"I pressed a button that calls for the Creators," Malkia muttered, shuffling her unsteady feet beneath her. "We need to continue on with our mission. Our only chance of stopping the Creators from descending and annihilating all of us, is to destroy what they call the All-Seeing Eye on Theia."

"What are we waiting for?" Mataya snapped, trotting past Damon, her eyes filled with a look of dread as she moved past Malkia.

The three of them lugged the scrolls outside of the pyramid and Malkia and Mataya surrounded the building with its original incantation, before racing back to the ship with their arms full of crates overflowing with the knowledge of the Elvens.

NINE

Connecting with Esaki

"WHY DO YOU insist on doing everything by yourself?" Damon shouted, his bloodshot eyes searing Malkia with their accusations.

Malkia sighed, shrugging her shoulders, not knowing the proper words to speak to this man. She glanced at her sister who had her head placed in between her legs.

Damon maneuvered the ship into its landing space near the Domesca fortress and settled it onto the terrain. His face was as bright as a wildfire. Watching his every move, Malkia jumped up from her chair and moved toward him.

"Stop yelling at me," she said, gripping his arm. "I'm not your enemy, but ever since Thalia, you've treated me as such."

A growl rumbled up his throat and he twisted to face her. "My frustration lies with your impulsive behavior. You left me on Eris and when we were reunited, you promised you would discontinue being so foolish." He threw his arms up in the air and stepped away from her. "But here we are again. You needed to be alone and suddenly we have a new enemy to face."

"You think I did this on purpose?" she asked, simmering with frustration.

"No, I don't think you did it on purpose," he hissed between clenched teeth as he rushed toward the door. "You want to be alone, I'll leave you alone." The door slid closed after him, leaving her with her mouth agape and her pulse slamming inside her skull.

"He's right," Mataya suddenly spoke up, rising from her seat and staring at Malkia. "Why would you push that button?"

"I didn't know," Malkia muttered, her scalp prickling with shame. "Please don't be angry with me, Mataya. I needed more information and it seemed safe to explore everything in that pyramid."

"There's always a catch with you." Mataya sighed as her fingers raked through her dark locks. "If the Creators do decide to check in on their 'experiments,' we might as well call ourselves extinct."

Malkia hiccoughed. She stepped over to stop her sister from leaving but froze when Mataya shook her head and marched from the room. Sinking to the floor, she covered her face with her hands and shook from the sobs that quivered through her body.

It was only moments later when she felt arms curl around her shoulders and pull her into a tight embrace. "I'm here," Alyssa whispered, kissing the top of her head.

"Mom," her voice shook as she snuggled into her mother's warmth. "Everything I do is wrong. I didn't realize the button would cause the Creators advancement." A fountain of tears slid from her eyelids, and she wiped them, before wrapping her arms around Alyssa's waist. "Damon and Mataya are both on edge. I'm on edge. And the drama and bickering within our group is gnawing at my heart. I retrieved my abilities for a short period of time, but now my child has taken that as well." She paused as more tears filled her eyes. "Why can't I find the peace that I desire?"

Alyssa squeezed her and kissed her forehead, once again. "If you want peace, you must be peace."

Malkia leaned back, staring at her Esaki mother. "What do you mean?"

"We all have our moments of disarray, but in order for you to create the peace on the outside, you have to find it within first." Alyssa rose from the floor, offering her hand to help Malkia up. Gripping her fingers, she stood next to her, confused by her mother's words. "It's one of the simpler, but also strangely difficult tasks an individual will face in their lives. You will never find complete peace with those who surround you if chaos and conflict rule your heart and mind."

"Is this why you've been so quiet lately?" Malkia asked, the buzz of a conversation outside the vessel catching her attention.

"Your people have endured a troublesome and heartbreaking fight that stole the lives of their loved ones. Their home consists of cold corridors and rooms in which they fly from one destination to another, removing the connection with their moons' energy." Alyssa pointed to the outside, where the hum of voices had grown in strength. "They fight amongst themselves, because there is no end at sight. Any peace they once had has abandoned their spirits, and they see their leader lost as well. I'm working on my own peace, but even I struggle with grasping it when I'm in the company of so many wounded souls."

Malkia's fingers brushed her hair out of her eyes, and she wiped away the remnants of her tears. "I have to be the peace I want from others. Is that what you're saying?"

"Yes," Alyssa replied, a weary smile surfacing on her lips. "Any person out there is capable of finding the peace themselves, but when they see their leader demonstrating it, they will be more likely to follow suit."

"What about the Creators?" Malkia asked, a chill racing through her veins.

"Stop." Her mother grasped her hands within her own, locking eyes with Malkia. "Whatever problems we are required to face, they won't be any easier if your heart is afraid." She placed one hand on her own chest and the other on Malkia's. "Quiet your mind, calm your pulse, and look within for the answers. The Aletheians gave you this task because they know you're capable of succeeding, and they have confidence that you already contain the answers. Stop second-guessing yourself and lead your people."

Malkia froze, digesting this information her patient and loving mother was bestowing upon her. Her eyes scanned the tired eyes of the woman who had raised her but had her own demons to face. "We're all fighting our own inner battles, aren't we?"

Alyssa nodded, running her hand over Malkia's hair. "Yes. Now take a few breaths, search your heart for the answer, connect with your moon, and then go speak to your people. They need *you* to step up your game." She kissed her daughter's cheek and left the room without another word.

"Connect with my moon," she said out loud, her gaze fluttering around the barren and cold room. Drawing in a long breath, she trotted to the door and sprinted down the corridor.

Before long, she was outside and racing toward the trees, finally understanding what had to be done. Her people did need her. And she was useless to them at this moment. Her confidence had waned, her strength inward and outward had dissipated, and she felt disconnected from everyone and everything. It was time to take back her power.

She found herself in a quiet clearing, not far from Domesca but surrounded by vegetation and massive trees that stretched up into the sky. Sinking to the dirt, her hands burrowed into the soil and she shut her eyes, concentrating on the energy of Esaki. Almost instantly the magic poured inside her, as well, it flowed and twirled around her body, nipping at her hair and reminding her that it had always been here, waiting.

A grin rose on her lips and she felt her entire body pulsate with renewed powers and strength. She inhaled deeply over and over again, giving her body some much needed air. Her belly fluttered and she laughed, elation surging within every cell, including the child within her. He could feel her powers and although he was absorbing as much as he could, the energy was endless, enough for both of them.

Tilting her head toward the sky, her eyes flashed open, seeing the sway of the trees above her, their tips piercing the vibrant white clouds above. The bright lavender and mulberry leaves danced with the wind, their life force connecting with her.

"I remember," she announced to the spirit of Esaki, her teeth glistening with the suns rays as her lips parted in a wide smile. "Thank you." She rose from the earth and bowed to the vegetation around her, honored by the presence that permeated every inch of her skin.

Taking in another deep breath, she turned on her heel and strolled back to Domesca, feeling fully alive for the first time since they arrived on Thalia. Her smile returned when she approached the vessel and noticed many of her friends hovering near the cargo doors.

Esta bounced on her toes when she saw her mother approaching, grabbing Mataya's arm and pointing at Malkia. Her sister turned to see what the fuss was and burst out with laughter, as the joy swept across her face and all conflict between the two disappeared.

"*Malkia, you're glowing,*" she shouted as she and Esta raced to meet her.

Damon and Koleton twisted around to take in the view and both of their jaws dropped open, before they slowly began walking to greet her. Her daughter reached her first, flinging herself into Malkia's arms and hugging her tightly around the neck. Seconds later, Mataya's arms joined them, and she chuckled from the attention.

"I'm still me." Malkia set Esta down on the ground. "Just needed some time to remember my worth and my connection to the spirits of Esaki." She glanced around at the growing group of people drawing nearer to her. "We should all return to the fortress, where I can speak with everyone about our mission plan and the future of Domesca and Esaki."

Damon, Koleton and Apollo reached her, just as she spoke the last sentence and seemed perplexed by her sudden change. Holding up her hand to stop their questions, she shook her head and pointed at the stragglers behind them.

They nodded and turned back around, herding the mixture of humans and Artemisians back to the fortress. Malkia sighed as she reached for Esta's hand and gripped it within her own.

"Let's go." She winked at her daughter and curled her other arm around her sister's waist as they strolled toward the broken castle.

Tantiana and the hatchlings, along with several of the Nesoi, were watching them from the periphery. Her dragon tilted her head, lowering it toward her as they passed.

Did you fall into a glowing lake? She asked, half joking with her mistress.

Malkia patted her nose. *No, silly. This child is siphoning all my powers, but I forgot that Esaki's energy can be absorbed. Now to find a way to bottle it up, so I can take it with me on this mission.*

The dragon nodded, her wings fluttering softly against her scales. *You always have me to protect you.* Tantiana stepped back, allowing the Nesoi to gain a better view.

"I know," Malkia said out loud to the dragon, waving as she continued toward the growing crowd. "Do you hear the Nesoi, like I hear the dragons?" She peered over at her sister.

Mataya shrugged her shoulders, her eyes glued to the mysterious creatures. "I think they communicate differently. I feel what they want, versus hear what they're saying. And they don't connect with me as much as the dragons do with you. They're quiet, watching everything that is said and done, as if they are learning our ways." She paused, glancing back at the Nesoi for a split second. "Sometimes it's eerie and other times I sense a deep connection and knowing with them."

"They're ancient creatures." Malkia gave her sister's waist a squeeze. "Maybe they'll have more answers as we gain their trust. If they are, in fact, older than any other creature on Theia's Moons, then maybe they remember the Creators."

"Maybe," her sister murmured, her body tensing as she noticed the amount of people and Artemisians who'd gathered. "Are you ready for this?"

"Yes." A grin rose on Malkia's lips, her eyes sparkling with delight. "I just forgot. That's all. Now, I'm ready to rise up as the warrior I was destined to be and finish this conflict once and for all."

As they approached, the group's voices became whispers, dying out completely as she bounded up on top of a large boulder. "First, I want to apologize for my disconnection and selfishness over the past few months," she shouted over the tops of their heads, ensuring the entire crowd could hear her. "In the beginning, I believed my only true mission was to retrieve my daughter. I never really cared about my father's battle and had no desire for any part of his scheming, if it could be avoided." She rolled her shoulders back, her eyes sweeping across the different species arrayed before her. "Look at us." Her arms spread out to either side of her, including everyone who was before her. "We've gone from despising and executing one another, to working as friends and comrades. Today, our path has shifted. We have the upper hand and my father will pay for his transgressions."

A roar of approval rippled through the crowd. The Artemisians raised one fist to the sky, each pounding their chest with the other one. Her friends and family smiled and laughed, embracing one another and waving at one another. She waited patiently, until they quieted once more.

Clearing her throat, she laced her fingers together behind her back and paced the length of the boulder, staring out over the heads of her friends, family and allies. "We must play our next encounter with my father, wisely. No racing into battle without a plan. It's possible that more lives will be lost, but if we can avoid that by keeping our wits together, we *will* be victorious."

More cheers erupted from the crowd, and she smiled out at her comrades, elated by the surge of golden energy surrounding them. Parowan and the other pegasi stamped their hooves, while the hatchlings flew to the sky, twirling up and diving down and around the group.

She held up her hand and waited for silence. "We are the species of Theia's moons." Clasping her hands together, she brought them to her chin as she stepped up to the edge of the boulder. "Up until a few months ago, we were all being deceived in one way or another, and my father was intent on dividing us to the point that we would do anything to destroy one another. But now we are clear in our path. My father was foolish to believe he could destroy so many civilizations, burning bridges between species, and still escape unscathed. His greatest mistake in all of this, was his inability to acknowledge our intelligence. His deceit has bonded us together, uniting us as a solid front. And everything he set out to avoid will be delivered to him when we meet him on the battlefield." A smile crept across her face, brightening her emerald eyes with the realization of his failure. "His actions have created a force to be reckoned with." Another roar erupted from the crowd and her entire face lit up as she waited to speak again.

Seconds later, Koleton whistled and pointed at her. "Where do we go from here?" he asked, crossing his arms over his chest.

Malkia nodded toward him. "The ones who can, will leave for Hemera. It's our last stop before venturing to Theia, where we believe my father has taken up refuge with the Elvens who abandoned their people." The whispers grew and she held up her hand to silence them. "I have one last thing to say before we end this." She paused, affection glowing in her eyes as they locked on several of the faces in front of her, coming to rest on Ustarum and Mataya, who stood side by side. "From the moment my memories were returned to me, I knew my journey would lead me to my daughter, but I had no idea I would be surrounded by such an abundant family. And that's how I see all of you. As family." Her words broke as the emotions swelled in her heart. "I'm ready to defend all of you. Whether we are victorious or not, I'll keep fighting until my very last breath in order to halt the tyranny of the Elvens and my father's dominion over the civilizations of Theia's moons."

The crowd was silent. She rose her arms above her head, just as everyone burst out with whistles and cheers, rushing to the boulder to help her down. Drawing in a deep breath, she laughed as she flung herself into the crowd and let them swallow her in their embraces.

TEN

Staying

"DOMINIQUE?" MALKIA TROTTED toward her old friend, touching his forearm. "May I have a word in private?"

He nodded and waved good-bye to the group with whom he had been conversing. "What can I do for you?" he asked, holding out his arm for her to take.

She linked arms with him, and they strolled toward the eating edifice. "Before we leave in the next few days, I would like to work with you and your people to create a foundational structure upon which you can build the rest of your fortress." Pausing midstride, she twisted to face him, squeezing his arm with her fingers. "I realize you have made peace with the Artemisians and I find your forgiveness encouraging. I've loved seeing everyone work side by side, rebuilding Domesca. I hope that, moving forward, we can all find a diplomatic way to continue in a peaceful manner."

"I agree," Dominique replied, tilting his head down to gain a better view of her. "Ever since Nedra's death, I've surrounded myself with busy tasks, to erase her burnt corpse from my mind."

"I know the feeling," she murmured, her eyes glazed over in thought.

He gripped her hand within his own and kissed the top of it. "The

Artemisians were following the orders of your father and had been fed a lie that caused our fight. If they can forgive you, and I'm so grateful they have, we can forgive them." Turning back toward the edifice, he began his slow walk again. "Nedra's death was at the hands of the Elvens, and although so many were lost by the Artemisians, my revenge lies with those pointed-ear heathens." He gave her a sideways glance. "And your father."

She nodded and sighed. "Mine, too."

He was quiet for a few moments, appearing to be deep in thought as they neared the tables in front of them. "We would love your help finishing what we can of the fortress," he finally spoke in a hushed tone. "Having the Artemisians here this past couple of weeks has helped us clear away the debris and larger rocks, giving us the room to recreate the castle as it was before it was destroyed. And with the extra hands from your group, I believe we could build the first floor within a matter of days." He held out a chair for her to sit in and then sank into his own chair across from her. "How long do you have?" He pointed at her burgeoning belly.

She glanced down and smiled, her fingers trailing over her core. "Another six months, maybe a little less."

"How will you fight with the child draining you of your powers?" he asked, lifting an eyebrow.

"I'll use the energy of the moons and Theia. And if that isn't enough, I'll have the warlocks to assist me." She leaned back in her chair, toying with a lock of her hair.

"And what it all that isn't enough?" he asked.

She shrugged, shaking her head. "I'll leave the battle. The children will be with us, but we are planning on settling on Theia and then taking the fight wherever my father is hiding. If fate delivers us into another circumstance and I'm unable to protect myself, I'll take the children and leave."

Leaning forward, Dominique rested his arms on the table in front of him. "I believe in you." He shot her a crooked smile. "I always have. Even back in our tiny town of Lancaster, I stood by you, knowing you had something within you that not many others possessed. Your inner strength shines through as brightly as the suns and I'm honored to have known you for as long as I have."

Malkia chuckled as tears brimmed in her eyes. "Thank you, Dominique."

"You're welcome, my dear friend." He rose from his chair and patted her on the shoulder as he stood over her. "Speak with Cormac, as well. If you and your group can remain here for a few more days and help us rebuild the first floor, we would forever be indebted to you."

"We will stay," Malkia answered, knowing Damon would be furious because of the threat of the Creators. But in her gut she knew this was the right choice.

He smiled down at her. "I'll send Cormac over to speak with you."

She nodded as he walked away. Alexa and Mataya were walking toward her, with the four children straggling behind them. Sitting up straight in her chair, she waited for them to reach her.

"Great speech, Malkia," Alexa said. She pulled out a chair, its legs scraping against the pebbles on the ground. Sitting down, she folded her arms over her chest, a wide smile plastered across her face.

"Thank you," she replied, setting her elbows on the table. "I see that you two have become acquainted." Her gaze danced between the two women.

Mataya nodded, crossing her leg over her knee and leaning back in her chair. "I've been teaching her how to focus her powers. She's quite powerful."

Twiddling her thumbs, Alexa smiled widened. A crimson spark shot between her palms and Malkia sat up straight again, watching the energy in Alexa's hands. "I knew I possessed something I didn't understand fully. Too bad I didn't realize my abilities when I was being abused by my oppressive spouse." She rubbed her hands together, extinguishing the light and looked over at Malkia. "With my powers as strong as they are, I would love to travel with your group and learn as much as I can, before we face your father and the Elvens. Would that be a possibility?"

"What about your children?" Malkia asked, her brows furrowing.

"I would bring them with us. They can remain with your children on the ship or wherever we settle." Her ice blue eyes closed for a moment, before refocusing on the women. "I realize it's a risk on all our lives, but I need to leave Esaki and I want to make a difference in our civilization's future. You're planning to remain on Theia, and I believe that's where I belong as well. I know I can assist, if Mataya and the other warlocks wouldn't mind teaching me."

"As long as you understand the danger you're placing your children in," Malkia advised. The scent of a newly made campfire wafted past her nose and she twisted around, her eyes sweeping across the area. "The day is nearly over." She released a long breath, leaning back in her chair, once again. "I would like to help with our evening meal and then spend the night preparing for tomorrow. I've told Dominique that we will remain here for a few days and help build the first floor of the fortress, giving them a head start on their construction."

Mataya froze in midrise from her chair, shooting a pointed look at Malkia. "Are you sure that's wise?" she questioned, her hazel eyes growing wide as she straightened her stance.

"I know that it's the right move, if that's what you're asking," Malkia responded, pushing her chair back and rising as well. "I need to speak with Cormac and Damon, but I'll see you both at dinner. Welcome to our team." She tapped her fingers on the table and nodded at Alexa. Waving good-bye to the ladies, she turned to face Cormac, who had been patiently waiting a few yards away.

Strolling toward one another, she embraced the robust man, inhaling the sweet scent of honeysuckle mixed with freshly ground tree foliage. "It's great to see you again," she murmured, stepping back and examining his face. His sapphire eyes were weary but happy and his long hair was pulled out of his face into a low ponytail. "Still sporting the full-beard, I see." She grinned as he ran his hands down it and a smile rose on his lips.

"It's easier to just let things grow, these days." He folded his arms across his chest, drawing in a long breath. "I enjoyed your speech and I'm grateful for your desire to protect our people." He paused and she tilted her head to the side, waiting for his caveat. "But I think you're a fool to rush into this war while you're with child."

She nodded, raising an eyebrow and continued to wait for him to say more.

He sighed and threw his arms up in the air. "Nothing? No come back?" he asked, perspiration shining on his brow.

"Cormac, I appreciate your concern, but we always knew if I didn't defeat my father on Thalia, I would continue this quest." She planted her bare feet on the ground and allowed the peace of Esaki's spirit to rise within her. "I don't want to argue with you. It's already been decided. And besides, if I don't show my face, my father and those arrogant Elvens will come looking for me. Don't you know this would be the first place they would search?"

"It still doesn't make it right," he muttered, tears shining in his eyes. "You're like a daughter to me. How will I know if you survive?"

She leaned in and wrapped her arms around the hefty man. "I'll make sure you know, even if I have to return and give you the news myself."

"Maybe I should just accompany you to Theia." He held her tight, patting the back of her shoulder with his large hand. She felt like a child in his arms.

Shaking her head, she stepped back. "You're needed here. Dominique needs your help with these people and the rebuilding of Domesca. I would be selfish to take you with me."

He lowered his eyes and drew in another deep breath as he nodded. "How long until you leave?"

"I agreed to stay until the main floor of the fortress is completed." Her gaze darted over to the kitchen area where the clang of metal pans reverberated, and the smell of fresh bread filled the air. "I would like to assist as much as possible while we are here. Is there something you need help with, aside from rebuilding walls?"

"The children need to be wrangled together and given a basic education. Food needs to be prepared. Firewood has to be gathered. Livestock requires attention and feeding." A horse neighed in the distance, just as he spoke. He chuckled. "See? They know what they require. We will take any assistance you can offer, while you remain with us. You're more than welcome to spread your people out and work until you drop."

A couple of dogs sprinted past them, heading toward the smell of food. "I think I'll join them in the kitchen," she said, jabbing her thumb at the mutts.

"I'll see you at dinner, then." He tugged her into another squeeze and patted her on the shoulder before walking away.

Making her way toward the sound of dishes and the scent of cooking meat and baked bread, she smiled and waved at Esta, who was still playing with the other children. She was eager to move on with their mission but delighted her daughter would have some time on the moon she adored the most.

ELEVEN
One Last Night

LANDON'S SCREAMS BROKE into Malkia's deep thoughts. Wiping the perspiration from her brow, she jumped to attention, scanning over the other end of the fortress where he was crouched against a tree, sobbing as he held his foot. Dropping the tools she had in her hands, she raced toward him, sliding to a halt in front of him and stooping to his level.

His tear-filled eyes stared back at her as his chin quivered. "My foot," he whispered, tears swimming down his cheeks. "I dropped that rock on top of it." He pointed to massive boulder, nearly twice as big as his head.

"You picked that up?" she asked, her hands sliding his foot from his grasp.

He cried out, his whole body tensing as she eased his foot into her lap. Closing her eyes, she placed her hands over his limb and sent her light into it as she channeled the energy of the moon through her. She could feel his muscles tighten and he squeezed her wrist, before relaxing. Hearing him sigh, she opened her eyes to see him leaning against the trunk of the tree, his foot completely healed.

"What happened?" A hand curled over her shoulder.

Peering up, her eyes met Damon's. "He crushed his foot with that rock." She pointed to the boulder, lifting his foot off her lap and rising from the ground. Reaching down, she helped Landon to his feet and brushed the leaves and dirt from his clothes and hair.

Damon shifted around her and bent down to look Landon in the eyes. "That rock is extremely heavy. Why did you pick it up?"

"It's not that heavy," the boy whispered, taking a deep breath before continuing, "At least when I picked it up, it wasn't. But when it slipped from my hand and landed on my foot, it felt like fire rushing through my body."

Damon glanced up at Malkia, before hugging his son tight. "Be careful, boy. You have my strength, but gravity still exists and our bodies are susceptible to damage." He leaned back. "I'll teach you how to protect yourself." He kissed Landon on the forehead and rose up to meet Malkia. "Thank you, for healing him."

"Of course," she replied, gripping his bicep. "We leave tomorrow, and I'm afraid these children are stepping into a warzone we aren't prepared to meet."

"We will hide them away." Damon tousled Landon's hair and shooed him away from the work area that surrounded the fortress. "But on our journey to Hemera, we will need to teach them how to protect themselves." He paused, his eyes glazing over as he stared towards the children. "And each other."

"If Landon's abilities are surfacing, I'm wondering how much more Esta is capable of doing. Her telepathy is improving, and I believe she's able to push into others minds as well, just like Misty." She wrapped her arm around Damon's waist. "These children are our legacy, and we must end this for them."

He nodded, his mind a million miles away from her. Squeezing him tight, she shook her head, knowing he was worrying enough for the both of them. She kissed his cheek, bringing him out of his reverie. Smiling down at her, he planted a kiss on the tip of her nose and swept a wisp of her hair out of her eyes.

"You're right," he whispered, his eyes taking in her entire face. "Let's cleanup for the evening meal and prepare for our journey tomorrow."

The second sun was dipping down on the horizon, spreading purple hues across the opposite mountain. Malkia surveyed the work they had done over the past few days and smiled. The entire first floor had been repaired or rebuilt, leaving the Esaki people a safe place to reside as they continued building onto the fortress. One of the original walls remained standing, so they had also reinforced that, ensuring it didn't topple while they worked around it. By the time she returned, the fortress of Domesca would be whole again.

Leaving Damon, she grabbed a cleaning cloth, and headed toward the stream. Gingerly walking down the trail, she picked her way over the rocks and into the hidden pool she had been using since they arrived.

Scrubbing every inch of her body, she hummed a quiet tune and watched the scurrying wildlife around her. The connection with Esaki was always strongest when she was alone and this moment was no different. She could feel the energy swirling around her, sweeping past her naked body and whisking her tresses around her neck. Dipping low into the pool, she washed her hair and swam around the water, enjoying the warmth cradling her body.

She missed Damon and wished he wouldn't be so distant with her. He struggled with his words and always needed time to hash through his emotions, before speaking with her and the wait drove her insane. These past few days, she'd spent alone, only gaining his attention if something was needed. If only he was there with her now. They made a great team and just thinking of his arms around her, aroused her in ways she never knew possible until she met him.

Rising from the depths of the pool, she stood waist deep and allowed the breeze to rush across her bare chest, enjoying the sensations it created in her body. Smiling to herself, she stepped up the rocks and sank onto the giant boulder at the top. Lying on her back, she closed her eyes and allowed the air to dry her body, while she listened to the chirping crickets and the scampering of small animals.

She must have dozed off, because when she opened her eyes, the stars were twinkling between the branches of the trees and the suns' light had disappeared completely. Although the air was chilly, she was in no hurry to return to her last night on Esaki. Instead, she continued to lie still, absorbing more energy.

It wasn't long before the smell of meat cooking wafted past her nose, sending her empty stomach into a frenzy of bubbly gurgles, pleading for nourishment. Sitting up, she slipped her clean shirt over her head and tugged her trousers over her hips, securing them around her waist. She could hear her stomach growling as she tiptoed up the trail, pushing her faster toward the fortress.

Dropping her dirty items at the ship, she trotted over to the eating area and was happy to see that everyone was already bustling with the end of the day energy. Landon and Esta appeared out of nowhere, each of them grabbing one of Malkia's hands. She glanced down at them and smiled, her eyes trailing over to Damon, who wore a matching smile.

TWELVE

Reunited

THE VESSEL WAS quiet as Malkia strolled down the corridor toward the bridge. Esta and Landon were tucked away in their beds. Before they'd departed Esaki, she had connected with the energy once more and was still high from the powers brewing within her.

The doors to the bridge slid open and she stepped across the threshold, ready to speak with Damon for the first time in over a day. He was sitting at the helm, lost in thought as his eyes stared blankly out into the space.

"I miss you," she whispered, sinking into a nearby chair and waiting for him to acknowledge her.

His jaw twitched as he twisted in his seat to face her. "Why didn't you tell the Esakians and Artemisians that the Creators have been notified of your presence?"

"Because I'm going to stop the Creators." She sighed, crossing one leg over the other. "We must first focus on my father and then I'll put a halt to the Creators' return."

"How will you stop them?" he asked. His hands reached up to his temples, rubbing them with his thumbs.

She rose from her chair and walked over to him. Standing behind him, she placed her hands on the sides of his head and kneaded it with her thumbs. "I have to destroy the All-Seeing Eye on Theia, but I also believe if I can find a way to contact my grandparents again, they can give me the information I need to stop them."

"It was a great speech," he murmured, moaning under his breath as she pressed near the base of his skull. "I can understand why you wanted to escape this life after retrieving Esta. Now that I have Landon back in my life, I feel the same way." He leaned forward so she could massage his neck. "But I'm standing next to you, through all of this. No matter what happens."

Malkia nibbled on her bottom lip, focusing on the sore spots on his neck and shoulders and not really wanting to interrupt his thoughts. The silence filled the room as she kneaded the knots in his upper back.

"I miss you too," he spoke up a few minutes later. "My anger isn't really toward you, although I've been directing it at you." He reached back and clutched one of her hands, twisting around and kissed the top of it. "With this child inside you, absorbing all of your powers and making you weak, I feel powerless to keep you safe. And that is the most petrifying fear I have. The thought of Ginny or Dario or your father laying their hands on you, creates a rage within that's difficult to manage. And after what happened on Thallassa, I'm terrified that side of me will emerge again."

Stepping around the chair, Malkia settled onto his lap and pressed her lips to his, wrapping her arms around his neck. His hunger for her overrode any other emotions, as his hands strayed up and down her body and his tongue explored her mouth. Clasping her about the ribcage he rose from the chair and she wrapped her legs around his waist, not once breaking the seal of their kiss.

He stumbled toward the wall, pressing her back against it as she slid down, connecting the soles of her feet to the floor. "What if someone walks in?" she asked, running her fingers through his dark hair.

"They'll leave," he replied, chuckling for a moment, before his eyes darkened and a devilish grin rose on his lips.

Sliding her trousers over her hips, she moaned as his fingers traveled down her thighs, pleasing her in all the right places. She grinned as he tugged her to the floor and left a trail of kisses across her chest and torso, driving a moan from her lips over and over again.

Moments later, they collapsed in each other's arms, laughing from the absurdity of their location. They were completely exposed, with the bright lights shining on them and the possibility of any one of their family or friends walking in on them.

Damon propped himself on his elbow and kissed the tip of her nose. "It's probably a good idea to put on some clothes before we become the talk of our small and suffocating community."

Chuckling at his words, Malkia nodded, kneeling on the chilly floor, thankful she wore long pants today. Once she was dressed again, they returned to the helm and Damon checked their coordinates.

"We haven't passed by Thalia, yet." He pointed at the screen that showed each of the moons' locations. "Once we have Thalia at our backs, it will be about seven days before we arrive to Hemera."

"And there's no way to for this big piece of scrap metal to move faster?" she asked, her eyes glued to the stars outside the ship.

"If there is, I haven't figured it out yet." He sighed, sinking into his seat and stretching his legs out onto the edge of the control panel. "Apollo is resting, but he agreed to work on the ship, once he woke."

"What about the Artemisians' ships?"

He shook his head. "They have the capability of flying much faster, but they aren't leaving Esaki for another few days. What we should have done is taken their ship to Hemera and had them fly this vessel to our meeting point on Theia."

"There has to be a way," she muttered, walking around to the other panels and reading what each screen and control panel's function was. "When you found this ship back on Eris, do you know who you took it from?"

"It was your father's," Damon replied, watching her examine his machine.

She froze. "Stop it. Really?" she asked, turning to face him, her eyes wide. "Where was it? And do you think he's using it to spy on us?"

"I found it in a nearby bunker from your father's fortress. There were a few smaller ships there as well, but this one had the space we needed. I didn't think he would miss it."

"But what if he knows we have it and he's able to tune into our frequency? What if this vessel is the reason he's been one step ahead of us?" she questioned, a small bit of fear clawing at her insides.

Damon's eyes glazed over in thought. "It's a possibility," he said, slowly, his eyes focusing as they swept around the room, halting at the control panel at the far end of the room. "Apollo and Koleton are the experts—and maybe Asha. Once they're all awake we will need to have a meeting."

THIRTEEN
Brilliant Artemisian

"HOLY, MOTHER OF Artemis," Apollo cursed, scowling up at his audience while he rubbed his sore head. "I swear, you're all watching me for the entertainment of seeing me injure myself." He growled as he focused back on the switches underneath the panel he had torn apart.

Koleton chuckled, running his hands through his beard and leaning forward in his chair. "I thought you knew how to make this engine purr," he jested, winking at Esta, who was grinning over at him from her seat on the floor.

"Your puny human controls are impossible for my fingers to maneuver," Apollo grumbled, not taking his eyes off of his current task, but kicking a leg out toward Koleton.

Bursting into a fit of laughter, Koleton tumbled to the ground, clutching onto his knee in mock demonstration of Apollo's threat against him. Malkia chuckled, her eyes watching Apollo glare up at his comrade, drawing his lips back into a snarl.

"Just you wait, Sir Koleton," he mumbled, returning his attention to the wires he had just tugged out from the wall.

"Shaking in my boots, my favorite half-god." Koleton hopped up from the ground and shook his foot above Apollo's torso.

Swiping his leg up and across, Apollo brought Koleton down on his back in a split second, without even pausing in his work. "Now what, grunt?"

Koleton groaned and shot Apollo an icy glare, before picking himself off the floor. Glancing over at her mother, Esta's eyes were wide, but she burst out in giggles when Malkia smacked her own forehead, shaking her head in amusement.

"This half-god just kicked your ass, in one swift move," Apollo muttered under his breath, as Koleton drew his finger across his throat and then pointed it at the Artemisian.

"This isn't over, not-good-enough-to-be-a-full-god." Koleton pranced around the room like a pony, flashing Esta and Landon a thumbs up as he made his way to a half-smiling Damon.

Apollo scooted out from underneath the control panel, replacing the cover, before turning to face everyone in the room. His eyes fell on Koleton. "Hey, small nugget, I bet you have no idea how to shift this boat into full-speed." A devilish grin spread across his thin lips and he rubbed his palms together, his eyes daring Koleton to challenge him.

Koleton slapped a hand over his mouth, his eyes growing wide in mock horror. "Is it possible? The great and glorious less-then-god has achieved the impossible?"

Apollo growled, tossing a lever toward the imbecile's head. Koleton's hand flew up, curling around the object before it connected with his skull, glaring at the Artemisian as he lowered his hand back down. "Insert that into the orifice, on the main control panel and the screen will instruct you how to increase your speed," Apollo coached, pointing behind Koleton.

The small group laughed and cheered. Malkia rose from the ground and curled her arms around the creature's waist. "You did great,

Apollo." She peered up into her friend's face and smiled. "Thank you."

"You're welcome," he replied, hugging her in return, while tossing Koleton another look of contempt.

Koleton was examining the lever, his eyes flashing between it and the control panel. Snatching it from his grasp, Damon whistled softly as he pointed at the Artemisian. "We all want to hear it, Koleton. What do you say to Apollo?"

Twisting to look at Damon, Koleton glowered at his friend before facing the rest of the group and Apollo. "You're the master of all ships, oh mighty half-god of our galaxy." He stood up straight and mock saluted the Artemisian, before placing his finger up to his skull and pretended to shoot himself in the head.

Apollo plucked at the cuffs of his shirt. "Don't tempt me, you filthy beast." His straight-laced expression remained still, but as the silence grew, a smile spread across his face and he chuckled. "You should see your faces." He tossed one of Damon's tools over to Koleton. "If you desire my expertise further, I will be resting my weary head in my quarters."

The group burst into laughter and Koleton snickered, throwing a few fake punches as Apollo sauntered past him. Apollo reached up and covered Koleton's entire face with the palm of his hand, pushing him just enough to make the man teeter on his feet, before continuing on his way.

Malkia stepped over the Asha and curled her arm around her shoulders. "You didn't want to be a part of that conversation?" she asked, grinning over at her adoptive mother.

Asha laughed, the lines around her eyes crinkling with delight. "I figured it was time to let the male inhabitants shine. And didn't they do a marvelous job of demonstrating their talents?"

"They did," Malkia joked, toying with a lock of Asha's silver hair. "You knew how to make it work ages ago, didn't you?"

"Yes, I did," Asha responded, tossing her a warm smile. "This was far more entertaining, and it gave me some time to sit with you and the children. These are the moments I'll treasure."

"Me, too." She turned to face Asha, taking in a deep breath and looking sideways, gathering her thoughts. "I'm also glad you were able to verify that my father wasn't using anything to track us. The thought of him having that ability was terrifying."

"Yes, it was." Asha's fingers grazed across her cheek. "Is there something else you would like to ask me?"

Shrugging her shoulders, Malkia locked eyes with Asha. "With the loss of my mother and Skye, a weight had settled onto my heart, causing me to lose focus. And when Esta and I were reunited, I wanted to walk away from this war completely." She sighed, sagging against the wall behind her. "Back on Esaki, I felt whole again, for the first time since before this journey began. I have a connection with that moon, like no other, and now that we've departed I'm afraid I won't be able to re-manifest my powers while I'm carrying this child. The thought of not being able to protect my loved ones, including my own body, terrifies me."

"I'm not going to lie," Asha replied, pushing her hair over her shoulders and glancing over at Koleton and Damon. "If we make it to Theia, and the energy there doesn't revive you, you'll need to sit this one out. We can't take a chance on either of your lives. These children need you alive." Reaching over and clutching Malkia's hands, she passed her own magic from herself and into Malkia's body. "There are several of us here that can help keep you feeling well, but we won't be able to recreate your powers. Those come from within you and until this child is born, you will have to learn alternative ways to adjust. Esaki possesses a special energy, unlike any of the other moons I've lived on or visited. Your connection with the spirits there is something to be admired, as I've never heard of anyone regenerating like you have." She paused and swept a wisp of Malkia's hair away from her eyes. "It would be thrilling to find out why."

Nodding, a smile crept across Malkia's lips as Asha's powers eased a slight discomfort in her gut and helped her focus on the mission. "Let's hope Theia provides us with more answers than questions, and truly is the place where my father will fall."

Damon held up his hand and motioned for Malkia to join him and Koleton. Tugging Asha along with her, they halted in front of him.

"It's time," he told them, pointing at the screen with the lever pushed into the panel. "Apollo is a genius. We are just now passing Thalia, but once we give the machine the coordinates, it will increase our speed in order for us arrive in less than one day."

"The big goof is brilliant," Koleton chimed in, setting his hand and chin on Asha's shoulder and throwing them a wide smile. "He might only be a half-god, but he's our half-god."

Asha laughed and pushed Koleton away. The kids giggled as he stumbled to the ground and rolled right to them, kissing each of them on the nose before bouncing back up. "Even the great warlock can't keep me down." He winked, before slipping out the door.

"On to Hemera." Malkia's hands gripped the edge of the panel and watched as Damon began typing in the coordinates. "This will be the farthest I've ever been away from home." She turned to look at the two kids and then back at Damon and Asha, who both smiled at her. "I'm just grateful it's with all you misfits."

FOURTEEN

Twin Statues

THE VESSEL HOVERED above the moon, Hemera, pausing in high orbit as the entire group clustered onto the bridge. Ustarum stood closest to the window, staring down at the dark and rocky moon, while the others spoke around him. Watching him from across the room, Malkia attempted to reach him telepathically, but he was blocking contact and she didn't want to press. Stepping gingerly around each person, she made her way to her mentor.

"What do you think?" she asked, her gaze locking on Hemera as her thoughts turned to Tantiana.

Ustarum's gaze shifted to her, and he smiled. "You wanted into my mind a moment ago, didn't you?"

She nodded, clasping her hands behind her back. "I wasn't wanting to know your personal thoughts. I just wanted to speak to you without everyone else hearing," she whispered, throwing him a sideways glance.

"I see," he replied, returning his focus to Hemera. "I've been here before." He held up his hand as she began to speak, halting her words. "And so has your Esaki mother. Our history together runs back more years than I can remember, and our shared secrets are many. But this one, has to be spoken, especially now that Mataya has finally learned the truth."

"What are you saying?" Malkia asked, pinning him down with her piercing, green eyes.

He twisted around and stared out into the group, his eyes lingering on Mataya and Alyssa. "Alyssa," he called out, waving at her when she looked up. "It's time."

Damon and Koleton both stopped talking and turned around. Following her mother, Mataya appeared calm, a smile twitching on her lips as she wiggled Esta's nose and then leaned over and kissed her on the forehead before continuing after Alyssa. The rest of the room quieted, their attention focused on Ustarum.

A crimson flush crept up Alyssa's cheeks and she rolled her eyes as she neared Malkia and Ustarum. "Why do you always have to make a big scene?" she asked Ustarum, grumbling as she stood next to him.

"Isn't that why you fell for me?" he asked, holding his hands out for Mataya to take.

Alyssa chuckled. "Hardly." She shook her head and glanced over at Malkia. "I'm going to say this, before he reveals my past. I hope, when I was raising you, that I was a good enough mother to make up for my misdeeds."

"I'm not worried, mom," Malkia replied, watching as Mataya grasped Ustarum's hands and leaned in to give him a kiss on each cheek.

She stepped between Malkia and Ustarum and turned to face the crowd as well. Ustarum cleared his throat and ran his hand down his beard, scanning over the faces in front of them.

"Now that we've arrived to Hemera, I have a warning for all of you." He wrapped his arm around Mataya's waist and drew her close.

"But first, I need you all to know that your friend, Mataya, is my biological daughter."

The silence in the room became deafening. Even Koleton was speechless, his jaw agape as his eyes widened. A few moments passed and Esta coughed, jolting the group out of their shocked state.

"What?" Justin spoke up, shifting through the crowd and pausing a few feet away. "Why am I just finding this out?"

"Because I've been sorting it out in my head," Mataya responded, her smile faltering for only a moment. "Receiving this news was shocking, but after I had some time to digest it, I was able to understand myself better. And really, what kid wouldn't want their dad to be a part of their life?"

Malkia's heart lurched and she swallowed back the sudden pain from Mataya's innocent comment.

"You just found this out?" Justin asked, shifting from one foot to the other and folding his arms across his chest.

"A few days ago." Mataya waved a dismissive hand. "You and I can speak privately about this, as Ustarum has some more information to divulge."

"Now that we let that cat out of the bag, let's continue," Ustarum started, tossing Justin a stern look before turning to the others around him. "Alyssa and I spent many weeks together when we first conceived Mataya. On one of her visits, we stopped by the Dellanti statue on Eris and discovered a portal by accident."

"What kind of portal?" Koleton interjected, stepping closer. Apollo followed suit, hovering just over his shoulder. "Good grief, Giganto. Could you give me some breathing room?" He glanced back at the Artemisian.

Apollo pursed his lips, as if he was considering the request and then shook his head and turned his attention back to Ustarum. "Don't interrupt the story, little man."

"Continuing on," Ustarum interrupted, irritation sweeping across his face. "The portal was similar to a wormhole, except it's always there, created a long time ago, either by our Creators or an extremely ancient civilization. But it only connects to Hemera, which makes sense. They are nearly polar opposites from one another, and this moon is farther out than any of the others. Whoever constructed this portal, did it in order to have an easy connection to this rock. What treasures are hidden here, I do not know, but there's a reason it was built."

"This is what you needed to tell us?" Malkia asked, her feet growing tired from standing. Shuffling away from her sister, she sank into the nearest chair.

Ustarum's eyes narrowed, and he threw her a pointed look. "No, Malkia. That's the information leading up to the plot twist. What have I told you about being patient?"

She grumbled, her shoulders slouching as she looked away. Damon stepped over to her and kneaded her sore and tired shoulders as both their attention returned to Ustarum.

"Alyssa and I entered the portal, arriving on Hemera within a few seconds. On the other side was a similar statue to the Dellanti one and a valley filled with tall and thin pyramids. It was an astonishing sight, but we had no idea where we were. At first, we thought that we could easily explore, believing we had remained on Eris, but as night began to fall, we realized there were actual creatures that go bump in the night." He stopped short, his gaze falling on Landon and Esta. "I know the children will remain on the vessel, but we need to keep an adult with them at all times. And if for some reason the ship is infiltrated or damaged, we have the portal through which to escape."

"What would infiltrate the ship?" Damon asked, leaning up against Malkia's chair.

Alyssa waved her fingers in the air. "I have the answer to that." Everyone's eyes swept over to Alyssa. She patted Ustarum's shoulder as she stepped forward. "Ustarum and I quickly discovered that night arrived a bit faster on Hemera. As we were racing back to the statue, we noticed in the shadows there was movement, as if something or someone was following us. We called out to it, determined to protect ourselves, when this two-legged creature, about two or three feet tall reached out of the shadows and with the strength of a ritter, dragged me kicking and screaming into the darkness."

Mataya's hands covered her mouth and she looked over at Malkia. "Did it look like the small statues in the pyramids?"

Alyssa ran her fingers through her hair, as her eyes darted between Malkia and Mataya. "Maybe," she whispered, looking upward to the ceiling. "Actually, yes, I think it was. I only saw its face for a split second, before it was concealed in the shadows, but yes, I honestly believe it could resemble those statues."

"What happened after it dragged you away?" Koleton asked, waving his hand to coax her into continuing. "We can talk about statues later."

"It bit me on the thigh," she replied, licking her lips.

"The little bastard bit you?" Koleton eyes widened, completely enthralled by the story. "Then what?"

Ustarum curled a hand around Alyssa's arm and nodded toward the kids, reminding them there were young ears listening. "I was able to pull her out of the shadows, but the little devil was preparing to pounce again, once the second sun finished its descent. Out of nowhere the Nesoi slipped up next to us and nudged us toward the statue. One of them carried Alyssa, after she collapsed from the poison in her veins." He shook his head and his eyes glazed over, returning to that day in his head. "I was terrified. We had just discovered she was carrying our child and she was planning on leaving her husband for a life with me." He refocused as he turned to peer at Malkia.

"What about me?" she asked, her stomach knotting up. "And what about our brother?"

"You and he would've joined me and Ustarum." Alyssa's lips melted into a frown. "We planned on residing on Esaki, but leaving the town that your father lived in."

"And what about him?" Mataya asked. Her foot tapped rapidly against the floor. "You were going to rip away his children?"

"It's not that simple," her mother replied, scratching her arm as she crossed them over her chest. "And this part of the conversation should be done in private."

"As I was saying." Ustarum pulled Alyssa protectively next to him. "We had just found out Alyssa was with child and now she'd been bitten by an unknown creature. The Nesoi's presence was instantly calming, but it didn't remove all the dread writhing in my heart as I watched the love of my life lose consciousness." He tightened his grip around Alyssa's shoulders. "As we reached the statue, the Nesoi paused and gathered around Alyssa and one by one they began to breathe this blue energy across her body. Not long after, her eyes fluttered open and she was able to stand with my assistance. We returned through the portal and never ventured that way again. It wasn't until later that we discovered we had traveled to Hemera. By then Alyssa had returned to her husband and our families' feud was her reason for breaking ties."

"I was petrified to return to Eris," Alyssa whispered, peering up at Ustarum. "It was only an excuse to protect myself." She released a deep sigh and swept her gaze across the room, looking at each individual, eventually locking eyes with Mataya. "Because of what the Nesoi did for me, I believe this is why you have the ability to communicate with them, along with bending space with the help of your sister's channeling. And me—I changed that day as well. Not only was I more fearful, I was able to create magic I'd never known existed. The Nesoi are the ones who gifted my ability to shapeshift. And because you grew within me, their energy permeated you, as well. Once you arrived on Eris and gained that connection, the pieces to your heritage slid right into place. You're one of a kind—a gem who was graced by the magic of the mysterious Nesoi."

Mataya's eyes twinkled. "They are quite magical. I'm grateful they protected and healed you." She stepped over to her mother and planted a kiss on her cheek.

"After that long story," Ustarum said, holding up his hand to quiet the whispering crowd. "We want you all to protect yourselves, while we gather the information we need on Hemera. Malkia, if you're unable to use your protective light, I suggest you remain on the ship."

"I'll be fine, as long as you or Asha or Mataya stays with me." Malkia rose from her chair and stepped over to Esta. "But we need two or three adults to stay with the ship and keep all intruders locked out."

"I'll stay," Alyssa volunteered, waving her fingers at Malkia. "I'm in no hurry to step on that terrain again."

"Who else?" Malkia asked, nodding at her mother as she sank to the floor and pulled Esta into her arms.

"I can stay." Bella stepped forward. "I haven't been feeling well, and I could use the down time. The kids are much more fun, anyway." She threw Malkia a weary smile before sliding back to her seat.

"Me too." Alexa raised her hand from the chair she was sitting in. "I'm still learning how to use my powers and I don't want to make a mistake out there that could endanger everyone else."

"Okay, good." She turned toward Apollo. "Is it possible to fit seven of us in your vessel and leave this ship in high orbit?" she asked, wringing her hands together.

He shook his head. "I wouldn't advise leaving your ship up here, with only the three women and four children to protect it. But to answer your question, yes we could all fit in my vessel if needed."

"What do you think, Mom?" Malkia's gaze drifted back to Alyssa, her fingers trailing through Esta's hair.

"I think we should park this beast on the moon and be near, in case you need anything." Alyssa touched her hand over her heart. "I know my two daughters and sister are capable of protecting themselves, but I would be devastated if I knew I could have helped but was too far away. Let's stay close to one another."

"Do we know which pyramid holds the map?" Koleton asked, lifting on eyebrow towards Malkia.

"There are hundreds of pyramids on Hemera," Ustarum interrupted, folding his arms over his chest and tapping his foot. "It would take us days, possibly weeks to explore them all. Is there something in those scrolls that can help us?"

"I'm fairly certain I know where the map is," Malkia answered, pointing over to a pile of scrolls in a container near the main control panel. "I've studied every scroll that contains information about Hemera, and there are two strange things. Never once are those two-legged creatures mentioned, but they speak of the spawn of the Illumanti several times. I'm not sure what Illumanti are, but I'm fairly certain they aren't pleasant, considering they describe their bite to be the fire of a hundred dragons rippling through every cell of one's body." Her eyes fell on her mother. "Does that accurately describe your experience?"

"One hundred percent, yes." Alyssa's nose crinkled and she shivered, rubbing her hands up and down her arms.

"What about the second strange thing?" Esta questioned, peering up at her mother.

"This is the one moon where the scrolls point directly toward the pyramid that contains the map. In fact, there is more written in these scrolls about why they broke the map into pieces than anywhere else." She rested her chin on the top of Esta's head. "What makes Hemera so different from the other moons?" Her eyes danced around the room, finally settling on Damon.

He shrugged. "We have the Nesoi and the dragons as allies. Although I agree the children should stay on board, I'm not too worried about these spawns, as you called them." He nodded toward Malkia. "One thing is certain, we have arrived earlier than planned and Tantiana might not even be prepared for our landing. I suggest we spend some time surveying the terrain and reading over the scrolls. Then, once we spot our dragons and the Nesoi, we can begin our search for the map."

Koleton groaned. "You mean I have to spend more time in these cramped quarters with you people? And this imbecile?" He stabbed his thumb toward Apollo.

"Who says we want to be stuck with a half-twit like you," Apollo muttered, running his finger across his neck, after making sure the kids weren't watching.

"*See*?" Koleton cried, pointing at the Artemisian. "I'll be dead before we have any fun."

"Grow up, you two," Ustarum barked, a crimson flush rising in his cheeks. "I know you think this is funny, but we need to start making plans. Either get in the game or leave."

"Woah, touché," Koleton muttered, standing up straight and throwing Apollo a pointed look. "You're hurting the half-god's feelings over here."

Apollo snickered, punching Koleton in the arm and sending him sprawling to the ground. "I apologize, tiny man. I forget my own strength sometimes." He rubbed his fist and walked away to join the others who were reading through the scrolls.

Malkia grinned over at Koleton, loving how Esta fell into fits of giggles over his absurdities. She swore he was doing it just to please the child. He blew Esta a kiss and picked himself off the floor, sauntering after the Artemisian.

"I'm taking the ship into the atmosphere," Damon warned, securing his restraints over his shoulders. "I suggest everyone takes a seat and buckle up, since we are about to enter the unknown."

Everyone in the room stopped what they were doing and found an empty seat. A few moments later, they entered into a dark and gray storm system, tossing them to and fro, and making it difficult to gain their bearings. Esta gripped Malkia's arm, her eyes wide, before slamming them shut and dragging her knees up against her chest to hide her face.

"Hold on," Damon yelled above the thunder and wind. Shifting the vessel to the right, he flew it around an obstruction he could only see on his radar. His eyes widened and Malkia held her breath as she stared at his clenched jaw, inwardly cursing herself for not waiting for a clearer day to venture into this mysterious atmosphere.

FIFTEEN

Welcome to Hemera

HER HEART DRUMMED in her ears, her breath coming in short as she gripped the armrests. Glancing around the room, she could see Landon crouched in his chair. His eyes were widening with each passing breath.

"Landon, look at me," she called out, holding out her hand. "Take a few deep breaths and focus on my voice. Your father is an excellent pilot and if anyone can land us safely, it's him."

Landon's eyes darted to meet hers and then snapped back to the viewing window. "How can he see where he's going?" his trembling voice nearly drowned out by the rush of the wind.

"Look at me," she demanded again, reaching for him. "Give me your hand."

He stretched out and clutched her hand. "*I can't see anything,*" he cried, tears spilling down his cheeks. "Are we going to crash?" His other hand covered one of his eyes as he peeked over at her, avoiding the outside world.

"Your dad has a guide that tells him what's in front of him," she replied, squeezing his hand. "Now look at me."

The young boy tore his eyes away from the window and stared at her. "How does it work?"

"The radar?" Malkia asked, receiving a nod from the child. "If there is anything drawing near, it shines red on the machine, showing him which way is clear. Once we fly out of these clouds, he won't need it as much, but he's always watching that screen." She quieted, glancing out the window just as they broke out of the storm system and the winds calmed around them. "See? We made it." She pointed at the mountainous terrain jutting up around them. "He always knew where we needed to fly."

Damon drew in a long breath and peered over at her, mouthing "thank you" before turning back to the view. They flew into the valley and she examined the rocky ground below. The vegetation was nearly non-existent. The cracks in the valley seemed to spiral downward for miles and they gave up trying to see the bottom as they flew up and over the first mountain.

Rising into the sky and away from the stormy clouds, the group gawked at the dreary sight before them. This area of the moon was covered with rugged peaks, whose mottled black and gray faces were devoid of life and stretched on in every direction, for as far as the eye could see.

"How will we find the pyramids in this mess?" Alexa asked, leaning forward in her chair and letting go of the hands of her children.

"We have a machine for that as well," Malkia replied, unbuckling her restraints and rising from her chair. "The coordinates are listed on the scrolls." She rummaged through the bins until she found the right one and handed it over to Damon. "It will take us right to them. But first, we want to explore for a while and find up what we are really up against."

"This is the home of the dragons, but I don't see anything flying in the sky." Koleton stepped up next to Malkia and Damon, his eyes searching the gray background before them.

"Don't get too eager to see the dragons," Malkia admonished, tucking her hands in the pockets of her trousers. "We have enough to worry about, without running away from their breath."

"Can't you just speak with them?" Mataya asked behind her.

Turning around, she could see the rest of the group hadn't budged from the chairs, except Apollo who was reading one of the scrolls. "Most likely, but just like Sirath, I don't know if they'll listen. We do need to go to the pyramids and find Tantiana, but on our way I would like to explore as much as possible. This moon is different and there's a reason why so much was hidden on it."

"We need someone to be on watch for dragons and any other creatures that might see us as a threat," Apollo spoke up from the corner in which he stood. His fingers ran down the parchment in his hands and then he pointed. "Just from reading this one scroll, I'm apprehensive about anything that moves on this moon." He glanced up at all the staring eyes. "It's filled with the terrors of nightmares."

Malkia turned back to Damon and stepped lightly toward him. "Maybe exploring is out of the question. Let's head toward the pyramids and see what Tantiana has discovered."

Inputting the coordinates into the vessels mainframe, he smirked when it lit up the spot on the screen. Placing the vessel in auto-pilot, Damon leaned back and released a loud exhale.

"Were you really surprised it wasn't as easy as you hoped?" he asked, staring up at her.

She shook her head. "Apparently, I'll never learn." She moved away and stopped in front of Alexa's chair. "It's a good time for you to learn more. I might need you out there, or at the very least, I'll need you assisting Bella and Alyssa in protecting this vessel and all those children."

Mataya's hand curled around her forearm. "We have this covered." She nodded her head at Ustarum. "Are you ready, Alexa?" she asked, smiling down at the woman.

"Yes, of course." Alexa rose from her chair. "Do you want all the children to come with us?"

Malkia nodded, waving at Landon and Esta. "Thank you, Alexa. I'm grateful you decided to join us."

"It's my pleasure." She smiled before following after Mataya, towing the children behind her.

Turning back to the outside view, she watched as the terrain swept beneath them, never seeing any creature venture out from the many caves. *Maybe they don't care if we're here*, she thought, scanning every inch of the ground that she could see.

They care, Tantiana's thoughts interrupted hers. *Sirath was able to bring some of the dragons to your side, but for the most part, we're on our own.*

Malkia bounced on her toes, seeing her dragon's shadow sweep across her view outside. *You found us!*

You're hard to miss, Tantiana replied. *The Nesoi have all gathered near the pyramids awaiting your arrival. Sirath, the hatchlings, and a few other dragons are waiting there as well.*

We'll follow you, she replied. Malkia hurried over to the window and pointed. "Follow Tantiana," she told Damon, glancing back at him.

"I'm going to kiss that dragon on her nose, when I get my hands on her," Koleton boasted, smiling wide as he circled around to see everyone left in the room "Apollo, what are you and your half-god abilities going to do for us today?"

"That's for me to know." Apollo didn't stop reading or even look up at Koleton, which apparently only increased his desire to aggravate the Artemisian.

Malkia watched her friend's smile fade slightly and chuckled, knowing the battle between those two would never let up. Walking over to Damon, she curled her hands over his shoulders and kneaded the knots on both sides.

"Don't ever stop," Damon moaned, relaxing against her fingers.

Another storm flashed off to the far left. The forks of lightning lit up the sky, one after another, striking the ground several times as Malkia watched. Tantiana and the ship steered toward it, flying into another rocky valley. Over to her right, she noticed a large shadow and balked as the face of a massive creature emerged from a hole in the mountainside. Malkia's body tensed as the ice blue eyes of a beast, five times the size of her dragon, followed their passage, its nostrils flaring and frigid contempt rising in its expression.

"How would we ever battle a creature that enormous?" she asked out loud, a chill rushing down her body.

"What creature?" Damon eyes snapped open and he leaned forward in his chair, searching the dark terrain.

That one won't bother us, Tantiana replied. *It hates everyone and everything, but it's too lazy to venture from its cave. It's the other dragons that might be an issue. And the Illumanti spawn.*

Have you seen the spawn? She replied, looking down at Damon's bearded face.

Yes, Tantiana answered. *Stay far away from them. If they're able to capture you, you won't survive.*

A sigh rushed across her lips. "I'm the only one paying attention to the outside, apparently. We just flew by a giant creature—far larger than Tantiana." She glanced around the room, seeing a few others had gone and Koleton was resting in his chair. "Apollo, did you see that monster outside?"

His head flew up and his reptilian eyes narrowed. "No, I did not." He dropped the papyrus he'd been reading and stalked toward her. "What was it?"

"Tantiana says we don't need to worry about it, but seriously, you two should be paying attention as well. Not just me," she scolded them, facing the outside world again. "We need to know what we're up against." She pressed her hands against the glass, searching for any other creatures.

"I apologize, Malkia." Apollo halted next to her, setting his large hand on her shoulder. "We were all lost in our own worlds for a moment there. Especially the lazy, waste of space back there." He gestured toward Koleton. Twisting around, he threw a wadded piece of parchment at his head, striking Koleton in the forehead and jarring him awake.

"What happened?" Koleton stuttered, his gaze sweeping the room, landing on Apollo. His eyes narrowed and his hands balled into fists, slamming them both down onto the armrests. "Alright, big guy. Let's take this outside."

"Can it wait until we land?" Malkia spoke up, nodding toward the window.

Koleton glanced over Malkia's shoulder and back at Apollo. "Or we can take it downstairs to the dragon's quarters. There's plenty of room down there for me to kick your ass."

Malkia chuckled and Damon threw another wadded parchment at Koleton. "Get up, you slothful man. We have a job to do."

"Aye, aye captain." Koleton saluted Damon and with his other hand pretended to shoot Apollo. Rising, reluctantly from his chair, he stumbled over to the others and peered out the window. "What do you need me to do?"

"Watch for anything attempting to eat us, kill us, or blow us out of the sky," Malkia ordered, patting his shoulder.

"No problem," Koleton replied, shooting her a devilish grin. "Just my specialty."

"We figured as much," Damon shot back, winking at the red-haired man.

The storm continued to fester and it appeared as if the red blinking dot was just on the outskirts of the whirling winds. Malkia cringed, watching the lightning strike in quick succession, never letting up and filling the darkening sky with blinding light.

Are we going to seek shelter soon? She reached out to Tantiana.

It's just a little farther, and there's a cave in the mountain, right above the pyramids that the vessel will fit into.

Malkia nodded and glanced over at Damon. "Tantiana will lead us to a cave where we can ride out this storm."

"I was beginning to wonder what her plan was," he murmured, messing with some functions on the control panel. Gripping the controls, he took it off auto-pilot and guided the vessel toward the cave as it came into view.

Moments later, the ship was nestled inside the cave and the group had ventured outside the ship. Tantiana, Sirath, and the hatchlings were settled into the far corner of the nook, along with five other dragons. It didn't take long for Malkia to connect to each one of them and they greeted her kindly, bowing before her.

She returned the gesture and then kissed her dragon on the nose. *I missed you.*

And I, you. Tantiana replied.

Turning to face the other end of the cave, she noticed there was a large group of the Nesoi huddled together, eyeing the ship and the storm beyond. *They're used to these storms,* Tantiana interrupted her thoughts. *The Nesoi reside as the majority species here on Hemera and have protected its lands for thousands of years. They thrive in these storms. Just watch.*

Malkia did just that, sinking to the ground and leaning up against Tantiana's body. As the storm began to build just outside the cave, the Nesoi rose from their hiding place and shifted around the ship, heading for the opening. Jumping up from the ground, she followed the tail end of the group, followed by Mataya.

When they reached the edge of the cave, Malkia paused and a smile rose on her lips. She watched the Nesoi glide off the cliff and disappear into the thick, gray clouds. Every so often, one would emerge, diving to and fro as they communicated with a high-pitched whistle. It was intoxicating to watch their music unfold.

"Have you ever seen what I can do with lightning?" Malkia asked her sister, turning to face her.

"No," Mataya answered, her fingers curling around Malkia's. "Don't do anything foolish. Remember that child is draining your powers."

"This energizes my powers." She turned to face the opening to the cave and then stepped outside, holding her hands to the sky and concentrating on the energy and magic in the air. "This place is pulsating with an intense spirit and something tells me, you possess this ability as well."

Just then a bolt of lightning connected with her hand and using her mind she seized hold of it, shifting it around the sky and making it dance right alongside the Nesoi. Glancing back at her sister, she laughed when she saw her wide eyes.

"Can you feel it?" she shouted, flinging the bolt of lightning out into the storm in front of them, illuminating the twin statue of Dellanti, showing her wings piercing the clouds and brightening again with each new strike.

Mataya nodded, laughing and pointing at her sister. *"You're drenched,"* she shouted over the winds. "Aren't you freezing?"

Shaking her head, Malkia waved for her sister to join her. "You won't regret it. The Nesoi have given you this ability. Just search for the magic in the air and then hold onto the traveling light."

As Mataya stepped out into the open, Ustarum wrapped his arm around her waist and hauled her back into the cave. Malkia ran after him, her eyes narrowing as she stalked toward them.

"Why did you stop her?" she yelled at him, her drenched hair clinging to her cheeks.

He whirled around to face her. "Just because you possess this ability, doesn't mean your sister does. Why would you be so reckless?"

"I could feel it," Mataya shouted, her hair already plastered to her face and a crimson heat suffusing her cheeks. "You may be my natural father, but you don't have the right to tell me what to do."

"How do you know that lightning won't obliterate you?" Ustarum yelled back, stepping closer to Mataya.

"Do you really believe I would ever put my sister in harm's way?"

Malkia questioned, her brows furrowing, following closely behind him.

Ustarum ignored her, putting his hand up to stop her from continuing. "Answer me, Mataya. How do you know?"

Mataya stood frozen, her teeth chattering from the cold and her eyes darting between Ustarum and Malkia. "*I don't know*," she cried, tears springing from her eyes. "But I could feel the magic in the air and if my sister can do it, why can't I?"

"Because you're not the same." Ustarum wrapped her in an embrace. "If you want to find out if it's possible, then let's do it in steps. Malkia was able to figure it out on her own, but her ways aren't always safe. It's imperative to be careful and logical when you're dealing with the energies of these moons. If you're not capable of absorbing what they offer, it could destroy you."

Malkia shook her head and turned back to face the storm, furious with Ustarum. With her, he had pushed her to the edge, nudging her over several times. But with Mataya he coddled her as if it would make up for all the years he had missed. Grumbling to herself, she watched in silence as the storm system slowly dispersed and the air began to clear over the pyramids.

Stepping to the edge of the cave, her hand flitted up to her mouth, astonished by the number of pyramids spread out across the valley floor. There had to be hundreds. And not only were they a magnificent rusty red, they also glittered from the newly fallen rain. Not too far off, she could now see the twin statue clearly and bounced on her toes with excitement. She was about to dig up some ancient secrets.

A hand wrapped around her waist and she turned to see Damon staring out into the valley. "This is amazing," he said, tightening his hold on her. "Don't even think of leaving without me."

She laughed and rose up on her toes, planting a kiss on his cheek. "You know me too well. But I'm not leaving without you. You're my ride." She slapped his backside with the palm of her hand, just as the Nesoi began gathering below them in the valley. "Do you think they want us to go to the pyramid tonight? The suns are already setting."

"They'll have to wait," Damon replied, clutching her hand and towing her away from the edge of the cliff. "We need to retreat to the ship and start again at first light."

Malkia glanced over her shoulder, before trotting behind Damon and catching up to the rest of the group who were already boarding the vessel. Closing the cargo door, with the dragons and Nesoi remaining outside, she climbed the steps to the corridor and followed her friends and family to the upper levels.

SIXTEEN
Malkia's Pyramid

"ARE YOU POSITIVE this is the pyramid?" Damon asked, his brow glistening with perspiration.

Malkia glanced over at him, wiping her own forehead with the back of her arm. "Where did this heat come from?" Her mouth was parched and she licked her dry as a bone lips. Tasting the salty sweat from her skin, she forced herself not to gag. "And yes, this has to be the right pyramid. If not, I'm a complete idiot and so are Ustarum and Alyssa."

Damon nodded, his own lips cracking from the intense heat. "The atmosphere is different here. Extreme weather patterns and unusually short nights. This moon must tilt and rotate differently than any of the others." His surveyed the terrain, searching for the others. "*Finally.*" He pointed past Malkia. "Here come Mataya and Asha."

She pressed her hands against her knees and let her head hang low as she caught her breath. This place was a nightmare. The sounds that arose after the suns set were the worst that she'd ever heard. The eerie yelps and roars that rushed by the cave opening, along with what sounded like a cross between a wolf howling and a human shrieking continued to invade her thoughts, even after the suns had risen. Morning couldn't have arrived faster.

And now this. The heat was unbearable, and she had nearly fainted while waiting for the others to join them. Damon and she had polished off the water they had brought with them nearly an hour before and had been waiting for the rest of the team to bring more. To finally hear their voices as they approached brought her foggy mind back to reality.

"Are you ready to break into this structure?" Mataya asked as she strode toward them.

Malkia twisted around to see her sister and before another word could be uttered, she vomited on her shoes. Swaying with exhaustion, she felt Damon's arms wrap around her body, and suddenly, her feet were swept off the ground and she was peering up at his face.

"I'm taking her back to the ship," he barked at the others, pushing past them. "I warned you this was a mistake to send her out first, but no one listens to me." He growled, glancing down at her for a brief moment. "Especially her."

"Give her to me," Ustarum demanded, his voice grating on Malkia's nerves. She watched Damon's jaw clench just as her eyes closed.

She felt her body shift to the ground and several hands were placed on her body and forehead. Suddenly, her mind was relaxed and a soothing sensation swirled from her head and down to her stomach, easing the nausea and exhaustion that had overcome her body. Drawing in a deep breath, she opened her eyes and stared up at her group.

"I swear," she said, propping herself up on her elbows and slowly sliding into a seated position. "If I survive this pregnancy, I'll never have another child again."

She held up her hand, shielding her eyes from the suns' light with her other hand. Damon reached down and gripped her arm, helping her to her feet and holding her against him as she looked out at the concerned faces that surrounded her.

"I'm fine. Thank you for easing my nausea." She waved a dismissive hand. "Let's finish this, so I can leave this heat."

Mataya stepped forward and grasped her hands. They closed their eyes and began chanting their incantation. Connecting with the magic in the air, Malkia sensed it was different than the others. There was a silkiness as it slid against her skin and rushed inside her, swirling through every cell in her body, and suddenly exploding from her like a bright star. Gasping, she jumped back, releasing Mataya's hands as her eyes snapped open.

"What was that?" she croaked, glancing around at the others.

The entire group, except for Mataya, was shading their eyes. Her sister shook her head and pointed toward the pyramid. "I don't know, but it worked."

Traipsing over to the entrance, Malkia peered in as far as she could see, but only a wall of darkness met her. Searching for her inner light, she felt nothing and sighed with disappointment. Her eyes met Ustarum's. "Will you light up the path, please?"

"You don't have any energy remaining within you?" he asked, stepping around her and tossing his light into the void. "What I just witnessed says otherwise."

"There's nothing left. It drained me of everything I already possessed." She pouted, moving into the pyramid. Her heart leapt into her throat as a sticky cobweb clung to her face and her eyes focused in on the abundant residue covering the entrance. She shrieked, flailing her arms around and swatting at the strands as she scampered back outside where the group was watching with smirks smeared across their faces.

"Not much luck, I can see," Ustarum jested, plucking a cobweb from her cheek.

She scowled at him, feeling the weariness slide through her body once again. "I'm not in the mood for your tone, Ustarum. If you have a plan, let's hear it."

Mataya wrapped her arms around Malkia's shoulder and helped her to the wall, just inside the pyramid. "Sit down and rest. Here's my water." She handed her sister her bottle and turned back toward the rest of the group. "Spit it out, Ustarum. We all know you have something you want to say. Stop berating my sister."

A smile rose on Malkia's lips and she peered around Mataya to see Ustarum's face. Unfortunately, his daughter's lecture didn't faze him and he still wore his lame, lopsided grin.

He winked at Malkia. Turning his attention to Mataya, he pointed into the pyramid. "Obviously, this moon has altered magic. It was readily available, but as Malkia is now witnessing, if it's going to give something, it requires a payment in return."

Malkia's hand fluttered to her belly. "Did it hurt my child?" Her voice quivered as she realized the possible ramifications of her actions.

"No, it didn't," he replied, holding up his hand to halt her assumptions. "I sense his powers more strongly than before. Hemera's spirit gave an abundance of energy to him. Probably more than you want him to have, but it most definitely didn't hurt him." He paused and waved for the rest of the group to join Mataya and Malkia. "What it procured was what remained of your own abilities." He held up his hand again, signaling that he wasn't finished. "However, it's possible you might have them returned to you, before we depart. If not, your powers will forever be lost to you."

A silence filled the air and Malkia realized she was holding her breath. Releasing it quickly, she inhaled deeply, her wild eyes dancing to each of the others faces. "Are you serious?" she asked, pushing up from the ground and sagging against the wall.

Ustarum nodded. "Come here."

She obeyed, stepping quickly toward him. His hand rested right above her heart and he closed his eyes. A few moments later, he opened them and refocused on her.

"They're gone. Like I said, your child still possesses a significant amount of power, but as for you, there's nothing." He shook his head, releasing his hold on her. "I'm sorry. Unless the spirit of Hemera chooses to return your powers, you will be without them for the rest of your life."

A sob rose in Malkia's throat and she turned away from them as the tears tumbled from her eyes, streaming down her cheeks. She wiped them away, collapsing to the ground and silently cursing her father for forcing her hand. Now she would be the one to pay. Again.

"It's not over," Mataya whispered in her ear, her arms encircling her shoulders. "We will find a way to have your abilities returned."

She shook her head. "We can't deviate from our mission. As much as I want my powers, I survived the majority of my life without them and I can figure out how to do it again."

"What about Tantiana?" Mataya asked, wiping a lone tear from Malkia's cheek.

"I don't know," she replied, numbness saturating her body as she pressed up from the ground and brushed the dirt from her trousers. "It's not about me. We need to keep pressing forward and finish what we came here to do."

Damon stepped forward and kissed her on the forehead. "I'll lead the way, my love. Just take my hand and we'll do this together."

She nodded, pursing her lips together and gripping tightly to his hand. Moving into the pathway, Damon used his dagger to cut through the cobwebs, guiding them all down a slight slope. After several minutes, they reached a steel door, preventing them from venturing farther. Damon tugged on the handle, but it didn't budge. Clutching it with both hands, he pulled harder, clenching his jaw as nothing happened.

Asha spoke up from the back. "Maybe you should push inward, instead."

A laugh burst from Malkia's lips and she quickly covered her mouth with her hands. Damon twisted around, shooting her a dirty look. "I'm glad my troubles are amusing you." He leaned over and kissed her on the nose. "Although, your laugh, even at my expense, is the best thing I've heard all day."

Turning back around, he shoved himself against the door. The groan of the door echoed down the pathway, pausing their movements as they glanced behind them. Pushing harder, the door creaked as it eased open the rest of the way, revealing another dark room.

Ustarum shifted around the others and threw his light into the room. The space spread beyond their view and stretched upward to the tip of the pyramid. Malkia followed the two men into the room, just when they heard Koleton's voice yelling for them.

"Are you all down in that dark abyss?" Koleton's voice was heard again.

"Yes," Asha shouted in return. "Hurry up. We're about to leave you behind."

"Don't you hurry me, woman," Koleton yelled, even though he was

already half way down the path. "I've had to drag this massive brute around with me, and let me tell you the chore that has been."

Malkia glanced back just in time to see Koleton sprinting toward them, waving his hands for them to clear the path. Right behind him, Apollo was barreling after him, his eyes glued to the back of Koleton's head.

"Here they come," Malkia announced, stepping to the side and letting Koleton fly by her, followed by Apollo. "I'm so glad you two could finally join us."

The two of them halted a few feet past the doorway, gazing at what stood before them. A statue rose up in the middle of the room, stretching to the top, with its dagger nearly piercing the ceiling. Malkia tilted her head to see the face, but the woman was looking heavenward, with her hair trailing all the way down her back, hitting the tops of her legs. She wore the armor of a warrior, her boots rising to her knees and her arms covered to her wrists, similar to the gear Malkia had worn on Thalia. Her importance must have been significant, but they were out of time, and Malkia really was in no mood to remain on Hemera any longer than was needed.

"Let's spread out and find the map." She trotted away from the group, searching the walls. Her eyes moved as high as she could see, but being unable to fly was incredibly irritating in this moment.

"How can I help you?" Damon asked.

She swung around to face him. "I just want the map found so we can leave."

"What if they want you to figure out how to reacquire your powers?" he questioned, peering over her head and crinkling his forehead. "*Sweet mother of Theia.*"

Malkia whirled around, searching for whatever he was looking at. "What?" she asked, her eyes darting from one drawing to the next.

"Focus on the images," Ustarum spoke up from behind them.

She stepped forward, just as Ustarum shone his light directly on the image in front of her. It was an etching of a sleeping dragon, with a woman leaning against it. Shrugging her shoulders, her eyes moved upward to a cottage behind the dragon, trees surrounding it in every direction. She froze. The next image was of a vessel, just like the one they were using, with three people walking up to meet the ones emerging from the ship. Her fingers hovered over the image, as she moved to the next one.

The Guarding Statue of Eris. And two women standing near its rear door, holding one another hands. She swallowed hard, her stomach churning with what little remained in it. Shifting over more, a group of people stood, surrounding the dragon and grasping hands. She paused and slowly turned to face her friends, her eyes trailing up the body of the statue in the middle of the room as her blood froze within her veins.

SEVENTEEN
Hidden Message

"THIS ENTIRE PYRAMID is my story," she whispered, listening to her heartbeat ram inside her skull. Sweat trickled down her spine, and she shuddered with a sudden chill that swept across her arms. "Am I hallucinating?" She stepped forward, one foot after another, halting at the base of the statue and tilting her head to see the top. "This is me? When? Where?" She wiped her brow, her hands trembling as her feet became glued to the floor beneath her.

"We'll search for those answers," Ustarum replied, the pressures of his fingers around her forearm, forcing her to focus on him. "Malkia, you knew you were foreordained. Someone went to great lengths to document your every step until you set foot in this pyramid."

"How do you know it doesn't foretell my future?" she asked, finally twisting fully to face him.

"Come see." He held out his hand and led her to the next wall, tugging her to the corner and pointing to the section a few feet off the floor. "This is where we open the pyramid."

She knelt down and examined the painting. Her gaze moved to the final image and there she stood, just below the statue, staring up at the dagger. "They knew my every move." She hiccupped as she blinked back the tears threatening to spill from her eyes. Rising from the ground, she whirled around to see everyone staring at her. "My entire path was already planned. Everything, down to this very moment." Her shrill voice echoed throughout the room. One hand clenched the other, knuckles white and the tendons of her wrist stood out sharply beneath the skin as she begged her powers to emerge.

"Malkia, stop." Mataya shifted in front of her, running her hands up and down Malkia's arms. "Give us a minute to look at everything. Maybe this structure holds answers that we haven't discovered."

She nodded, wringing her hands together and directing her attention to Damon. Rushing into his arms, she leaned against his chest. He held her tightly, running his fingers through her hair as she allowed all the emotion of the moment to pour from her. She could hear the others whispering and walking around the room, and it brought her a sense of peace, knowing her friends weren't stopping until they understood why this was here.

Relaxing into Damon, her heart calmed and she sighed, inhaling his musky scent that she loved. Leaning back, she wrapped her arms around his neck and dragged his face down, pressing her lips to his.

After a long, deep kiss, she released him, her gaze locking onto his dark eyes. "Thank you."

"No, thank you," he whispered, giving her another squeeze. "It's nice to know you still choose me."

"Always," she murmured, stepping back and smiling up at him.

"We found the map," Asha announced from the other side of the room.

Malkia zipped toward Asha, twisting around a hidden corner, skidding to a halt in front of the etching of the map. "Let's copy it over to parchment and leave this place."

Koleton dragged the parchment from his pack and patted Malkia on the shoulder as he handed it over to Apollo. "We have your back. I hope you know that."

"I do." She peered up at him and smiled. "I'm lucky to have all of you."

"When I first met you back in the forest on Esaki, who knew our path would lead us to this place?" he said, watching Asha and Apollo work on the map. "Well, someone knew." He chuckled, glancing over at her. "Sorry, I couldn't help myself."

"Don't be sorry," she replied. "It's just a strange feeling to discover my whole life was already prearranged. Every step."

"I can only imagine." He ran his fingers through his hair. "Does it make you wonder what's inside all the other pyramids?"

"Yes, it does," she whispered, thinking back to the moment the light burst through her body and her abilities were sacrificed. "The spirits of Hemera always planned on taking my powers. They had to, as it was foreordained. And if they hadn't, I really believe my anger would've demolished this place."

"Do you think it would be wise to break into the other pyramids?" he asked, his eyes wandering around the room.

"I doubt we could force our way into any of them, unless you're the owner of the story inside," she mused, one corner of her mouth lifting into a smirk.

"You think?" He turned to face her, toying with the end of his beard.

"Absolutely." She laughed, the fine lines crinkling around her eyes, as a tickle of delirium rose in her belly. "My story. My path. It led me to the scrolls and they pointed directly to this exact pyramid. Who else has a path similar to mine?"

"It's possible there will be or have been others like you," Ustarum interjected from behind them.

Malkia and Koleton twisted around. "What would their mission be?" she asked, a fresh non-ability energy soaring throughout her body.

"Anything the Aletheians need to be accomplished," he explained, folding his arms across his chest. "I imagine there have been several adventures that led a warrior to their story, reminding them that they were called to perform a certain task for our people. This one is yours. The Aletheians need you and with everything that has happened and still needs to happen, you need them."

"I think you're right." Rolling back her shoulders, she left the men and walked over to the walls, stepping alongside each one and examining every image, until she could no longer see them high above her. "Knowledge is power, right?" she called out to the group. "I think there's a message within these images. One that will lead me to my grandparents or to the Aletheians or to the most direct way to end the Elven's voyage and cruelty."

"Maybe the message is on the statue," Damon suggested, his eyes surveying the base of the statue.

"It could be anywhere within this structure," she said, glancing over at him. "An image that doesn't belong. Words written in a language that only I can read. Or maybe another map." Her voice lowered to a whisper as she examined the paintings near her. "Something that doesn't belong."

"I think you're on to something," Ustarum's voice echoed from the other side of the room. "Everyone who isn't already doing a task, start searching every inch of this pyramid."

She didn't know how she knew, but something had sparked within her the moment she remembered the light that shot through her. They were leading her to a message. If only she had her power to fly, so she could reach the higher levels of the room.

"Look what I found," Mataya shouted near the same corner where the map was tucked away. She pulled out a long ladder. "There are two of them over here. We can start searching higher."

Koleton trotted over to Mataya and grabbed the ladder she was holding, leaning it up against the wall. Ustarum moved around them and pulled the other ladder out from its hiding spot.

"Why didn't they just let you keep your flying ability?" Koleton asked, as he made his way up the ladder, looking at each image as he climbed.

"Good question," Malkia mumbled, following Ustarum. Gripping the rungs of the ladder, she pulled herself up and rose one step at a time, examining each painting.

They searched each wall over the next hour in silence, and found nothing out of the ordinary. Moving to the statue, Malkia took the front and Ustarum examined the back. Losing hope, Malkia's eyes had grown weary and each time she came up empty handed, her desire to return to the ship increased.

"I think I found something," Ustarum called out from his side of the statue.

"What is it?" she asked, pausing in her search.

"Another painting," he replied. She could hear him moving down the ladder. "You'll need to take a look, as I don't know if it's anything that has happened yet."

She hurried down the ladder and rushed over to his, climbing as quickly as she could. Halting in front of the image, she tilted her head to the side and examined the vast painting before her.

A blue ocean was off to one side, with a white sandy beach in the middle. She was standing on the beach, facing an older man and woman. Her grandparents. The Aletheians hovered back within the trees, watching her as she seemed to be speaking. Her eyes darted from one end of the painting to the other, searching for any other clues, and locked onto some writing just above it.

Stepping up to the next rung, she leaned over and studied the words. It was written in another language, but as she attempted to say them out loud, she instantly knew what they meant. "Your Grandfather's message will assist in amending the path for the people of Theia's Moons. Find him." She spoke the words several times, engraving them in her memory, before easing her way back down the ladder.

"What was it?" Mataya slid up next to her, concern etched across her features.

"Another image," she replied, patting Mataya's hand. "I have to return to the Blue Planet. I believe my grandparents have a message for me."

"That's what the image told you?" Ustarum asked, pressing his palms together in front of his lips.

"Yes, as well as the words above the image." She pointed up and sighed. "It's done. We have what we need and now it's time to depart. When we find the pyramids on Theia, I must find a way to speak with the Aletheians and insist that they transport me to the Blue Planet. There's a reason this message was placed for me, and I'll only receive my answer when I speak with my grandparents."

Everyone nodded in reply, exhausted from the long day. They returned the ladders to their hiding spot and gathered up their items, just as a shriek echoed down the path and whisked through the doors of the room. The entire group froze, remembering where they were and what was waiting for them when they emerged from the pyramid.

"What are we going to do?" Asha whispered, looking over at Malkia.

"We'll have to make a run for it," she replied, glanced around at the rest of the group. "The dragons and Nesoi are waiting to protect us. The moment we are outside, we don't look back until we are safely inside the ship."

"Should we just wait it out until morning?" Koleton spoke up from just inside the door.

"We can't leave the ship unprotected all night," Mataya reminded him. "Those creatures will destroy it and everyone inside."

"Let's move," Malkia ordered, stepping toward Koleton.

Damon and Mataya flanked her as they tiptoed to the next doorway, noticing the shadows casted against the other pyramids, indicating the second sun was setting. Pausing at the threshold, Koleton and Apollo peered around the corners and waved for everyone to start moving.

Dashing from the entrance, they sprinted through the maze of pyramids, racing up the hill to their ship. Ustarum and Asha stayed to the rear, protecting them with their magic. The dragons swooped down and in this moment, Malkia wished she could communicate with Tantiana. However, the Nesoi seemed to connect with Mataya and surrounded them on every side.

As they emerged from the cluster of pyramids, Malkia relaxed. She saw the ship in good condition, and no giant creatures, other than the dragons surrounded it. The Hemera statue loomed up on one side of the vessel, and, in the rays from the sun, she appeared to be watching them.

Malkia slowed for a brief moment, gazing up at the massive statue, reminding her of the one on Eris. The only difference was this one had long, flowing hair that swept over her chest, and she held a staff to her left side. There had to be an importance to this specific spot, to have someone go through all the trouble of creating a direct route to it. What else was this moon hiding? Or were the pyramids and their secrets all it guarded?

Shaking her head, she pressed forward, sprinting across the rocky terrain with Damon only a step ahead of her. In her peripheral vision, she cringed as she watched him twist his ankle, stumbling on a loose stone and falling face first into the rocks. Smacking the side of his head, he was knocked out instantly.

EIGHTEEN

Her Light Within

MALKIA SCREAMED FOR Apollo, running back to help Damon. That's when she saw the movement behind the Nesoi. A small figure flashed past the group of them, its clawed hand ripping into Damon's leg and dragging him away right before her eyes.

Apollo and Ustarum gave chase, seizing hold of Damon's arms and hauling him back from the shadows. The Nesoi bent down and breathed a blue smoke at the creature. It screeched, just like the one that had been near the pyramid, and released Damon's leg.

Tossing him over his shoulder, Apollo whirled around and sprinted back up the hill, followed by the rest of the group and the Nesoi. Moments later, they closed the cargo door and Koleton took control of the vessel, steering it back to their cave in the mountain.

Laying Damon on a bed in the infirmary, Ustarum and Alyssa bandaged his wounds and sent healing light into his body. Malkia watched, helplessly, from the corner of the room, biting her nails as she paced the floor.

"Go tend to the children," Alyssa ordered, looking over at her. "They need you more than Damon does."

"Are you sure?" she asked, her gaze shifting between her mother and Damon. "What if my powers return? I can help him heal."

Ustarum shook his head, drawing in a deep breath. "If that time comes, we'll give you the space you need to help Damon, but for now you're only in the way."

Taking in a sharp breath, she pivoted on her heel and trudged out of the room, heading toward the children's play room on the other side of the ship. Her heart thudded inside her skull and she struggled to draw in a full breath. Halting midstride, she leaned against the wall, sliding to the floor and placed her head in between her legs, as the tears rolled down her cheeks.

A sense of helplessness spiraled through her mind. The image of Damon being torn away from her grasp thundered through her memories as she gasped for breath. Gripping her hair, a sob tore up her throat, shaking her body as terror slithered relentlessly through her core.

How am I to win this battle, if I can't protect the ones I love? It was a thought that consumed her. She felt completely and utterly alone for the first time in months.

Glancing down the corridor, she wiped her face with the back of her hand and rose to her feet. She hurried to her quarters, where she locked the door and stumbled into the powder room. Knowing their water supply was low, she ran the water in the shower for only a minute, washing off the dirt from the pyramid and the tears from her face. Tugging on clean clothes, she then brushed her wet hair, examining her reflection in the mirror.

Her emerald eyes sparkled, even though she felt a weight of grief on her shoulders. Setting her brush on the table in front of her, she pressed her palms flat against it and leaned closer to the mirror. Somehow she had to find the strength to continue. A sudden white light shone around her body and drawing a quick breath in, she smiled.

"There I am," she spoke to herself, watching the light intensify.

It wasn't her powers, knowing those were still gone. But it was her soul, an eternal fire that could never be extinguished, no matter what anyone else did. The darkness she had consumed on Enyo was never an issue. Her spirit was always there, never-ending, regardless of the events that took place during her physical life. At the nadir of her powers, she finally remembered who she was.

Breathing in the light, she stood up straight and grinned at her image in the mirror. "I can do this."

Prancing out of her room, she skipped down the hall, elation feeding every cell in her body. Opening the door to the children's play room, she laughed when she saw Esta's wide eyes staring back at her.

"Mama!" her daughter exclaimed, racing toward her and throwing her arms around her neck as Malkia stooped low. "I was so worried about you."

Alexa smiled from the other end of the room, waving for her to join them. "We've been playing every game in this place to keep their minds off your absence. How did the mission go?"

"It was a success," Malkia replied, setting Esta back onto the ground.

"Where's my dad?" Landon asked, rising from the floor and embracing her with a tight hug.

Malkia sank to her knees and held his face within her hands. "He was injured on our return to the ship, but he's being bandaged up in the infirmary and will be good as new before you know it."

"Everyone made it back safely?" Alexa asked, concern washing over her expression.

Malkia's head bobbed up and down, pursing her lips as she glanced around the room. "We're all fine. It was the most bizarre experience of my life, but we each returned in one piece."

"I want to hear more," Alexa said, shifting around the kids and pointing to the couch against the other wall. "Why was it so strange?"

The kids resumed their playing, laughing at Zoe's choice of dress-up clothes. She was sporting a top hat, mustache and bright orange jumper suit. Malkia chuckled, settling into the cushioned seat and turned her attention to Alexa.

"The heat out there was excruciating. I wanted to give up, but Ustarum and Asha gifted me more healing light, enabling me to continue." Her eyes traveled heavenward as she nestled farther into the cushion and recalled the day's events. "When Mataya and I channeled the spirit of Hemera, it did open the pyramid door. But in return, it stole all my abilities. They're completely gone." A laugh vibrated up her throat, and she peered over at Alexa.

"But you're not upset?" Alexa asked, twisting around to face Malkia more fully. "And your skin is glowing. How could that be, if your powers have been extinguished?"

"I was angry and frustrated, at first," she replied, wringing her hands together. "When we returned to the ship and Damon was hurt, my mother and Ustarum excused me from the room because they believed I was useless to his recovery. I have to admit, that stung." She licked her lips and brought her leg up onto the couch, turning enough to face Alexa directly. "But as I spiraled down a path of self-loathing, I suddenly caught sight of my Eris mother in my own eyes and my entire outlook shifted. My powers are not what define me. And neither does the outcome of this mission. My soul is eternal, and that's what you're witnessing in this moment. Whether or not my abilities are returned, I'll always carry the energy of my own spirit, which is just as powerful as the magic that surrounds us."

Alexa's eyes widened, her head nodding over and over again. "Can you practice the craft?"

"I don't know," Malkia answered. "I always believed you had to possess that blood in your veins, but it wouldn't hurt to test it out." She locked eyes with Alexa. "But that will have to wait. The children should retire to their beds, so we're prepared to leave Hemera at first light."

"What about the pyramid? What happened inside?" Alexa questioned, leaning forward and squeezing Malkia's leg.

"Awe, yes." A smile rose on her lips, laughing at the memory. "If you could only see what we discovered. I was blown away by it." She paused, her eyes darting over to Esta, making sure the children weren't listening, before focusing back on Alexa. "The entire pyramid was a story of my life. It had drawings of significant events, from the moment I was conceived to the exact spot that I was standing when I realized what I was seeing. And in the middle of the pyramid stood a statue of myself, clutching a dagger that nearly pierced the top of the structure."

"Those pyramids are tall," Alexa gasped, leaning back against the armrest. "Who would take the time to carve that statue and outline your entire life?"

"That's the question of the day." Malkia sighed, running her fingers through her damp hair. "And if each one of those pyramids contains someone's life path, along with their statue, what does it all mean?"

Alexa nodded. "Strange, indeed," she mumbled.

"Anyway, I'm grateful we made it back." Malkia turned to face the kids, setting both feet firmly on the ground. "Landon and Esta, it's time to clean up your mess and say goodnight to your friends."

Waving good-bye to Alexa and her children, she strolled down the corridor and opened the door to the kids' room. Tucking them both into their beds, she planted a kiss on each of their foreheads before turning down the light and securing the door behind her. Her next stop would be to see Damon.

Placing her hand on the door, she stepped over the threshold once it opened and over to Damon's bed. Ustarum and Alyssa had gone, leaving him alone to mend internally. She eased herself onto the bed next to him, laying her head on his chest and settling against him. Closing her eyes, she was out before she realized how exhausted she had become.

NINETEEN

Sacrifices Will Be Made

WAKING WITH A start, Malkia's gaze flashed around the room, wondering why she had awakened so suddenly. Peering over at Damon, he hadn't moved an inch all night, his eyelids still glued shut with the bandage covering his entire forehead. She rose from the bed and left the room, examining the darkened hallway to either side.

A sudden, protracted shriek pierced her ears and shook her to her very core. Turning into a strangled screech, it echoed again and again as if it was circling their vessel. Sprinting down the corridor and up to the bridge, she flew into the room, halting when she came face to face with Koleton and Apollo.

"What is out there?" she asked, her hands shaking. Her attention fell on the covered window.

"We don't know," Koleton whispered, sliding into the captain's seat and lowering the protective cover on the window. "We just arrived ourselves."

The outside world was dark, aside from a stirring in the back of the cave. "Can we use the surveillance equipment to find out what is making that sound?" she asked, gathering her hair up on top of her head and securing it in place as she stepped up next to Apollo.

"Already working on it," Koleton muttered, his fingers running over the control panel.

Apollo stepped around her and switched on the outside lights, causing the Nesoi to rear up and shake their heads toward them. Quickly turning the lights off, he glanced over at her with wide eyes.

"They're terrified," he breathed, signaling for Koleton to shut the cover. "Whatever is out there has no intention of letting us see it."

"Should we leave?" Her hands continued to tremble and she held them up to her chest to keep them from shaking.

Koleton shook his head, his eyes squinting at the screen in front of him. "Whatever is sniffing around the ship has friends waiting on the outside." He pointed to the red spots on the screen. "There are thousands of creatures wandering the grounds. If we move, it might attract them to our location, causing them to attack the ship in the air." He paused for a moment and swallowed hard, as he closed his eyes and finished, "Or possibly lash out on our creature friends outside."

"We'll have better luck switching everything off and cooling the engines," Apollo suggested, just as Justin and Mataya emerged from the hallway, sporting bleary eyes to match the rest of them.

"Agreed," Koleton nodded, pressing on the screen in front of him and sliding his finger down. The vessel powered down, encasing them in darkness.

"I'm going to the children's room," Malkia announced, walking past her sister and squeezing her arm. "If they're awake, I'll bring them here."

"It's important that we stay as quiet as possible," Apollo whispered loudly, his words stopping her in her tracks.

She pivoted on her heel, facing him. "Do you think it can hear us?"

He nodded, putting his long finger up to his crimson lips. "Refrain from speaking and step lightly. Pass the information on."

Drawing in a quick breath, she turned back around and tiptoed off the bridge, leaving the door open so they wouldn't have to continue opening it. Hurrying down the corridor, she took the stairs down to the children's room, entering the darkness. Leaving that door open as well, she checked on Landon to find him fast asleep, before tiptoeing over to Esta.

"Mama?" Esta whispered, the blanket pulled tightly around her face. "What is that noise?" Her fingers were white, clutching the edge of her covers as her inky irises widened, revealing the whites around them.

Malkia settled onto the bed next to her daughter, holding a finger to her lips. "Stay quiet. We don't know what it is, but we have turned off all power in the ship to mask our whereabouts. It's best to remain still and as quiet as possible. Morning will arrive soon and we'll be able to leave this moon."

Esta nodded, tears shimmering in her eyes. "I'm frightened," she whispered, barely loud enough for Malkia to understand.

"Me too," Malkia responded, climbing over Esta and curling up next to her. "But I'll protect you. Don't you worry my sweet child."

The screeching began to grow more distant and after some time of lying in Esta's bed, it receded completely. Breathing easier, she sat up, leaning against the wall and looked down at her sleeping child.

"Crisis averted," she muttered to herself, sliding off the bed and leaving the room.

Lightly stepping up the stairs, she strolled onto the bridge, expecting to find everyone more relaxed, but instead came to an abrupt halt as she stared at the terrified faces of her friends. "What happened?" she mouthed to Mataya.

"Something was slaughtered right outside the window. We heard the fight and whatever it was nearly struck the ship as it dropped to the ground." Her voice shook as she covered her face with her hands. "It was horrible. The worst sound I've ever heard."

"How long until the first sun rises?" she questioned Justin, who was already checking a hand-held device.

"Soon," he mumbled, his hands quivering as he set the device on his lap and drew a shaky breath. "I hope it wasn't one of our dragons." A crimson heat was rising up his neck as he hung his head and covered his face with hands. "We can't keep going on this way."

"I didn't hear anything in the children's room." She turned toward Ustarum and Alyssa, just as Alexa and Bella strode in with all four of the kids in tow.

"Something woke my kids and I didn't want to leave yours alone down there," she mumbled, waving at the kids to find a quiet spot near Mataya. "What happened?"

"I'm not sure." Her eyes scanned everyone's faces. "I just left Landon and Esta a few minutes ago and I thought whatever was roaming around outside had left."

"It did leave," Apollo replied, turning to face her. "But not before it killed another creature. Whatever died was large. I'm surprised you didn't feel the entire ship shake as it slammed into the ground."

Malkia shook her head, surprised by what he was saying, but petrified by the possibility of it being Tantiana. "Mataya, are the Nesoi speaking to you? Can you find out what they're seeing out there?"

Mataya shook her head. "They've cut me off. At first, all I could feel was the necessity of staying inside the vessel, but when the fight outside began, my connection with them was severed." The color drained from her face as she fought back tears. "Whatever happened out there, it was one of ours who paid the price. They are blocking me from knowing which one of them perished."

Whirling around, Malkia tiptoed over to Koleton. "We need to open the cover."

"No," he replied, rising from his chair and blocking her from the controls with his large stature. "If we turn anything on, we could attract that monster back to us and there will be others who will pay a steep price. Is that what you want?"

Her pulse pounded in her ears and she slammed her eyes shut, shaking her head at him. Reaching within, she searched for her powers, but only found the light of her soul still beaming from her heart. As grateful as she felt to have rediscovered her true nature, it wasn't helping in this moment. Gritting her teeth, her eyes flew open and she surveyed the people in the room with her.

"Where's Asha?" she asked, searching the room for those purple eyes.

"She never came up here," Justin whispered, handing his device to Mataya and rising from his chair. "We need to find her."

"Stay here." Malkia pointed at Esta and Landon, before racing from the room and hurrying down to the infirmary. "I'll check on Damon and if I don't find her there, I'll start searching the lower floors."

Justin nodded, turning down the opposite corridor and sprinting to the first open room as she moved into the infirmary. Damon was still asleep. His hand had fallen off one side of the bed, dangling at a strange angle as if someone had been holding it and left in a hurry. Rushing over to his side, she set his hand back on his chest, running tender fingers down his cheek.

His skin felt warmer than usual and she placed the back of her hand on his forehead and then his neck. Leaning down, she set her ear against his chest, listening to his weak pulse.

"Why aren't you healing?" she asked out loud, standing up straight and jumping from movement at the other end of the room.

"Because he's been infected," Asha said, her voice shaking as she crouched in the corner. Moving the palms of her hands up the wall, she rose and instantly sagged against the wall, rubbing her eyes with her fists. "I'm sorry. I'm so dizzy and after hearing and feeling the death of the creature outside, I'm unable to gain control of my body."

Malkia rushed over to her, curling her arm around her waist and leading her to the other bed in the room. "Lie down and tell me what happened."

Asha sank onto the bed, curling into a fetal position and closing her eyes. "I was in here, checking on Damon, when a pain began to gnaw at the base of my skull. I could hear the commotion outside and I dropped his hand from the shrill cry I heard in my head. Something was being murdered and for some reason it connected with my thoughts in its final moments." Her hands trembled as she wiped fresh tears from her eyes. "And then it was over. But now I know why Damon is worse. Somehow, he has contracted a venom that is slowly killing him."

The muscles in Malkia's body tensed, her eyes shifting between Asha and Damon. "How do we heal him?"

"I don't know, yet," Asha replied, rubbing her temples with her fingers. "But we need to leave, sooner rather than later. Once the suns have risen and we've secured our dragons on the ship, we need to leave for Theia."

Malkia patted Asha on the leg, before racing out of the room and down the hallway, nearly smacking into Justin as they met at the door of the bridge.

"Did you find her?" he asked, catching his breath as he leaned his hand against the wall.

"Yes." She gripped his forearm. "She's in the infirmary. We need to leave as soon as we can." She looked over at Ustarum. "And you're needed by Asha. Damon has been infected with a poison that's killing him."

Ustarum didn't hesitate, racing past her with Alyssa and Bella hot on his tail. Turning back to the bridge, she fell to her knees as a wash of vertigo swept over her. A hand steadied her and she opened her eyes to see Apollo lifting her off the floor and setting her in the chair next to Mataya.

"Have the suns risen?" she asked, holding her head in her hands.

"The first sun is beginning its rise," Koleton answered her. "But I don't want anyone to leave until we are clear of the shadows outside of the cave."

Malkia bit down on her bottom lip. "We need to open the cover to the window and find out what was executed." She tilted her head to the side and peered at Koleton. "Please."

"As you wish," he replied, rubbing his bloodshot eyes, before pressing the button to the cover.

TWENTY
Tough Love

SIRATH'S PEARLY SCALES glistened against the rising sun, laying still against the window. Apollo leaned his forehead against the tempered glass, sobs shaking his entire body as the palms of his hands pushed against the barrier between him and his friend.

"I need to go out there," Malkia insisted, rising from her seat. "Tantiana and the hatchlings are in there somewhere and we need to bring them safely into the ship."

"Just wait," Koleton barked, the color draining from his face. "I know you're eager to save them, but if we make our move too soon, we could lose you. Or someone else." He looked away, clenching his jaw. "Please, be patient."

She sank back into her seat, glancing over at Esta's wide eyes, her hand holding tightly to Zoe's. Shaking her head, Malkia cradled it in her hands, willing the ache that was pulsating inside her skull to disappear so she could focus.

What a nightmare this journey had become.

Apollo slid to the ground, his forehead still pressed to the glass, and Mataya joined him on the floor, her tiny arms wrapping around his giant body. The group was silent for several moments as they watched the light of the sun dance across the surface of Sirath's body, sliding to the rear of the cave.

Sudden movement caught Malkia's eye and she jumped from her chair, stepping toward the window as Tantiana's face came into view. A gash ran from her right ear all the way to her nostrils. But she appeared to be well, despite their horrific night.

Racing from the room, Malkia ignored Koleton's warnings, sprinting to the stairs and down to the cargo entrance. Punching in the code to open the door, she tapped her foot waiting for it to stop. Holding her hand over her heart, she stepped toward the entrance just as the hatchlings rounded the corner at a sprint and slid into the ship, pausing long enough to glare at her before disappearing into their quarters.

Turning her attention back to the entrance, she cried out, seeing Tantiana limping up the gangway. Throwing her arms around the giant beast, she wept against her, shaking from head to toe and wishing she could communicate with her friend.

"My powers are gone," she said to the dragon, tapping on her chest. "But I'm going to find a way to hear you again."

Tantiana's eyes drooped, nodding as she shifted past Malkia and stepped into the dragon's area, not looking back even once. Drawing in a sharp breath, guilt flooded over her for not bringing the dragons in to the ship before the suns had set. How would she ever make amends for the death of Sirath?

The door to the corridor opened and Apollo, followed by Mataya and Bella walked out. Their eyes traveled over to the dragon's quarters, pausing for a moment before turning back to Malkia.

"Are they okay?" Bella whispered, hurrying over to her friend and enfolding Malkia within her arms.

"They're alive," Malkia answered, trembling within her friend's embrace. She stared at Apollo's as he stepped toward the outside, and the tears suddenly spilled from her eyes. "I'm so sorry, Apollo. We should have been more careful." She stopped talking, her gaze dropping to the floor. "I should've been more careful."

"Don't place the entire blame upon yourself." He plodded down the plank and disappeared around the corner.

"I'll stay with him," Bella assured, squeezing Malkia's wrist. Turning away, she sprinted after the Artemisian.

Malkia stared after her, unmoving, wondering how the mission turned on her so quickly. Once again, she was on the losing end and not much closer to finishing what they had begun.

A scream ripped up her throat as she crumpled to the ground, pounding her fist into the metal floor. "When will it end?" she cried out to the crisp morning air.

Mataya settled next to her, patting her back. "We'll figure it out," her sister whispered, a hint of defeat fluttering in her voice.

Malkia whirled around, glaring at her, a deep anger welling up within her. "*That's all we ever do*," she cried, jumping up from the floor. "Every time we make any kind of move to finish the ridiculous war, I'm punched in the gut by a force that I'm unable to see or battle, for that matter. My abilities have disappeared, this child is draining every ounce of my energy, and now we've lost another of our comrades." She danced around the room, kicking anything in her way and throwing a tantrum that only made her angrier. "*I'm done.*" Racing from the ship, she headed to the entrance of the cave, pausing long enough to throw her arms out wide and scream into the valley below, before sprinting down the path alongside the precipice.

"*Malkia*," she heard her sister yelling at her from the cave, but she kept running.

Rounding the corner, she glanced up the rocky terrain and slid to an abrupt halt, scampering back up the trail and hiding behind a large boulder. Stepping across the top of the mountain was one of those giant beasts she had seen on their flight across the terrain. Its head was shaped like a dragon's, but the mouth was wider and its sharp teeth hung over the edges of its mouth, revealing multiple rows. Its scales were bright red and a sparkling ivory, gleaming in the suns' rays.

She watched it move along the top of the mountain, pausing here and there and swatting at some nuisance buzzing around its head. Realizing it didn't have wings like the dragons and Nesoi, she breathed easier as it turned its back to her, whipping loose rocks with its extremely long tail.

Sinking to the ground, Malkia realized she was still the fool who made rash decision. No wonder she was on the losing end at every turn. After discovering her own inner light, one that didn't require the powers that were bestowed upon her in her mother's womb, she believed it was going to be easier from here on out. But once again, she was the sucker, who made a choice based on her naivety.

Sighing, she leaned against the boulder behind her, looking out at the pyramids across the valley. "I can't do this," she said out loud.

"Sure you can," Ustarum announced, strolling toward her. "This wasn't your fault, but if you keep running off, whatever happens next, will be." He leaned down and gripped her elbow, forcing her to her feet. "Follow me back to the ship and spend ten minutes on the edge of the cliff and then I want your head back in the game. You don't have the luxury of choosing to quit."

Stomping back up the trail, Malkia kicked the pebbles along the path, listening to them ricochet over the cliff, striking others as it fell to the valley below. She knew he was right and hated that she had just reacted like a two year old. Embarrassment coiled within her stomach, and she wished she could just disappear instead of facing her people.

Ustarum paused at the mouth of the cave and pointed to the edge. "Ten minutes and then we're leaving. However that looks for you is up to you, but it will be done," he scolded her as if she was a young child.

She nodded and moved around him, sinking to the terrain and dangling her feet over the ledge of the cliff. Inhaling deeply, she closed her eyes and took one breath after another, focusing on calming her mind.

Suddenly, a warmth rushed into her body, heating her from within. Snapping her eyes open, she scanned the landscape, turning her body to see behind her, but seeing she was alone. Drawing her legs up, she scooted back a few feet and took another deep breath, shutting her eyes once again.

The warmth continued, snaking its way through every muscle and stretching from her toes all the way to the top of her head. She snickered from the sensation. It prickled down her spine and brightened like the stars in the heavens, bursting from her skin and shining in every direction. Her eyes slowly opened and she rose from the dirt, opening her arms to the heavens and twirling as relief washed over her. Her powers had been returned.

TWENTY-ONE

Back On Track

THE NESOI HAD retreated to their home underground, communicating to Mataya that they would join them on Theia when they were able. There was no argument, as the ones who had ventured out of the ship returned to it and watched the beasts disappear over the cliff. The Nesoi had transported Sirath's body to the graveyard of the dragons, but before they took him, Apollo released his spirit to the winds, uniting him with the ones who had gone before him.

Malkia returned to the infirmary, just as they lifted into the air and left the Hemera atmosphere. She settled into a chair next to Damon and remained there for hours, waiting for him to open his eyes.

Her thoughts consumed her, tumbling back to Esaki and the days leading up to Damon coming into her life. Her entire path had not only shifted, but had been flipped upside down and inside out. What if she had agreed to join her father? Would her mother still be breathing, along with so many others?

Leaning her head against the cushion of the chair, she stared at the wall across the room, licking her lips a few times, before finally allowing her eyes to close. She drew in a deep breath and exhaled as her mind and body relaxed.

Jerking awake, she jumped from her chair as Damon groaned. He rubbed his head with the palm of his hand. "You're back!" she exclaimed, leaning over him and hugging him tightly.

"What do you mean I'm back?" he asked, tensing his shoulders and squinting up at her.

"You were knocked out on our way back from the pyramid." She turned down the lights enough for him to open his eyes all the way. Stepping next to him again, she touched his cheek. "You're really hot. Lie back and let me see if I can give you more healing energy."

"Your abilities returned?" he asked, laying his head back on the pillow.

"Just before we left." Steadying her breath, she placed her hands on his chest and closed her eyes, focusing on her healing light.

It slid through her arms and into her hands, rushing from her to Damon. She could feel the blackness of the infection within him, and, as she searched for its whereabouts, she realized it had spread to every inch of his body. Furrowing her brow, she pressed farther, giving him everything she had within her. After several minutes, her knees wobbled, and she snapped her eyes open just as her joints gave out on her.

Damon gripped her elbows and pulled her back up, situating her in the chair. "Too much, I take it." He shook his head. "I'll be fine, but I'm starving. Let's go find some grub, and then I want to speak to Koleton."

She nodded, rising from the chair and holding onto his arm as they strolled to the kitchen. The room was bustling with the kids and Alexa, who all grinned when they saw Damon and Malkia enter.

"*Dad*." Landon jumped up from his seat and hugged his father. "You're so warm." The boy leaned back and peered up at his father's face.

Esta waved from her chair, stabbing her food with her fork and taking a large bite. Dishing up some vegetables and bread for Damon, Malkia handed it over to him, and then filled her own plate with food. He quickly ate, shooting her pointed looks every so often, but kept most of his attention on the children.

Alexa and the children finished first, and they waved as she marched them back to the playroom, mumbling something about Bella waiting for them, so she could have a break. After they left, Damon set down his utensils and leaned back in his chair.

"How are you feeling? You've been picking at your food," he pointed out, as he crossed his arms over his chest.

"So much happened while you were out," she replied. She was quiet for a minute, pushing her food around on her plate with her fork. Damon waited patiently, his silence comforting to her. "That night, after our adventure at the pyramid, another creature ventured into the cave and made an uproar that brought the hairs on the back of my neck to a standing salute. It was frightening." She set her fork on the plate, raising her gaze to meet his. "The creature killed Sirath."

His eyes widened and he sat up straight in his chair. "Was anyone else hurt?"

"Tantiana has a few claw marks on her face and body, but for the most part she's fine." She hung her head, rubbing her eyes with the heels of her hands. "We shouldn't have left them out there. He was protecting us from whatever was out there and paid the ultimate price for his bravery."

"It's not your fault," he said, leaning over and grabbing her arm. "Stop blaming yourself for every mishap. Who knew the dragons would be attacked on their home moon? They didn't insist being on the ship for the night, did they?"

"I don't know. That's the thing, I didn't have my ability to speak with the dragons, so I have no idea if they wanted to board." Her fingers raked through her hair and she rose from her chair, tossing away what food was left on her plate. "We still don't know what the beast looked like, but based on what Tantiana showed me in her mind, it was one of those small, two-legged spawns."

Damon stood up, his eyes narrowing. "If she was clawed by that creature, is it possible she's been poisoned?"

"The Nesoi healed her before we departed." She walked around the table and touched his shoulder. "Should we go see Koleton now?"

"Yes." He held out his hand for her to take. "I hope you aren't blaming yourself. We needed to find the map, and discovering the message left by whoever constructed that statue is important as well. Everyone dies, but before our time comes, it's important that we leave behind a safer and more peaceful place to live." He looked down at her and smiled. "That's our destiny."

Walking onto the bridge, Justin, Asha and Apollo stood in the center talking quietly to one another.

"Where's that red-headed fiend who's supposed to be flying this beast?" Damon asked, strolling toward them with Malkia in tow.

"You're awake," Asha said, a tired smile rising on her lips.

"It's good to see you up again." Justin gripped Damon's wrist and leaned in, giving him a pat on the back.

Damon grimaced slightly, but before Malkia could say anything, it was gone and he was all business again. "Who's keeping an eye out?" he asked, stepping around the group and dropping into his seat at the control panel.

"We've been taking turns," Apollo replied, throwing her a concerned look. "Koleton has barely slept over the past couple of days, so Asha insisted that he take a break."

"Good thinking," Damon murmured, examining the ships log. "We left Hemera, less than a day ago. How long until we reach the pyramids of Theia?"

"Just over a day." Asha pointed at the screen display of their destination. "We only have a general location, but this spot should bring us close."

He nodded, scanning over everything else, before turning to face the small group. Malkia's heart dropped into her stomach. Damon's eyes crawled with deep crimson veins and perspiration covered his brow, glistening against his jaundiced skin. He reached a trembling hand up to wipe the sweat away.

"I'm not feeling so well," he mumbled, leaning his head back against the chair. "What's wrong with me?"

"We need to return him to the infirmary," Asha ordered, curling her hand around the back of his neck. "He's ice cold."

Apollo lifted Damon off the chair, throwing him over his shoulder and hurried to the infirmary with Malkia and Asha following behind. As the door was shutting, Malkia could hear Justin speaking to Ustarum on the intercom.

Back in the infirmary, Apollo set Damon down on the bed and Malkia helped him rest his head on the pillow. Ustarum burst through the door, his eyes wild as they locked onto Damon.

"The infection must have been more serious than we believed it to be," he blurted, tugging Damon's socks off his feet, while Malkia eased his trousers over his hips.

Apollo turned to exit the room, giving Malkia a pat on the back before departing. "I'll return soon to see if there's anything I can do to help."

She nodded, barely noticing him leave. They covered Damon with a warming blanket and Ustarum instructed her to remove her clothes and lie next to him under it. "Skin to skin contact is the fastest way to warm him up."

She didn't question him. Removing everything but her undergarments she slid underneath the blanket, wrapping her arms and legs around Damon.

"Not the best time to get fresh with me," he joked, his voice barely a whisper.

"You just relax and let me do all the work," she replied, rubbing his chest with her hands.

He twisted his face and peered down at her. "Promise?" He chuckled, forcing a cough from his throat. He turned away quickly. "Sorry," he mumbled, lifting the cloth he had over his mouth and showing it to Asha.

"He's coughing up blood," she told Ustarum, her purple eyes glancing from him and back to Malkia. "What could possibly be ailing him?"

Ustarum lifted the blanket by Damon's feet and pointed. "He was bitten by that creature. We need the Nesoi."

TWENTY-TWO
Healing Damon

MALKIA'S PULSE DRUMMED loudly in her ears. She clenched her jaw as she twisted her head to see Ustarum. "Let's return to Hemera. *Now*," she ordered.

"They're meeting us on Theia." Ustarum shook his head. "If we return now, we might miss them and by the time we turn around and make it Theia, it could be too late."

"What about Mataya or my mom?" she asked, panic thundering through her mind and heart. "They have the magic of the Nesoi within them. Maybe they can help him."

"I'll page them," Asha responded, slipping from her view.

Malkia examined Damon's pallid face. His eyes were closed and his raspy breath was unnerving. "I've got you," she whispered in his ear, clinging tightly to him. "Don't you dare give up on me, do you hear?"

He nodded, swallowing with difficulty and turning his head as he coughed some more. She laid her head on his shoulder, nearly lying on top of him with her feet rubbing up and down his legs, begging the Gods and Light Beings to heal the man she loved.

The door slid open and Mataya and Alyssa hurried in, both sets of eyes gazing at Damon and Malkia. "What happened?" Alyssa asked, rushing over to the side of the bed.

"He was bitten on Hemera and we just discovered it," Ustarum told her. "It's too late to return to the moon. We don't know when the Nesoi plan to meet us on Theia, and we can't chance missing them." He stood in between her sister and mother, holding their hands above Damon. "We need you to see if you can channel the Nesoi's blue healing magic."

Mataya nodded, but Alyssa yanked her hand away. "It's not possible," she stammered, stepping backward.

"How do you know?" Ustarum asked, clutching her shoulder to prevent her from moving any farther.

"I just do." She glared at Ustarum and shoved his hand away. "It could kill Mataya if she attempts to channel that kind of energy."

Malkia shot out of the bed, rushing around, digging her fingers into her mom's upper arm. "This is not the time to be cryptic. *Tell us what you know*," she cried.

Alyssa shrank back, trembling from head to toe. "*How dare you yell at me.*"

"*Mom*," Mataya snapped, joining her sister. "Stop it. Why won't you just tell us?"

"*I used it once and it killed the person*," she screamed at them both. "Now let me go. I refuse to use it ever again."

"Who did it kill?" Malkia asked, holding her hands up as she stepped back.

"Your father on Esaki," Alyssa whispered, sinking in the chair behind her.

"What?" Mataya's eyes widened.

She nodded, hanging her head in defeat. "After those bombs

destroyed our home, I regained consciousness in the rubble, with your father next to me, weak but living. I leaned over him and channeled that blue magic, remembering how it healed me." Closing her eyes, she rubbed her hands down her legs and paused when she reached her knees. "He sputtered up a mouthful of blood and died right before my eyes. And the energy it took to make that attempt, rendered me unconscious."

"You lied," Malkia hissed, pressing the palms of her hands against the foot of Damon's bed railing. "You told me that you tried to protect us with a spell and it backfired, putting you in a deep sleep. Why do your stories keep changing?"

"I didn't want you to know that I was the reason your father died," she admitted, peeking up through her eyelashes to look at Malkia. "The Nesoi magic did place me into a deep sleep. It did backfire. I just wasn't completely upfront with the entire storyline."

"Of course you weren't," Malkia muttered, sliding back under the covers, her pulse beating rapidly as she focused on Damon's waxen skin. "This isn't the same circumstance. Maybe that magic was never meant to heal a person who had been struck by debris."

"I'll do it," Mataya said, stepping up to the side of the bed and slipping her hands under the blanket and onto Damon's bare chest.

"*Mataya, no,*" Alyssa begged, jumping up from the chair.

Ustarum wrapped his arm around their mother's waist and pulled her away. "I believe Malkia's right. This is *not* the same circumstance, and if anything goes wrong, I'll stop Mataya from continuing."

Mataya had already began chanting, searching for the Nesoi magic within her and channeling their blue energy. Shifting her body away from Damon, Malkia watched as a blue mist drifted from her sister's mouth, flowing toward Damon. She slipped out of the covers and knelt next to the side of the bed, taking his hand within her own as the mist streamed from Mataya to Damon, covering his body as they moved the blanket out of the way.

As if he suddenly took a deep breath, the mist drew quickly into his mouth, disappearing inside and leaving Malkia's mouth gaping. Damon's eyelids flew open and he gasped, coughing out a small amount of the mist. Leaning forward, into a seated position, his fingers dug firmly into his chest.

"What happened?" he croaked. His gaze darted frantically around the room, finally seeing Malkia.

She stared back, unable to find the words as she looked over at her sister, whose own shocked expression was glued to Damon. Shifting Mataya to the side, Ustarum stepped up next to Damon and placed his hand on his forehead.

"Your temperature has returned to normal," he announced, looking over at Malkia. "The Nesoi energy is powerful. It even has the influence to steal the words from Malkia's lips." He winked at her, turning his attention back to Damon.

Mataya chuckled, as her hand flashed up and gripped Ustarum's forearm just as her knees wobbled, threatening to give beneath her. He grabbed her arms and shifted her to the chair. Malkia tugged her shirt over her head and rushed over to her sister, kneeling in front of her.

"Are you dizzy?" she asked, gripping her knee. "Do you need some water?"

"I feel sick to my stomach," Mataya whispered, taking in several deep breaths as her hand flitted across her stomach.

Asha handed Mataya a glass of water and Alyssa swept her

daughter's hair from her neck, feeling the side of it. "She's clammy," she grumbled, glaring down at Malkia.

"I'm fine," Mataya grumbled, pushing her mother's hand away. "It just took a lot of energy, not unlike many of the healing spells. Give me some space to catch my breath."

The three women stepped away, and Malkia refocused her attention on Damon, who had leaned back on a stack of pillows. "How long was I out?" he asked Ustarum, closing his eyes.

"Not long," he answered, covering Damon with a regular blanket. "You should rest. Whatever poison was in your system has drained your energy. Mataya's magic only washed it from your body, but it won't heal the side effects. Sleep will be your best medicine."

"I need to check on the ship," Damon insisted, pushing at Ustarum's hands and sliding his legs out from beneath the covers.

"Stop resisting, Damon," Malkia snapped, pressing his shoulders back against the pillows and forcing him to stillness. "Koleton and Apollo, along with Asha are all experienced pilots. They can handle the ship while you rest." Her fingertips trailed down his cheek, gripping his chin and twisting his face toward her. "Your children need you alive, so don't you dare leave this bed until your body is properly healed."

He nodded, his eyes taking in the terror etched across her features. "You won't lose me. I promise."

She swallowed hard, subduing a rising sob as she wiped away a lone tear. "Don't make promises you can't keep. Just rest and do what Ustarum instructs you to do. Please."

Gripping her hand, he kissed it and nodded. "Of course. I'll be right here until he gives me the all clear."

Her teeth grazed her bottom lip as she glanced over at her sister. "I'm going to check on the children and let everyone know you're well," she said, patting his shoulder and focusing on his face. Leaning over she sealed her lips to his, kissing him softly. "I'll be back soon." She searched his eyes, pleading silently for his quick recovery, before breaking away and leaving the room.

Her walk down the corridor was foggy, her mind drifting from Damon to the pyramid on Hemera, focusing on the small creature who had chased them to their ship. What was their significance to the pyramids? Guardians? An alarm for the Creators? Their symbolism and actual presence on Hemera was a mystery she intended to unravel.

Peering into the playroom, she caught Bella's eye and waved at her. Esta glanced up as Bella was approaching her and tilted her head with a smile, before returning to her play with Zoe.

"Is everything okay?" Bella asked, curling her fingers around Malkia's forearm.

She shook her head, and covered her mouth as she cleared her throat. "This mission is an utter mess."

Bella tightened her grip, her expression darkening. "*Stop it*," her voice was lower and harsher than Malkia had ever heard it. "You did well on Esaki and somewhere inside of you, that connection with your higher self remains. This journey might feel like a complete failure, but I want you to remember how far we've traveled and all that we have accomplished. No victory is achieved without loss." She leaned in, lowering her voice even more. "Hold your head up high and don't you dare succumb to the defeat you're feeling in your heart."

Staring wide-eyed at her friend, Malkia's mind raced from the stern words thrown at her. "This is one of the reasons I appreciate your friendship," she whispered, the edges of her lips twitching into a half-smile. "Thank you. Damon is better and we're finally on our way to Theia. Despite the battles and death, we have achieved more than I ever thought possible." She embraced Bella, hugging her tightly. "I appreciate your directness and the smack across the face."

Bella chuckled, planting a kiss on Malkia's cheek. Leaning back she grinned up at her friend. "That's what I'm here for, to keep you in line." She patted Malkia on the hand and stepped back. "Now, go take care of your people and leave the children to me. If you're unable to return before their bedtime, I'll make sure they are tucked in for the night."

"Thank you, Bella." She glanced over Bella's shoulder at the children. "I'll do my best to return soon. If not, someone will announce when we are nearing our destination."

Bella nodded and walked back to the kids, kneeling on the floor to resume a game she was playing with the two boys. Blowing a kiss at her daughter, Malkia left, heading back to the bridge.

TWENTY-THREE

Theia

"WE'LL BE ENTERING Theia's atmosphere in the next thirty minutes," Koleton announced with a cheshire grin plastered across his face. His cheerfulness had been restored by ten hours of sleep.

Malkia pried her eyes open and she squinted over at him, raising her chair into a seated position. "How long was I out?" she asked, a yawn overtaking her face.

"Maybe two hours. You've been snoring for almost an hour of it." He chuckled to himself as he swiped one of the screens in front of him.

"Anything to annoy you brings joy to my heart," she replied, stretching her arms above her, turning to scan the room. "Where has everyone gone?"

"Your loud ruckus scared them away. It *was* a bit terrifying." He didn't take his eyes off the screen, but his lips twitched into a smile and Malkia threw a waded piece of parchment at him. He deflected it, his jaw dropping in mock surprise. "After everything I've done for you." Shaking his head, he turned back to the screen, ignoring her growling.

"You're impossible." Rising from her seat, she stepped over to the window and stared down at the stunning planet. "This is a dream come true," she muttered, twisting a lock of her hair around her finger and remembering her childhood with Palma. It had been her sister's dream, too. Her chest tightened from the memory. Their father had stolen so much from them.

She turned back to Koleton. His brows raised in thought. "I bet most of us believed we would never travel this far." His eyes drinking in the scenery behind her. "I know Skye would've loved every moment of this journey."

Another dagger twisted in her gut. She sighed, turning back to watch. "Yes, she would have."

The silence between them overtook the room, with only the hum of the machines around them, keeping the air from growing stale. She made her way back to her seat, securing her restraints after Koleton announced over the intercom that they were entering the atmosphere. It was a bumpy ride, but far smoother than Hemera. As they shot through the clouds, Malkia gripped her armrests, her eyes wide with astonishment at the beauty before her.

"Are you seeing this?" she asked, entranced by the scenery sweeping by them.

"It's difficult to miss," he replied, pressing on the call button. "Ladies and not so gentlemen, if you can walk, run or crawl, I suggest you make your way to the bridge. This is a sight you won't want to miss."

Malkia released her harness and tiptoed to the window. Excitement raced through her, invigorating every cell in her body as she watched the terrain below them. She knew this was where the Aletheians had brought her, back when she was on Enyo. Having it verified right before her eyes, made her squirm with eagerness.

The mountains' peaks spread across the horizon. The boughs of trees stretched toward the sky, crowded with blooms and foliage in a prismatic display of botanical exuberance. Crimson blossoms overtook the cliffs to one side, while lavender and auburn burst from the fields in the valley to her right. And as they flew over the next peak, the turquoise waves of the ocean crashed into the diamond sands at the base of the valley, washing back out to the sparkle that stretched as far as the eye could see.

Esta appeared next to her, sliding her fingers within her mother's grasp and resting her forehead on the glass. Damon's arm curled around her waist, and he kissed her on the cheek before turning to watch the terrain rush beneath them.

"We're nearing the area where this pyramid is supposed to be," Koleton interrupted her reverie, drawing her back to the present moment. "Once I land, we'll have to navigate our way into the forest and do the remaining search on foot."

She nodded and smiled over at Landon, who had his arm draped over Esta's shoulders. Their family was nearly complete and bonded, just as soon as the incubus was born. Malkia smiled to herself, running her hand over her belly, grateful the nausea and weakness hadn't fully returned. Hopefully, Theia's spirit would ease the discomfort and weariness and restore her powers, so she would be prepared to face her father.

Koleton set the vessel down in a field covered with sapphire flowers, crushing a number of them under its landing gear. Frowning as she stepped down the opened cargo door, she scanned the vegetation for any living creatures, who might become a problem. Not seeing anything dangerous, her toes burrowed into the dirt and she closed her eyes, skimming her hands across the tall blossoms.

The wind whistling past her and birds chirping in the trees vibrated in her ears, and she inhaled the sweet scented air, searching for her connection with the planet. She growled in frustration, feeling weaker by the second. Theia was refusing to unite with her.

"Maybe it's different here," Apollo remarked, touching her shoulder with the tips of his fingers.

She sighed, wringing her hands together as the rest of the crew and dragons alighted. "I don't feel anything. Not even a fraction of magic or intense energy."

"Give it some time." Asha's purple gaze locked with her own. "Let's find this All-Seeing Eye. Maybe there's something you'll find along the way that will connect you with her spirit."

Malkia stretched her feet out in front of her as she slipped on each of her boots, scooping up her items, she looked up at Bella, Alexa and all four of the children.

"Are you sure you don't need someone else to stay back with you six?" she asked, running her fingers through Esta's hair as she hugged her close.

"We'll keep the ship locked up tight and ward it with our magic. No one will bother us while you're away," Bella replied, reaching for Alexa's hand. "We will be just fine."

Malkia nodded, leaning down and kissing her daughter on the forehead. "Keep them safe. And practice your abilities. My mind will remain open to you, in case you need to contact me telepathically."

"Come back to me, Mama," she whimpered, embracing Malkia again.

Malkia closed her eyes and gave her daughter a squeeze. After a long embrace, she turned to Landon and folded her arms around him. "Watch over her." She peered into his eyes and smiled. "When this is all said and done, we will find a life here, as a family. Okay?"

He grinned and nodded, clasping Esta's hand and leading her back into the ship. Malkia waved good-bye, pivoting to face the others as the cargo door closed behind her.

"Let's go," she ordered, gesturing for them to move forward.

Tantiana and the hatchlings jumped into the air. *Let me know what you see.* Malkia shielded her eyes from the sun, watching them disappear over the forest.

The vegetation is thick, Tantiana replied. *Be careful.*

Just be prepared to pick me up, once you find the pyramid. An insect buzzed just above her eye and she ducked down to escape it, trotting to catch up to the others.

Asha and Apollo led them into the trees, cutting away the overgrown vegetation with their hatchets to clear a path for the others. Taking up the rear, Malkia scanned the area, listening to the noise of the wild and paying attention to anything that wasn't one of them walking through the forest. Her father must know they were closing in on his position. At the very least, he would expect pursuit.

For now, they had to find the All-Seeing Eye and she needed to speak with her grandfather before they destroyed all paths that led to the blue planet. Afterward, her father would have to pay with his life, and, if the Elvens refused to live in peace, they would follow him to the grave.

We discovered an ancient city ahead, Tantiana's thoughts interrupted her own. *The vegetation is too thick to land, but there is definitely a city underneath.*

Pick me up and show me where we need to go, she instructed her dragon.

Is there a clearing near you? Tantiana asked, swooping over Malkia's head. *I think I see you, but I'll need some space to land.*

"Tantiana's found a city," she announced to the rest of the group, trotting up to Mataya and Alyssa. "I'm going to find a spot for her to land, so she can show me where it's located."

Ustarum waved his hand up in the air, raising an eyebrow. "Without your ability to fly, shouldn't you keep your feet on the ground?"

"Why?" she asked, setting her hands on her hips.

"If you fall and she doesn't catch you in time, you won't survive and neither will your child," Alyssa replied for him, wiping a drop of sweat from her chin.

"What do you suggest?" she asked, tapping her fingers against her thighs.

Alyssa glanced over at Damon. "One of us could go."

"No," Malkia snapped, shaking her head to stop her mother from continuing. "It's a short trip and I'm not placing anyone else in danger. Let's keep going. I'm through with all the delays." She stomped away, frustration thundering through her. None of them would survive if they fell from Tantiana, but she's the only one who was being told not to go, as if she was still a small child.

A short trek through the vegetation and the trees opened up to field of blossoms, with a shallow stream running through the middle.

"This is perfect," Malkia whispered, peering up into the sky. *Tantiana where are you?*

I see you, she replied. *I'll land soon.*

One of the hatchlings, Vasuki, landed first, followed by Tantiana and then Pythios. Malkia sprinted over to the beast, leaping up her dragon's leg and gripping tightly onto her scales, swinging her leg over her upper back.

Let's go, she told her dragon, waving at the others in her group and not giving them a chance to object.

The brisk air greeted her face, and she realized this was the first time she hadn't possessed her light to shield her from its cool rush across her cheeks and neck. Leaning in close, she smiled at the view just above the trees. Tantiana swept just above them, heading farther into the dense area of the vegetation, when Malkia noticed the tip of the pyramid.

"I see it," she yelled, pointing at no one in particular. "Is there any place you can land?" She patted the side of Tantiana's neck.

We looked already, her dragon replied, throwing her a sideways look. *If I did land, I'm not sure I'll be able to spread my wings to fly again.*

We could cut out a spot for you, Malkia replied, examining the area. *Or maybe not. How are we going to cut through all of that?* She surveyed the length of the city, thick with vegetation that covered every rooftop.

It will take some time. Tantiana flew over the city one last time, turning around and heading back to her group.

"Why would anything be easy?" Malkia grumbled to herself, cuddling into Tantiana for some warmth.

Once the dragon landed, she slid off her back and into Damon's arms. "I know the way," she told him, patting him on the shoulders and shifting around him. "I can lead us toward the city, but it will take some time digging our way through the overgrown brush. The city is covered in dense foliage."

"How long?" Koleton asked, leaning on his newly carved walking stick.

"We might make it to the outskirts before the suns set," she replied, tossing her pack over her shoulders. "But breaking through the inner area, might take us another day."

"Well, we'd better start hustling." Koleton picked up his stick and pointed it at the group. "I'm not suited for sleeping outdoors. The elements don't agree with my porcelain skin." He growled under his breath, turning to face the trees and began the trek back into their shadows.

Malkia sighed, her stomach gurgling with hunger and nausea all at once. "I'm right behind you," she murmured, pressing forward, one foot at a time, determined to not be voted out of the group before they arrived at the pyramid.

TWENTY-FOUR
The Perfect Pyramid

MALKIA SANK TO the rock behind her, wiping the spit from her mouth and cradling her head in between her legs. She could hear the others yammering around the campfire, oblivious that she had snuck away. The smoke from the fire had been her breaking point and she no longer could hold what was gurgling in her stomach. Her dinner lay at her feet. And Theia's spirit was still refusing to connect to her.

Rinsing her mouth with a swig of water, her toe nudged a broken twig as she inwardly winced with self-pity. Mataya, Asha, Ustarum, and her mother had no issues linking with the magic ebbing and flowing around them. It was abundant, but she was unable to touch it.

They had reached the edge of the city before nightfall. It hadn't been easy breaking through the thick vegetation, but they'd managed to move into an area of this ancient civilization where homes had once stood. Whatever species had lived here before had been hundreds of years more advanced in technology and intelligence. What remained of the structures was unlike anything she had ever seen, with walls made of a nearly unbreakable metal. Very few remained standing, while most others had crumbled from thousands of years of neglect and the depredation of vegetation. Deeming the ruins unstable, they had chosen to make camp away from them.

She focused on a partial wall that stood not too far from her position. It was difficult to imagine the lifestyle and ways of the long-vanished inhabitants, but she was moved by a sense that this was once a thriving community. It would be interesting to see what remained in the city. On her earlier flight, she'd noticed many tall buildings clustered around the pyramid, and she knew if they remained intact, they would be made or more resilient material than these dwellings.

"Are you feeling ill again?" Asha spoke, squeezing her shoulder.

Malkia looked up at her and shot her a weak smile. "The smoke was overwhelming. I lost all my dinner to this blasted shrubbery."

Asha chuckled, finding a seat on a nearby rock. "The wild greenery seems to be the dominant vegetation around these parts." She pursed her lips as she stared at the structures to Malkia's left. "I had no idea this kind of civilization ever existed in our star system, let alone on the mother of our moons."

"Did you notice how perfectly straight their house foundations are?" Malkia asked, pointing at the wall she had been staring at before. "And the glass in those windows hasn't cracked. I didn't even know windows or mirrors existed until the Enyoans brought them to Esaki. This entire world is perplexing to me and I can't wait to dig farther in tomorrow. Hopefully, there will be answers when we reach the city."

"And what sort of answers are you looking for?" Asha asked, leaning forward, resting her arms on her knees.

"Where did the people or species that lived here before go? Was this the Creators' home before they left or someone else's?" She sat up straight and pointed to the side of a building they could see in the distance. "What happened to the technology? I have dozens of questions. If the city doesn't hold the answers, I intend to ask the

Aletheians."

Asha shivered, rubbing her hands down her arms. "And what if they don't want to answer?"

Malkia rose from her seat, helping Asha up next to her. "I don't know. But I'm sure they know by now, I'll keep asking until I find answers."

"You definitely don't know when to stop, that's for sure," Asha joked, knocking her hips into Malkia's as they picked their way through the brush.

Laughing out loud, Malkia reached over and hugged Asha around the shoulders. "You know me well."

She left Asha at her sleeping area and crawled into the cocoon that held Damon. He wrapped his arms around her waist and rested his head against her back, breathing softly as he fell asleep almost immediately. Her mind raced with dread and worry, with a small dash of excitement, imagining what the next day held in store for them.

"*We've broken through,*" Koleton shouted, waving his arms at the others.

Apollo was squeezing past the broken branches and twigs, glancing back at Malkia and giving her the thumbs up. Returning her hacksaw to her belt, she waved at Ustarum and Alyssa who had been using their magic to untangle the thick undergrowth. It had helped them move faster, but she wished her own abilities would return, as she believed her heat would have been far more useful.

Tantiana had offered to burn the entire area with her breath, but Malkia had feared they wouldn't have been able to stop the blaze, and it would destroy anything left of value within the city. After nearly of day of breaking the vegetation apart and using the warlocks' magic, they had finally found an easier path that lead them to this spot.

With just enough room for each of them to slither through, she could see the structures on the other side. They seemed to call for her to hurry. As she waited her turn to move through the hole in the branches, her eyes scanned the forest, and she wondered when the Nesoi and Artemisians would arrive. She knew they were ahead of schedule, but the days were beginning to run together and she couldn't remember how soon they had agreed to meet them.

She twisted around, with her back to the others, gazing up through the tree branches at the turquoise sky above. Her mind reached out to the dragons, who had circled back to the ship to check on the ones who stayed back. Pythios had remained, to keep an eye out for any intruders or allies. She locked onto his mind, as he would be her warning.

"Are you coming?" Damon's hand rested on her shoulder.

Tilting her head, she nodded and turned to follow him into the darkness of the canopy. A stillness slid over her as she stepped onto a broken trail of black rock. It was wide enough to land a small ship and led into the heart of the city.

"This place is massive," Alyssa whispered. She wrapped her arms around her chest, shivering from the chill.

Ustarum draped a blanket over her shoulders. "Now that we're in here, we can use our incantations to push the vegetation away. Let's move to the center of the city, or at least farther in, and set up an area where we can begin working."

Koleton, Asha and Damon had already ventured farther down the broken path, with Apollo not far behind them. Helping gather the rest of their items left on the ground, Malkia trotted after with Mataya and Justin by her side.

Examining the buildings, she realized they were entering a place that possessed advancements in technology she couldn't even imagine. The structures all had a dark gleam to their exterior, but varied in blacks, grays, and blues. Even with the broken walls and vegetation running through each building, it was obvious how well the ancient civilization had once lived.

As they traveled down the trail, she watched the others pause midstride and peer down a crossroad. Hurrying to catch up, she came to an abrupt halt next to Asha. The suns' rays broke through the thick canopy, just enough to illuminate a small section of the road. A squat animal was raising up on its back feet, baring its front claws and hissing at the group. But that wasn't what surprised them. Behind the creature, were several wrecked warrior vessels or at least that's what they appeared to be at first glance.

The animal fell onto its front paws and skittered down the trail, dodging the ships until it disappeared in the shadows. Malkia stepped toward the first vessel, when Damon's hand shot out and took ahold of her wrist, tugging her back to him.

"Wait," he said, swinging her around to look at him. "Please."

"There isn't anyone here," she replied, waving her hand at the ships. "What are you worried about?"

"Just let me check, first. The child you carry is mine as well, so please give me the opportunity to ensure your safety." His expression was etched with worry as his eyes darted around to the others in the group. "We can spread out and move down the road. All I ask is that you don't go first."

Giving him a slow nod, she stepped back as her arm fell to her side. Damon shifted around her, raising his laser weapon, followed by Asha and her weaponized magical hand, illuminating her entire arm. Malkia fell into line behind her, holding her daggers in front of her chest, her eyes dancing from one vessel to the next, excited to see them up close.

Sliding along the broken path, Damon paused at the first one and slid his arm across the side of it, revealing a section of glass that had been covered in a thick layer of dust, dirt and leaves. Wiping it away even more, he motioned for Asha to shine her light so he could see inside.

Leaning closer, he peered through the window and shook his head at the others. "It's empty. And it only contains two seats. I'm not even sure it flies."

"How would it move, if it didn't fly?" Koleton asked over Malkia's shoulder.

She walked around Asha and looked through the window. "Let's find out." She picked up a rock and pounded it onto the glass. "*Ow,*" she cried, when her hand bounced back.

"*Stop it,*" Damon snapped, gripping her arm and holding it away from the glass. "Until your abilities are restored, you're officially off-duty."

"What's that supposed to mean?" Malkia questioned, pushing against his chest to move him away from her.

"Malkia." Her sister grasped her elbow. "I know you want to match us step for step, but you need to let us do the heavy work, while you keep your baby safe. He is your main concern."

Exhaling a defeated breath, Malkia held up her hands and dropped the stone. "I would like to find a way into the vessel. It might hold answers."

"What about contacting the Aletheians?" Apollo asked, pointing toward the spot she had said the pyramid had risen from the trees. "You're losing focus. We can return to these, once we learn more from your grandfather and have been reunited with my people."

She gritted her teeth, frustrated with her lack of powers and feeling like she was the least capable person in the group. Humility was not something she wanted to embrace, but as she trudged alongside her sister, she realized it just might be her only choice.

They passed several more of the strange vessels concealed in vegetation and a thick layer of dust and grime. If anyone had remained in the city after the majority had abandoned it, their remains were either buried in the accrued debris and dirt or lost within the buildings. Malkia's eyes strayed up each building, some with their windows still intact, while other were just shells of the past.

Torn fabrics lay among the ruins, decayed or withered beyond recognition. Randomly picking through pieces, Koleton shook his head over and over again, before giving up entirely.

"How will we ever discover anything in this mess?" he asked. He peered from one end of the road to the other.

"Some of it will be preserved," Malkia answered, turning to face him. "The small vessels have been closed, possibly protecting whatever is inside. And the pyramid will be sealed as well."

"But what lies within might only bring more questions, not answers," he grumbled, jumping as a rodent skittered passed him.

"*Woah.* I'll protect you," she jested, skipping in between him and the creature. He stuck his tongue out at her as she ignored the dirty looks from the others. "Even if there are more questions, the Aletheians have promised an ending to all this madness. It might not be the one we wish for, but at least we know there's an end in sight."

He groaned and rolled his eyes, throwing his pack over his shoulders. "We should hurry. The sooner I see the suns again, the better I'll feel."

Each of them picked up their pace, trotting down the lane, until they could finally see the edges of the pyramid. It was unlike any of the others they had seen. While they had been made of rock, this one was plastered with the glistening and smooth material that enrobed all the other buildings. As they neared it, Malkia paused several times, unsure of how she would ever find a way to speak with the Aletheians. There were no drawings or etchings anywhere on the outside of the structure.

Damon's fingers ran along the base of the pyramid. Glancing over at her, she could see he was thinking the same thing as he shook his head. Shifting around the others, she released her held breath. Her gaze wandered up to the apex that barely pierced the canopy, just like she'd seen it from the air.

"There has to be something here that will connect me with the Aletheians." Meeting Damon's stare, she could see the doubt warring within his irises. "They wouldn't just abandon us. We've come too far to give up now, so stop looking like we're defeated and keep searching."

She stalked away from him, following Alyssa, Mataya, Asha and Ustarum, who were finding a place to set up their herbs. If they could open up this area it would help their cause. Passing them by, she continued to walk along the base of the pyramid, searching for any clue that might lead her to the feather.

That lame feather. Why did they choose that symbol? To this day, after all this time, there were so many unanswered questions and she couldn't see those angels divulging anything they felt was unnecessary.

As she turned the corner of the pyramid, she glanced back to see Damon trailing behind her, with Apollo and Justin not too far behind. Her eyes darted back to her path, hearing some rustling within the tangle of vines that covered a section of the pyramid and the structures ahead of her. An animal, nearly the size of Parowan, squirmed from the confines of the vegetation, and galloped toward her. Spooked by her presence it reared up and suddenly veered off into the broken building across from her path.

Watching it recede into the darkness, her gaze focused in on the vegetation it had just escaped. The corner of her lips twitched into a smile, admiring the deep crimson and purple flowers, reminding her of her own light that she missed immensely. Her hand flitted over her abdomen, feeling the flip-flops of the tiny fetus within her. It was going to be long five months until she would be able to regain control of her body and powers.

She picked her way over more substantial boulders of one of the buildings. Through the branches and vines, she could see a slight inward dip in the base of the pyramid. Bouncing over the foliage, she raced to the spot and skidded to a halt in front of a set of massive doors. Spreading across both doors was the etching of an eye staring down at her as if it were boring into her soul. The iris was a brilliant sapphire, standing out against the whites of the eye and reds and purples that were splattered and smeared around it were similar to the face painting of an Esakian warrior.

The other three paused behind her, breathing heavy as they surveyed the doors and eye. "What do you want to bet, *that's* the All-Seeing Eye?" Malkia glanced back at Damon, puffing out her cheeks and blowing out the air in her lungs. She pointed behind them. "The path is extra wide leading away from the pyramid. Once we clear out the brush, I believe it allows the eye to see to the end of the city." Her fingers tapped against her cheek as her mind raced. "Or even farther." She twisted back to the eye, examining the entire doorway for any other inscriptions.

"Is that what the Aletheians want you to destroy?" Koleton asked over her shoulder, his breath warm on her cheek.

She shook her head. "I doubt this is the actual eye they were referring to, but it would be great if I could find a way to communicate with them." Tilting her head back, she met his gaze. "Just in case I'm wrong. Which, by the way, is rare." She winked and focused back on the pyramid.

"Right." He chuckled, pushing her lightly on the shoulder, before walking around her. "How do we break in?"

"Mataya can help me. And possibly one of the other warlocks. I need their energy to lock onto mine." She leaned back to look around the brush, searching for the warlocks. "The canopy hasn't budged, so I'm going to assume they're still working on that problem."

"I'll check on them," Apollo spoke up, stepping away. "Will you please have Tantiana search the area for my people?"

She nodded, her eyes raising to view the sky. *Tantiana, have you seen the Artemisians?*

No other ships have arrived, although I thought I saw a vessel on the other side of the forest a short while ago. But when I checked, I couldn't find anyone. Her dragon answered, as her shadow swooped above them. *I flew over our ship and everything is still as it should be, but the Artemisians and Nesoi haven't arrived.*

If you do see them, please let me know immediately. And if you see those Elvens, have Bella fly the ship away from here with Pythios. When we are free and clear, you can have them return. Malkia's breath came in short, when Damon suddenly grabbed her shoulder. "*You frightened me,*" she exclaimed, swiping his hand away.

"What are you doing?" he asked, as he shifted in front of her, waving his hand in front of her face.

"I was talking to Tantiana, like Apollo asked," she answered. Her hands settled on her hips as she glared up at him. "What did you think I was doing?"

"Your lips were moving. I walked around you several times and you never blinked." He scratched the top his head as his gaze swept down her body. "Are you sure you're okay?"

"Yes," she mumbled, breaking eye contact with him and licking her lips. "Sometimes I go into trances when I speak to the dragons."

"Since when?" he asked, crossing his arms over his chest.

She sighed, frustrated with the questions. "I don't know. Maybe I'm just tired. Give it a rest." Trudging away from him, she continued to search the doors, realizing the light from the suns was dimming. "What is taking them so long?"

Just as she spoke those words, the branches above them began to shift and crackle. Her gaze followed the movement, watching the twigs and foliage unwind from one another and shift away from the area above the pyramid. The sunshine spread nearly halfway down the structure, when the vegetation stopped moving and the air around them grew still once more.

TWENTY-FIVE

Unlike Any Other

"IT APPEARS THAT'S all they can do for now," Damon said, staring intensely at the warlocks' position. "They're all heading our way."

"Finally," she muttered, her eyes heavy from the long day. Dropping her pack on the rock below her, she opened it and rummaged through until she found the bread she had wrapped up earlier. Ripping it open, she chewed one bite after another, waiting for the others to join them.

Mataya emerged first, followed by Apollo, Justin and finally the other three. Justin's eyes darted back and forth, from the pyramid and then down the path that faced the All-Seeing Eye. Giving him one last pointed glance, Malkia turned her attention to her sister. She brushed her hands against the sides of her legs and gripped Mataya's hands.

"I might need some assistance from one of you." Her eyes landed on Ustarum and then moved to Alyssa and Asha.

Ustarum moved first, planting his feet next to hers and curling his hand around her forearm. Drawing in a deep breath, Malkia's stomach settled and the weight on her shoulders disappeared, as his calming effect swept across and down her body. Exhaling a thankful breath, she channeled her light and for the first time in days, it rushed through her, connecting to her sister. They closed their eyes and began chanting their incantation.

A sudden wind blew past Malkia's face, bringing with it the dust that covered the city. She sneezed, halting the incantation. Feeling the warm bodies of her friends circling them, they continued on, despite the intense windstorm forming around them.

The groan of the doors threw her off again and she rushed to catch up with her sister, listening to the whistle of the winds and the creak of the old door. Her grip on Mataya's hands tightened, just as the winds dissipated and calm surrounded her, once again.

"It's open," Ustarum whispered in her ear, his hand on the back of her neck, feeding her more energy.

"Thank you," she breathed, her eyes remained closed as her body absorbed the powers and healed her achy muscles.

She felt the tug of a hand on her arm. "Let's go," Damon said.

Her eyes fluttered open and she stared over at the doorway. The inside was pitch black and the cool draft sent shivers down her spine. Scooping up her pack, she threw it on her back, drawing out her daggers and holding them firmly in front of her. She followed the others, tiptoeing into the dark space and waiting for one of the others to light up the room.

Asha and Alyssa flung their light orbs into the pyramid. Everyone paused in place, taking in the sight before them. This structure was nothing like the other pyramids. As its doors had been sealed, there was only a thin veil of dust coating each figure throughout the room. A massive pillar rose up from the floor, stretching into the darkness of the pyramid's apex. Around the pillar was a spiral staircase that led to walkways above.

Tilting her head to look up, Malkia stepped farther in, examining the end point to the walkways. They led to more than a dozen corridors that skirted the periphery of the structure. In places, they were fully enclosed, but elsewhere only a light railing marked the walkway.

"What was this place?" Mataya whispered, her fingers absentmindedly reaching out to her sister.

"I have no idea," Malkia answered, stretching her gaze upward and seeing that the walkways circled all the way to the tip. "Was there a purpose to it? A meeting hall? It doesn't make sense. What are we supposed to discover here and how will we ever find the All-Seeing Eye?"

"Maybe the one painted on the doors is the only one that exists," Ustarum suggested. He scanned the main floor as he ran his fingers through the end of his beard.

"It's a library." Asha had moved to one of the walls, lighting it up. Books lined it from top to bottom, with a ladder that slid back and forth so each of the books could be reached. She tugged one of them out, blowing the dust off the top of it and opening the delicate pages. "I can't read this language. It's unlike any that I've seen before."

Malkia hadn't budged. Her heart was racing, and she realized, she hadn't been inside a library or even held a book in her hands since she was a child on Eris. The nostalgia rushed through her as she remembered the stories her mother would read to her, and her hands trembled.

"They preserved their history." Damon remained next to her, his voice low with amazement. "Very little remains on the outside of this building, but their words are unspoiled. Why?" He glanced over at her, his brows furrowing as if she would know the answer.

"It will take ages to rummage through these books," she muttered, wringing her hands together to calm the shaking. "How will we ever finish anything, if we're stuck in here for the rest of our lives?"

"I don't know," he answered, following after the others. "But we won't make any progress if we just stand around."

She watched him walk away, her eyes dropping to the floor. A layer of soil covered it, but with the footprints stirring it up, she could see that there were various colors showing through. Sinking down, she ran her hand over the dust and gasped when she saw a painting underneath. Tugging out her blanket from her pack, she wiped at the grime, cleaning up as much as she could, before stepping back and staring at the art at her feet.

The suns had dipped down below the other buildings, making it difficult for her to see anything, but she swore it was a painting of Eris and Enyo. She needed a better view, but first the rest of the floor would require cleaning.

"I think I found something," she said, her eyes rising to find the others. They had all moved to the other side of the massive room and couldn't hear her. "*Hey*," she shouted, waiting for them to turn to face her. But they kept walking away as if they had forgotten her.

TWENTY-SIX

The Blue Planet

"MALKIA," A THUNDEROUS voice spoke behind her.

Whipping around, she covered her ears and jumped when she came face to face with an Aletheian. "*You're here*," she exclaimed, her eyes squinting from their bright light.

"We told you we would be." Another Aletheian emerged from behind the first one, stepping closer to her. "You must find the All-Seeing Eye and destroy it."

"Where is it?" she asked, waving her hands out around her.

"It's close. But only the Illumanti know its final resting point," the second Aletheian replied.

"The Illumanti?" She shook her head. "You're the Light Beings. How do you not know where this Eye is?"

"They've warded it from our view." Another Aletheian stepped in front of her. "You must speak with your grandfather. He possesses the answers."

"*Yes*," she gushed, bouncing on the balls of her feet and glancing back at her comrades. "Why can't they see you?"

"They don't need to see us, so they don't," the third Aletheian told her, waving what appeared as a hand. "We will take you to your grandfather on the planet, Earth. We've transported you there once before, but it's a forbidden act that we are *not* comfortable performing." The stature and energy of this one, gave her the impression it was male, but she wasn't entirely positive if they even had sexes. "The Illumanti are a powerful force and if they discover our treachery, their influence could blind us from all the secrets of the Universe."

She shook her head, confused by his words. "What? The Illumanti are more powerful than you?"

"*No,*" the first Aletheian thundered, giving off a more feminine aura. "But they possess magic far more sophisticated than that to which you're accustomed. It can even damage the sight of our species, making it difficult to perform our duties as your guardians."

"Why do they care if I go to this Earth?" she asked, her eyes darting from one Aletheian to the next.

"The answers lie with your grandfather," the female Aletheian replied, shifting around her so she was surrounded by the rest of them. "We're running out of time."

"What about my friends?" she asked, realizing they wouldn't know where she'd gone.

"We will return you to this moment or not long after." The first Aletheian huddled in closer and for the first time she clearly saw their faces. Their wide eyes shone like the suns, while the outward appearances glistened with a copper tone, sparkling against their own light. They were stunning and the energy surrounding them intoxicated her.

Her body became weightless and the light enrobed her. She closed her eyes, settling into the warmth of their auras and feeling the rush as she whirled away from the pyramid. Moments later, her feet connected with solid ground once again and she opened her eyes to the bright rays of one sun. It appeared closer to this planet than her suns or it was far larger, and the air was heavy, weighting her down like the last time she'd arrived to this place.

Surveying her surroundings, she could see the white sands through the tree line. The crash of the ocean surf rang in her ears. Taking a step forward, she followed the sound, knowing her grandparents were near.

The Aletheians had disappeared, but she knew they were watching her. In that moment, she realized they'd never needed the feather to connect with her. It was all a story she had created in her mind, from the first time she'd contacted them. But why would they not divulge this information to her?

The soil gave way to sand and she leaned over, yanking off her bulky boots and allowing her toes to sink into the tiny, glittering specks. "What a gorgeous planet," she said out loud, smiling as she twirled around in place, extending her arms up to the light blue sky.

"We're glad you like it," a deep voice stopped her mid-twirl.

She glanced over her shoulder, her heart hammering against her ribs. Standing a few feet away were her grandparents, grinning over at her. "Did they tell you I was coming?"

They nodded and her Mamu glided over to her, running her hands over Malkia's cheeks. "You look just like your mother," she whispered, a lone tear running down her cheek. "I'm sorry I've missed seeing you grow up. Both you and Palma."

"You knew my sister?" she asked, quivering from the memory of the last time she saw Palma.

"We don't have much time," her Grandfather replied, taking hold of her Mamu's hand and waving for Malkia to follow. "We'll give you as many answers as we're allowed, but first we must speak about our

People and the All-Seeing Eye."

They hurried up the steps to their cottage and over the threshold. Malkia's gaze swept over the interior, astounded both by the differences and similarities in their home structures. The walls rose higher than a typical home on Esaki, but seemed similar to the ones on Thalia. This one was open to a sitting room and eating area, with a corridor that lead off to the right and another in the back. She eyed the black glass that hung on the wall, noticing that it looked similar to some of the devices on Enyo and Eris.

"Introductions first?" her Mamu suggested, beckoning Malkia farther into the home.

Malkia nodded, easing her way closer to her Grandparents as she threaded her fingers together.

"Has your mother mentioned us before?" her Mamu asked.

"Haltia had secrets that I'm only now learning," Malkia replied, wiggling her toes against the hard floor surface. "I knew of you, but not of her biological father." She shifted her gaze to her Papa.

"My name is Cosimia and your Papa's name is Theodore," her Mamu spoke up, running her fingers down Theodore's arm.

"But call me Ted for short," her Papa interjected. A wide smile broke across his face as he dug his hand into the pocket of her trousers. He handed her a green piece of parchment. "I don't mean to cut this short, Malkia, but we have a lot of information and not much time. Look at that carefully. What do you see?"

She twisted it around, pursing her lips as she took in the details. "A face of a man. Is he important?"

"Not anymore," he replied, pointing at the papyrus. "Look closer. Is there anything that's familiar?"

Drawing in a deep breath, she examined it further. "I can't read or understand these words," she said, holding it closer. It was then she saw it. Her breath caught in her throat as she pointed at the pyramid with the All-Seeing Eye above it. "Here." She turned it toward them.

"Yes." He reached out and took the piece of parchment, stuffing it back in his pocket. "The Illumanti are watching."

"Who are the Illumanti?" she asked, crossing her arms over her chest and tapping her foot against their floor. "And why does that parchment have the painting of the pyramid and eye?"

Cosimia waved for her to take a seat, handing her a glass of water. "My dear, *we* are the Illumanti."

The room grew silent as Malkia froze, aside from her eyes that danced between their faces. "What?"

"Let's be quick." Cosimia glanced over at her Papa, crossing her leg over her knee. "If we keep her here too long, the others will discover our treason. We must hurry."

"Malkia." He reached across the table and covered her hands with his own. "We are the Illumanti. And *you're* the Illumanti. Many thousands of years ago, our people arrived on the moons of Theia, to find them desolate and unable to grow life. It was the perfect star system to begin an experiment, so one by one they terraformed each of the moons, aside from one, creating life as they went along, while living on Theia. They stayed for hundreds of years, watching their creations evolve, until they finally decided to move on."

"Wait." She raised her hand up in the air to stop him. "This is why the Illumanti are called our Creators?"

"Yes," Cosimia responded, nodding her head. "Each moon was seeded with different species of vegetation and animals. As they evolved, they all formed differently, which in our experience is normal within the explored universe. There are many thousands of different species, ranging from primitive to complex, some with the intelligence and lifespan similar to our own."

Ted leaned forward, his palms firmly resting on the table. "When our People abandoned the moons of Theia, we knew the species would evolve and their intelligence would flourish, which meant they required a watchful eye. But no one was prepared for the many Illumanti who secretly returned to plant their own seeds. With their knowledge of the whereabouts of our communication center, they began shaping evolution, right under the Commanders nose." He swallowed hard, glancing out the window and then back at her. "And I was one of them. But I didn't arrive until after several others had already produced multiple lines of descendants. Cosimia was the progeny of two Illumanti who had remained on Eris for many years, until they were summoned to return by our Commander."

Malkia's jaw dropped, staring at her papa. "My mother was a full-blooded Illumanti? Was she as powerful as all the other Illumanti?"

"Yes, your mother was a pure-blood and had the ability to summon the magic from the atmosphere, just like any Illumanti," her Mamu replied. She brushed her hands together as sadness clouded her features. "However, when Cerce discovered who she was, he had her powers stripped from her."

Malkia's eyes widened as they darted between the two of them. "How is that possible?" She leaned back in her chair, struggling to wrap her mind around what they were telling her. Focusing in on Ted, he broke his hold on her gaze and leaned forward, cradling his face in his hands. A deep sigh was all she heard as the seconds ticked on by.

TWENTY-SEVEN

Her Heritage

AFTER SEVERAL SILENT and long seconds, her Papa straightened up in his chair, a look of anguish plastered across his face. "He used the dark magic of the Elvens, combined with the essence of an Angel. They tapped into an energy that even the Illumanti refrain from using, and gave him the ability to dissolve her powers," Ted quaked, closing his eyes for another moment as if he was holding back a flood of tears. "She was my child and I had to leave her in the arms of the enemy."

Malkia nodded, knowing the heartache all too well.

He coughed and quickly glanced down at the floor as he cleared his throat. "Her abilities could've been returned to her, but Cerce possessed the container that restrained them. He hid it too well, burying it in a place no one has yet found. When your own father discovered it was a possibility, he attempted to find the source of this magic, but was never able to attain the proper incantation." He shot her a pointed look. "They came close several times, but their attempts never managed to rob you of your powers for more than a short period."

"I have the Illumanti blood flowing through my veins." Malkia sat up straight, suddenly realizing what they were saying. "But I'm not a pure-blood. Only half."

"Your father was half," her Mamu told her, nodding. "With the help of Cerce, it was that very heritage that gave him the influence he had over the Eris government. And he was chosen, specifically by Papa." She looked over at her partner and back at Malkia. "Your other Papa, I mean."

"Call him Cerce," Malkia grumbled, rubbing her hands down her legs. "He wasn't my Grandfather."

Ted's lips twitched with a smile as he nodded and leaned forward again. "Cerce found your father and raised him through the ranks of his guards, giving him the power to take over after his passing. His mortality would never be as prolonged as our own. He needed someone to marry his daughter—" his voice shook as he reached over and gripped Cosimia's hand. "Our daughter. Someone who would be able to control her and possibly enable him to find a way back to Earth. Cerce was intent on destroying the Illumanti. He was disgusted that he wasn't one of us. Even though he adored Haltia, he hated me and despised your Mamu. It enraged him to know he would never be as powerful as even the least among us."

"Why is Earth so important to the Illumanti?" she asked, her gaze shifting over their shoulders, out at the blue ocean.

"This is our home," Ted murmured, reaching over and raising Cosimia's hand to his lips. "Or better yet, it's our home base. Our influence on this planet has been taxing to its people. But our Commander is intent on keeping the primitives under control, and invisible to our existence. We were here first. We have allowed them to evolve, helping them along as much as possible, but preventing them from discovering too much about the history of their planet."

Malkia's eyes narrowed, a sudden reminder of the turmoil her people have endured. His words were a slap in the face. "That's what you do," she rebuked, clenching her fists to calm her nerves. "You keep everyone under your thumb, molding them to your liking and never allowing them true freedom. That's what I'm hearing."

Cosimia shook her head. "That's not what we're saying." Her silky, ivory hair fell in her eyes and she swept it away, securing it behind her ear. "This planet is different from Theia and her moons. It's special and we need to protect it. There are forces far more dangerous than the Elvens and your father. If the Commander discovers that anyone is threatening our planet, she would destroy entire civilizations to protect it." She glanced over at Ted. "The Illumanti are not a force anyone wants to battle. If your father knew how powerful he truly was, with the blood of the Illumanti running through his veins, he could devastate the moons of Theia." Nibbling on her bottom lip, her eyes locked onto Malkia's. "*You* could obliterate every species that lives on those moons."

"Why would the Illumanti want to extinguish what they've created?" she asked, not taking her eyes off Cosimia. "It makes no sense to me."

Her papa patted the table, making her jump and shift her attention to him. "Not everything will make sense. We don't have the time to explain every detail." His voice was agitated as worry flitted like a cloud shadow across his features. "But I'll tell you this. Earth connects with every planet or moon that the Illumanti have touched." Balling his hands into fists, he then flattened them against the table again, gritting his teeth as the noticeable anxiety grew in his expression. "We have to protect our evolution, our progress, and our secrets from those who would use them against us. Nothing is more important. That's why you must cut all ties to Earth."

"By destroying the All-Seeing Eye on Theia," she mused, playing with a lock her hair as her eyes glazed over. "But where do I find the correct Eye?"

"Extinguishing the Eye on Theia is just the beginning." Her Papa rose from his chair, pacing the floor behind it. "Once it's obliterated, you must wipe out all the other pyramids on Theia and on the moons." He locked onto her gaze. "Especially the one on Esaki. Its communication center is how we update ourselves on the progress of evolution, while the Eye provides sight."

"You can actually see us?" Malkia asked.

"Yes and no," he replied, continuing to pace along the dark floor. "It calculates movement. Once the Esaki pyramid is activated, the Eye on Theia awakens. It connects with the pyramids and their guardians, sending reports back to Earth of any movement on all your moons. If motion appears to derive from flying vessels or speeding vehicles of any sort, the Illumanti army are instructed to return. Upon their arrival, they'll evaluate your evolution and intellectual progress. And if your people exceed their limits, they have been ordered to eliminate all intelligent life."

Malkia's heart skipped a beat. Slowly rising from her chair, she leaned the palm of her hands against the table and stared at her grandparents. "Where's the Eye?"

Cosimia's hand slid across the table, settling over Malkia's fingers. "You'll have to destroy the entire pyramid." Squeezing Malkia's hand, a haunted look swept across her features. "The Eye lies underneath the foundation. To access the area, you must take the stairwell in the center of the structure and unbind the magic that protects it."

"If you've seen the model Earth that floats within the Esaki pyramid, you'll recognize that the Eye does the same." Ted had moved over to her side, tilting his face to peer over at her. "It hovers underneath the column, encircled by an enchantment and bright light, along with the spiral staircase. In order to unbind the powers, you'll require the magic of four, standing at each corner of the pyramid and speaking the words that are inscribed at their feet, all at once. After that's complete, the rest is just a matter of demolition. You won't be able to move the Eye, so once you obliterate it underneath, the pyramid will collapse around it."

"Easy enough," Malkia replied, straightening and watching her mamu rise gracefully from her chair. "If you don't mind my asking, how old are you?"

Cosimia chuckled, glancing over at Ted, and touching her prayer hands to her lips. "I'm two thousand and thirteen years old," she whispered, her emerald eyes twinkling. "As an Ilumanti, you will age differently than those who are not. It is why our leaders permit only minimal interbreeding with humans. Over the past two hundred years we've increased their lifespans to one hundred years, give or take a decade, depending on how well they honor their bodies."

"Why did you not have children until you were older?" Malkia asked, confused that someone would wait hundreds of years and then decide to have a family.

Nodding as if acknowledging her confusion, her lips blossomed into a wide smile. "When my parents left Eris, they took me with them. I was raised here on Earth and met Ted first. In our earlier years we had seven children over a span of eighty years. Life for us is different and you'll understand once you begin seeing your loved ones without

Illumanti blood die." Tears shimmered in her eyes. "Sometimes it's not easy to live for such a long period of time."

Malkia's gaze fell to the ground. The timeline still confused her. "How did you meet Cerce if you lived on Earth?"

"I returned to Eris to deal with my parent's estate. Once they passed away, the Commander discovered their life on Eris. She demanded that I tie up loose ends and return to Earth without divulging my true origins to anyone," her Mamu whispered. She picked at her nails and glanced over her shoulder at the world beyond the window, before capturing Malkia's gaze with hers once more. "But I met Cerce and he swept me off my feet. At that time, my path diverged from Ted's. We were both bound to our careers. It made it easy to find another lover, once I arrived on Eris. Cerce didn't know who I was until after your Papa appeared years later and revealed himself." She leaned her hands against the back of her chair as she glanced over at Ted. "But Cerce was unable to sire children, and Ted and I reconnected, conceiving your mother."

"Did Cerce know my mother was not his from the beginning?" she questioned, her breath unsteady as her thoughts wrapped around all the information from her Grandparents.

"No, he didn't," Ted answered. He pointed at Cosimia. "Our relationship was rocky during this time and we both struggled to stay faithful. That is our responsibility. Because of our relationship problems, we created the hateful flame of vengeance that burned within Cerce, and consequently passed to your father."

"And the Elvens are just pawns to your father," Cosimia added, stepping around the table. "They believe this is all a ploy to give them eternal life, but your father's only desire is to wreak havoc on the people Cerce despised. It's an act of vengeance and you're all his playing pieces to bring him to Earth and finish what Cerce could not."

"There is one more piece of information we must divulge before you return," Ted interjected, gripping her elbow and turning her to face him. "The child you carry, he possesses the pure-blood of the Illumanti."

She stepped back, shock prickling her scalp and furrowing her brows. "How? If I'm not a Pure-Blood and Damon isn't an Illumanti, how could he possibly be one of you?"

"Damon's natural parents are unknown, but based upon his DNA scan, he *is* a Pure-Blood," her Papa told her, stepping closer and holding tightly to her arm.

Wiping the perspiration from her forehead, she drew in a deep breath and held it for a few seconds, letting it out in a huff. "That makes sense," she whispered, nodding meditatively, thinking back to Damon's powers and strengthening abilities. "But that doesn't explain me."

"When Asha infused the magic of the Angels into your mother's womb, she gifted you with the missing link in your DNA. Although the Aletheians don't fully understand how it occurred, they are positive about your genetics." He pushed his white hair away from his forehead and placed his hands on her shoulders. "Your child will be the next step in your personal evolution, and he must be protected at all costs. Destroy all connection to this planet. Sever the communication with our people. If the Commander makes the voyage to Theia, she could decide to remove you and your child, and destroy everything left as they drag you from your home. I don't trust her motives." His hand grazed her cheek and he tugged her into an embrace. "You're my granddaughter, my blood. And I'll do everything I can to keep you and your family safe. Return to Theia and do what is needed." He leaned back and peered into her eyes. "Your father must perish, along with any Elvens who are intent on traveling to Earth. It is the only way to ensure your safety."

Malkia gulped back her grief, struggling to find the words to reply. Instead, she nodded and hugged the Grandfather she would never have the chance to know. Stepping away quickly, she followed Cosimia from the house, hurrying across their sandy yard and pausing near the tree line.

Turning to face them both, she could feel the heat gathering in her cheeks, a combination of regret, sadness, and fear filling her heart. "Thank you," she stammered, tears streaming down her face. "I would've liked to have known you both and to learn more about where I come from, but I'll do what is needed. Especially if it means I'll protect my home and family."

Cosimia turned away, covering her mouth as a sob burst from her lips. Malkia wrapped her arms around her waist and kissed her cheek. "I'll never forget you."

Her Papa edged up beside them, sweeping Malkia's hair out of her face. "You have many years ahead of you and someday your sacrifice will enable a new, intelligent civilization to flourish." He embraced them both, kissing her on the forehead, just as the light of the Aletheians shone in their eyes. "And just a side note, your actions, if successful, will bring freedom to more than the moons of Theia. Remember that as you journey down this path."

Malkia nodded, wiping away the tears that continued to flow. "I'll do what I can. And," her voice trembled, "I'll never forget either one of you." She blew them a kiss, turning to face the trees and following the Light Beings, forcing herself to not look back.

"*Wait*," Ted yelled.

She paused, turning her sorrowful eyes to meet his.

He stood just inside the trees, his hands held up to his lips. "Do *not* destroy the pyramids on Hemera."

"Why not?" she asked, taking a step back toward him as he held up his hand to stop her.

"Just listen," he said, shaking his head as his own face was flooded with tears. "Your life *was* foreordained, but it wasn't planned out step by step as you believe. Return to your pyramid and you'll understand what I mean." His gaze fell on the Aletheians behind her and he took a step back. "Whoever built those structures arrived on Hemera long before the Illumanti. Our people withdrew their forces from that moon, fearful of the demons and nightmarish life forms we found. We were intelligent enough to know that some things are best left alone. However, those pyramids possess ancient secrets of a mysterious civilization, and, for some reason, they prophesied your life." He hung his head, wiping his face with the back of his arm, just as the Aletheians surrounded her.

She waved her fingers around the light of the Aletheians, watching the faces of her grandparents melt with grief as she was whisked away.

TWENTY-EIGHT
The All-Seeing Eye

RETURNING TO THE same spot she had been before the Aletheians arrived at the pyramid, Malkia trembled and began to sob. An intense grief rocked her from side to side, their brokenhearted faces before they disappeared still fresh in her mind. Pressing her hands over her mouth, she could see the others on the opposite end of the structure, pulling various books from their shelves and showing one another their findings. Her eyes trailed to the column in the middle. She moved toward it without hesitation, as if an unknown force were pushing her forward.

Halting next to the stair railing, she sighed with relief when she spotted the opening that lead to the sublevel. She clasped her quivering hands to her chest, closing her eyes and burning the image of her grandparents into her memories.

A hand suddenly gripped her shoulder and she jumped, snapping her eyes open and whipped around. Damon stood wide-eyed behind her.

"I know where to find the Eye," she whispered, her voice faltering. More tears streamed from her eyes and she reached up, wiping them away with the backs of her hands.

"What happened?" he asked, his expression softening as he

wrapped his arms around her.

She nestled against his chest, allowing his energy to calm her heart. "The Alethieans were here."

"They were?" His head swung around, searching the room for the Light Beings.

"I was transported to the Blue Planet." Her lower lip trembled as she stepped away from him, numbness spreading throughout her body. "I have so much to tell you—" Her eyes darted over to the others who were headed their way. "But first, we have to destroy the All-Seeing Eye and move forward with obliterating every pyramid on Theia and her moons." She paused, raking her hands through her hair and spinning back to look at Damon. "Except the ones on Hemera."

"There's a history in this structure that I never knew existed," Asha interrupted, curling her arm around Malkia's shoulder. "What a treasure we've discovered."

A lone tear tumbled from Malkia's eye and she hurriedly wiped it away, sniffling as she shifted away from Asha. "It has to be destroyed," she whispered, her breath catching in her throat. Her eyes locked onto Asha's. "I've been to the Blue Planet. We cannot delay any longer, as the Creators have been alerted that something is off about our moons."

"You left?" Alyssa asked, stepping closer. "We didn't see you depart. Are you sure you aren't mistaken?"

"Stop." Her voice shook as her hand shot up to forestall her mother's advance. "Please. I have so much to tell you. My Grandfather told me all about the Creators and why it's imperative we halt their decision to return to our home. We're running out of time, so please just listen."

Alyssa nodded, crossing her arms over her chest and shifting back to Mataya and Asha. The rest of the group remained quiet.

"The All-Seeing Eye is located beneath this structure, and it's surrounded by intense magic. In order to disconnect the Creators connection to Theia and her moons, we have to unbind the incantation and destroy the entire pyramid." She pointed to the spiral stairs, her eyes trailing down into the darkness and seeing a flicker of light as she concentrated. "Each pyramid is connected to that Eye and must be demolished as well. We have a lot to accomplish. Once we complete our work here, I'll divulge everything my Grandparents disclosed."

She paused and waited. No one spoke, but a few nodded in response. Shifting around the others, she eased her foot down the first step, breathing deeply as she descended.

As the upper floor moved above her, the light below her brightened, and the closer she drew to it, the more intense it became. She shielded her eyes, just as the white light swept across her face. The All-Seeing Eye hovered, just as her Papa had said, rotating within the confines of the spiral staircase.

The entire group made their way down to the last step, each shrinking away and shielding their eyes, while still catching glimpses of the relic. Ustarum was the last one down, his amber irises glistening from the light as he turned to face Malkia.

"Now what?" he asked, his face more relaxed than the others.

She beckoned to Mataya, tugging Asha and Alyssa to her sides. "To disarm the Eye, the four of you must stand in the corners of the pyramid, invoking the spell etched at your feet."

Asha whipped her head around, as the others slowly turned to stare at the corners. "That's all it takes?" Asha asked, running her hands over her silver hair and pulling it back out of her face.

"Are you positive it's not a trap?" Alyssa asked, shifting her feet nervously as her hand rested on Malkia's shoulder.

"What choice do we have?" Malkia wiped the beads of perspiration from her brow with both hands, glancing in the direction of the light. "This heat is overwhelming." She released an exhausted sigh. "And we're wasting time. The Aletheians wouldn't place us in a situation that would eliminate us, unless they want to find a new group of chumps to do their dirty work."

Ustarum nodded, his arm wrapping around Malkia and kissing her glistening cheek. "You've been through something. I can see it in your eyes and I'm here for you, once you're ready to talk." His gaze shifted to the others. "We will do the incantation and release the Eye from its protection. When that's complete, we will require materials to demolish the structure." Licking his chapped lips, he pointed at Justin, Koleton, Apollo, and Damon. "Please go back outside and search for anything that can assist us in this task."

"No need," Apollo replied, holding his pack up in front of him. "I already brought Artemisian devices that can be set down here, as well as in specific spots on the main floor that will tear apart this entire pyramid."

Malkia's eyes narrowed for a moment, unsure of Apollo's original reasons for bringing along something so dangerous. Shaking her head, she turned to Ustarum. "I'll go with them, but if you need anything, you know how to reach me."

He nodded, stepping toward one of the corners and gesturing for the three women to do the same. Mataya embraced Malkia, her forehead pressing against her own.

"Be safe," Mataya whispered, gripping her sister's shoulders. "We will win this war."

Malkia swallowed hard, closing her eyes and remembering her Papa's words. "I hope so," she murmured, kissing Mataya on the forehead and watching her walk away.

Twisting back to the staircase, Malkia took a few steps up, her eyes fixed on her sister as she reached her chosen corner and turned around to face her. Sinking to her knees, she ran her hands over the floor, appearing to read what was written on it. Unable to deal with the suffocating heat, Malkia gave her sister one last glance, before rushing up the stairs and following the others who conferred near the entrance.

"Why did you bring a device like that on the ship?" Koleton barked at Apollo, wrapping his fingers around the Artemisian's wrist.

Shaking his hand away, Apollo was unfazed by the backlash. "They're harmless, until I arm them. And keeping them secret, kept them safe from anyone's imprudent hands." He focused on Malkia as she approached them. "Do you really believe I would do any of us harm?"

"No, I don't," she replied, halting next to Damon. "But I can't lie. I was shocked to hear that you possessed these devices." She paused, tilting her head to see the upper floors of the structure. "But, honestly, I'm more relieved. We don't have time to search for anything to bring this monstrous structure down. My grandparents warned me of the Creators destructive tendencies, and reasons to keep the Blue Planet secure from outsiders. It's imperative we keep them from traveling here and even more important that we stop the Elvens and my father." Entwining her fingers with Damon's, she locked eyes with Apollo. "What do you need us to do?"

The Artemisian opened his pack and withdrew four small boxes.

Setting his finger on the top of the first one, it glowed a brilliant blue, the light running down the length of his finger and then back up, beeping when it was complete.

He stretched out his arm, handing it to Malkia. "Place this at one of the corners. It will adhere the moment you set it against the wall, so ensure you situate it as close to where the floor meets the wall as you can." She wrapped it in her hand, concealing it completely within her palm. He pointed to the farthest corner. "That's your corner. We will each do one, with Koleton keeping watch by the stairway, and then we'll all return to the sublevel to place four more around the eye. Once we are free and clear of the building, I'll use the final device to bring the entire structure crumbling to the ground."

Swallowing the rising dread in her throat, Malkia nodded slightly and turned to see her corner. With every step she took, her reluctance to destroy this place of knowledge settled more firmly on her shoulders, a burden of impossible weight. Reaching the other side, her eyes trailed around the structure, admiring the books that lined each shelf, holding thousands of year's history within them. They truly were destroying a treasure. But what choice did they have?

She slipped one of the books from its spot on the shelf, blowing away the miniscule amount of dust on its spine. It was blank. Opening the maroon cover, the crisp pages inside rustled and flapped open. Her eyes skimmed over the words, not understanding anything that was written, but growing more intrigued by what these books had to offer. Closing her eyes, she inhaled the scent of the ancient parchment, burning the smell into her mind, before sliding it back into place on the shelf.

Kneeling in the corner, she withdrew the device from her satchel, turning it over in her hand. It was a cold to the touch and almost appeared to be a rock, shiny and smooth as if someone had polished it after molding it into a perfect rectangle. Wrapping her fingers around it, she scooted as close to the walls as she could and leaned over, pressing the device firmly to the stone. It did exactly what Apollo had said, adhering to the floor.

She pushed herself up from her cramped position, giving the book one last glance, before trekking back to the column to meet the others. As she neared, she could see the light from the Eye spilling brightly up the staircase and a buzz was reverberating from its aperture. Picking up her speed, she sprinted toward it, terrified by the possibility that her sister could be in danger.

Pausing at the top, Damon grabbed her wrist and pulled her back. "Let me check first," he said, stepping in between her and the stairway, with Justin right behind him.

"Wait," she replied, "I can speak to Ustarum telepathically." *Ustarum?* She reached out in her mind, holding up her finger to the two men. *Are you all okay?*

We've all repeated our incantations five times, and the only reaction is the brightening of the light and intensity of the heat. Are you positive this is what your grandfather asked you to do? Ustarum asked in his mind.

Yes, she replied, closing her eyes to recount her Papa's words. *"In order to unbind the powers, you'll require the magic of four, standing at each corner of the pyramid and speaking the words that are inscribed at their feet, all at once."* Her eyes snapped open, stepping toward the staircase, ignoring Damon's pleading eyes. *Are you saying it in unison?*

We are, Ustarum thought. *We will keep going. Just wait upstairs.*

TWENTY-NINE

Eliminating the Threat

WRINGING HER HANDS together, she turned away from the staircase that led downward. Her gaze lifted to the levels above. "I need to clear my mind," she told Damon, patting his arm and pointing up. "I'll be wandering the corridors until they finish."

Without waiting for a reply, she eased away from him, taking the stairs two at a time until she reached the first walkway that led over Damon's head. Stepping onto it, she waved down at him and Koleton, seeing Apollo staring from the corner he had placed his device. Justin was nowhere to be seen. She rushed down the bridge, pausing when she made it the corridor and looked both ways at the hundreds of books spread across the shelves in both directions.

Skipping to her left, she halted in front of a bright green book and slipped it from its spot. Running her fingers over the leather binding, she could make out words on the front, but she still couldn't understand them. One after another, she looked at the books, searching for anything that was familiar.

"Malkia?" Apollo shouted from the main floor.

She moved over to railing and peered over. "Have they finished?"

"I don't think so," he replied, twisting around to see her. "Damon and Koleton are on their way up to find you. Stop being so quiet."

She laughed and dismissed his comment with a wave of her hand. "Then stop being so overprotective." Turning back around, she caught a glimpse of a yellow book that sat on a lower shelf a few bookcases down.

Setting the book she had in her hand back on the shelf, she hurried over to the yellow book and pulled it from its spot. Turning it over, the front cover had one word on it.

Theia.

She understood that word. Opening up the cover, her eyes trailed over the first page, which only contained, Theia's Secrets, sprawled in curvy lettering. Flipping the first few pages, her breath caught in her throat when she saw a picture of all the moons and Theia. Another few pages and the words of an ancient personage sprang from the pages, directing the reader to various coordinates across the surface of this planet. Malkia drew in a deep breath, hugging the book to her chest and twisting around to see Koleton and Damon staring at her.

"Take a look at this section," she said, pointing at the shelves next to her. "I'm beginning to believe each area of this pyramid has writings from different species throughout our universe. That's why the languages are so different from one another, but this book is written in our words. Maybe we should grab some of these, before the structure is demolished."

"We don't have much time," Damon grumbled, peering at the books in front of him as his fingers traveled across their spines. "If you want to take some, do it now and read them later." He gave her a sideways look as he gritted his teeth.

"I'm not trying to annoy you," she replied, slipping a few of the other books from their spots and stuffing them in her pack. "Please just help me. I'm not asking for much. We can each take a handful of books in our packs and bring them to the ship later." She pulled a few more out and filled her pack, throwing it on her back as she cradled six more in her arms. "These are for Apollo and Justin." Responding to the quizzical expression on Damon's face.

The men each slid a few books each into their packs, grabbing a couple of extras for the rest of the group to hold. Following Malkia across the walkway, she could hear Damon muttering under his breath. Ignoring his griping, she stepped lightly down the stairs, her eyes focused on the opening that led to the sublevel and noticed that the light had disappeared completely.

Not stopping when she reached the main floor, she signaled to Apollo with a nod of her head to follow her down the stairs. He removed the books from her grasp without any disagreement, shoving them into his pack and shifting ahead of her as they moved down the steps.

As they reached the lower floor, Malkia's gaze locked onto the Eye that was still hovering above the ground but was no longer surrounded by the light. Her sister was a few feet away from them, leaning over with the heels of her hands pressed against her knees.

Malkia rushed over to Mataya, kneeling down in front of her. "Are you okay?" she asked, brushing her sister's hair from her face.

"Barely," she whispered, peering over at her sister and settling onto the hard surface. "Whatever magic was used to ward this Eye, was the most intense energy I've ever encountered." Her breath was raspy, while her eyes carried a deep weariness and had sunk into their sockets.

Ustarum dragged his feet, heading toward them, followed by Asha and Alyssa. "We will need assistance to leave this structure," he told them, his hand trembling as he wiped the chilled perspiration from his beard. "The magic that surrounded this relic was not only intense, but it was deadly to anyone who was near it. The reason it took four of us, was to ensure our survival, as the words that we chanted were all the same."

Justin bounded down the stairs at that moment. Helping Mataya up from the floor, he curled his arm around her waist and followed Apollo and Alyssa up the stairs. Malkia paused a few steps up, giving the room one last glance before ascending the remainder of the way. One by one, they stepped onto the main floor, moving toward the entrance. Once outside, Apollo and Koleton returned to finish laying the last four explosive devices around the sublevel area.

"We need to move away from the structure," Damon instructed, holding Asha up. "I know you're all weak, but it's imperative that we find shelter on the outer edges of the city."

Malkia nodded, her own energy at its lowest as her mother sagged against her. "Let's start walking." She nodded at the entrance. "Koleton and Apollo will catch up." Straightening her spine as best she could, she pressed forward, her mother shuffling next to her, with Ustarum, Justin and Mataya right behind them.

It wasn't long before Koleton and Apollo were by their sides, helping them move more swiftly down the road as the warlocks strength began to return. Malkia's energy only decreased as she eased to the back of the group, clutching weakly to Asha's arm and doing her best to not reveal her debilitated state.

They returned to the first roadway that held the small vessels. Damon, Justin, Apollo, and Koleton continued down to the other side, pointing for the others to rest next to one of the smaller buildings.

Ustarum, Mataya and Alyssa followed for a moment longer, finally pausing midway and settling into a small nook on one of the buildings. It appeared as if they were deep into a conversation, so Malkia and Asha remained where they were, resting beside one another and leaning against the wall of the structure behind them.

Malkia could see Damon at the far end of the road, talking to Apollo before stepping back and peering over at her. He waved and held up a finger, indicating they would be blasting the pyramid soon. She bobbed her head up and down and smiled, closing her eyes and feeding off the small amount of energy that had returned to Asha.

The explosion struck Malkia's ears a moment later and her eyes snapped open. Her muscles tightened as she brought her knees to her chest and her hands to her ears, peering over the vessel in front of them and seeing the dust and debris fly down the crossroad.

She wrapped her arms around Asha and both of them hid their faces behind their knees, waiting for the dust to soar over them and the ground shaking to dissipate.

A light filled Malkia's core, the sudden sensation rushing through her as her powers poured into every cell and her long-lost strength returned. She glanced over Asha, catching sight of Damon trotting towards her. But as he passed her sister, he paused next to her, shaking his head, a look of confusion plastered across his features.

Rising from the ground, a wide smile rose on her lips, a feeling of rejuvenation traveling across her muscles as she helped Asha to her feet. They turned toward the others, just in time to see a look of terror melt down Damon's face.

"*Dario*," he bellowed.

As an impulse to that name, Malkia jerked her elbow backward, but didn't connect with anything solid. The pinch in her neck and the iron grip around her waist, caused every muscle in her body to tense up. As the murkiness of the liquid concoction blackened her vision, she reached her arms out to the blurry shadows of Damon and Mataya sprinting toward her.

THIRTY
Asha and Thane

SHE GROANED, HER hands shifting to touch her head, which was pounding with her pulse. Her eyes fluttered open to a darkened room, the only illumination was the gloaming of twilight through a distant window.

"What happened?" she muttered, attempting to sit up, but feeling the tug of something cold and hard wrapped around her ankle.

Scooting to the end of the cushion she was sprawled on, she finally rose to a sitting position and reached down to her ankle. Whatever shackled her, was connected to a long rope or cord that traveled over the edge of the cushion. As her eyes adjusted to the dark, she could see it was a coiled cord and a black brace. She grasped the brace, pulling with the little energy that remained in her muscles. Releasing her breath and the brace, she leaned back onto the cushion, gasping for air and searching her mind for the memory of how she became shackled in a dark, strange place.

Damon and Mataya were running toward Asha and her. He had yelled something, but she couldn't remember what it was. Twisting to her side, she stared at the window and suddenly realized there were bars lining the area in front of her, traveling from the floor, all the way to the ceiling.

Her hands covered her mouth as she suppressed a sob. *Dario,* she thought. *He was there and now I'm their prisoner. How did he know where and when to find me?*

Movement on the other side of the bars caught her eye as someone shifted on the floor, moaning as they rose to a seated position. Catching the glimpse of silver hair, Malkia shot back up, moving as close to the bars as her chains would permit.

"Asha?" Her eyes focused on the person, just as they shifted away from the wall. Light from the stars danced across Asha's bruised face.

"Where are we?" Asha asked, groaning more as she scooted toward the bars.

"I think my father has us," Malkia whispered, tugging on the cord, but unable to release more so she could move closer. "Damon yelled Dario's name just before I blacked out."

"Fantastic," Asha mumbled, sarcasm lacing her tone. She leaned against the bars, peering over at Malkia. "Are you okay?"

"I'm weak." Holding her trembling hands up for Asha to see, she winced from the effort it took. "Whatever new concoction they've given me, it's depleted most of my energy and once again removed all my powers." She sighed, running her hands over her stomach. "Just when I was receiving them again."

"Your powers returned?" Asha questioned, her brow furrowing as her hand gripped one of the bars.

Malkia nodded, easing her head back onto the cushion behind her. "Moments after the explosion, I could feel them racing through my body. I was just about to tell you, when I saw the dread on Damon's face." Her gaze traveled back up to the window and then across the room. "Where do you think they've taken us?"

Asha closed her eyes, rubbing her fingers on her temples. "I'm sure we're still on Theia. Where on this planet is the question. And why they've imprisoned us, instead of killing us, is beyond me."

"My father wants my child," Malkia whispered, covering her core with her hands. A sense of terror was rushing through her veins, chilling her to the bone. "He'll wait until I've delivered him, before he murders me." She paused, suddenly rising into a seated position. "But you—he has no reason to keep you alive. Unless he believes you have information for him."

A door on the other side of the room slid open, revealing the large stature of her father and a lanky male standing next to him. Chills raced down Malkia's spine as she scooted back to Asha, reaching for her as the men stepped into the room.

"*No,*" she cried, knowing exactly what was about to happen. The sadness swimming in Asha's purple irises told Malkia that she was already aware of her circumstances.

"You look well, my dear daughter," Thane spoke up, as a bright light flooded across the room. "How is my grandson doing?"

Malkia didn't take her eyes off Asha, pleading silently for her warlock mother to fight. Asha shook her head, a deep weariness veiling her expression. An Elven strode over to Asha, towering over her with his thin proportions. He yanked her up by her arm.

"*Leave her alone,*" Malkia screamed at the barbarian.

Another Elven stepped in front of Asha, staring at Malkia with his ash gray eyes. "How long until the child will be born?" he asked, peering over at Thane.

"With the mixture of spells and the incantation of your magic, your doctors have calculated three to four weeks until the child is fully developed," Thane answered, his deep voice crushing Malkia's heart as she twisted around to see the face she despised most in the universe.

"What?" she croaked, shifting as far away from both of them as was possible. "I have months before he's ready." Her eyes darted between her father and the Elven. "What have you done?"

"Nothing for you to worry about," her father informed her, moving around the corner of the bars and standing next to the Elven. "Once the child is born, we will have her stripped of all her powers and returned to Esaki. Will that suffice, Dasco?" His eyes were locked onto the Elven, who continued to examine Malkia.

Dasco nodded as the edges of his lips twitched into a smile. "If you're positive this child is the key to finding the Blue Planet, I'm fine with however you deal with his mother." Dasco winked at Malkia, before twisting to look at Asha. "What about this witch? Are you willing to do what needs to be done?"

"It will be my pleasure," Thane replied. His cheshire smile stretched across his lips as he waved the other Elven away and gripped the back of Asha's neck, holding her in front of his chest. He leaned forward and whispered in her ear and Malkia quivered as tears streamed from Asha's closed eyes.

Thane drew a large dagger from its sheath. Screaming at her father, Malkia bounded to her feet and rushed toward the bars as he brought the sharp edge to the tender flesh of Asha's neck and sliced it clean open. Falling to the floor, Malkia shrieked, her sobs rocking her body as she watched the blood gush from the wound in Asha's neck. Her body struck the floor with a thud, convulsing before relaxing completely.

The tears burst from Malkia's eyes and she strained against the shackle on her ankle. Even sprawled on her stomach, her hand barely grazed the bars that separated her from Asha's body. A copper stench filled her nostrils, making her gag as the nausea returned.

"Now that's out of the way," she heard her father say, wiping the blood from his dagger with a large rag, "I can begin searching for the others and eliminate them one by one."

She jumped to her feet again, her wild eyes staring down her father and her hands holding onto her queasy stomach. "Please, leave them alone. You have what you need, just leave the rest of my friends alone."

He chuckled as he stepped over Asha's body, careful to avoid the crimson puddle. "I told you I would take everyone you love and I do *not* distribute empty threats. It's the only reason I'm leaving you alive, after you deliver my new grandson." Folding his arms over his chest, he stood tall, attempting to intimidate her with his stature, like he did when she was a child. "You thought I was being merciful, but I never intended to leave you whole. Your heart will be crushed over and over again, until the only thing left is an empty and miserable shell, unable to retaliate because your powers will be bottled up just like your mother's."

She hiccupped, clutching her trembling hands together. "Why do you hate me so much?" she asked, drawing in a raspy breath.

"Because you chose her over me," he barked, shifting away from Asha's body and snapping his fingers at the Elven. "Clean up this mess and burn the body." Without another look he exited the room, leaving Malkia to watch the obedient Elven remove Asha's body.

The silence filled the room as she sank onto the cushion and closed her eyes, pleading to the Aletheians for their help. With no response, she turned to face the wall, weeping quietly for the loss of another one so dear to her heart.

"Time for your next dose of love," Dario's voice was like daggers to her heart.

She didn't bother to even look at him, knowing her mind and heart couldn't handle another jab. Not budging from her position, she waited until she heard the creak of her prison door, cringing when his firm hands held her leg down.

He leaned in close, his lips brushing her ear. "Maybe I'll be in later for a nightcap." His hand slid up her leg pausing on her hip, just as she connected her fist with his nose. Jumping away from her, he wiped the blood from his nose, smiling down at her. "Feisty as ever." He chuckled, beckoning at another Elven who stood on the other side of the bars.

The Elven stepped forward, carrying a black bag and a wary expression, giving Malkia the impression he would be an easy target. "Please don't do this," she pleaded, scooting away from him.

"It won't work," Dario replied, shifting around the Elven and sitting on the cushion, his firm grip holding her hands and legs down. "You're too weak and this man's family is in jeopardy if he doesn't comply. Those Angels might have convinced most of the Elven population to cease fire, but the ones still on task won't be listening to you."

"I hate you," she hissed through clenched teeth.

He laughed and nodded as the doctor stuck her with a needle in the neck. "This won't hurt your child," the doctor whispered, his gaze never leaving hers. "But it's speeding up his development, so you'll be able to deliver in the next few weeks. I'll be in here several times each day to keep an eye on you and measure your expanding belly." He rose to his feet, nodding at her abdomen. "As you can see, the results from your first shot are already showing. Good luck to you, Malkia." He glanced over at Dario, before backing away and leaving the room.

Dario's lips twitched, watching her weary eyes droop. "We added some sleeping agents to their mixture to keep you from straining yourself too much." His hand slid up to her belly, covering the tiny bump entirely. "If my Mamu has her way, you both will be dead before dawn," he whispered, licking his lips as he rose from the cushion. "You'll need all the luck you can obtain."

Her eyes followed him as he locked her cage and left the room, closing the door behind him. Forcing her eyes to stay open, she noticed Asha's blood had been cleaned up and she was now completely alone. A moment later, the lights switched off and she finally allowed her eyelids to close.

THIRTY-ONE
Making Allies

"HOW LONG HAS she been out?" She could hear her father's voice close to her. She struggled to pry her eyes open.

"Nearly the entire day," the Elven doctor replied. "Whatever Dario is adding to my mixture, it's causing her adverse side effects."

"What do you mean?" Thane asked, a growl rumbling up his throat.

Malkia opened one eye halfway and focused on the two men who were a few feet from her. Her father's cheeks were steaming, with a crimson heat and fury in his eyes.

"I don't think his intentions are pure," the doctor stuttered, stepping away from her father. "He and Ginny speak quietly when they prepare it, but I've heard the word "kill" several times and after Malkia was unable to be roused to eat, I realized you needed to be warned."

Thane's lips set in a straight line as he glanced down at her and noticed she was stirring. "Look, she's opening her eyes." He pointed, peering back at the doctor.

"He's right," Malkia murmured, her voice barely audible.

"What did you say?" her father questioned, stepping closer to her.

She pushed up from the cushion and with the help of the doctor, leaned against the wall behind her. "I said, he's right." She swallowed with difficulty, her throat filled with the dry cobwebs of sleep, forcing a cough from her mouth. She covered her face with her hands, pausing until she could speak again. "Ginny attempted to murder me back on Thalia and if she's here, I'm sure she's intent on trying again."

Thane's breathing became ragged. Taking a few steps backward, he gripped one of the bars with his hand, his eyes darting around the room as if he was searching for something. "Make sure they haven't harmed my grandson and serve her some food and drink." He waved his hand toward Malkia as if she was another one of his animals. Leaving her cage, he exited the room without another word.

The doctor sank down onto the cushion with a sigh, his pale pink irises locking onto her own. "It's not often I have you alone, but now that you're awake, we can actually speak to one another."

"Why are you being so kind?" she asked, scooting to the edge of the cushion and twisting around to face him. She reached around her side and rubbed her aching lower back. Everything hurts more than usual.

"I'm not here willingly," he answered, revealing a new needle. "My expertise in this medicine and magic constitute my only value, and if I don't comply my family's lives will be terminated."

"Sounds like my father has no desire to keep any allies, once his plan has been completed," she mumbled, drawing in a deep breath and running her fingers through her knotted hair. "Would it be possible to shower sometime soon?" Her stench was surrounding her like a rotting ritter.

He nodded, placing the needle back in his medicine bag. "I will have some food and drink brought in first. Afterward, one of the ladies will escort you to the shower and return you back here, in time for you next injection." He wrinkled his nose and his eyes rose to look at the ceiling. "Ginny has your father's ear and I doubt he'll retaliate against her, even though her desire for your child's death will infuriate him. If Dario or Ginny returns, you must fight and show your father the harm they wish upon you." Rising from the cushion, his gaze returned to her, bowing his head before taking his leave.

After the door closed, she studied the cord that was connected to the brace around her ankle. Tugging on it, she could see it was infused with magic and without her abilities, it was most likely unbreakable. Despite knowing the possibilities, she bent it in half, kinking it and hoping that would block the spell that surrounded it. Instead it sparked, forcing her to drop it.

Shifting off the cushion, she walked over to the entrance to her cage, examining the lock. It had a finger imprint, which made escape nearly impossible. If only she could knock out Dario and use his fingerprint.

Shaking her head, she strolled around her cell, checking for any weaknesses in the bars, but not finding any. Her father wasn't foolish enough to place her in anything that would potentially have an escape route. Even though she was aware of this, she kept searching, pulling the cushion away from the wall and surveying every inch of the metal wall.

As she was sliding the cushion back into place, the door swung open and a petite female Elven stepped inside, holding a tray filled with bread and cut fruits. Her expression remained passive, holding out the tray and sliding it through a slot on the floor. A lanky, male Elven walked in behind the female, eyeing her carefully with his lavender irises before handing her a glass of water through the bars.

Malkia smiled, pulling the items over to the cushion and watching the two retreat, securing the door behind them. The food was the best she had tasted in days. She chewed slowly, enjoying the flavors. Once she washed it all down with the water, she set all the dishware near the entrance and settled back on the cushion, waiting for someone to return for her.

She didn't have to wait long. The petite female escorted her across the hall, letting out more of the cord from the wall so she could make it to the bathing room. The Elven sat on a chair in the corner, only giving Malkia the privacy of a thin fabric curtain as the warm water cascaded over her body.

A sigh escaped her lips, and she felt a bit of relief as her focus strayed down to her expanding belly. Her child was swimming around, kicking every so often and reminding her that he was with her. A few tears tumbled from her eyes and she closed them as she sank to the floor and wept, a deep sorrow settling over her heart.

As her eyes opened again, she noticed a shadow on the other side of the fabric. Quickly wiping away her tears, she scooted to the corner. The figure sagged against the wall and slowly slid to the ground.

"I'm sorry for what you're enduring," the Elven spoke quietly, her voice barely a whisper. "The ones who are against these actions will do what we can to make the transition as seamless as possible, but with the threat to our own families, it's all we can offer." She paused, her hand easing around the fabric. Malkia grasped it and felt a squeeze. "We are with you. There are several of us, and once they're finished with you, we intend to ensure your freedom." She withdrew her hand and rose from her spot on the ground, returning to her seat across the room.

Malkia finished washing her hair and body, wiping away any tears that remained on her face, before stepping out of the shower with fresh new clothes. The pants were loose around the belly, allowing them to slide below the expansion. As well, a lose shirt was provided, along with a warm, open sweater to keep her arms covered.

Smiling sadly at the Elven as she returned to her feet, Malkia followed her back to her cage, peering down the corridor before reentering the room. It was dark, but she noticed several other doors and a crossway corridor. Whenever they allowed her to shower, if she kept examining the area, maybe she would have an idea of where to run once she escaped.

"My name is Elisa," the Elven whispered as Malkia walked passed her and stepped into the confines of her prison. "I'll send word to the doctor that you're ready for your next injection."

Malkia reached through the bars and clutched Elisa's arm. "Promise me, if you find a way for me to escape before my child's born—a way that will appear as no one's fault—you'll assist me."

A look of dread rushed over Elisa's pale pink irises. "I can't do that. There's too much at risk, but I'll do what I can if I find a way to free you. I cannot make any promises."

"Fair enough," Malkia whispered, releasing Elisa from her grasp and stepping a few feet back. "Thank you, Elisa."

Her eyes wandered around the room, landing on the dark crimson stain on the hard floor and her heart wrenched. Asha's last moments weighed on her mind. What had her father whispered in her ear? The sorrow eating at her mind, drowned her in a familiar grief as she sank onto her only means of comfort and curled up in a ball, pulling the cord up with her.

She stared off into space, petrified by the thoughts of her future and the well-being of Esta and the rest of her family and friends. If only the Artemisians would arrive. Her brain throbbed every time she attempted to reach past the barrier they had placed on her telepathy, so that wasn't a viable way for her to warn them. The Artemisians' army and the Nesoi were their only hope.

The door opened, once again. Sitting up, she stared at Dario, a wide grin smeared across his face as he sauntered into the room. "How're you doing, sugar?" he asked, licking his lips as his eyes traveled down her body.

"I've wiped the smile from your face so many times, I've lost count," she replied, rising to her feet. "I dare you to rattle my cage without the locked door protecting you."

He chuckled, clearly understanding her double meaning, before leaning forward and pushing his face in between two bars. "You don't scare me, little witch."

She didn't hesitate, bringing her foot up to connect with his chin. "Idiot." He flew back and hit the wall behind him, sliding to the floor as he held his bleeding chin and mouth in his hands. "I warned you," she muttered, settling back down on her cushion and watching him race from the room, holding his face in his hands.

"You're going to create your own mess, if you keep that up," the doctor stated. He stood in the doorway, watching Dario stumble down the hallway.

"What do I have to lose at this point?" she asked, shaking her head in disgust. "And I warned him. He never learns."

"I'll post a guard at your door and have your father order them to not allow anyone else in until further notice," he replied, opening the door to her prison. "That's the best I can offer you."

"I appreciate the gesture, but if Ginny and Dario want me dead, they'll find a way." Snuggling back onto the cushion, she tugged her thin blanket around her. "Unless I escape, one way or another I'm doomed."

"This mixture will help you sleep through the night, but you'll actually wake in the morning, instead of being drugged until our last meal is upon us." The doctor pulled out the syringe as he settled next to her on the cushion. "Don't give up hope yet," he whispered, locking eyes with hers. "We know the Aletheians are in contact with you and I don't believe they'll allow your demise."

She shrugged, frustrated with relying on everyone else to save her, while her father rained the terrors of the universe upon her people. "If they show up, I won't turn down their assistance."

The needle pierced a vein, the thick substance sliding in to mingle with her blood. She looked up the doctor one last time, before the darkness melted across her vision.

THIRTY-TWO
Ginny's Deadly Mistake

THE RATTLE OF the door woke her. Malkia's eyes snapped open and she stared up into Ginny's baleful gaze. Shifting backward, she sat up and leaned against the wall, eyeing the woman's every move.

"Sleeping beauty has woken," Ginny said, strolling along the edges of the bars, twisting around to face Malkia. "Your behavior is unladylike and I believe I owe you for how you treated my grandson." Her fingers trailed down the front of the pendant worn around her neck.

Malkia's eyes narrowed as she noticed her necklace. "Bring it, coward," she growled, rising from her cushion with clenched fists.

Ginny laughed, her eyes dropping to Malkia's fists. "I won't need to touch you, as I still possess my abilities." Her white light shot from her body, sliding toward Malkia, crackling as it approached.

Closing her eyes, Malkia focused on Esta's face, pushing all thoughts of Ginny from her mind. A few moments passed and nothing happened. Flashing her eyes open, she stared at a dumbfounded Ginny.

"I don't need my powers to beat you at your own game," Malkia jeered, squaring her shoulders. "Leave this room. I don't want to see your face again."

Ginny gaped as if forgetting herself, belatedly snapping her jaw shut with an audible click of the teeth and glaring at Malkia. "I don't think so." She stepped toward her, tugging a dagger from its sheath and twisting it at Malkia's face. "One way or another I'm going to cut that child from your womb and exterminate the parasite."

"You'll do what?" Thane bellowed, his brawny stature filling the entire doorway.

Ginny whipped around as the edges of Malkia's lips twitched with a smile.

"I didn't mean it the way it sounded," Ginny stammered, ramming the dagger back in its sheath and walking toward Thane. "Your daughter kicked my grandson in the face and I was reminding her who was in charge around here."

"As cocky as Dario is, I'm sure he deserved to be kicked in the face," Thane roared, a crimson flush creeping across his features as he glared at Ginny. Opening the cage door, he yanked the woman through the doorway and wrapped his large hand around her throat, leaving her feet dangling inches from the floor. "I'll rip you to shreds, woman."

Ginny attempted to shake her head as his grip tightened. Throwing her to the far side of the room, her body struck the wall, slamming the side of her head against it before she landed with a thud against the floor. She gasped for air, her snow-white hair hanging in her face.

"Lock her up," he ordered the long-legged Elven who was standing behind him. "I'll deal with you later." He shot Ginny one last glance before storming from the room.

"Not your best move," Malkia mumbled, chuckling to herself as she settled back onto the cushion.

"Shut it, you obnoxious witch," Ginny shrieked at her, flinging her hair out of her face and pushing the Elven away from her. "Touch me, you insolent fool and I'll slice you up for my dinner." She shot him a frosty look as she scooted away.

Ignoring her threat, he gripped her wrists and snapped a brace around both of them. His hand reached behind him, muttering words Malkia didn't understand, and another cord flew from the wall to his reaching hand. Connecting it to the braces, Malkia couldn't help but smile, seeing the terror in Ginny's eyes.

"This might be my favorite day, here in captivity," Malkia told the dreadful woman, smiling wide as she twirled the ends of her hair with her finger.

"Time for breakfast," Elisa announced, her gaze on Ginny. Sliding the tray through the slot, she then handed Malkia a glass of juice through the bars. "Why is she locked up?"

"She said the wrong thing at the wrong time. Now she has the honor of experiencing my father's wrath." Her eyes narrowed at Ginny, as she sipped on her juice. "A fabulous luxury I've endured for the past half year."

Malkia chewed her bread and fruit, slowly, staring at Ginny's bruised face. The woman sat against the wall, her legs bent in front of her with her arms resting on her stomach, glaring at Malkia without blinking.

As she was polishing off her plate, Thane burst into the room, followed by Dasco and Dario. Storming over to Ginny, he yanked her off the ground, turning her to see her grandson. A look of terror flashed through Dario's eyes and for a split second, Malkia felt sorry for him, but she quickly regained her wits and leaned forward to watch.

"If you ever cross me again, I will slaughter you without another word," Thane barked at Dario, yanking at the pendant and breaking the clasp. He threw it off to the corner of the room, and held his dagger against Ginny's throat.

Dasco grinned and clapped his hands, apparently not a fan of the woman. Swallowing hard, Dario nodded, holding out his hand to interject.

"*Don't say one word, boy,*" Thane shouted, spit flying from his clenched mouth. "My grandson is the key to our entire voyage. If you dare lay a hand on my daughter or grandson, *you* will face the same fate."

With a flick of his wrist, the dagger sliced open Ginny's throat, her hands flying up to stop the bleeding and choking as she dropped to the floor. Feeling no remorse for the woman, Malkia watched her struggle to breath, sputtering blood from her mouth as the life pulsed from her hateful body.

"Step into line, Dario," Dasco said, a smile twitching on the edges his pale lips. "We are too close to the end game to squander our efforts with tiny feuds. You now know what's at stake." He patted Dario on the back, before turning to face Malkia. "I wouldn't be overjoyed by this extermination. If you even breathe wrong, I'll have you bound up so tightly, you won't be able to budge until that child is cut from your womb and you're abandoned to bleed out in the last spot you saw him."

He tilted his head in amusement, his smoky gray irises dancing with joy as he watched the fear travel across her expression. Tugging Dario along with him, they exited the room, leaving her alone to stare at the lifeless body of the woman she detested most in the universe.

THIRTY-THREE
Renewed Energy

TIME FLOWED BY unmarked and Malkia begun etching a line on the wall, to remind her how many days she'd been held captive. Now there were twenty-three lines and that didn't count the first few days. Ginny's body, along with her pendant, had been removed only after it lay abandoned for an entire day on the other side of the room. She had been grateful for the sedative, so she could erase the memory of the dead body from her mind.

Her belly had expanded significantly and her little boy was wiggling within her womb, kicking at her organs and ribs throughout the day and relaxing with the injection at night. It helped her have restful sleep, but she was growing more terrified at each passing day, knowing the moment would come where her father would rip her child from her arms, once again.

She felt completely alone. The Aletheians hadn't appeared and there had been nothing but silence beyond the walls of her prison, making it difficult to gain any knowledge of her whereabouts. Her father had been thorough in his choice of a hiding place.

Pressing down on her baby's foot that was rammed into her ribs, she paced the floor of her prison, glancing over at the brightly lit window. One thing she did know, the trees didn't cover her area of the building, as the suns' rays shone in from early morning to late evening. She had nothing better to do than to count her way through the day.

They fed her well, but she knew it was all in hopes for a healthy baby boy and not because they cared about her health. She had just finished her mid-meal and was waiting for Elisa to return for the tray and glass. The doctor and Elisa had spent her entire stay searching for a hiding spot to conceal her, if they had the opportunity to help her escape, but had come up empty handed time and again. She was hoping for better news today.

The door slid open and Dasco stepped across the threshold, his eyes swimming with mischief. "Hello, Malkia. How are you feeling today?" he asked, his hands behind his back as he stepped to her cage.

"I'm fine," she muttered, only giving him a sideways glance as she continued to pace. "Why are you here?"

"It would be rude for me to not stop by from time to time and check on the well-being of my guest," he replied, a smile twitching on the edges of his lips.

"Your guest? For a chump, you're a horrible jokester," she snapped, pausing with her steps and glaring at the leader of the Elvens. "I've warned you of the dangers our moons are facing, if we don't stop the advances of the Illumanti, but here we still remain. Why torture me with your phony kindness and concern?"

"I've placed no one who matters in danger," Dasco said, his hand touching his chest, mocking her with his shocked expression, before lifting the edges of his lips into a wide smile. "Once we have the child, we will leave this star system and travel to this Blue Planet, where I'll discover the secrets of the Creators, followed by obliterating their precious Earth, as you called it."

Malkia stuck her tongue out at him, weary of his irrational replies. "Go away," she grumbled, sagging against the far wall.

"Before I do, I wanted to inform you of our plans to take your daughter with us as well." Malkia's head whirled around, her eyes narrowing as she pushed herself away from the wall and stalked toward him. He laughed, waving a dismissive hand at her. "You won't mind, will you? I mean, if I have my way, you'll be flying with those disloyal Alethieans instead of confined to your useless body. You're very welcome for being so merciful." He winked, pivoting on his heel and sauntering to the doorway.

"If I ever escape, I'll strangle you with my bare hands," she hissed, gripping hold of the bars and glaring at the Elven. "Don't mistake my pregnancy for weakness."

He didn't turn to face her, but shook his head as he chuckled, exiting the room and leaving her to chew on his words. Unclasping her shaking hands from the bars, she screamed at the top of her lungs, unable to hold in the frustration and terror any longer. Her hands raked through her hair, gripping it by the roots as she screamed again. Sinking to the ground, she freed her hair and cradled her belly, weeping for the child she feared she would never know and the one that could possibly be taken from her, once again.

Dario swung open the door and peered down at her, a smirking parody of a smile stretching his mouth, obviously relishing in her misery. Feeling a rush of fury slither through her veins, a sudden flame ignited within her and with one swift move she bounded to her feet. Dario stumbled back a few feet, surprised by her sudden move, his eyes narrowing just as she became aware of her hands glowing with her crimson light.

She welcomed the darkening light with deep relief. The fate of her children rested in her hands and without another thought, a bright red aura erupted from her body, enveloping her. Dario sputtered, his jaw dropping open as he fumbled to run away but instead tripped over his own feet.

With a flick of her wrist, her light flew from her hand, striking him directly in the chest as he whirled to face her. His body flew through the doorway, smacking into the wall and embedding him within the metal particles. She snapped off the brace binding her ankle and stepped from her cage, following after him and curling her hands around his throat, squeezing as hard as she could.

Gritting her teeth, she could see her father in her peripheral vision, emerge from one of the other rooms. She was done playing nice. She gripped Dario's head with her other hand, watching as his eyes widened with fear. Pausing for just a moment, she screamed in his face. Before she could break his neck, his eyes rolled back and blood sputtered from his mouth, boiling with an intense heat as his flesh began melting from his bones and his organs liquefied beneath his crisping skin. Dropping him to the floor, she watched as the flames she had ignited consumed him, from the inside out.

Her eyes traveled down the corridor, realizing her father had disappeared. Not waiting for permission, she sprinted in the opposite direction, twisting around the corner and down another corridor, finally flinging open the door to the outside and rushed out into the clean, crisp air.

The suns' rays hit her protective light as she surveyed her surroundings, seeing the tops of the city buildings across a massive meadow. Soaring into the air, she aimed for their skyscrapers, reaching out to Tantiana in her mind.

Where have you been? Tantiana asked.

My father had me, she explained, concentrating on the spot she remembered the pyramid had been. *Where are all of you?*

We've met up with the Artemisians and the Nesoi at the same place we landed the ship, along with a number of your own people from Esaki. After you were taken, we scoured the area, but never found any place that wasn't already vacated.

I'm on my way, she thought. Her crimson light was darkening and she feared the murkiness closing in on her heart. But the safety of her people was too close to stop now. Flying over the city, she stared down at the hole in the center, feeling like that moment was ages ago, instead of only four weeks.

Glancing back at the building that had been her prison, she could no longer see it and wondered if a spell had concealed it from sight. Shaking her head, she twisted around, focusing on the direction of her ship and zoomed toward it.

Seeing the crowd on the ground and the vessels beyond it, a grateful smile rose on her lips. The Nesoi were gathered just inside the forest, with Tantiana standing tall, craning her neck to see her.

There you are, her dragon thought. *I've missed you.*

And I've missed you, she replied, feeling a sense of joy whirl through her heart.

Someone pointed as she neared and she slowed down, wishing for her purple light to appear. With only her thoughts, the color melted into her warm purple, with silver sparks flickering from one end to the other. "Finally," she breathed, grateful her abilities were at last restored.

Alighting on the lush grass of the meadow, she allowed her power to dissipate, hugging herself as she twirled around. Mataya bolted through the crowd, throwing herself at her sister and embracing her so tightly that Malkia could barely breathe.

A moment later, she felt the small hands of Esta wrap around her giant waist. Releasing her sister, she pulled the weeping child in her arms, squeezing her firmly. Damon emerged from the onlookers, his eyes wide as he rushed over and curled her into his embrace.

More faces emerged, but one in particular brought her to a standstill. Jayde stood with the Artemisians, waving her fingers at Malkia with a wide smile smeared on her face. Setting Esta on the ground, she walked toward her old friend, throwing her arms around her neck and tugging her in as close as her belly would allow.

"Where have you been?" she asked, stepping back and holding Jayde's hands.

"It's a long story," Jayde replied, glancing over at the creatures who flanked her. "I made new friends and have been traveling the skies. My hawks have kept me in the loop, and when we heard that the Esaki pyramid needed to be destroyed, we returned to the moon and did the job."

Malkia drew in a quick breath, realizing all the scrolls they'd left behind, were now dust in the wind. "Thank you." She embraced her friend once more. "It was a job that had to be done. And I'm glad you decided to join me here."

"Now," Damon interrupted, pulling her to his side. "Where have you been?" His eyes strayed down her expanded belly. "And how are you this pregnant in just a few weeks?"

"My father." She twisted to look at the crowd that was slowly dispersing. Her eyes locked onto Alyssa, who was sprinting toward her. "I need to speak with my mother," she whispered, easing away from Damon and Jayde. "Privately."

"Where's Asha?" he asked, suddenly realizing she was alone.

Malkia shot him a sideways glance, pressing her lips together to prevent the tears from falling. His eyes widened, swallowing hard and stepping away with a nod of his head. She focused back on her mother as she trudged toward her, feeling a sudden weight land on her shoulders.

Alyssa threw her arms around Malkia, sobbing into the crook of her neck. "Where have you been? We've been terrified?" Releasing Malkia, her eyes swept down to her belly and gasped. "What happened?" she asked, her breath coming in short as she held her hands over her heart.

"Mom," she gripped Alyssa's shoulders, giving her a pointed stare. "You know my father and Dario captured Asha and me."

Alyssa nodded, glancing over Malkia's shoulder, searching the crowd. "Where's my sister?" she questioned, stepping to the side, her gaze darting around.

"Mom, look at me." She gripped her mom's arm, twisting her back to face her. "Thane—" Swallowing hard, she closed her eyes. "My father executed her." Her eyes snapped open as the tears flooded her eyes, unable to halt them any longer. "I'm so sorry."

Alyssa stared blankly at Malkia, blinking a few times as her arms fell to her side. "What?" The color drained from her face. "What did you say?"

Malkia stepped closer, sweeping her mom's brunette hair away from her cheek. "I'm sorry, Mom."

"*No*," Alyssa snapped, her eyes narrowing as she pushed Malkia's hands away. "*He wouldn't dare.*"

Malkia's eyes fell to the ground, drowning in her own grief. "He did. Right in front of me."

Alyssa's hands rose, sliding her hair back from her forehead as she shook her head. "It's because of you, isn't it? He wants to hurt you."

Nodding her head, Malkia felt the dread snaking its way through her stomach as she stared at her mother's devastated expression. "You're all in danger. He wants to take everything and everyone from me." She licked her lips, shuffling her feet as they began to ache. "They will kill you all, and take away my children, leaving me to rot on Esaki."

Alyssa's head snapped up, her eyes boring into Malkia. "I won't let that happen," she hissed, her eyes narrowed as she reached out and clutched her daughter's arms. "My sister won't die in vain and I'll protect my grandchildren and my daughter to my very last breath." Tears tumbled from her eyes, coursing in unbroken rivulets down her cheeks as she inhaled several times, before refocusing on Malkia. "We will not quit." Dropping her arms to her sides, she shifted around Malkia. "I need to be alone for a moment."

Malkia remained still, only rubbing her hand over her belly, the kicks of her child soothing her broken heart. The crowd had dispersed, leaving her completely alone with the flowers and tall grass. Sinking to the dirt, she gasped in a lung full of air, the memory of Asha's death still vivid in her mind, along with the pain on her mother's face. A deep and intense fury stirred within her and she stared down at her hands, noticing the crimson light had returned.

Swallowing her grief, she stuck her hands into the soil, digging her way down until her connection with Theia enveloped her entire body. Drawing in one deep breath after another, she concentrated on the faces of her loved ones, and the sacrifices so many had already made. There was no quitting in this journey. She had known the threats that had awaited her. And denying that Asha hadn't known as well, would be discourteous to her memory.

She took time to draw a few more breaths and rose from her place on the ground, surveying the area her people had made their home. Strolling across the meadow, she paused several time to take in the blossoms' scents and gather her wits, before revealing Asha's death to the others.

Koleton and Apollo stood just outside the vessel, their backs turned to her. A few feet away, Esta sat on the plank, dangling her feet over the edge and laughing with Zoe, while Landon and Branston wrestled on the dirt below them. The neighboring ship had dozens of Artemisians surrounding it, with Jayde perched on a tree stump, her face lighting in response to something one of her friends had said.

Her army had grown overnight. And she would need every single one of them, because she knew her father would come. Her child was too important to him.

Strolling up to Koleton and Apollo, she embraced each one of them, letting them each rub her belly as she laughed at their jibes. Her heart was hurting, but being with her people again was the only medicine she needed.

"I have something to tell the group," she finally said to the two of them. "Do you know where Mataya, Justin, and Damon are?"

Koleton froze, his eyes darting over to Apollo. "Justin? I thought you knew," he said, clenching his jaw and fists.

"Know what?" she asked, twisting her hair up into a messy bun on top of her head as she grinned over at Esta.

"Justin's a traitor," Koleton growled.

Malkia's head snapped back to face her friend, her eyes growing wide as they danced between Apollo and Koleton. "What are you talking about?"

"Did you not see him when you were being held by your father?" Apollo asked, his hand curling over her shoulder.

Shaking her head slowly, the beat of her heart drummed ferociously in her head. "No. You're kidding, right?" she questioned, a desperate tone rising in her voice.

"Damon and Mataya saw him drag you two away," Koleton responded, stepping closer as he waved for the kids to go inside the ship. "Dario and he both jumped onto the plank of a ship, holding Asha and you."

Her hand flitted to her mouth, a soft sob escaping her lips. "Justin did this?" Her voice trembled, realizing her sister's partner was the reason Asha was dead.

"Let's go inside and find Mataya and the others," Apollo suggested, placing his hand firmly on her back, leading her up the cargo door.

The three of them were silent as they made their way up to the bridge, where they found Damon and Ustarum speaking quietly near the window. Their sudden silence was a knife to Malkia's heart, a deep distrust filling her gut.

"She didn't know that Justin revealed our position to her father,"

Koleton announced, moving toward the two men with Malkia in tow.

Damon's eyes locked onto Malkia's, his expression falling with grief. "We thought you knew," he told her, wrapping his arm around her shoulder as she halted next to him.

She shook her head, struggling to breathe as her baby kicked her in the ribs again. Pressing down on his foot, she bent slightly backward attempting to move his position while the others watched her. "He's nearly ready to be born," she moaned, rubbing her hand over her belly. "The Elvens sped up his development with their magic, giving me this gravid body you see before you." A low chuckle rippled up her throat, but the amusement ended there, as her heart was far from happy. "I didn't know about Justin. I never saw him while I was with my father and Dario, and it's nearly unbelievable that he would do such a thing." She covered her mouth with her hands, attempting to hold back the heartache. "I can only imagine how painful this must be for Mataya."

"She was devastated," Ustarum replied, running his hand down his beard, his amber eyes holding a sadness much like that of the others. "But she was more terrified with the prospect of what they would do to you and Asha. Speaking of—" He turned to look at the door. "Where is Asha? Did you not bring her with you when you escaped?" His focus returned to her and as soon as they made eye contact, he took a sudden step back, shock melting down his face. "*No.*" His voice was barely a whisper as he leaned over, pressing his fists against his knees and rocking back and forth.

"What?" Koleton asked, twisting around to look at Malkia. "What is it?"

"My father executed Asha," she whispered, her voice quivering as a sharp pain clutched her stomach and spread up her back and down into her hips. "*Ow*," she yelped through clenched teeth, her fingers wrapping around Damon's arm as she sank to her knees.

Ustarum sprang forward, gripping her beneath the arm and helping her back to her feet as a tidal wave of pain raced through her body. Staring wild-eyed at each of them, Koleton remained frozen, until Apollo shoved him out of her way as they half carried her to the infirmary down the corridor. Lying on the bed, she sat straight up again as more intense pain thundered from her core and across her entire body.

"What do you need me to do?" Koleton finally spoke up, standing uselessly in the middle of the room.

"Go find Alyssa and Mataya," Damon barked, pointing at the door as he scooped up an armful of rags and returned to the end of the bed.

Koleton bolted from the room, without another word. Grimacing at Apollo, who was clutching her hand, she tensed up as the agonizing pain ebbed and flowed. Damon held her knees up, asking her to push as Ustarum sat on a chair and checked on her baby.

She screamed, another rush of agony pressing down on her hips and spiraling up her entire back and sides. Biting down on her bottom lip, tears swam down her cheeks. She wasn't ready for this. Dasco and her father would be coming, and the terror of protecting an infant in this war was crushing her, just as a new tidal wave of pain rippled through her.

THIRTY-FOUR

Delivery

"PUSH, MALKIA," USTARUM urged. He peeked up at her and nodded.

Another shriek tore across her lips as she clenched her fists and pushed with every bit of energy she could muster. Panting afterward, she settled against the pillows Damon had set behind her.

"I forgot how exhausting this is," she whispered, wiping the perspiration from her brow with the palm of her hand.

"I've got you," Damon answered, trading places with Apollo. He ran his hand over her hair, before planting a kiss on the top of her head.

Just as she was catching her breath, another pain rose in her pelvis and the urge to push was greater than ever. Clutching the blanket in her fists, she cried out and pushed again, the pressure building in her back.

"You're doing great," Ustarum said, checking for the baby. "He's close. Maybe a few more good pushes."

She nodded and drew in a shaky breath, when another contraction came on suddenly. Holding her breath, she didn't have a moment to think of pushing as she tried to roll over to her side. The pain was excruciating.

"*Ahhhhhhh*," she screamed at the top of her lungs, releasing the shallow breath. Her fingers wrapped around Damon's forearm and she shrieked again, struggling to catch a good breath as the agony continued in one tidal wave after another.

Ustarum jumped up from his chair and leaned forward, grabbing both her knees. A slight ease of the pain cascaded from her legs and swept into her hips, allowing her a moment to inhale deeply. "Breathe, Malkia," he coaxed, staring intently at her.

Trickles of sweat ran down the sides of her face, but she was finally able to relax again, drawing in one deep breath after another. "Thank you," she mumbled, releasing her death grip from Damon's arm. "Sorry." She stared at the red handprint spread on his skin and shook her head.

"What did I say?" Damon asked, raising her hand to his lips. "I've got you. We're in this together."

A weary smile lifted on her chapped lips as her focus returned to Ustarum. He raised his eyebrows in question and she nodded. "I'm ready."

Releasing her knees from his hold, he settled back on the chair and Apollo stepped forward on the other side of the bed, holding her other hand. "You may squeeze as hard as you need to," he told her, patting her forearm with his other hand.

"His head is crowning," Ustarum choked, peering up at Malkia. "He's coming fast, so be prepared."

She nodded, the muscles in her jaw clenching as she squeezed Apollo's hand. The door suddenly slid open and Mataya rushed in, followed by Alyssa and Koleton.

"Push, *again*," Ustarum shouted, over the commotion in the room.

Closing her eyes, she pushed as hard as she could, only stopping when she heard Ustarum say the baby was out. Snapping her eyes back open, her ears perked up as her baby cried out, his wails filling the space around her. Ustarum lifted the child over her legs and set him on her chest, covering him with a blanket.

Malkia's heart soared, staring at his beautiful face as his cries stopped and he burrowed his face into her chest. Glancing up at Damon, she grinned at her partner. He sank to a chair next to her, his hand covering their child's head. Alyssa and Ustarum cleaned up around them, covering Malkia completely with a warm blanket.

"He will need to eat soon," her mother said, pausing next to her and smiling proudly at the newborn. She wiped away the sweat from Malkia's forehead and cheeks with a damp cloth, and brushed her hair away from her face.

Malkia nodded after she was done. "Thank you, mom." She turned to face Damon and tugged her shirt up. Her baby latched onto her nipple immediately, suckling until the cream flowed to his mouth. Damon's hand ran down her hair, staring at her face as she looked down at their baby.

The mood had shifted and although she hadn't forgotten about Asha and Justin, the only thing she wanted to concentrate on was her little family. "Apollo, will you fetch Esta and Landon, so they can meet their baby brother?" she asked, staring up at the Artemisian.

Apollo beamed with pride, puffing out his chest as if he had been asked to participate in a warrior's mission. "It would be my honor," he replied, bowing to her.

She chuckled, turning her attention back to her hungry baby. His tiny fingers flexed and relaxed against her breast and his eyes remained closed, completely lost in dreamland as he continued to eat.

"Malkia." Her sister came up beside Damon, her gaze focused on the baby. "I thought you knew about Justin." Her voice quivered and she glanced away for a few seconds. "I had no idea of his plans. I hope you know that."

Sticking her hand out, Malkia gripped Mataya's arm. "Of course I know that," she whispered, squeezing her wrist. "Whatever his reasons, this is all on him. My abduction and Asha's death will forever be his fault."

"Asha's dead," Mataya croaked, her eyes darting over to her mother. "Does mom know?"

"Yes," Malkia nodded, twisting to her other side and switching her son to her other breast. She glanced over her shoulder at her sister. "It's a lot to digest. Every time I close my eyes, I see my father slit her throat. And now that I know Justin brought this upon us, my vengeance has only expanded."

"Mine too," Mataya muttered, brushing the tears from her cheeks and moving around the bed, followed by Damon. "He was my best friend. To be deceived by the man you love—" she paused, peering over at Malkia. "Well, you know how that feels."

Malkia nodded. "We'll finish this. One way or another, Justin and my father will pay."

"What about Dario?" Damon asked, his jaw clenching as he sank into a seat.

Raising her brow eloquently, Malkia shrugged her free shoulder. "I killed him when I escaped," she said, settling her baby more securely against her body.

"*Thank, Theia*," Alyssa muttered, her praying hands rising to the ceiling. "One down."

"Two down, actually," Malkia replied. "Thane executed Ginny as well. She slipped up and threatened to slaughter my child and me. Unfortunately for her, my father overheard her. As usual, his own agenda is far more important than anyone's life, including his lover. She met the same fate as Asha."

"I can't say I'll miss the wench," Alyssa said, her expression softening as she stared at the baby. "She wanted my grandson dead, along with my daughter, more than anyone else. I despise your father, but I would've patted him on the back for that execution." She stepped over to the bedside, seeing the child had finished eating and was now sleeping in Malkia's arms. "May I bathe him?"

A grin broke out on Malkia's lips and she nodded, lifting him up for her mother to take. "Can I have some time to rest?" she asked, feeling an intense weariness settle over her body and mind.

"Of course," her mother replied, cradling the baby in her arms. "Do you have a name yet?"

Malkia glanced at Damon. "When I wake, our family will decide on a name together."

Damon rose from his chair and kissing her on the forehead. He tucked her in and shooed everyone out of the room, ushering the sudden appearance of the children and Apollo down the hall to stare at their new baby brother.

The lights were lowered by Ustarum, just before he slid the door closed and left her to sleep off her adventures.

THIRTY-FIVE
Hidden Allies

HER EYES FLUTTERED open. The first thing she noticed was the lights were extinguished, aside from a soft white light under the cupboards on the other side of the room. Not knowing what time it was, but finally feeling rejuvenated, she slid her legs out from underneath the blanket and planted her feet on the icy floor. Her toes curled away from the chill as she stepped over to a pile of clothes on the chair.

Slipping on some clean trousers, she slid them over her hips and was delighted to see that her healing powers had nearly shrunk her stomach to its normal size. She yanked off her dirty shirt that had been given to her when she was in her cage and pulled on a clean, black shirt, followed by an oversized sweater to wrap herself in.

Now to go find her baby.

Stepping over the threshold of the doorway, she looked both ways, wondering why it was so quiet. She hurried down the corridor toward the playroom, swinging it open and was greeted by darkness. Pursing her lips, she swung around and sprinted to the children's room, sliding the door open and exhaling a breath of relief when her eyes fell on Damon and all three children.

She smiled, staring at her infant wrapped in Damon's large arms as he slept on a cot, near the children. Tiptoeing over to him, she slipped the newborn from his embrace and kissed her partner on the forehead. She gave Landon and Esta one last look before leaving the room.

Her baby stretched, his eyes opening just a little bit and turning his face toward her chest, his mouth suckling and searching for his food. She slipped up her shirt as she was walking and he latch on without much coaxing.

Strolling down the hallway, she made her way to the bridge, hoping to find some company there, but was greeted with darkness once again. Outside the twilight twinkled and she could see one of the moons through the window. Standing next to the glass, she surveyed their surroundings, more determined than ever to finish what they'd started. Her children's future depended on it.

Sinking into one of the chairs, she smiled down at her tiny boy, already madly in love with him. His perfect face, with his button nose and rosy cheeks, brought a newfound joy to her heart. For the first time in days she felt a peace envelop her.

She finished nursing, snuggling him close to her body and rising from the chair. The first sun was beginning to rise, lighting up the clear sky, forcing the stars to withdraw behind its sparkle. The Artemisians were already stirring as she noticed their cargo door open and a few of them step onto the terrain, stretching and chatting as they worked.

The door to the bridge slid open and Damon stepped through, his forehead crinkled in worry. "You should have awakened me," he breathed, hurrying toward her. "I was terrified when I woke and he was missing."

"You had to know I would come take him," she replied, a sparkle dancing in her eyes as she smiled up at him and then back down at their baby. "What should we name him?"

Exhaling loudly, the worry melted from his face, replaced by a softness in his gaze. "The kids voted on Tristan, but I'm not too fond of that name," Damon told her. His palm covered the newborn's head and he leaned down and gently kissed him on the forehead. "We created this." A wide smile rose on his lips and he drew Malkia in for an embrace, followed with a kiss on the top of her head. "He's perfect."

"Exactly what I was thinking," she whispered, tilting her head back to look at Damon. "What about Zeke?"

Damon stepped back, nodding his head as he thought about the name. "I love it," he replied, focusing back on her with a small smile. "Should we run it by the kids?"

She shook her head. "I don't think they'll mind too much. And besides, he looks like a Zeke."

"Our tiny Zeke," Damon murmured, twisting around when the door slid open.

Koleton stepped through rubbing his eyes and jumped when he saw the two of them standing in the room. "Seriously, you two. Can't you find a better place for your private sessions?" He stretched his arms over his head and halted in front of them. "I guess it wasn't that kind of meeting, since you're sportin' the little one." Chuckling to himself, he swiveled away from Damon's fist, dancing toward the pilot's seat.

Grinning at Damon as he swatted at her backside, Malkia followed Koleton over to his seat. "My father won't stop," she told them, staring out the window. "Today, we need to take the time to plan our attack strategy. The building I was in, was hidden by the Thalian magic and without an idea of where to take this war, I'm worried we will be on the losing side."

"We have begun planning." Damon settled into a nearby chair, wringing his hands together as he leaned forward. "While you were away, we had a surprising ally show up."

"Who?" she asked, hoisting Zeke up in her arms.

"It's more fun to show you," he replied, sharing a knowing smile with Koleton.

"You're going to make me wait?" She glared at him, tapping her foot on the floor.

Damon laughed and nodded. "It will be far more exciting this way."

She growled as her eyes narrowed. "Oh, that's right. I need more excitement in my life after the last few weeks I've had."

"You'll like this surprise," Koleton interjected, nodding in amusement when she threw him a dirty look.

Both men burst out laughing from her disapproving stare, as her eyes darted between them. Finally nodding, she walked over to Damon and handed Zeke to him. "I need to shower and eat. Then I'm free to see your surprise." Walking from the room, she hurried down the corridor, making her way to the eating hall.

She ate quickly, cringing from the smell that was wafting from her body. Thinking back to the last time she'd showered, she realized it had been at least two or three days. She was surprised Damon didn't plug his nose when he was near her earlier. *Oh well, he deserves to smell my ickiness.* Chuckling to herself, she finished chewing the last of her food and slipped from the eating hall and down the hallway to her room.

Although the shower was cramped, having the water cascade over her and knowing she was not only free again, but her powers were restored, made it the best shower she had experienced in a long time. She sighed, leaning her forehead against the shower wall and closed her eyes, enjoying the warmth of the water.

Stepping out of the shower a few minutes later, a joyous smile danced across her face, and she couldn't help but laugh out loud. Losing her powers had been a burden on her soul, knowing she had to rely on others, but having them returned made her treasure them even more. And having a healthy and strong, baby boy in her arms was worth the heartache of having her abilities lost to her for the time he needed to develop.

She dressed in stretchy, long pants, and a form-fitting black shirt. It was time to arm up and bring the fight to her father, before he advanced upon the place that held all their children. Wrapping her belt around her waist, she snapped on the sheaths, followed by another one that circled her left thigh. Her daggers sank into each of the three sheaths, and she bent to tug on her tattered, black boots.

Examining herself in her mirror, she quickly braided her hair, letting the ends fall to the small of her back and sweeping the wisps of hair around her face behind her ears. Her bow and arrow seemed useless, after everything she had been through. She picked up the bow, trailing her fingers down the carved wood. She had made this one herself back on Esaki, so many years ago. Now, that life seemed like a dream. She set the bow down and searched for the laser weapon that Apollo had given her. Her powers were far more advanced and she had never needed it, but today she intended to be fully prepared for any outcome.

She clipped the sheath and laser gun on the back of her belt, knowing it would be there if she needed it. A knock on the door brought her focus back to the others, and she stepped lightly to answer it. The door slid open and her mother stood on the other side, holding a bundled piece of fabric.

"How are you feeling this morning?" she asked, her gaze

scrutinizing her attire and laughing at all the weapons she had strapped to her body. "Are you preparing to meet your father?"

Malkia nodded, raising her brow in a smile. "I'm feeling like I'm on top of the world and yes, I'm done playing nice with that man. Today, his cruelty ends." She stepped to the side and signaled for her mom to come inside.

"What if we don't find your father today?" Alyssa eased over the threshold, sinking into a nearby chair. She held out the fabric for Malkia to take.

"Then we keep searching until we do find him," she answered, her fingers sinking into the fabric as she held it up. "Is this a satchel of some sort?"

"I made it last night from some discarded clothing." Alyssa smiled and pointed. "Hang it over your neck and put your baby inside. Here, let me show you." Her mother sprang up from the chair and clutched the baby sling, slipping it over her neck and right shoulder. She held it open and showed Malkia. "This way, you can keep him with you until we leave to find your father. And then when we're done, you have the means to carry him next to you."

"*That's great*! I love it," Malkia gushed, hugging Alyssa and taking the baby carrier from her. "Thank you for this." She slipped it over her head and patted it against her torso. "Let's go find that little guy."

She grabbed her mom's hand within her own and dragged her from the room and up to the bridge, where Zeke and Damon were hanging out in the same place she'd left them. Alyssa cooed at Zeke, picking him up and cuddling him into her chest.

"He's perfect," she whispered, pressing her lips against his bald head. "So perfect."

Malkia smiled, just as Landon and Esta rushed into the room. "Hey, you two," she said, waving them over to her.

"I want to hold him." Esta's gaze danced between Alyssa and Malkia, waiting for her turn to snuggle with Zeke.

Malkia helped Esta settle onto one of the chairs and Alyssa set Zeke into her lap, standing close to watch, while Malkia spoke with Koleton and Damon.

"I want to go see your surprise," she said, pressing her hand against the window and searching the area beyond the Artemisians ships. "How soon can we leave?"

"We're just waiting for Apollo to return," Damon answered, messing around with the screen in front of him and glancing over at her. "Then we can take you to meet our friends."

She groaned, sagging against the console to her left and realizing her patience was depleted. Her father's desire to destroy her was stirring up a maelstrom of turmoil inside her mind. Being so close to finishing this journey wasn't helping. "The suspense is killing me," she muttered, sinking to the floor and focusing on Zeke and Esta. Landon stood next to her daughter, holding Zeke's hand and rubbing it with his thumb. "Do you want to know his name?"

Everyone in the room turned to face her. "You already named him?" Esta asked, pulling Zeke closer to her chest.

Malkia nodded, jumping up from the ground and walking toward her daughter. "The name just popped into my head and we both knew it was the one." She looked back at Damon, who smiled at her. "His name is Zeke," she told them, rustling Landon's blonde hair and peering into Esta's inky irises.

They nodded, both of them smiling and looking down at their

brother. "I like it," Landon whispered.

"I'm so glad," Malkia said, embracing him into a sideways hug.

Apollo rushed through the door, with Alexa, Bella and Mataya in tow, followed by Braxton and Zoe. "They're ready," the Artemisian announced, his eyes flashing around the room and pausing midstride from all the stares. "What did we miss?"

Without missing a beat, Malkia answered, "How could you, Apollo? I trusted you."

Apollo's reptilian eyes widened as he took a step toward her. "Malkia, I don't know what you're speaking about. What have these baboons told you?" He glared at Koleton as he crossed his arms over his chest.

"Don't deny it, Apollo." Malkia growled deep in her throat and Apollo puffed out his chest, eyeing her with caution.

Koleton twisted away, suppressing a smile as he pretended to work on the monitor in front of him. Taking a few steps toward the confused Artemisian, Malkia wagged her finger at him as if he was a small child.

"They told me everything," she replied, pointing at each person in the room. "You've been keeping a secret from me."

Apollo's breath spilled from his lips as his shoulders relaxed. "I don't know what that half-twit over there has told you." He jabbed his thumb toward Koleton. "But, I was the one who told them not to wait until today to tell you the news." His eyes focused on Damon and then jumped to a grinning Koleton. "I'm going to kick both of your asses."

Laughter burst from Malkia's lips as she doubled over, her hands on her knees as she sputtered, attempting to speak but unable to form the words. The room roared with the group's laughter, excluding Apollo and Zeke. The baby was shaken from his sleep, wailing in fright from the sudden volume change in the room. Malkia glanced over at a shocked Esta, who held Zeke out for Alyssa to take. Apollo grumbled, throwing Malkia a hateful look. She fell to the floor in a heap of giggles.

"You're too easy, my friend." Malkia managed to finally say, looking at the Artemisian with tears in her eyes.

"It's good to see you back in fine form, Malkia," Apollo muttered, stalking toward the two men with his hands balling up into fists. "I'll take care of you, after I deal with these two mutts."

Damon and Koleton ducked around the brawny Artemisian, racing for the door as Malkia slipped Zeke into his carrier and winked at Esta. She laughed at Apollo, watching him pivot back around and barrel after the two men.

Mataya's brow lifted toward her sister, a smile teasing the edges of her lips. "What did we miss?"

"Nothing. I have no idea who these allies are, as Damon and Koleton thought it was more entertaining to make it a surprise. Apollo was just collateral damage." Making her way to the door, she twisted around to look at the children. "Who's coming?"

Esta bounced off her chair and the rest of the group laughed as they followed behind, hurrying down to the gangway where the men were still making jabs at one another. Zeke squirmed in the carrier, snuggling into the soft fabric, and Malkia made sure the strap around her neck was secure before approaching the others.

"Let's go see these friends of yours," Malkia said, planting her feet in front of Damon, whose smiling eyes met hers. "We've wasted enough time on fun and games. It's only a matter of time before my father brings the fight to us."

"Always so serious," Koleton joked, poking her in the side as he walked by. "What are you waiting for? Let's go."

The troop followed after the red-haired man, with Apollo waving at some of his friends to join them. As the crowd grew, Malkia's eyes swept across all those who surrounded her and a smile rose on her lips. In all of this, not only had she gained an entirely new and expanded family, but hundreds of allies and friends. With the destruction of Artemis and the extermination of so many Artemisians, she had believed her life would never find a peaceful ending. But now, she not only possessed a powerful army, she was on the home stretch of finishing this conflict and settling down as a normal mother and partner.

They strolled past the Artemisian's ships and Malkia glanced back, growing more confused as their path took them toward the roar of the ocean surf, leaving behind their established and now vulnerable position. Speeding up her pace, she caught up with Damon and Koleton, twisting her head to stare at their determined expressions.

"Where are we going?" She pointed forward, shaking her head. "There's nothing up there except the beach and ocean."

"Patience, my lady," Damon said, curling his arm around her shoulders. "Do you trust us?"

She groaned, her eyes meeting Zeke's as they opened just enough to peek at her face, before closing again. "I'm beginning to like you both less and less," she mumbled, thrusting her hips to side and connecting with Damon's leg.

He hopped away, laughing. "We know you love us," he choked out, attempting to steady himself, and fall back into line with the group. "We're almost there, lover." He grinned wider when she scowled at him.

Her eyes focused back on the path, seeing the edge of the white-sanded beach and coming to dead stop as a flicker of light caught her attention. "What is that?" she asked, taking a step backward as a snake of dread wormed its way through her insides.

THIRTY-SIX
United

DAMON TWISTED AROUND and beckoned her forward. "That's where we're going," he told her, seeing that she'd fallen behind. "Come on, they don't bite."

Shaking her head in confusion, she took a few small steps forward, her focus glued to the flicker of light that slowly expanded as she grew closer. A smile broke out on her lips when she saw Cormac and Thora sauntering toward them and a massive ship coming into view.

"You sly devils," she whispered, settling Zeke more firmly in his carrier and sprinting forward, passing Damon and Koleton. Meeting her two friends halfway, she embraced Thora first, careful to not squish Zeke in the middle. Taking a step back, she handed the baby over to Thora, and threw her arms around Cormac. "When did you all arrive?" Her eyes darted between the two, suddenly confused. "And how in Theia's name did you two connect with one another?"

Cormac chuckled, taking Zeke from Thora and cradling him in his massive arms. "You have powerful folks as your allies, Malkia. I didn't see this one coming, until she was standing right in front of me." Nodding his head toward Thora. "Scared the living daylights out of me."

Thora smiled, careful to keep her voice to a whisper. "We were able to shift the remaining citizens of the Elven community to our side, after Dasco, your father, and their followers fled Thalia." She jabbed her thumb behind her, showing Malkia the crowd of humans, Elvens and Fallen Angels who were gathering. "Once we established a firm army of our two species, we agreed to take our voyage to Esaki first, and gather anyone who wanted to join our ranks. Cormac was the first to volunteer, followed by several others." She glanced over at the large brute and grinned. "He's become a great friend and we've promised to return him and his people to Esaki, once your father and Dasco have been exterminated."

"Where did you find such a spectacular vessel?" Malkia asked, her eyes darting from Thora, over to the ship, and finally coming to rest on the approaching crowd.

"It's one of the Elven ships," Thora replied, twisting around to look at it. "They have several others, but this had plenty of room for the team we were bringing."

"I'm thrilled that you're here. My father should be shaking in his boots." Malkia linked arms with the female Angel and smiled at the many familiar faces in the crowd around her. "Let's go find a spot where I can speak to everyone."

"I have just the place," Thora replied, leading Malkia through the throngs of people.

Stepping toward a metal platform, Malkia took Zeke from Cormac and followed Thora up the stairway to the top. As she turned, she gasped at the multitude of people gathering. Peering toward her own ship, she could see a line of Artemisians still making their way over as people were already jostling for space near the platform.

"Where did everyone come from?" she muttered, glancing back at

Thora. "There must be well over a thousand people here." The Angel nodded as she raised her brow.

Damon stepped up to the platform, followed by Mataya and Ustarum. Easing up to her sister, Mataya wrapped her arm around Malkia's waist and smiled over at her.

"And the crowd just keeps growing," she whispered. "You did this." Nodding her head toward the gathering. "They're here because you've given them hope and a reason to fight. They believe in your ability to stop this bloodbath with your father."

Malkia drew a deep breath, her heart hammering against her chest and for the first time ever, felt completely intimidated by the stares from more people than she could count. Running her tongue over her lips, she stepped forward and waved her hand, waiting for the chatter to die down.

"I have to say, this was the best surprise I could've received," she shouted out into the crowd, hoping her voice would carry to the back.

"What did you say?" A brawny Artemisian yelled back.

"Here, use this," a towering Elven suggested, handing her a metal stick.

"What does this do?" she asked, turning it over in her hand.

The Elven chuckled, taking the stick back and raising it to his lips. "Can you hear me?" His voice traveled far and wide and Malkia's head whipped around in amazement as the entire crowd nodded in unison.

"Wow!" Her gaze locked onto the stick. "Is it magic?"

Thora burst out laughing and the Elven's smile spread from ear to ear. "No, it's a microphone. Technology," he replied, shrugging as he handed it back to her. "When this is over, I'll teach you all about it."

She nodded, fascinated by such a small object, creating so much sound. Holding it up to her lips, she twisted back around to face the crowd. "Let's do this again," she said, taking a step back when she heard her voice echo. Zeke squirmed in the baby carrier and she patted his back with her free hand. "First off, I'm thrilled you're all here. I never imagined our journey would bring us to this place, with three other species of our moons. I look out at all your faces, and I realize that my father has already failed." The crowd roared jubilantly, some of them saluting the sky and others jumping into the air. Grinning at all of them, she paced along the platform, locking eyes with a few of the people near the front. "I don't recognize every face, but I hope that once this battle is over, we will all be standing here again as not only allies, but as family." More cheers erupted from the crowd, and she leaned her head back and laughed at the sky, joy rushing through her heart.

Cormac had risen up to the platform and was beckoning her to give him the microphone. Walking over to him, he gripped it in his hand as she fell back next to Damon.

"My friends," he began, strolling up to the edge of the platform. "Aside from the tragedy that took place on Esaki, this is my first time being a participant in this war. But I've known Malkia since I came to her aide on that moon, many months ago, and there is no one more determined then herself to halt her father's tyranny on your people." He pointed to the sky, walking along the platform and then pointed out at the crowd. "She will lead us to fight her father and his Elven followers and although it might be a brutal and bloody battle, I'm confident we will be victorious."

As applause exploded from the horde, Koleton bounced up the stairs and sprinted over to Cormac, whispering into his ear. Cormac's face broke out into a wide smile, followed by a laugh as he pushed the goofball away from him. Wagging his finger at Cormac, Koleton grinned beneath his beard.

Cormac lifted the microphone back to his lips, turning back to the crowd. "I apologize. I did leave out some information." He pointed over at Koleton. "This man, my friend and comrade, assisted me in rescuing Malkia back on Esaki, when she was being abducted by a rare breed of creatures, called the Fenrir."

The crowd laughed as Malkia's eyes narrowed, never realizing the mutts were an actual species. "Wait." She held out her hand to Cormac. "Where do the Fenrir reside?"

The microphone dropped to Cormac's side. "Let's chat after this later and I'll tell you more."

She nodded as he handed the microphone back to her. Her gaze swept over the crowd and hope kindled within her core. "Who's ready to end this?"

Hands rose and many clapped enthusiastically, while the Artemisians pumped their fists in the air. She raised her own hand. "I know I'm ready. My father is here—or he was yesterday. He wants my baby boy and my daughter for his own, knowing they were born already possessed with my powers. When he held me captive, just on the other side of the city, he used the Thalian magic to conceal our whereabouts and I believe they have the same ability with their ships. I ask the Elvens here, does this ship have a similar cloaking mechanism?" Her attention turned to the Elven standing on the platform.

He nodded, stepping closer. "Everything your father and Dasco are able to do, we can do with this vessel," he informed her, stopping a few feet away from her.

"Well, there you have it. If we can find my father's location, as I'm sure he vacated the other one as soon as I escaped, we will have the means to keep ourselves concealed until we can surveil his circumstances." She paused, waiting for the cheers to dispel. Zeke's eyes opened and met hers, his mouth suckling for nourishment. "I would like all the generals, leaders, and commanders to meet in the Elven ship within the next hour. Let's gather together and work out an idea to move us forward, to advance upon my father and his followers." Pointing over to Damon, she continued, "My partner will begin the meeting until I return from feeding my child. Thank you, everyone, for being here, to ride into battle, giving us the advantage of ending this, once and for all. You're the true heroes and warriors of this story. When we reach the end, we will celebrate as the species of Theia."

The roar of applause and cheering, reverberated through the air and although Zeke was whining, searching for his source of food, she paused and smiled widely at all their faces. Reaching her hand up to her mouth, she blew a kiss and waved as she walked off the platform.

The tall Elven led her inside their ship, guiding her to a private room. Stepping inside the sitting room, she waited until Esta, Landon, Mataya, Ustarum and her mother entered, before shutting the door.

Sinking into one of the couches, she tugged up her shirt, allowing Zeke to find her breast and relaxed once he latched on. Her eyes met Mataya's and she sighed, a tear tumbling from her lashes. Mataya rushed over to her sister, sliding up next to her on the couch and wrapped her arm around her shoulders.

"What's wrong?" she asked, keeping her voice low as the other four played at the other end of the room.

"I'm relieved. Frightened. Excited. Terrified." Twisting slightly to look at her sister, she shook her head. "Look at him." She nodded down to Zeke. "He's absolutely wonderful. And all of them, outside—how amazing is that? We are so close to ending this conflict that I can taste it. And at the same time, it seems like it will never end."

Mataya's palm rested on Zeke's bald head and a smile tugged at the corners of her mouth. "He is beautiful." Her gaze rose to meet Malkia's. "And he's wonderful. Those people out there have traveled to support you and our mission. They want the end of this war, even without knowing the Creators are threatening our very existence. Peace between our moons is their prime objective." Her fingers brushed away a wisp of Malkia's hair, tucking it behind her ear. "Having all these mixed emotions is expected, and I completely understand. But as a leader, you will need to ground yourself and be prepared to address the commanders of these various species."

"You're right." Malkia nodded, picking up Zeke and switching him to the other side, where he immediately latched on to her other nipple. "He's such a great eater," she murmured, gazing down at his tiny features. "Give me a minute by myself, while he finishes eating. I'll find a way to sort out my mind."

Mataya patted her sister's shoulder and rose from the couch, smiling down at her. "I'll take them back to our ship and we'll see you after your meeting." She strolled over to the others, and after waving goodbye, they exited out the door, sliding it securely shut behind them.

Closing her eyes, Malkia leaned her head against the back cushion, concentrating on her inner light. It was churning within her core. Focusing on the energy, she pushed it down to her toes and up to her arms, where it flowed down to her fingertips. Suddenly, a surge of warmth traveled from her chest, uniting with her own energy and bursting from one end of her body to the other.

Her eyes snapped open and she focused on the sapphire light filling the room around her. It sparkled like a gemstone, ebbing and flowing as if it was the oceans of the Blue Planet. Dropping her eyes to Zeke, a peaceful sensation slid through her mind, calming her anxiety about her father and her ability to lead the people to war. Zeke's face and hands glowed with the blue light, connecting with her own powers.

He is *more powerful than I am*, she thought, her thumb trailing down his cheek as he finished eating and fell asleep from her touch. "We're connected little guy. Thank you."

The light around them dissipated, but the calm remained in her heart. She drew in a few deep breaths and rose from the couch, setting Zeke inside his carrier and straightening out her shirt. Strolling from the room, a female Elven was waiting on the other side of the door.

"Follow me, please," she requested, her silky lavender irises focusing on Malkia. She twisted away, leading Malkia down the corridor. "My sister is with your father." Her voice was barely a whisper, her breath coming in quick, shallow pants.

Malkia gripped her shoulder, twisting her back around and immediately noticed her trembling chin. "Is her name Elisa?"

"*Yes*," she exclaimed, her eyes lighting up. "Did you meet her? Is she well?"

Nodding her head, Malkia clutched her hands. "She was my friend, along with Velem, the doctor who injected me with the serum. We're going back to rescue them." She wiped a tear from the Elven's pale cheek. "I promise I'll do whatever I can to make sure they survive this and return to their families. What is your name?"

"Eternity. But most call me Ty for short." The elven gave her a shy smile, beginning her walk down the hallway again. "Thank you, Malkia. Dasco was never fair to his people. It's refreshing to have new leadership, who actually care about our wellbeing." Ty halted in front of a door. "You'll be meeting her today."

"I look forward to it," Malkia said, embracing her new friend. "I hope to see you soon, Ty, and thank you for escorting me to the meeting."

"You're welcome," she replied, bowing her head and taking her leave.

Malkia placed her hand on the door, seeing that it had similar technology to the doors on Enyo and suddenly recalling the Elvens assistance to Errandor. He knew more than he'd ever reveal, but he was another person she would need to speak to at some point, very soon.

THIRTY-SEVEN
The Leader's Meeting

THE DOOR SLID open and Damon greeted her, as did the six others in the room. The three Artemisian Commanders rose from their chairs, holding their hand perpendicular to their chests in a salute. Chantum and Thora nodded and smiled, and the final leader rose elegantly from her chair, a wide smile gracing her features. She bowed her head like Ty had done, her long, snow-white hair flowing softly to her waist.

"It's a pleasure to finally meet you, Malkia," the Elven leader said, holding out her hand.

Malkia stepped toward her, gripping the Elven's wrist and bowing in return. "You must be the new appointed Elven leader," Malkia replied, letting her hand fall to her side. "And what might your name be?"

"My name is Hope." A small smile tugged on the edges of her lips as her prayer hands were brought to her forehead, touching right in between her eyes. "I bless you, dear Malkia, with the fortitude to lead us into a battle that, with its victory, will transform our stars." Her hands came down to her heart center and Hope closed her eyes. "Your presence was foreordained by the ancient beings of our moons, and, although you feel like a normal person, you're far from ordinary."

Hope's eyes fluttered open, locking onto Malkia's. "We are here because of this. Your father knew his adversary would come, but never suspected it would be his own daughter. When his reality had to shift in order to destroy his child, you became my ally."

"Thank you, Hope," Malkia said with a nod. Settling into the chair next to the female Elven, she glanced around at the others. "Is there anything that has been decided?"

Damon nodded, sitting in the chair next to her and gesturing to the three Artemisians. "Before we continue, I would like to introduce you to the three Commanders. This is Rashuta." He pointed to his right, then shifted his hand to the one sitting at the end of the table. "And Jordan. And this is Maltese." His thumb jabbed toward the Artemisian on the other side of the table.

"It's an honor to meet all of you." Malkia reached across Damon and gripped all three of the Artemisian's wrists, before lifting the baby carrier over her head and handing Zeke over to Damon. "Your turn," she muttered, leaning forward in her chair after he took the baby. "It's also wonderful to see Chantum and Thora." They had settled in the chairs across from Malkia and Damon, wearing black attire, similar to her own.

"Malkia, as I believe you've already mentioned, it's imperative that we strike soon," Chantum spoke softly, his fingers entwined in front of him on the table. "In order to find your father, we will require the help of several others so we can diversify our search. I don't believe he would stray too far, as his prime objective is to return for your children and destroy whatever you hold dear. Am I correct?"

"Yes, you are," she replied, nodding as her eyes darted around at the others in the room. "However, Dasco has his own objectives, and we should be mindful that if my father doesn't deliver on his end, the Elven wouldn't hesitate to create his own havoc. He needs the map to the Blue Planet, which has been locked away from all eyes. Only I, and a select few, hold the key. There are a number of other items that he would require for the journey, starting with the journals of the Creators. Unfortunately for him, I believe most of those went up in smoke when the pyramid was demolished. At this point, Dasco and my father are both volatile and persistent foes, who intend on fighting their way through and altering the lives of our people in the most destructive and devastating way possible." Her gaze shifted to Hope. "This won't end until both of them are dead."

"We've established this," Rashuta grumbled, his large stature overwhelming the chair into which he was settled. "As you're the leader of this crusade, we require direction from you. Do we separate, sending multiple parties out in different directions to find these enemies or do we remain as a united front, waiting for them to make their first move?" One of his hands balled into a fist as his expression hardened.

Malkia twisted her chair enough to gain a better view of the Artemisian Commander. "Maintaining a united front is still possible, even if we send scouts out to search for my father." She examined each individual around the room one by one. "I'm not here to take prisoners, and I'm most definitely not waiting for these adversaries to strike first. If we must, we will defend our people, ships, and location with any means necessary. But if I've learned anything about my father, he will take us down in bites, sapping our strength. He will begin with something small, giving us the illusion that we still have the upper hand by only wounding us."

"But, he already knows our whereabouts," Thora muttered. Her eyes narrowed. "Why has he not striked?"

"He will," Malkia responded, "And we must be prepared. Once he weakens us, he will return with his army, plowing us down with all their forces, and eliminating as many lives as possible. His final move would be to pick off the survivors, one by one until I no longer have the support required to defeat him." A smile twitched on the edges of her lips, bringing on the charm that had always come so easily to her. "We *are* united, when we establish a solid plan that we all agree upon and strike quickly. When I know that everyone at this table and the ones who follow us, are here to win a war against tyranny and repression, determined to lay down their lives for this victory, then and only then, will we truly be united."

Jordan's crimson eyes sparkled as he moved forward in his chair, leaning against his elbows as they pressed into the table. "I'm already here to follow you, Malkia. My people didn't hesitate, once we discovered the true nature of your father. The destruction of our moon is a burden you must carry, but the freeing of the Enyo people was justified and everyone at this table agrees with me. We were not included in that persecution, nor would any three of us, participate in such horrendous actions." He pointed at the other two Artemisians. "If you want us to send our people out to find your father, we will obey and do it with pride for our Chosen Heir."

She scowled over at him, shaking her head. "Don't call me that."

A chuckle rumbled up his throat. "I can only imagine the irritation that might create, being called the Chosen Heir, but we all want you to know how serious we are in this venture. The spirits of Theia's Moons have called you to be their champion and we will follow you to the very end."

"Alright, enough." Malkia rose from her seat, pushing her chair away from her, her annoyance flaring. "Thank you for your kind words and desire to end this battle." She gave Jordan a slight nod and smile, before focusing on the others. "But I'm not here for the praise. It's presumptuous to believe I'm capable of leading this army more skillfully than a room full of seasoned commanders." Drawing in a deep breath, she entwined her fingers together, resting them against her core as she stepped away from the table. "I agree with the Angels. We must send scouts out to find Thane's whereabouts, but our camp will require a guarded outpost, as well."

"And who will be the guards?" Maltese spoke for the first time, his voice low and gruff.

"We will take shifts," she answered, focusing on the Artemisian. "We will need outposts in several areas around our ships." She pointed upward, tilting her head slightly. "Is this the only ship that can be concealed?"

Maltese and the other Artemisians nodded. "However, we have our shields and at night they are always activated," Jordan answered, crossing his arms over his chest as he leaned back in his chair.

"This is what I propose," Malkia said, pacing the floor just beyond the others. "We are always armed. As well, the children must remain indoors until our scouts return and we are able to take the fight to another location." She held up her fingers, touching one after another as she went through each idea. "Since the Elvens have the ability to send anyone into a deep sleep, we need to be vigilant and remain near the ships."

Hope rose slowly, her graceful movement drawing all eyes upon her. "If our brothers and sisters use the spawn's venom on you, we possess the elixir to cure it." Her hand settled on her abdomen, a smile stretching across her flawless face.

"It's the spawn's venom that creates that slumber?" Malkia asked, tapping her fingers against her lips.

"Yes," Hope replied, bowing her head.

"The Nesoi are capable of curing the bite of spawn." Standing behind Damon, Malkia rested her hands on his shoulders, peering down at Zeke, who was immersed in a peaceful nap. "We still need to avoid it, as it's not a pleasant recovery. However, it's reassuring to know what it is and that we have two cures for it, right at our fingertips."

Hope remained standing, giving Malkia a courteous nod. "Being that our ship is cloaked, if you would like to transfer all the children and anyone who is injured or sick to our vessel, we will find room for them."

"Great idea," Malkia responded, resting her palms on the table and looking around at the others. "We begin now. Pick five of your finest scouts from each group and they will leave within the hour." She nodded toward Chantum as he rose from his chair.

His muscles rippled beneath his clothing as he straightened and shifted around the table. "Damon and I will lead this covert mission," he instructed. He patted Damon's shoulder as he walked by and turned back to face the group as he stepped next to Malkia. "Our team will find Dasco and Thane and establish vantage points around their base. We will stay in contact with Malkia, as the moment we find their army, the bulk of our people will move out for our first attack."

"Will we be using the other ships?" Maltese asked, rising from his seat as well and crossing his arms over his chest.

Malkia nodded, her prayer hands touching her lips. "Yes. Take ours and one of yours, but the Elven's vessel will definitely remain. It will be our base, not only cloaked, but warded from any outside dangers by the warlocks who remain with the children. Is everyone in agreement?"

All three of the Artemisians nodded, followed by Damon and Thora. Hope remained quiet and still, waiting patiently for them to turn their attention to her.

When all eyes were upon her, she spoke, "My people are anticipating a new beginning on the moon of Thalia." She ran her long fingernails through the ends of her hair, keeping her voice calm and steady. "Our race has spent many years replenishing our numbers, from the time the humans slaughtered so many of us. We aren't asking for much, except peace and the ability to spread out across the moons and Theia, just as the humans have done." Her eyes came to rest on Malkia.

"The permission is not mine to give." Malkia shook her head, disgusted by the behavior of her ancestors. "We will no longer tolerate the injustice and separation our lineages have brought upon our moons. We are one People—the species of Theia's Moons—and we have united to halt the oppression of our past. I suggest from this day forward, every moon and the planet, will be available for all to settle upon." She nodded at Hope, before turning to the others. "Is this a path we can all walk down together, once we finish this absurd conflict?"

Once again, the group nodded in unison, including Hope. Damon handed Zeke over to Malkia, adjusting his sheaths and weapons, while his gaze shifted around the room at the others. She could see he was anxious and after securing their son's carrier around her neck, she curled her arm around his waist.

"Are you ready for this?" she asked, her voice barely a whisper as her free hand pressed Zeke against her.

Damon nodded, kissing her on top of the head. "We need to move as quickly as possible. While we organize the scouts, please reach out to your sister and have everyone from our ship meet you over here."

"I'll take care of it," she whispered, patting his back as she slid away. "I love you."

Cradling her face in between his palms, he sealed his lips over hers, kissing her with the love of a man staring death in the face. "I love you, my one and only," he whispered, after he broke away.

She nodded as he straightened his stature and swept the room with his brilliant dark eyes. Leaving Damon to gather his team, she found her way to the outside door and stepped into the sunshine. She was starving and needed her friends and family to join her, knowing the scouts would be leaving soon.

Concentrating on her sister, she reached out to her and seconds later Mataya was standing near her, speaking to Esta inside their ship. "Hello, ladies," Malkia greeted as they turned to face her. "Will you gather up our group and bring everyone back to the Elven ship? We need to prepare for any attacks. And we are sending out scouts to track down my father's group."

"We're on our way," Mataya answered, motioning at someone who was beyond Malkia's viewpoint. "Do we need to bring anything with us?"

"Pack any belongings you might need over the next few days." Malkia blew Esta a kiss and waved before letting the vision dissipate.

Focusing on her surroundings, she noticed the Artemisians and a few humans were gathered just beyond their ships. She could see Jayde perched on a tall boulder, with a hawk resting on her shoulder and several others hovering in the skies above them. The meadow and beach were calm and serene and she couldn't imagine a battle being fought here. Now if they could only find her father quick enough.

"The others are heading out to pick individuals from their crew and meet me in the clearing just up ahead," Damon interrupted her thoughts as his hand wrapped around her waist. He gestured toward the meadow where Jayde and the others were conversing.

She watched the Artemisians and Angels stroll past them. "When you're out there, look for the shimmer. I worry, because the Elvens are already so familiar with the cloaking and might still be able to discover this ship. You'll need to think like them. Search for that light that bends and you'll find their hideout."

"We'll return soon," he whispered, nuzzling her neck, followed with a sloppy kiss on her cheek. "Take care of our little ones." He smacked her backside with his palm, winking at her as he sauntered away.

THIRTY-EIGHT
Closing In

"WILL YOU BE checking in with Damon and Apollo soon?" Mataya asked. Her forehead puckered as she chewed on her nails.

Malkia's group had arrived just as Damon, Chantum and the scouts were departing. The Elvens had six fighter vessels that they used, along with one of the Artemisian ships, flying them across the lands, first. If their reconnaissance turned anything unusual, they would return and comb the territory on foot.

Glancing up from feeding Zeke, Malkia surveyed the beach and ocean, noticing there were a few others wandering outside their ships. "As soon as I finish here, I'll reach out to him," she answered, lifting Zeke. She cooed at him, flashing him a big smile, before settling him against her other breast. "Once we have an idea of where they are, I will need you to remain here with the children."

"No," Mataya interjected. Her hands dropped to her sides as her eyes narrowed. "My powers are strong and fierce. Bella and several of the Elvens are already staying behind, and I don't want to miss out on this battle like I did on Thalia."

Fear twisted relentlessly in Malkia's gut. She opened her mouth to speak, but Mataya waved her hand to stop her.

"I don't want to hear it, Malkia." Threading a hand through her hair, she settled her locks against her back. "I'm going." She rose from the ground. "Not only am I old enough to make my own decisions, I'm insisting that I have my turn to face the man who deceived me."

Releasing a long breath, Malkia nodded. "If that's what you want to do," she mumbled, biting back the words she really wanted to say as her thumb grazed over Zeke's cheek. "I can't say that I won't be terrified, knowing that you're in harm's way, but I agree, you are old enough to make your own choices."

"Thank you," Mataya muttered, relaxing her fists and slowly sinking back onto the ground next to her sister. "I can do this. My powers strength has only improved, especially since Ustarum, Alexa, and I have been working together."

A few moments later, Malkia lifted Zeke and tucked him away in his carrier, rising to her feet with the help of Mataya. Focusing on Damon, he zoomed into view, crouched behind a tree with one of the Angels next to him. Seeing her, he raised his finger to his lips, pointing with his other hand behind the tree.

Her eyes scanned across the vegetation, noticing a few of the Artemisians who were also crouching within the brush. That's when she saw movement at the edge of the tree line and an Elven, who wasn't among the scouts, stroll on by with one of their weapons held loosely at chest level.

Damon shook his head and waved her away. The vision disappeared and she turned to Mataya to tell her what she'd seen.

"They found it," Mataya spoke, before she could say anything.

Malkia was caught off guard by her sister's words. A laugh bubbled up her throat and across her lips as she remembered that Mataya had the ability to bend space and walk through it, just like the Nesoi.

"What's so funny?" Mataya asked, settling her hands on her hips.

"You *are* ready," Malkia answered, her eyes twinkling with delight. "I don't know why I always just see you as the little sister, who needs protection. And to be honest, that might never go away completely, but your magical abilities and connection with the Nesoi makes you as powerful as I, if not more so." She shook her head, strolling toward the door of the ship. "It will be a daily reminder for as long as I—"

She halted, the smile melting from her face as her gaze settled on a vessel zipping straight for the Artemisians' ship and the people who were still outside. Just as she opened her mouth to scream, a light shot out of the craft, striking the terrain near the Artemisian ship.

The scream tore itself from her lips, startling Zeke. Mataya held out her arms for the wailing baby, cradling him close as she ran for the Elven ship.

"*Go stop them*," she cried, her run turning into a sprint. "I'll meet you over there."

Malkia jumped into the air, zipping toward the vessel that was turning around in the air, returning for a second shot. Surrounding herself with her light, the shots from the vessel didn't slow her down, and it veered sharply to one side. She twisted around and raced after it. Another shot was fired, hitting one of the ships' shields. Flying just above the vessel, she couldn't see inside, but realized they could see her as its speed increased.

Matching the speed, her hands slipped against the blackened metal, but she finally found a spot that she could hold. With everything she had, she slowed and felt the pull of the vessel as the pilot attempted to maneuver from her clutch. Gritting her teeth, she forced it to turn away from the other ships, moving it to the city. As they reached the spot where the pyramid had been, she tilted the ship toward the ground and shoved it down.

Tightening her light around her, the explosion washed across her bubble, rumbling through the air. She inhaled a few deep breaths, calming her racing pulse as hot tears stung her cheeks. This was her fault. She had known her father would strike, but instead of insisting everyone hide within the safety of the ships, she had allowed them to decide what was best for each of their groups.

She tore through the air, landing hard against the ground and sprinting toward the people who had been outside during the attack. Her eyes fell on an Artemisian, lying face up in the dirt. The others had turned him over, as his face was covered in the filth, with blood smeared from his mouth and across his cheek. Searching for his wound, one of the female Artemisian's curled her hand over Malkia's shoulder.

"He's gone," she told Malkia, holding her back from continuing. "We will take care of our dead."

Malkia nodded and rose to her feet. "Are there any injured?" she asked, her eyes straining as they darted across the faces in the crowd around them.

Jayde pushed through the crowd, waving at Malkia. "There's one elven wounded over here. Come quick."

Jumping back into the air, Malkia flew over the crowd, landing on the other side and seeing her daughter already kneeling next to the wounded male. Her hands were pressed against his torso, filling him with a light so white, it blinded Malkia.

She covered her eyes and peeked around the edges, recognizing the elven as Mapesh. He had been assisting the Artemisians with some Elven weapons, giving them instructions on how to use them. Stepping back into the crowd, she watched Esta's powers ebb and flow, demonstrating a power far greater than her own. The light enrobed both her daughter and Mapesh, pulsating with the beat of her heart, and slightly lifting them from the soil. It was enchanting to witness.

As she saw the Elven's body begin to heal, she heard Mataya instruct the others to retreat to safety, in case more of Thane's ships arrived.

A cough and a sudden twist of the elven, kept Malkia's focus on her daughter. The light faded and Mapesh settled back on the ground. As he opened his eyes, she rushed forward and helped him to his feet.

"Return to your ship," she insisted, patting him on the shoulder. "You should be fine, but check in with your doctor, please."

Mapesh nodded, his hands straying down his own body, searching for the wound that was no longer there. "Thank you," he said to Esta, bowing several times before sprinting back to his ship.

Malkia scooped up her daughter and squeezed her tight. "You did wonderful," she whispered in her ear. "I'm so proud of you." From her peripheral vision she noticed Jayde hurrying toward her. As Malkia searched the sky for more invaders, Esta wrapped her arms tightly around her mother's neck.

"We need to meet up with Damon," Jayde gasped, shaking her head as one of her hawks landed on her shoulder. "I've been tracking them from afar and it's obvious they found the compound. I don't know why they aren't returning as instructed, but we need to bring our full force upon that army."

"You're right," Malkia agreed, nodding her head. "Let's go arm up. I'll reach out to Damon again and let him know we're on our way, as you have the coordinates."

They raced to the Elven ship, colliding with Koleton and Ustarum, who were both already geared up and ready to leave. "Where's Damon?" Koleton asked, securing the sheath belt around his waist.

"We're all going together," Malkia said, racing past him with a firm grip on Esta. "Where's my mother?"

"She's meeting us at the ship," Ustarum yelled after her.

The three women found Alyssa and Alexa, with Bella and a handful of the Elvens and Angels, securing the children in one of the inner rooms where the monitors could see every entry point of the ship. They had instructions to leave the area if they were discovered and meet them on the small island that could be seen from the shore.

Jordan stopped Malkia on their trek back to the ship. "Koleton says we are leaving. Did you speak with Damon?"

"I did earlier," she responded, waving Jayde and Mataya to proceed without her. "They had reached Dasco's hideout, but they couldn't speak. I'm going to contact him again and let him know we're on our way, as Jayde's hawks have discovered the compound as well and can lead us to them." She paused, seeing a few Artemisians stepping down the gangway and watching the two of them converse. "Do you trust me to lead you to the right place?" Her gaze met his, just as Tantiana landed in the meadow.

"Yes, I do," Jordan replied, giving her a nod and turning his attention to the dragon. "Will you be riding her?"

Malkia nodded, throwing Tantiana a look over her shoulder. "We take the ships in low and land them away from their compound. We need to rescue as many Elvens as we can from their captivity, before we slaughter everyone else."

The muscles in Jordan's jaw twitched. "That might be a foolish move. It's never a wise choice to save a few, when it could cost us hundreds or thousands of lives."

"This isn't up for discussion," Malkia muttered, stepping away from the Artemisian. "If there comes a point where we can't justify saving those in my father's servitude, then we will use your approach. But until that moment, this is how we are playing the game. I need to go." She pointed at her ship. "Once I make it back to Tantiana, we'll be ready to leave. Prepare your warriors and watch for my signal."

She could feel his eyes boring into her as she raced away from him, but knowing what the doctor and Elisa had done for her was enough to know this was the right move. Her feet were loud on the metal cargo door as she pounded upward. She paused when Koleton and Mataya stepped out of the corridor and met her.

"Good," she said, running her palms over her forehead and pushing her hair out of her face. "I wanted Mataya here when I reached out to Damon."

She twisted to face the outside, focusing on Damon's image and took a small step back when the vision burst out in front of her. None of her abilities were truly predictable, but this one still had a tendency to startle her.

Damon was walking with a few Elvens and Angels, when he noticed her. "We've found their hideout." He paused midstride, waving away the others. "We attempted to close in and at least obtain an idea of the infrastructure or the whereabouts of the Elvens of which you spoke, but they have the area locked up so tight with spells and wards that it would trip an alarm if we broke through it."

"That makes sense. That's exactly what I had Bella do once we left the Elven ship." Malkia glanced over at her sister. "Jayde knows your whereabouts and we're coming to meet you. We can use those smaller vessels to move in closer, but I think our best bet is to surround the compound and move in quickly. Once we have Elisa, the doctor and any other captives, the rest of our army and the dragons can finish them off."

"But first, we have to break down their incantations." Damon's eyes narrowed, growling at her inattention. "We can't move in without making them aware of our presence. We need a diversion or a way to break through their spells."

"I understand," she replied, nodding her head. "You forget we have the Nesoi and my sister to move us around, if needed. When we arrive at your position, we can figure out a plan to move forward."

He nodded as she turned away from him and let the connection fall away. "I'll follow you on Tantiana," she told Koleton and Mataya. "This is it." She grasped both of their hands, her heart thumping against her chest.

Koleton raised his eyes to the ceiling. "Don't start with the sappiness, Malkia. You're going to make me cry and I need all my manliness right now." He jabbed her in the side.

"Crying is manly," she murmured, a hint of a smile tugging at the edges of her lips. "May Theia's light shine upon us today." She focused on them both, first patting Koleton on the shoulder and then kissing Mataya on the cheek. "I'll see you two soon."

Without another word, she sprinted down the gangway. She could hear it shut as she raced across the meadow, bounding lightly upon Tantiana' back. "It's show time, my love." She patted the dragon's scales as they shot into the air, circling back around to follow the vessels that were ascending to the skies.

THIRTY-NINE

Her Father's Hideout

IT DID NOT take them long to catch up with the others. Settling onto a grassy plain, alongside the smaller vessels, Malkia flew from Tantiana's back and landed in Damon's arms. She hugged him close, a deep longing whispering through her, followed by gratitude for his safety. Leaning back, she laughed when he nuzzled her neck with his whiskers, reminding her everything she had to live for, and the necessity of this fight.

Ustarum, Alyssa, Alexa, and Mataya stepped off their ship, followed by Koleton and Jayde. Cormac, along with several of her Esaki people, joined them from the Artemisian ships. Before long, she was surrounded by many others. The Nesoi had arrived, most of them keeping their distance within the shadows of the vegetation, while a few settled closer to the crowd.

"Mom, will you be able to work on their magical barrier?" Malkia asked, glancing over at Alyssa and the other three warlocks.

Ustarum stepped forward, not giving Alyssa the chance to respond and nodded his head as he clasped his hands in front of his body. "If Damon will show us where their hideout lies, we'll begin working on breaking down their walls. We can possibly give the warriors a section to advance upon without tripping any alarms."

"Follow me," Damon said, waving his hand and maneuvering toward the forest. "I'll take the warlocks in, with a handful of others. The rest should wait here until we know more." He glanced over his shoulder as he walked away. "But be prepared to strike as soon as they break through."

Malkia waited for the few who were accompanying the advance party to follow Damon into the brush, watching as nearly half the Nesoi beasts scattered outward, staying near the warlocks. She pressed her lips together as she turned to face the others. "We might have to enter at the same point if that's all the warlocks can give us, but once inside, we'll need to spread out. Find the ones who are being held captive and bring them to our ships. Then, our pitched battle will begin."

Malkia saw several smiles in the crowd as the Artemisians beat one fist against their chests and stretched the other toward the heavens in a unified salute. Stepping away from them, she moved into the safety of the trees and observed Damon's group slinking in the direction of Thane's compound.

"What if we move around their hideout and encircle it completely?" Thora asked, stepping next to Malkia, clutching her bow in her hands.

"If we can't break through their barrier, then that would only be a waste of time." Malkia's eyes strained to see the Damon's vanishing back, losing him completely as he shifted around a cluster of trees and vegetation. "I'm anxious to make our move, but if we strike too soon and announce that we know their whereabouts, we could lose our advantage."

"But if they break through and we aren't in a position to strike, could it be possible that their incantation will repair itself too soon for us to all advance on them?" Thora spoke half in question, tilting her head to peer over at Malkia.

Malkia paused, chewing on the angel's words, before pivoting on her heel and staring at the crowd hunkered near the ships. "How soon could we spread everyone out?"

"Not too long, and we won't take many with us. I'll place a handful of warriors at six points around their hideout, and, if we're able to move in, we will signal with a burning arrow in the sky," Thora told her as she pointed at several of the warriors in the crowd. "I'll arrange the groups and we'll set out in just a few minutes."

"I would like to create a signal chain that can begin from our position here." Malkia held up her hand to forestall Thora's departure. "I'll stay in contact with Damon and the warlocks. The moment they break through the spells, I'll signal the first person in the chain and they will pass it on. This way, my father and the Elvens won't be able to see any indications in the sky that will alert them to our presence."

Thora nodded, slinging her bow over her back. "Good idea." She pointed to a spot that was on the outskirts of the forest, but near the boundary of the compound. "I'll place my first scout right there and keep them within eyesight of one another as we encircle the enemy's position."

Malkia watched as the angel warrior gathered her group and within a few minutes they were stretching across the meadow. They headed for their designated positions, with about a dozen Nesoi following behind. Whatever the Nesoi planned to do, she hoped they would be more help than hindrance.

Drawing in a few deep breaths, she focused on her connection with Theia and the magic pulsating in the air around her. She balled her hands into fists, and then fully extended her fingers. Over and over again, she did this until her mind calmed and she could see the first scout take her position in the designated spot.

Reaching out with her mind, she connected with Damon's location and stood her ground when the vision of him and the warlocks burst in front of her. Damon was apparently expecting her as he pressed his back into the bark of a tree and pointed over to one side, without speaking a word. Shifting her view, she could see the four warlocks huddled near the edge of the magical ward, which was now visible to the naked eye because of their incantation.

Their eyes were closed, and together they were muttering under their breath, while grasping one another's hands. Damon inched closer to her and mouthed, "Bring in our warriors."

Not wanting to leave the ones who had encircled the compound, she beckoned Koleton and Jayde over to her side, while she continued to watch the warlocks. When a small group had gathered around her, she diverted her eyes long enough to make eye contact with the leaders.

"Move in to Damon's position," she told them, pointing over to the tree line. "The warlocks have nearly broken through the Elven defenses, and, the moment they do, you must begin the invasion of their compound. I'll wait until I've given Thora and her team the signal they require and then join you." She paused, her gaze shifting to the visible shield sparking within her vision. "Move quickly, but quietly."

Without a word, the warriors broke into teams, spreading out just inside the canopy. One by one they disappeared within the foliage. Malkia remained alone with the restless dragons, along with the angel warrior who watched Malkia's every move. Slowly raising her hand toward the angel, she held out a finger and paused, watching the barrier spark and shatter in small sections, but still holding together in the most crucial areas.

The warlocks' mouths moved faster, their words like the susurrus of the ocean surf against Malkia's ears. But the shield was sparking brightly in several areas and Damon covered his head with his arm as flashes of light struck the ground around him. Holding her breath, she forced her eyes to remain open, just as the barrier closest to the warlocks crumbled completely, creating a crack over the bulk of the shield. Seconds later, it shattered in its entirety.

Releasing her held breath, Malkia's arm flew up into the air, waving at the angel. She waited until the signal was passed on, before bolting into the forest and sprinting through the vegetation toward Damon and the rest of her people.

Tantiana, wait for my call. I might need you to remove the innocents and return them to the ship near the ocean, she ordered her dragon, glancing back at her position before the dragons were completely out of her sight.

Dodging the trees and brush, she leapt over a large boulder, realizing the canopy was thickening the farther in she went. The sky faded above her until the light from the suns was fully blocked, forcing her to shine her own to guide her forward.

A few more moments of running and she could see the tail end of the warriors as the pressed into the compound. Levitating, she flew over their heads and landed inside the now breached and inactive barrier, the soles of her boots striking the terrain with a thud.

It was another ancient town, swallowed by the vegetation of the planet. With the magical barrier in place they hadn't seen the symmetrical structures. Even if it hadn't been warded, encroaching vegetation and the simple time had destroyed anything that had risen above the trees. She froze and her warriors crept around her, searching the nearest ancient buildings.

It was quiet within the compound, and Malkia's gaze darted from one broken building to the next before focusing on a distant structure. Sprinting toward it, she belatedly noticed the guards placed near it and skidded to an abrupt halt, diving behind a large, crumbled section of one of the buildings. Inhaling a quick breath, she beckoned at Jayde and jabbed her thumb in the direction of the guards, allowing her to speak to the others around her.

Glancing around the corner, she could see the guards were unaware of their invasion. They had no idea their protective barrier had been shattered as they continued to stand at attention, nor were they aware of the forces that were encroaching on their positions. To the side of the building, she noticed movement as Thora zipped behind a boulder, followed by several others. Two Nesois leapt onto the roof of a small structure, but blended into the background before drawing any attention to themselves.

They were now all inside the bounds of her father's hideout.

Making eye contact with Thora, she held out her hand and counted down, starting at five. As her last finger curled down within her palm, the arrows from five bows flew from various positions, striking the five guards in the hearts.

Too easy, Malkia thought. Her eyes darted across the other buildings, before twisting around and beckoning to Damon and the others.

They moved in fast, sliding open the front door and peering within. Crossing the threshold Malkia paused when she heard the buzzing of electricity. Inching forward she peered over the railing in front of her. The bustle and noise of the Elvens on the lower floor was an indication that they still didn't know their enemies were inside. She pointed down the corridors to each side and hid herself behind a round column that still stood, fully intact, even after the hundreds of years of neglect.

With her hands hovering over the hilts of her daggers, she glanced around the column and searched the crowd below for any allies who had befriended her while in captivity. Her heart drummed against her ribs as her gaze landed on her father who was speaking to a shorter, female Elven, oblivious to their presence. Gritting her teeth, she swallowed hard when Justin appeared from a lower floor doorway and strolled nonchalantly toward her father.

The traitor, she growled silently. Her eyes flashed over to the corridor to her left and saw Mataya crouched behind another column, glaring at the man who had betrayed her.

Waving her fingers at her sister, she nodded when Mataya's gaze met hers. "You've got this," she mouthed.

Mataya shoulders stiffened in response, twisting back to see Justin and Thane conversing as if they were old friends. A sickening knot twisted in Malkia's gut and she wondered how long her friend had been in contact with her father.

Thora's face appeared on the other side of the round room, hidden between two large boulders. Nodding at the angel, she searched the rest of the corridors, seeing that their warriors were all in place. Creeping down the hallway to her right, she used a small fraction of her powers to ease herself down the closest staircase, sliding behind another wall with two closed doors behind her. Peering around the corner, she could see her father only a few feet away with his back turned toward her. Ustarum and Apollo crouched up above, hidden mostly by another column, but carefully observing her from their position.

It was now or never.

FORTY

Confronting Him

SWALLOWING THE BILE of terror rising in her throat, she concentrated her light into her hands and peered up at Ustarum as he did the same. Nodding her head, she stepped out from the shadows, quickly ensnaring her father and yanking him toward her.

Justin's head snapped up and over, making eye contact with her as dread bleached his features. Before he had the chance to move, Mataya had flung herself over the railing, landing with the grace of a panther directly in front of Justin. Her sister grabbed the back of Justin's head, slamming it down into her knee, before tossing him from Malkia's view.

Suddenly the room exploded with noise and furious motion, shots being fired and striking the Elvens working on the devices in the room. A few Nesoi beasts leapt over the railing, ripping apart the bodies of her enemies.

Thank Theia. Her fingers curled around her father's throat, squeezing as she leaned forward. "How does it feel to know you underestimated me?" she whispered in his ear, relishing in the fear she was witnessing in his face.

Thane's chest heaved and he coughed, attempting to wriggle from her grasp. Surrounding both of them with her light, she flew from the room and beyond the conflict. She slammed him against the uneven ground outside, pinning his face with her foot against his neck and held him immobile with her light.

"Where are Elisa and the doctor?" she asked. Flashes of red sparked over her light and she rolled her shoulders, relaxing the fury thundering in her heart.

He groaned, struggling against her powers. As she pressed her foot more firmly against his neck, he froze. "Why would I tell you anything?" he snarled, his irises peering up at her from the corner of his eye. "You're just going to kill me."

"That's true," she replied, brushing her hands together and nodding. She focused her attention on a smaller building farther down the lane, blazing with a newly lit fire. "If they die, your death will be slow and agonizing." She glanced down at the man who had done his best to destroy her entire life. "But if they live, I'll end your despicable existence quickly."

An explosion from another structure closer at hand made her jump, and she momentarily released the pressure of her foot against her father's neck. Fortunately, her light continued to pin him down, leaving him writhing with fury as she peered down the side pathway.

Several Elvens were escaping in a small craft, and from farther down she could see Dasco wave his long fingers at her. A smirk spread across his face, as he entered his own vessel. A growl throbbed in her chest and a bright spark flashed from her hand, but missed the ship by inches as it lifted through an opening in the vegetation. Stomping back to her father, she lifted him off the ground, dragging him up the stairs and inside the building where her people continued to fight.

A thin haze of smoke had risen from below and she stopped near the first column, attempting to gain her bearings. The only dead she found were Elven. So far, no one from her team had been slaughtered. She released a sigh of relief, until her eyes fell on Mataya.

Limping up the stairs toward her, her sister's face was smeared with blood and tears. Securing her father to the wall behind her with cords of light, she rushed over to Mataya and helped her sink to the floor. Mataya's face fell into her hands and she shook her head as the sobs rose one after another.

"What happened?" Malkia asked, running her hands over Mataya's brunette locks. "Are you alright?"

Mataya shook her head and wiped her eyes with the back of her arm, only smearing the blood across her cheek and into her hair. "I killed him," she choked out as another sob interrupted her words. She swallowed hard, clasping her hands against her chest. "He kept spewing apologies at me, begging for his life and claiming he would be better off if he had been able to leave our star system." She hiccupped as her narrowing eyes swept over to Thane. "*Selfish and greedy bastard*," she screamed at Malkia's father. "*All of you.*" Her eyes shifted back to Malkia's. "Including Justin. He was weak and now my hands will forever be the ones who ended his life."

"Where is everyone else?" Malkia asked, tugging a rag from her satchel and wiping the blood from Mataya's forehead and nose.

Shattering glass from the other side of the room interrupted them, and Malkia focused in on dozens of her people suddenly moving within the haze.

"Ustarum and Mom used a spell that immobilized some of our people," Mataya whispered, following Malkia's gaze to the far side of the room. "Most of the others trailed after the fleeing Elvens out the back. The battle isn't over."

Hauling Mataya off the ground, Malkia dragged her father behind them, her grip on his neck tightening as her anger writhed in her gut. Damon emerged from the smoke, followed by Apollo, Thora, and several other Angels and Artemisians. They had purposely not brought many of the Elvens, who were their allies, in order to keep them from being slaughtered during the battle. As she glanced around at the faces in the building, she realized the ones who had accompanied them were no longer with them.

Stomping from the building, she handed her father over to Apollo who wrapped a steel noose around his neck, followed by a magical chain, similar to the one her father had used on her. She raced around the building and ran into Chantum and Ustarum.

"Has anyone found Elisa and the doctor?" she asked, peering around them at all the other warriors still alive and sighing when she saw several of the Elvens among them. Elisa stepped out of the crowd and rushed into Malkia's arms.

"Thank you for rescuing me," she cried, tears wetting Malkia's cheeks as she pressed against her. "But Dasco took Velem, along with his family and a few other prisoners, with him when they escaped."

Malkia released Elisa and patted her softly on the shoulder as she twisted around to view her father. "We will execute my father and rendezvous back at the Elven ship."

Her father snickered, shaking his head in amusement. Malkia's eyes narrowed as she stalked toward him. "What do you find so amusing?" she snapped, gripping his obsidian hair and yanking his head back.

"You call me the fool," he said, wincing from the pain in his scalp. "But if you believe you'll stop Dasco, you're the foolish one. You caught me, but now all your warriors are here. Who's watching over my grandchildren?"

Malkia's heart skipped a beat as her eyes fluttered to the small section of exposed sky above her. *Tantiana, have you seen additional Elven ships anywhere near our people*, she asked her dragon, as a chill raced down her spine.

No. We saw them leave and gave chase, but they vanished into the clouds, so we've returned. I'm circling back around in your direction to double check on your security. Tantiana paused in thought. *But on second thought, I'm going to return to the Elven vessel.*

Do that. And let me know what the status is when you arrive. "Nice try," she hissed at her father. "String him up." She tossed her father forward and sauntered past him.

"How are you planning on ending his life?" Damon asked, watching Koleton and Apollo drag her father toward the front of the main building.

Her hand gestured back at the warriors following them. "He's ruined so many lives. They should all have the chance to make him suffer."

"What about you?" he asked, gripping her wrist and twisting her to face him.

"What about me?" her voice trembled and she pressed her lips together to hide her heartache. Shaking her head rapidly, she halted any other words Damon wanted to throw at her.

She shook her wrist free from his grasp and rushed to catch up with the others. Watching Koleton throw the chain over a broken wall, Apollo gripped onto the end and wrenched her father onto the tips of his toes. The Artemisians in the crowd roared with delight, while the

Angels remained unmoved by the demonstration. She held her hands over her heart, pushing back the tears that were welling in her eyes.

Mataya's arm curled around her waist, hugging her from the side. "You don't have to watch this," her sister whispered, brushing a wisp of Malkia's hair away from her eyes.

"Yes, I do," Malkia answered, inhaling a raspy breath as she chewed on her fingernails.

The crowd cheered as her father stared out with wide eyes, struggling to breathe as he attempted to steady himself on his toes. Koleton glanced over at her, waiting for further instructions.

Stepping forward, she turned to face her people and held up hand to quiet the masses. "First, I want to thank all of you for sacrificing your lives to prevent any more cruelty by my father's hands." She swept her gaze over the crowd, landing on Alyssa, Jayde, and Ustarum. "I won't stand in your way as you decide his fate and send him to the Aletheians to be judged. But I ask that you give me a moment before we end his life, to seek my own answers."

A leaden silence rippled across her team, followed with nods of approval as they walked away from her, allowing her the privacy she desired. Pity washed across Damon's face and she bit down on her lip to prevent herself from lashing out at the man she loved. Instead, she twisted around to face her father, unable to forestall the grief that was crushing her heart in that moment.

Her father eyed her with disdain, having been lowered a few inches. With his heels firmly on the ground, the hatred in his expression had returned.

"Was it worth it?" she asked, pausing a few feet in front of him and clasping her hands behind her back.

He chuckled and rolled his eyes to the heavens. "Death is only the next step in existence. I never cared for eternal life, like Dasco is intent on attaining, nor did the damage I inflicted upon you and your loved ones bother me in the slightest." His focus shifted behind her, returning to eye her with the same pity Damon had given her just moments before.

She winced under his stare, suddenly feeling like the small child who was intimidated by her powerful father.

His stare intensified as if he was reading her mind. "I learned a long time ago to not allow myself to become too attached to any person or thing, as the moment you do, your heart and life will be vulnerable. And being that I'm already able to manipulate most anyone that I please—" A sly grin rose on his lips, nodding his head toward Damon. "Similar to the man you call your lover, I wasn't about to place myself in a situation where the tables could be turned on me." He paused and waited for her to speak, but when she didn't he cleared his throat and chuckled again. "Don't worry, my dear, your sister meant very little to me as well. You were all a means to an end. Unfortunately, it appears I won't be leaving on the journey of a lifetime as I had planned. So, let's finish this already."

Malkia's eyes closed, and she drew in several deep breaths as her hands lifted in front of her. Her light grasped hold of the chain, yanking her father by the neck and dangling his toes inches from the ground. His desperate gasps for air only furthered her desire to end his life as a dark rage throbbed within her body.

Suddenly sensing the heat of the others gathering around her, her thoughts cooled, releasing the blackness and anger with an abrupt exhale of air. Warm fingers curled around her forearm and she opened her eyes. She stared into the hazel irises of her sister and relaxed her hold on the chain, allowing her father's feet to touch the ground once again.

"He means nothing to me," she yelled out into the crowd. "He's admitted to his evil actions, and by the grace of Theia, I believe his life is toxic to our star system. I can hang him now—" She paused, her eyes meeting her father's. "Or the ones in the crowd who have been most deeply affected by his actions, may take him apart, piece by piece." Her father's eyes widened, shaking his head rapidly as she shifted to view the people once again. "And then we will dance around the fire that burns what remains of him, celebrating our victory here today."

The Artemisians shouted and the rest of the crowd clapped and cheered, eager to see the execution of her father completed. Several Artemisians stepped forward, followed by all the Elvens who'd been held captive. After several moments, a handful of Angels shifted through the crowd, their gaze locked onto Thane.

Mataya gripped Malkia's hand, towing her away. They stepped to the side, allowing the others to pass by and walked away from the massacre that was about to take place. Within seconds, the air was filled with the screams of agony from her father as a few stepped forward and sawed off a piece of his body, throwing it in a pile beneath his feet, before following Malkia away from the mayhem of his death.

FORTY-ONE
Chasing Dasco

MALKIA STARED AT the dying embers, her eyes unblinking as she watched the lowered flames nipping at the charred remains of her father. The strong scent of burned meat saturated the air and it sickened her to know her father's last moments were filled with such horrific agony. Although there were only a handful who actually cut into his flesh, the fire that consumed him while he continued to breath, wasn't easy for her to witness. His final shrieks would forever be heard within her mind.

The peace she had hoped for, eluded her.

Most of the others had departed the empty compound, returning to their ships as the night swept in, bringing the chill of the winds. The Nesoi had opened their connection to Hemera and with one last good-bye to Mataya, had disappeared through it. They were on their own to finish off Dasco.

Malkia hugged herself tightly, and she concentrated on breathing evenly, determined to burn this moment into her memory and remember the sacrifices that had been made.

"Malkia," Damon's voice was quiet as he stood behind her. "Are you ready to leave?"

She turned to face him. A sigh swept over her lips and she nodded in response, leaning over to gather her possessions. She scooped them up, placed them in her satchel, and threw it on her back as she tossed the fire one last look.

Following Damon down the pathway, she could see Ustarum, Alyssa, and Mataya just up ahead waiting for them. Jayde, Apollo, and Koleton were sitting on a boulder at the edge of the village, watching them all approach. Stepping from the shadows, Thora, Chantum and several other Angels joined them on their walk into the forest. Her friends and family had waited for her, and in that moment she realized how precious they all were to her.

Making their way through the overgrown brush, Malkia fell behind the others and glanced back at the compound one last time. The farther away she walked, the better she felt. But what about Dasco? She knew he would return for her children, as he believed they were the key to finding and overtaking the Creators on the Blue Planet. He would need to be eliminated as well, along with any Elven who insisted that the path to the Illumanti's Earth was essential.

Something's wrong, Tantiana's thoughts interrupted her own.

Malkia halted. *What do you mean?* She asked, her eyes focused on the receding group.

The Elven ship is powering up, Tantiana replied. *Pythios says a group of Elvens rushed in from the brush, but he believed they were members of the original group. However, the vessel is now rising from the terrain.*

No matter what happens, do not lose sight of that ship. Malkia sprinted toward Damon, gripping his arm and wrenching him around to face her. "The Elven ship is leaving. Is it possible that the others from our team have arrived back and are leading them away for a reason unknown to me?"

Damon's eyes narrowed as he shook his head. "I'd be surprised if they've left the meadow. Can you reach out to the dragons or Esta?"

"Tantiana is the one who informed me they're leaving," she replied, her gaze shifting around the forest. "Give me a moment."

Her mind reached out to Esta and smacked into a magical barrier. Gritting her teeth, she pressed forward, eroding the weak barricade and finally breaking through. The image of Esta sprang up before her, and her daughter flinched when she noticed her mother's presence.

"Mama!" she exclaimed, jumping up from the chair she'd been sitting on. "They've taken Alexa and Bella. It's only Landon and I."

"Who took them?" Malkia asked, squeezing her hands into fists.

"The Elvens," Esta whispered, glancing around the room as Landon came into view. "But they were mean and they wouldn't allow Zeke to stay here with us."

Malkia's breath caught in her throat and she glanced over at Mataya. "Can you go to them?"

Her sister nodded, inhaling a deep breath. "What should I do?"

"Hide and keep watch over the children," Malkia told her, securing her weapons tightly in their sheaths. "I'll catch up to the dragons and keep in touch with Damon so the rest of our group can follow us to wherever Dasco is taking them."

Alyssa gripped Mataya's arm. "I'm coming with you."

"You can bend space, like Mataya?" Malkia asked, the delay creating a dread worming through her stomach.

"No. But if I stay connected to Mataya, I can go with her. It will be better to have us both on the ship." Alyssa's eyes strayed to Ustarum. "Find us."

Ustarum grimaced, but nodded in reply, as Mataya stepped through the vision with Alyssa beside her. Once they were on the other side, the two children clung to them as they scooped them into their arms.

"We will hide," Alyssa said, twisting to see Malkia. "But the children will have to remain here."

Malkia nodded at her mother and sister before allowing the connection to dissipate. "Go to the ships and when I reach a spot where I can connect with you, I'll let you know where to go," she told Damon. Twisting to face Ustarum, she grasped his wrist and tugged her toward her. "Keep an open channel. If I'm able to connect with you, I can direct your path without stopping."

"Yes, of course," Ustarum replied, embracing Malkia lightly. "May Theia guide you and keep you safe from the evils of that dictator."

Malkia pushed herself away, giving Ustarum a tight smile, before turning to Damon. "Go quickly." Her lips met his and she kissed him hard, holding tightly to his arms. "I love you."

"And I love you," he choked out in a whisper.

Without another word, she leapt into the air and broke free of the canopy. Her head turned from side to side, gaining her bearings as she reached out to Tantiana.

Have they left? Malkia asked, focusing on the spot the Elvens' ship was supposed to be as she bolted toward that area.

Yes, Tantiana replied. *Follow the ocean surf away from the meadow. The moment they steer away from it, I'll let you know. But Malkia, they are using their cloaking mechanism and I don't know if I can keep up with them if they increase their speed.*

I'm coming. Stay as close as possible, please. Malkia's light strengthened as her speed increased, making her more visible in the night sky. But she didn't care.

The light from the three moons in the sky helped guide her along the shore. Looking ahead, she couldn't see Tantiana or the hatchlings and her body tensed, fearing she would never see her children again.

What if he leaves the atmosphere? She gulped back the rising fear. Her hands balled into fists, digging her fingernails into the flesh of her palms, but she didn't notice the pain or the blood she was drawing.

Her only reassurance was that Mataya and her mother were on the vessel, along with Bella and Alexa. With the assistance of Hope and her followers, they might be able to stop Dasco. Unless he had slaughtered the new Elven leader the moment he entered their ship.

Pushing those thoughts to the back of her mind, she pressed forward. From far off shore, she caught a glimpse of a sea animal rising above the surface. A face twisted around toward her and she gasped when she saw it was a Whalian. Another one rose next to it and they watched her zip past, unmoved by the alien creature flying above them.

I'll have to return and speak with them at a later time, she thought. Her mind returned to Thallassa and the three species she had encountered. She had never stopped to think that Theia might still possess creatures of the sea.

Malkia? Ustarum's thoughts interrupted her own. *We've returned to the spot where the Elven ship landed. Down by the shore we found Alexa and her children.*

Are they okay? She asked, refocusing on the shoreline.

Alexa and Branston are bruised and battered by their drop to the ground. He paused and Malkia nearly stopped, realizing she had just left her friend and children to die. Suddenly Ustarum continued, *Zoe is badly injured. She struck her head on a rock and bled quite a bit before anyone found her. She's not responding to my healing powers and I have no one to assist me, aside from her inexperienced mother. I'm placing her in stasis, in hopes we can save her once we're together again.*

Follow the shoreline away from the meadow, Malkia instructed him. Her core was filling up with grief, thinking of Zoe's injuries and last moments before she'd been knocked out. What a fright for a small child. Focusing back on Ustarum, she continued. T*hey haven't steered away yet, but the moment they do, I'll let you know where to go.*

Can you see the Elven vessel? Ustarum asked.

No, but I'm closing in. I caught a glimpse of Tantiana a moment ago. I'll let you know when the ship is in my sight, she told him. She shifted her mind toward the dragons. *Tantiana, Pythios, Vasuki are you still close to the ship?*

Tantiana is the closest, Vasuki spoke in her head. *Pythios is right behind her and I'm trailing behind, but I still have it within my sight.*

I'm close, she replied, pressing forward harder and faster than she had ever flown before. *I caught sight of you a moment ago, but I've lost you again. Just don't lose that*—. Malkia heard the impact in her mind as if one of the dragons had groaned in agony. *What happened?* She cried out, attempting to connect with all three of them.

Tantiana was hit by one of the Elven weapons, Pythios thoughts broke through in haste.

Don't stop, Malkia ordered. *Is Tantiana still with you?*

I've fallen into the trees below, Tantiana's weak thoughts interrupted her. *Keep going, Malkia. Do not come find me.*

A wave of nausea struck Malkia and she screamed out into the night sky, her eyes darting to and fro attempting to find where Tantiana was lying. *Where are you?* She demanded, straining to see into the forest on the edge of the beach.

I'll be fine, Tantiana's thoughts were nearly a whisper. *Come back and find me, once you have the children.*

Don't you die on me, Malkia barked.

I'll do my best. Tantiana's thoughts quieted completely and Malkia could no longer reach her.

"*Damn it,*" Malkia shouted.

The ship is turning away from the ocean, Vasuki broke into her thoughts. *When you reach the river, turn away from the shore and follow it toward the high peaks.*

I see the river, Malkia replied. *I must not be too far behind.* She cut across the tops of the trees, rising just above the roar of the river and flew forward. Finally catching sight of the two hatchlings, not too far ahead, she breathed a sigh of relief. *Ustarum, when you reach the wide river that cuts through the forest, follow it to the high peaks. I can see the dragons. Soon I'll be able to break through the Elvens' cloaking bubble and keep an eye on their ship. Tantiana was hit near the river, so when this is finished, we will need to return and find her.*

Should we stop? Ustarum asked.

If you can find her quickly, yes, Malkia replied. *If not, continue on after us and we can return once the children and our people are safely out of reach of Dasco.*

Up ahead, Pythios and Vasuki were slowing and they twisted away from the river, diving into the canopy. Malkia caught a glimpse of the cloaking shimmer as the ship settled into a meadow not far from the base of the mountain. She eased herself down into the trees, landing on the pillow of forest loam, peering through the darkness into the eyes of the two dragons.

They've landed just beyond the tree line, Vasuki told her, his face turning to see the meadow. *What should we do now?*

Is there anything significant about this area? Malkia asked them, stepping through some brush and pressing her back against the bark of a tree as she noticed the structures that were built against the mountainside. *I see.*

They had a place to run to all along. I will reach out to Mataya and find out what they know. Start circling the area and let me know if you discover a way for me to advance unseen upon their position.

She watched as the two young dragons eased off into the shadows, their paths taking them in opposite directions. Sinking to the dirt, she rested her hand on a gnarled root that had pierced through the soil and twisted along the path, before pressing back into the ground. She shifted her gaze to the space in front of her and reached out to Mataya. Seconds strummed by as her mind pressed against the magical barrier obstructing her connection. She concentrated, using her light to dampen its powers. Trembling from the exertion, she finally exhaled as the block crumbled and her sister's face rose up before her.

"Their powers are strong," Mataya whispered, nodding her head toward something out of Malkia's view. "We were nearly discovered, but your daughter has some outstanding abilities and was able to divert them from our position."

"Are you still inside their ship?" Malkia asked, wringing her hands together.

Mataya nodded and Alyssa crept forward, huddling next to her. "They're disembarking and preparing for the executions of Hope and her followers. You'll need to intervene sooner rather than later," her sister warned, licking her lips as her gaze shifted around their hiding spot.

"What if I hand myself over to Dasco?" Malkia drew her knees up to her chest and straightened her back as she leaned against them. "Would that be enough distraction to halt the execution or will he just add me to the list?"

"Zeke hasn't stopped wailing since we arrived," Mataya said, placing her finger up to her mouth as a shadow passed over their position.

Malkia's pulse was deafening in her ears, and she tore at her fingernails with her teeth as she waited for her sister to continue.

"They're keeping him in a room down the hall, and Dasco has been shouting at his people to quiet his cries," Mataya finally spoke after several silent minutes. "He won't take a bottle, and they've failed at easing him into a slumber. I believe if you offered to nurse him, Dasco would keep you alive in order to quiet the child."

"That is what I'll do." Malkia brushed the dirt and leaves from her trousers as she rose from the ground, and unclipped her weapons belt from her waist. "I will give these to the dragons and surrender unarmed. When I'm with Zeke, I'll find a way to reach out to you again. If I'm unable to do so, your only objective is to free Landon and Esta and hide until the others arrive."

Mataya nodded. "Be careful."

Slipping away from her spot against the tree, the connection with her sister faded. Before she reached the treeline, she paused and decided to speak to Damon first. Her mind reached out to him and moments later he was in front of her, sitting tensely in his chair on the bridge of their ship.

"We didn't find Tantiana," he said, his weary gaze meeting hers. "We've marked the area that we searched and are currently flying along the river toward the mountains."

She nodded, forcing back the tears threatening to spill from her eyes. "Dasco has landed in a meadow at the base of the mountain. From the sounds of it, there must be a waterfall just inside the shadows of the rocks, which would explain why this town was carved into the mountainside." Her eyes closed and she gulped loudly as her palms pressed against her collar bone. "Find a spot to set down our ship that isn't too close to their position. I'm going to surrender and hopefully give Mataya and my mom the chance to escape with the older children. Did any of the Angels and Artemisians travel with you?"

"One ship remained back at the meadow," Damon replied. A crimson tint was rising in his neck and cheeks and Malkia could see the fear in his eyes. "The others are behind us, ready to assist where needed." He gripped his armrests and clenched his jaw as if he were holding back what he really wanted to say. "I trust your judgment, Malkia. But I have to tell you I'm terrified for your life. Please stay alive." His last words shook and a single tear trailed down his cheek. He quickly wiped it away with the back of his hand.

"I'll do what I can," she whispered, before lifting her hand and blowing him a kiss. His face swept away with the breeze.

Three massive wind turbines rose up to the right as she walked into the meadow. They were nestled next to the pathway that led to the river. One of the moons was rising above the mountain peak in front of her and she paused, noticing a swinging object from two posts up ahead. The Elven vessel was positioned to the left and was dark and quiet, but the structures embedded in the rock had flickers of light shining from the windows. Taking another step, her eyes remained glued to the swaying object.

Another few steps and her heart skipped a beat. She focused in on the object and realized it was a person—more precisely a female person. Malkia's gaze darted around the meadow, searching for traps or other people hiding in the tall grass. If there were anyone else out there, they were concealing themselves well. She slid closer to the hanging body and gasped when the long, black hair blew with the wind, revealing the face underneath. *Bella.*

Sinking to her knees, Malkia smothered her sobs with frantic fingers, falling to her elbows and screaming into the trampled vegetation. The ground below seemed unsteady as she trembled with grief and agony, sickened by the vision of her friend's lifeless body. Would the bloodshed never end?

Drawing several deep breath, she quieted her sobs and wiped her face with her palms. She rose to her feet and brushed off the dirt on her shirt, avoiding the sight of Bella. Her eyes trailed across the meadow, and found Vasuki. He was looking at Bella. Knowing the bond he had created with her, she realized his heart must be breaking. The dragon stepped back into the shadows, disappearing into a thicket.

Don't leave, Malkia thought, directing it at Vasuki. *I'm going to release her from the chains and bring her back to the forest. Please deliver her to Damon, who will be landing nearby. I'm surrendering to Dasco and will do what I can from the inside to end this once and for all.*

Vasuki didn't answer, but Pythios interjected on his behalf. *I'll meet you in the spot we landed. And don't worry about Vasuki. The Elvens just gave him more reasons to fight.*

Thank you, Malkia replied, rising into the air and moving toward Bella.

Lifting Bella's body, Malkia was able to loosen the noose around her neck and tug it over her head. Her friend's head sagged against her own and Malkia pressed her lips together, determined to keep it together. Losing control now would dishonor Bella's memory.

She flew back to the forest and settled to the ground, shuffling the last few feet before resting Bella's body on the soft terrain. Vasuki was already waiting, his head hanging low as he wrapped his claws around Bella's legs and torso, lifting her back off the ground. Within seconds he burst through the canopy and flew off toward their ship, with Pythios hot on his tail.

Malkia whirled around and raced out of the safety of the forest, sprinting toward the Elven ship. As she whipped around the side of it, she slid to a stop, facing three tall male Elvens. They peered down at her, with their hands clasped in front of them, unblinking as they regarded her with disdain.

"We were expecting you," the middle Elven said. As one they stepped back, revealing an opened door to the vessel. "Remove all weapons and allow us to inject our serum to block your abilities."

She held up her hand. "I've already removed my weapons, but my abilities won't be taken from me."

The middle Elven shook his head, his milky white irises glaring at her. "This isn't a negotiation. If you want to see your children, you will not decline our requests. It's a temporary displacement and your powers will be returned after you've served our needs."

Malkia sighed and stepped forward, sweeping her hair to the side and revealing the flesh of her neck. "If you're intent on killing me, nothing will stop my allies from invading this area and slaughtering everyone."

The Elven ignored her warning, pricking her with the needle and pressing the button to release the liquid inside. The serum slid into her vein and she sagged against the vessel as her world tumbled to the side. The other two Elvens wrapped their arms around her waist and lifted her into the ship, dragging her down the corridor as she heard the click of the door close and secure behind her.

FORTY-TWO

The Elven Scrolls

HER HEAD RESTED against the back of the couch that the Elvens had dumped her on. She struggled to keep her eyes open, forcing them to search the nearly bare room as the three Elvens whispered on the other side, occasionally throwing a look her way.

There was a round table across from her, with three wooden chairs around it. A mirror was embedded into the wall near her, along with a credenza below it. It held a basket of fruits that only grew on Theia's trees. She noted nothing else, and she wondered what they intended to do with her, as the whispers turned into an argument.

"*Stop*," a voice bellowed from the doorway.

Malkia shot up, her head swimming with a fog as she twisted to see Dasco staring over at her. He threw the three Elvens a frosty glare. They quickly stood in a line, their pale lips settling into frowns as they waited for instruction.

"I see our guest has arrived," his voice grated on her nerves, reminding her of the moments she was imprisoned by the monster. He stepped toward her, choosing to stand over her instead of taking a seat. "I'm allowing you to continue to breathe, as your child won't accept any nourishment from my people. As before, you're only a means to an end. I will bring you with me on our voyage and while we are placed in stasis, you'll continue to feed and raise your child until he has reached the age of five. This will be done under the watchful eyes of my loyal servants. At that time, I will be awakened and I'll end your life." He chuckled, waiting for her to have a reaction. When she remained still and unmoved by his words, his smile melted into a frown. "At least I'm allowing you to have five more years of life. For that I should be thanked."

Malkia rolled her eyes. "Do what you need to do, but bring my children to me."

He threw his head back in a roar of laughter. Stepping toward her, he leaned over and whispered in her ear. "Only your infant will see you. The other two will enter stasis with the rest of my crew, and you'll be unable to reach them while you're on board my ship, as I would be a fool to give you full access to your offspring." He straightened his posture, a sly grin rising on his lips. "Until we meet again, Malkia." He pivoted on his heel and left the room without another word.

The three Elvens hurried after Dasco, leaving her alone in the room. Her eyes flashed around, ensuring no one was watching and she reached out to Mataya. The vision of her sister burst in front of her and Malkia leaned forward, seeing that they were in another area then the last time she had spoken with them.

"Mataya," she whispered, her head swiveling to look at the mirror as a sparkle of light caught her eye.

Her sister's hazel eyes were wide and her breathing rapid. "Malkia," she choked out, attempting to catch her breath. "We have Landon and Esta, but Dasco knows we're here. I can come to you and bring them all with me."

"No," Malkia objected, narrowing her eyes at the mirror and

realizing they were watching her on the other side. "You're on your own. They're watching me and most likely planned for me to reach out to you. Whatever you do, don't allow them to capture you and the children."

Her connection fizzled and she sank back in the couch, a frosty glare scrunching up her face. A moment later, she could hear the wails of Zeke as they approached the room. She bounded from her seat, tapping her foot on the ground, impatient to see her baby's face again.

The door slid open and Zeke instantly calmed, his bloodshot eyes rolling in her direction as he sniffled. The female Elven thrust him out to Malkia and bowed as soon as she was free of the child. The poor lady appeared frazzled and exhausted. Bowing twice more, she raced from the room, leaving Malkia alone with Zeke.

He nuzzled her chest, searching for his food. She raised her shirt and he latched on immediately, suckling and closing his eyes as he hiccupped from his emotional frenzy over the past few hours. Malkia breathed easy, relaxing into the cushions of the couch as she leaned against the armrest and gazed down at her child.

As her thoughts became more rational, she began to piece together her circumstances. Dasco knew she would still be able to channel her powers. Did he do that on purpose? Had she placed her family in more danger than they already were? His last words ground incessantly through her mind. He had wanted her to know she wouldn't have a chance to see her other children again. If he already knew they had escaped, what was he planning? Especially since he knew she would attempt to find Esta and Landon.

A sudden sapphire light swept out from Zeke and her gaze snapped down to him. Raising him up, she planted a kiss on his nose and set him down on the other side to resume eating. His light filled the room and eased her anxiety. Their connection enabled her to function as if her powers were still intact. She would just have to create a solid barricade that the Elvens couldn't penetrate.

After Zeke had finished his meal, he snuggled in close to her and fell fast asleep. She chuckled to herself, running her thumb across his smooth and perfect cheek.

The door slid open and Dasco entered. Her smile melted. "You said he could stay with me. And I thought that was the last I would see of you for five years."

"Change of plans," Dasco hissed, waving his hand at the female Elven cowering behind him. "Take the child."

The Eleven rushed in and swept Zeke from Malkia's arms, departing from the room before she had a chance to object. She glared at Dasco, rising from her seat and stalked toward him. "*Bring him back, right now.*"

Dasco held out his hand and snapped his fingers, rendering her incapacitated. "I have to thank you, Malkia. When Justin was able to retrieve all the scrolls from your hideout on Esaki and arranged for my assistant to pick them up, I had no idea the treasures I would find in that mess. And when he also stole the ones from your ship, I was doubly pleased by the precious assets that were contained in their words."

A grunt escaped her lips and she wiggled her fingers, pushing against the incantation immobilizing her. Dasco snickered, relishing in her impotence as he sauntered around her.

"Yes, your friend turned to our side right after the battle on Thalia ended. He was through with your rule." Dasco's fingers tapped against his lips as they curved into a sly smile. "His words were harsher than that, but why bring up such nasty comments while we're having such a great conversation?"

Exhaustion spread numbly through Malkia's limbs and she paused in her attempts to free herself, realizing the more she fought the worse her situation became. Another Elven pranced into the room, raising his brows toward her as he frisked his way past her. He stopped in front of Dasco and whispered in the leader's ear.

"*Ah, yes,*" Dasco exclaimed, his smile widening. He patted the eccentric Elven on the shoulder. "Good work, Sully. How soon can we leave?"

"We are gathering up the items from the mountain and once they're loaded, we will set course for the next location," Sully boasted, lifting an eyebrow as his gaze strayed over to Malkia. "What should we do with the mother and sister?"

"Hang them," Dasco ordered, waving his hand to dismiss the Elven. "I don't need any more mouths to feed."

Malkia squirmed against her magical binding, terror exploding within every cell in her body. A spark of a flame was igniting quickly within her heart. Her fingers twitched and she circled her wrist, invoking her light to dissolve her bonds. It flickered, but the serum was stifling its expansion. Without thinking, a groan rumbled up her throat and Dasco's eyes flashed over to meet hers.

"Nice try," he chuckled, holding one palm outward, while the other circled it. She twirled around in place and flew into the corner of the other room, with her face pressed against the wall. "Stay there, my dear. I'll have the nurse return soon with your child, as the only reason you're alive is to sustain that child's life."

She heard the door slide shut and a moment later, her body relaxed and she was released from her invisible bindings. Twisting around, she reached out to her sister, pushing against another magical barrier and seeing it flex and spring back in her mind's eye without leaving a trace of cracking. Pressing again, her mind snapped as a black fog swirled into her thoughts and dragged her down into an abyss.

FORTY-THREE

Sapphire Light

A CRY WOKE her from her slumber. Malkia blinked, staring up at the pure white ceiling, with the fluorescent lights shining down on her. Sitting up, she sagged against the wall, her eyes darting around and searching her memory for a reminder of why she was in here. As she recalled her last moments, a sob rose up her throat and she slammed her eyes shut, screaming out into the room.

The door slid open and the frightened female Elven gingerly stepped in, with a wailing Zeke cradled in her arms. She frantically searched the room, relief rushing across her features as she noticed Malkia curled in the corner. "He's hungry," she whispered. Her chin quivered as she glanced down at Zeke.

Malkia jumped up from the ground and stalked over to the Elven. Smiling down at her child, he cooed as she snuggled him into her chest. Turning her back on the Elven, she lifted her shirt and gave her baby his nourishment.

"I'm—" the Elven stammered and Malkia swiveled her head to face her. A crimson heat stained her cheeks and suddenly Malkia knew this one was not her enemy, recognizing her as one of the Elvens who greeted her back at the meadow.

"I'll only be a few minutes, as he eats quickly," Malkia told her, giving a slight nod. "You can wait in here or if you're not allowed, I can call for you when he's finished."

The elven nodded, as fear flashed within her eyes. "I will remain here until he's finished. Dasco has ordered that you're never to be alone during the child's feedings."

"As you wish," Malkia muttered, nodding toward the couch. "You may sit with me, if you like. I don't bite."

"Your sister and mother are alive," the elven whispered, bowing her head to hide the movement of her mouth. "They managed to escape when my people were hauling them off the ship."

"My daughter too?" Malkia asked, kissing Zeke on the top of his head.

The elven's head shook. "No, they're being prepared for stasis. We are closing in on the last location that contain the items needed for the journey, and Dasco wants everyone who will be entering stasis ready for that moment."

Malkia puffed out her cheeks and released an exaggerated breath, focusing on the details of Zeke's chubby face. A tear slid down her cheek, landing on his hand. Without warning, his sapphire light burst from his body and enveloped Malkia within it. Opening his eyes, he stared up at her, continuing to nurse while spreading his light to enrobe the elven as well.

Rising from her perch, she shifted him to her other breast and stared at the Elven. "What is your name?"

The elven's gaze was wandering the room, rising to the ceiling to watch the flow of Zeke's light. "My name's Tess," she murmured, raising her prayer hands to her lips. "What is this?"

"Where's Dasco?" Malkia asked, ignoring Tess's last question.

"What will you do?" Tess locked eyes with Malkia.

"Whatever it takes to free us from this captivity. I won't allow him to reach the heavens," Malkia whispered, stepping closer to Tess. "Will you help me?"

Tess gulped in a mouthful of air, terror dancing across her face. "What do you need me to do?"

"Find my children," she replied, looking over Tess's shoulder and into the corridor behind the elven. "Take them to Velem and wait for me."

"Velem is preparing the children for stasis," Tess told her, shaking her head. "And Dasco will be close. He never allows the children to be alone for long."

Malkia nodded, her eyes flashing about as she thought of a new plan. "Do you know if any of my other people are following us?"

"Two small dragons were seen several times, even though the fighters have chased them off. But I don't know if they're still out there." Tess glanced behind her. Her hands trembled and she clasped them together to hide the shaking.

Ustarum? Malkia reached out with her mind, but saw her thoughts collide with another magical barrier. She groaned and pressed against it, closing her eyes to focus. Wrapping Zeke's sapphire light around it, she tightened her grip, crushing it with everything she could muster. The barrier exploded within her mind and she reached out to Ustarum again. *Are you there?*

Yes! Ustarum replied. *We have the ship in range of our radars and we aren't letting Dasco take you away. He thinks he won, but your sister was able to place a tracker within a wall of the vessel.*

He's taken my abilities with one of his blasted serums, Malkia told him, focusing her eyes on Tess again. *Zeke's powers are connected with me while he nurses, enabling me to reach out to you. Landon and Esta are being prepared for stasis, so I'll do what I can on my end to halt their progression. When we land, which we'll be doing soon, make your move quickly. This is their last stop before departing Theia.*

We will stop him, Malkia. Whatever it takes, Ustarum replied. *Just take care of yourself and those children.*

Rolling her shoulders back to release the tension, Malkia lifted Zeke up to her shoulder and straightened out her shirt. "When we land, please find a way to open this door for me. Take all three of my children out of the ship, without being seen and find my people. They will protect you and shouldn't be far off from where they set the ship. Can you do this for me?"

"I'll do my best," Tess replied, cradling Zeke within her arms. "Velem will be anxious to continue his process for stasis, as his own family will be in jeopardy if Dasco suspects his delays."

"I understand." Malkia raked her fingers through her messy locks. "But I know Hope and her followers desire their release as well. Gather some others whom you know will assist in the escape and do what it takes to free as many as possible. This is our last chance."

Tess nodded and bowed, stepping backward into the corridor. Her hand pressed against the wall next to the door and it slid closed, leaving Malkia alone once again. Her eyes flashed over to the mirror and waited for any commotion of flickers of light, but none came.

Zeke's light still shone within her. Settling onto the couch, she pushed past the mental barrier with ease, zeroing in on the two young dragons. *Vasuki. Pythios. Where are you?*

Not far from the Elven ship, Vasuki replied. *Pythios is trailing a bit behind, giving the Elvens the impression that I'm alone.*

We will be landing soon. Malkia leaned over and rested her forehead against her knees. If anyone was watching her, they would believe she was weary, grief-stricken, or ill and leave her be. *I've instructed one of the Elvens to free as many others as she can, including my children. If you see them escaping, please do what you can to hide them. If you don't see them, that means they were either caught or she turned on me. If that happens, I'll find a way to my children and bring them to you.*

We will wait and let you know where we are hiding, once we arrive, Vasuki told her.

She froze, hearing the door slide open. Lifting her head, she twisted and battled the urge to not the throttle the woman standing in the corridor. Bitterness filled her heart as she slowly rose from her seat, losing all thoughts of the dragons and her calvary riding fiercely to save her.

FORTY-FOUR
Working with the Enemy

"*YOU HAVE A lot of nerve*," she hissed, her stomach churning as her lips drew back into a snarl. Taking a step toward her visitor, she narrowed her eyes in an expression of icy disdain.

"What if I told you, I'm here to help you escape," Kelsey replied, crossing over the threshold, unfazed by Malkia's daggered eyes.

Malkia chuckled and rolled her eyes. "Your arrogance never ceases to amaze me. Let's go outside and finish this once and for all."

This time Kelsey laughed, shooting Malkia a sideways glance. "You don't scare me. In fact, I find your threats ridiculous."

"When I melted your brother's skin right off his bones, I don't think he was laughing at my threats," Malkia snapped, whirling around to face the woman.

"Listen, I forgive you for slaughtering my entire family," Kelsey replied, not flinching at the details of her brother's death. "I've grown weary of this entire conflict. I was only in it for ownership of Enyo, not a planet that may or may not possess the secret to eternal life."

She stepped around to the back of the couch, entwining her fingers behind her back. A devilish grin rose on her lips. "My Mamu was overreaching and your father was a greedy tyrant, just like you claimed. My brother was a lap dog, always jumping at the chance to do your father's bidding. I want out. I never wanted to go to this Blue Planet and now Dasco is insisting I prepare for stasis. If I assist you in ending this absurd battle, will you allow me to leave for Enyo?"

"What if they're listening to us?" Malkia asked, jabbing her thumb toward the mirror.

"No one's there." Kelsey settled onto one of the wooden chairs. "It was me for a while, and then Dasco became restless and demanded we begin preparations." She crossed her leg over her opposite knee, tilting her head to peer up at Malkia. "I've never cared for any of this." She waved her hand out toward the door. "I've been dragged around from moon to moon, trailing you and your family, and committing crimes that even sicken me. I'm never able to stop and enjoy my damn life for five seconds, before we're on to the next fight. It's just me now. Please let me leave with you. We can end this together."

Malkia sighed and sat on the couch, sweeping her grimy hair out of her face. "What are you thinking?"

A grin twitched at the corners of Kelsey's mouth and she leaned forward, resting her elbows on her knee. "When we land, I let you out of this room and you take me with you to safety."

"First, I need my children," Malkia reminded her.

Kelsey rolled her eyes. "We can't save everyone."

Malkia snorted and she threw Kelsey a dirty look. "Are you serious?" she snapped, balling her hands to fists.

A chuckle burst from Kelsey's lips and she shook her head. "No, but it was worth the look on your face." She chuckled to herself, another sound that grated on Malkia's nerves. "If we must save the children, I'll come for you right before we land and we'll sneak up to them. It will be easy."

"Nothing on this journey has been easy, but I'll take your word for it," Malkia muttered, gritting her teeth. "How long until we land?"

"Soon," Kelsey said, jumping up from her chair. "I'll return once I know the status."

Malkia watched her leave, before reaching out to Ustarum. *My old friend, Kelsey was just here and she says she'll assist in my escape. Based on our pasts, I'm wary of her true intentions, but if it allows me to really leave the confines of this room, I'll take it.*

Who's Kelsey? Ustarum replied.

I knew her on Esaki, but she was really one of Ginny's grandchildren. Taking me in for her Mamu to use and abuse. But she's alone now and claims she never wanted to be here in the first place. Her reasons are purely selfish, but if it helps us, then that's all I care about. Malkia glanced over at the mirror, but still couldn't see the movement and light she'd seen before. *It could be trap, but I have to take the chance. All I can ask is for all of you to be prepared.*

We're keeping our distance, but—, Ustarum's voice drifted away and Malkia felt the effects of the serum once again. Zeke's light had dissipated completely.

She closed her eyes and leaned against the back cushion, allowing herself to rest. It only felt like minutes, when the door slid open again and Kelsey strolled inside the room as Malkia's eyes fluttered open and focused on her visitor.

"Is it time?" she asked, a yawn overtaking her face.

"Yes, sleepy head. You can rest when you're dead, so rise and shine, baby." Kelsey laughed, twirling around and throwing out her arms to the sides, wiggling her fingers as she grinned over at Malkia. *"Let's move."*

Malkia peeled herself off the couch, brushing past the enraptured woman and peeked into the corridor. Seeing that it was clear, she stepped out and waited for Kelsey to lead the way.

Like a pouncing kitten, Kelsey burst through the doorway, winking as she landed gracefully. Malkia suppressed a smile, but was actually enjoying this side of her old friend. Not that she would ever trust her, but a little bit of fun wouldn't hurt her.

Following Kelsey down the hallway, she grinned as her companion crept along as if they were within the shelter of the vegetation. Crouching down low, she held her fingers up as if she was holding one of the Artemisian's weapons and joined in. If anyone were watching, she was positive they were shaking their heads and asking themselves why they would be afraid of such imbeciles. Kelsey had her brilliant moments, and this was one of them.

Malkia could feel the ship slow and begin its descent, settling onto the terrain below. Tugging her inside a darkened room, Kelsey pressed her finger to her lips, crouching in the shadows and beckoning for Malkia to follow her lead. Seconds later, a dozen or more Elvens swept past the doorway, racing for the exit to retrieve whatever was hidden in the city nearby.

"More lap dogs," Kelsey jested, rolling her eyes. "I'm surrounded by them." She peered into the corridor and waved her hand at Malkia. "Let's go."

Up a flight of stairs and dodging down a few more corridors, Malkia finally walked into the room where her children were sitting. Esta bounded from her chair, followed by Landon. Both sets of arms wrapped around her and she embraced them tightly, planting a kiss on both their foreheads. Velem had risen from his chair, his eyes weary and distraught. Handing Zeke over to her, he waved his arm and five other Elvens slipped out from behind a bed, stepping cautiously toward them.

"This is my family," Velem told her. "Take them with you, please."

"You're all coming with me," Malkia ordered, bundling Zeke into a warm blanket and slinging his pack over her shoulder. "Don't argue. There's nothing left for you here."

"Hope is still imprisoned," Velem argued, shaking his head. He shifted his family in front of him and pressed them out of the door. "Take them with you. I'll find Hope and the others and join you outside."

Malkia groaned. "I'll be returning," she muttered, shooing her kids from the room and following after them. "If I don't see you soon, I'm coming back."

He nodded and sprinted in the opposite direction. Kelsey's patience had been depleted, yanking on the Elvens' arms and forcing them to follow her.

"Hold onto my pockets," Malkia whispered to Landon and Esta. "If anyone attempts to stop us, take Zeke and run for the exit. Do you understand?"

The two children nodded their heads, terror flashing in their eyes. She inhaled a long breath and rushed down the hallway with her children latched onto her, following the others to freedom.

FORTY-FIVE
The Dark Warlock

THE TREE'S SHADOWS allowed Malkia and the others to hide from the Elvens pursuing them. Kelsey kicked at the dirt in front of her, her eyes narrowing at Malkia as they crouched behind a thicket of brush. Ignoring the woman, Malkia peered around the tree trunk she was pressed against and scanned the area for her dragons.

"Even if this turns into a fight, I'm not joining," Kelsey grumbled, rolling a small stone in between her thumb and finger.

"I'm not asking you to join," Malkia snapped, glaring at her old friend. "You held up your end of the deal and I'll hold up mine, as long as we all survive."

"Exactly." Kelsey tossed the stone into the brush across from them, cringing when it struck another boulder, pinging loudly between the other rocks. "You've given me no choice, but to fight."

Malkia peered down at Zeke who slept calmly against her chest, oblivious to the battle hanging over their heads. Dasco's shrill voice echoed in her ears as she listened to him threaten his people. She focused on the Elven leader, and she silently urged her powers to return to her soon as she imagined all the ways she would exterminate that barbarian.

"*Daddy*," Landon suddenly whispered, tapping Malkia on the back.

"I see him."

"Where?" Malkia asked, straining her eyes to see through the darkness. Her gaze darted around the structures of the ancient city that was nestled on the other side of the Elven vessel.

"Not that way," Landon replied, tugging at her arm. "He's inside the trees with us."

Sighing with relief, Malkia twisted to stare into the canopy and spotted the Apollo's large frame crouching low, pressed against a tree trunk. Sneaking to the next tree, he shifted slowly toward them. Right behind him were Jordan and Damon. "Finally," she breathed, beckoning for the others. "I'll lead you to my ship, but Kelsey you'll remain either with me or someone else who can make sure you won't steal my vessel."

"Wouldn't have it any other way," Kelsey replied, pressing her fingers to her lips and blowing Malkia a kiss. "Looks like we'll be joined at the hip for a little while longer."

"We have to rescue Hope." Malkia's eyes flashed back to the ship. "And Velem."

Damon swooped her into an embrace, crushing Zeke in between them as the infant's eyes flew open. Patting the startled child on the back, Malkia pressed her lips to Damon's. "Thank you."

"If you thought I was just going to leave my entire family in the hands of Dasco, you were sadly mistaken," Damon whispered in her ear. Landon wrapped his arms around his father's waist, squeezing him tightly. "Follow me," he instructed, patting his son's shoulder. "Mataya and Alexa will watch the children, while we finish this."

Leaving her children behind again brought a new rush of dread to Malkia's heart. She glanced back at their ship. It didn't feel right, but if she couldn't halt Dasco's journey to the Blue Planet, then this entire crusade would be for nothing. And Hope needed them. She wouldn't quit now, especially when she was so close to the finish line.

Tearing her eyes from the vessel, she sprinted after the others, eager to join the entire army that was waiting for them in the forest. The entire Artemisian clan had arrived, along with the handful of her Esakian friends and Angels. The flock of Elvens remained back at the ships, so they weren't confused with the enemy. Kelsey skipped along beside her, giving the impression that she was enjoying the battle more than she wanted to admit.

Pressing forward, Malkia's hand hovered above one of her daggers. She had been grateful when she saw Pythios had saved her weapons belt, including her Artemisian weapon, which was tucked against her lower back. Creeping through the trees, she could see her team ahead, prepared to attack as soon as they received her instructions.

Hope and Velem hadn't been able to escape the Elven vessel, along with several of their allies. Malkia had instructed her soldiers to pay attention to who they were attacking and that their prime objective was to execute Dasco and any of his followers who insisted they would continue with the journey to the Blue Planet.

Sliding into position behind a jagged boulder, she peered around it and noticed that Dasco was no longer in their sight. Swiveling her head, she looked over at Jordan and Apollo. "Where is he?" she mouthed, jabbing her thumb back at the Elven ship.

Jordan shook his head, his voice barely a whisper, "He went back inside the vessel."

Releasing a shaky breath, Malkia shook her head and searched the faces of the Elvens left outside. All of them were strangers to her and seemed to be guarding the entrance to the vessel as they waited for their comrades to return.

"We'll have to draw him out," she whispered over her shoulder at Kelsey and Damon. "He's obviously prepared to sacrifice the ones he left on the outside the ship. But, if he needs the treasures that the others rushed out to retrieve, he will be vigilant in protecting their path. We can go after the ones in the city or slaughter those guarding the vessel and hope he'll send out more for us to execute."

"Or he'll leave and find the Elvens in the city himself," Kelsey muttered. She rolled her eyes to the heavens and shook her head. "It's a good thing you have me with you. He will leave his people in two seconds flat and fly closer to the city. Our best bet is to find what they're searching for, first, and dangle it in front of his beady-eyed face like a worm on the end of a fishing pole."

A laugh escaped Malkia's mouth and she pressed her lips together to halt her bad form. "It's too bad I despise you, Kelsey. We could've been real friends if it weren't for your traitorous tendencies."

Kelsey patted her shoulder. "I'll survive. Let's go find those filthy heathens, so I can leave this miserable planet."

"I'll follow you," Malkia replied, waving at the others.

Damon shook his head. "She's right, but I'm not giving her the pleasure of knowing I think so."

"I heard that," Kelsey muttered, slinking behind another tree and shifting out of sight of the ship.

Malkia shrugged and followed after Kelsey. They hurried down a darkened path, pausing when they reached the city's shadows. Glancing over her shoulder, Malkia could see the others creeping after her, hiding behind broken boulders as they made their way to her position.

"We should split up," Malkia whispered, pointing at the heart of the city. "We don't know what they're searching for, but chances are they already knew exactly where to find it and won't be much longer. If we're lucky, we will catch them on their way back to their ship."

"Let's split into ten groups of five each. The remainder of our people should stay hidden, surrounding the Elven ship," Damon suggested, his breath hot against her cheek.

"Stop delaying," Kelsey grumbled. Her eyes flashed down the roadway in front of them as irritation puckered up her face. "If we're splitting up, let's do it quickly."

Malkia nodded and pointed at the first five, directing them down another pathway. Within a minute, she had nine search parties disappearing down their designated routes, while the bulk of her group returned to the trees or darkened positions just inside the city. Beckoning at Damon, Kelsey, Koleton, and Apollo, she crept forward, easing alongside the tall building. Peeking around the corner, her ears twitched from the unnerving silence as she paused for a few seconds, allowing her eyesight to adjust to the darkness.

Sprinting down that lane, she could barely hear the others behind her as she pressed her back against the corner of the next building. A crackle of magic splintered out of the roadway ahead and Malkia's breath caught as she crouched to watch the lasers of the Artemisian's ricochet off a distant stone. Whatever the Elvens had in their possession, was enabling them to return to their ship unscathed and was preventing her teams from stopping them.

She encircled her group within her newly returned light. Gripping tightly to the hilt of her dagger, she advanced upon the next building and snuck alongside it, until they reached the next path. Peering around the corner, her focus locked onto the three Elvens creeping backward, while two Angels, Cormac and two Artemisians faced them with their weapons drawn.

This was going to be easier than she'd thought. Malkia grinned back at Damon, jabbing her thumb back toward the roadway. Suddenly, her skull erupted with a raging inner fire, blinding her with a flash of light. She felt her powers snap, and then fade completely. Doubling over, a blackness edged its way across the light, threatening to collapse her consciousness completely. She swiveled her head, catching a blurred expression of horror melt down Damon's features. But he wasn't paying any attention to her. His eyes were glued to something beyond her, but as she twisted her body around, the heated agony exploded through her entire body and she crashed face first into the broken road beneath her. The crack of her jawbone echoed in her ears.

Her hands flew up to her cheek as she shrieked. Rolling to her back, her gaze focused on the stars twinkling above. She furiously blinked, fear clutching her chest as they faded in and out and the blackness chewed at her eyesight.

Someone's hands gripped her shoulders, dragging her away from where she'd fallen. Shaking her head, she blinked several times, willing her eyes to work. After several attempts, her vision returned, and she focused on a stone ceiling. Or was it a wall? Blinking again, she rolled over and glanced around the darkened room. Her eyes fell on a woman's back, who was peering over a ledge, staring out into the blackness. Kelsey had saved her. But where were the others?

Crawling over to Kelsey, she sagged against the broken wall and peered up into a pair of terrified eyes. "Did you see that?" Kelsey asked, her voice trembling.

Malkia shook her head, swallowing the bile that was rising in her throat. She cradled her head between her knees and wiped her thumb across her quivering lower lip, while her other hand urged her light to heal her broken cheek.

"Something else—" Kelsey choked out, squeezing Malkia's knee. "I've never seen anything more dreadful, in my entire life. It sucked away all the magic, your light—" She paused and gulped in a frantic breath. "—and set the Elvens and all the others on that path on fire."

"What?" Malkia's head snapped up, whirling around to face Kelsey. "Cormac? Everyone? What about our team?"

"I don't know," Kelsey stammered, licking her lips as she burst into tears. "It was utter mayhem out there. I saw you fall and suddenly the world around us exploded."

Malkia searched within for her light, but she sensed only a void. The air around them had been emptied of all magic. A chilling shiver ran down her spine and her legs trembled as she pressed herself off the ground.

"We have to go find my people," she whispered, her throat dry with cobwebs.

"Are you crazy?" Kelsey exclaimed, clapping a hand over her mouth. Her eyes flashed over to the broken doorway and she froze. "It will kill us." Her voice was barely a whisper.

"What was it?" Malkia asked, sagging against the wall and rubbing her temples with her fingers.

Kelsey shook her head and swallowed hard. "Maybe a human, but I swear it was larger. It rose out of nowhere, cloaked in a black robe and hovered a few feet off the ground. It radiated a light so intense, but darker than anything I've ever seen, as if a space of nothing surrounded it. As it raised its hands, your light shattered and you suddenly screamed." A sob escaped Kelsey's lips and she pressed her hand against her mouth to smother the noise. "Everything happened so fast. The fire. Your fall. The terrified screams coming from every direction. I just reacted. It was all I could do."

Stepping over to the woman, Malkia wrapped her arms around the woman's trembling shoulders and squeezed her tightly. "A warlock," she whispered in Kelsey's ear. "Maybe. I don't know, but we'll find out soon enough."

Releasing Kelsey, Malkia sank to the floor and searched for her powers once more. This time there was a tiny flicker and she used it to reach out to Mataya. The channel opened easily and her sister stood in the darkened bridge, staring wild-eyed at Malkia.

"What's happened?" Mataya asked, her hands pressing against her cheeks.

"I don't know exactly," Malkia whispered. "My powers are slowly returning, so I don't have much time. Take everyone who remained back at the ships and leave. Go to the island that was near the city with the pyramid and wait for us there."

Mataya opened her mouth to object, but snapped it shut and nodded. "I'll have one of the Elvens take us there. Please reach out soon. Don't leave me wondering if you're dead."

"I'll be in touch as soon as I'm able. Just leave quickly and stay in the ship. If the island is equally dangerous, leave it as well and when I channel you again, I'll find your location." Malkia's hands trembled as she squeezed them into fists. Her sister nodded and the vision fizzled away, taking what was left of her powers with it.

FORTY-SIX

Invasion

COMMOTION OUTSIDE CAUGHT the women's attention. They whirled around to face the opening in the wall. A shadow swept across, followed by several others. Malkia peered through the opening and sighed with relief when her eyes fell on Koleton and Ustarum. She waved her hand and the group paused as Koleton whistled for the ones ahead to stop.

A few moments later, a large crowd had gathered in the nook Kelsey had found. Damon's arms curled around Malkia and his lips pressed against hers. She winced from the pain in her cheek, but her yearning for his embrace kept her smashed against him. She'd been terrified she wouldn't see him again.

Cormac was alive, but one of his legs was charred from the flames. He muffled his cries with his fist as they set him against the far wall and Ustarum and Alyssa began a healing incantation, and the others caught their breath.

"Does anyone know what happened?" Malkia asked, her hand resting against her cheek. She twisted around to look at all the weary and frightened faces as some nodded, while others shook their heads.

"You didn't see him rise from the ground," Koleton muttered. The edges of his beard were burnt and his hair was filled with gray speckles of ash. "The moment you turned to look at us, he rose up from the soil and hovered above the Elvens who were attempting to escape our people. Cormac is lucky, as is Gentry." He jabbed his thumb over at the Angel sagging against another wall, her snow-white hair half gone on one side from the same flames that had claimed the lives of the others. "Everyone else on that roadway was burned to a crisp."

"Where did this warlock disappear to?" Malkia sank down to the hard floor in front of Koleton.

"Just like he appeared, he vanished before our eyes," Apollo told her, pausing midstride right behind Koleton. "Kelsey was dragging you away, and Koleton and Damon had been blown back several feet. I went to their aid, believing you would be easy to find. But Kelsey dragged you farther than we thought she would. You're nearly three blocks away from the blast."

Kelsey's eyes widened. "I didn't realize I had traveled that far," she breathed, her brows rising in confusion.

"Adrenaline does funny things to a person's strength and mind," Jordan answered, patting Kelsey on the shoulder. His gaze shifted around the room as he stepped forward into the center of the room. "Whatever Dasco was after has now been turned to dust. I'm surprised he didn't send in more of his warriors to find out why there was an explosion, but there's still time. When we passed the outer edges of the city, I caught sight of his ship, which means he hasn't abandoned his mission. I say we launch an attack on him and what remains of his people and finish this now."

A garish chuckle echoed from the opening in the wall and everyone whirled around to see who it was. A dark figure hovered just inside the room, its face covered by a hood, surrounded by an auric black void.

"Foolish people." Whatever it was, the low voice sounded like it belonged to a male. "Don't you know you've all been sent on a wild spawn hunt?"

Malkia's eyes narrowed, unafraid of this new foe, as she pressed up from the ground and shifted through the crowd, pausing when she was a few feet away from the stranger. "What do you know of our mission?"

"None of it matters," he muttered, a growl rumbling up his throat as he waved a dismissive hand at her. "I've only come to warn you. Attempt to steal my belongings again and I'll destroy all life in this vicinity." He lifted his head slightly, revealing a full, black beard. "This is my home, and everything contained within its boundaries belongs to me. Leave and never return." Without waiting for a reply, he swept out of the room and disappeared in a flash of smoke.

Malkia stood still, breathing heavily as she brushed her palms together, searching her memory for any stories from her childhood that would explain the darkened stranger. A hand rested on her shoulder and she turned her head to meet her mother's hazel eyes.

"He's a descendant of the Creators." She swallowed with difficulty as her gaze flashed over to where he'd stood. "Just like you, and from what I'm gathering, Damon as well. We all believed this man perished centuries ago, but it explains a lot that he's remained hidden on Theia. His powers are far superior than most of ours." She nodded her head back toward the others, her voice barely a whisper. "But the powers that were invoked within your body when you were a fetus, give you an advantage over him."

"I don't intend to fight him," Malkia replied. She patted her mom's hand that remained on her shoulder and twisted around to face the others. "Whatever Dasco was after, it's safe in the hands of that man.

He's not our enemy, but he's not our ally either. We will retreat from the city and find a way into the Elven ship. Jordan is right—it's time to end this."

The entire group nodded in unison, anxious to leave their hideout and put some distance between them and the stranger. Malkia assisted Cormac to his feet, his leg nearly healed. One by one, they crept from the building, hurrying toward the safety of the forest and their comrades.

Crouched just inside the city, Malkia watched as Apollo and another Artemisian hurried across the small section of tall grass, holding onto Cormac's large frame. As much as he wanted to fight, he would be sitting out this battle.

Dasco was standing just inside the lower doorway of the ship, speaking to one of his people. He waved his hand toward the buildings as a crimson heat swept up his pale neck and crawled across his cheeks. His voice grew louder, but Malkia could still not make out what he was saying. Closing her eyes, she pressed past their magical barrier and as it shattered, she heard Dasco's words loud and clear.

"…it again, or I'll rip your limbs from your body," he screamed, his breath raspy from yelling. "You've sent two groups into that city and both have failed to return. Give me results or die alongside the humans."

"Yes, sir," the other Elven stammered.

Snapping her eyes open, she focused on Dasco. Fear rushed across her face, like frigid water, as she realized he would retreat back into the safety of the ship again. This was their chance to invade.

Holding her hands, palms out, before her, she nodded at Ustarum and Alyssa. "We need to break down their defenses now, and stop that door from closing." Her light began to glow, as the stranger in black had released his hold on her powers as soon as he departed. When this was all said and done, she would return to him and find out how he disabled them, and how she could stop others from doing it in the future. She'd grown weary of being helpless and unprotected.

Ustarum and Alyssa stepped up next to her, placing Malkia in the middle. The remainder of the group either shuffled back several feet or moved off to either side of the warlocks, giving them plenty of space. Her eyes fell on Apollo and a soft smile rose on her lips, noticing he was calling his own Demi-God powers from the safety of the trees.

Drawing magic from the air around her, Malkia built up the energy within her body, pressing it down her arms and concentrating on the invisible barricade that protected the Elven ship. "On the count of three," she said, peering over at her mother who nodded back. "One… two… three."

Their combined light barreled through the tall grass and swept across the barrier, illuminating it against the night sky. Apollo's energy merged with theirs. Malkia closed her eyes, gripping the barrier with her mind and crushing it with a deep and unused force. The barricade flexed and held, rebounding against their energy, but fizzling in the same second. With another push, it finally crumbled. Without waiting for any instructions the entire group of warriors erupted into action, sprinting toward the surprised Elvens.

The twelve Elvens that had been guarding the ship stumbled back toward Dasco's position, but he was already closing the door. Koleton slung a boulder the size of his head, and it flew through the air, colliding violently with the metal door, leaving a gaping hole in its wake. Several of the Elvens scrambled through the hole, while the remainder drew their weapons and shot out as many arrows as they could, before they were over ran by the barreling Artemisians who led the invasion.

Malkia leapt over the fight, cringing at the bloodshed as the Artemisians tore apart the Elven bodies. They never had a chance. Bounding through the hole in the ship, she could hear the heavy breathing of the others right behind her as they raced down the corridors, each taking a different path.

Flying up the nearest staircase, Malkia rushed toward the area she believed Hope was being held, but when she attempted to open the door, a siren blared from the ceiling, flashing red lights in every direction. Cursing under her breath, she used her light to melt away the hand pad, forcing the door to open and revealing an empty room.

Damon pounded on another door nearby that finally slid open. Just like hers, no one was inside. "We need to find the bridge," she shouted over the siren, drawing a few deep breaths to calm her pounding heart. "Do you remember where it is?"

He nodded, leaning over and pressing his palms into his knees to catch his breath. "I think so, but this vessel is a maze. Give me a minute to think."

She whirled around and sprinted to the end of the corridor, looking both ways and seeing none of her people. Twisting to face Damon, she pointed to the right and he nodded as he straightened and hurried after her.

"This floor is quiet," she whispered in his ear as the sirens finally silenced. Chewing on her bottom lip, she tiptoed to the next door, forcing it open like the last one. Nothing. "It's possible Dasco had everyone ready for stasis. He might have even begun the process, thinking he would be long gone from Theia by now." She blinked several times, searching through her memories for the area where her children had been held. Everyone's medical care began there, but where did they go after that was complete? Locking eyes with Damon, she slowly shook her head. "It has to be another—."

An explosion shook the vessel, sending Malkia flying into the wall next to her. She watched in slow motion as Damon struck his head against the same wall, his eyes glazing as he fell to the floor. Screams echoed from a level above them and Malkia's head snapped up to look, just as smoke billowed from a vent in the ceiling.

Curling her arm around Damon's torso, she heaved him up and dragged him to the closest staircase. She encircled them with her light, flying up the stairs and through the doorway of the next floor. Koleton and Thora were huddled together a few feet down the hallway, their eyes darting down the corridor across from them. Malkia's gaze fell on an Artemisian body lying farther down the hallway, burnt to a crisp with wisps of smoke floating from his charred remains.

Setting Damon down next to Koleton, she noticed his lame arm, held protectively against his belly. She knelt in front of both the men, giving them each a small amount of her healing light. But before she could give them much, another explosion shuddered to her left and she enrobed all four within her light. She counted silently, waiting for the shockwaves to pass around them.

"You should go. Hope and your doctor, along with several others are being detained on the other side of the ship," Koleton yelled, pushing her away and pointing at Thora. "She's fine. I'll drag Damon out of the ship and find a place to hide until this is over."

Thora nodded at Malkia and patted Koleton on the head as she rose.

He glared up at her, sliding his functioning arm around Damon and dragging him toward the exit. Racing behind Thora, Malkia coughed several times as the smoke invaded her lungs. As they rushed farther into the thick smoke, she encircled them both within her light again. Not far ahead they ran into a throng of bodies, lining the floors in front of them.

"Hold on to me," she muttered to Thora.

The angel wrapped her arms around Malkia as they rose above the ground and shot over her deceased enemies, intermingled with several of her comrades. Thora pressed her face against Malkia's shoulder. Her sobs shook her body and she fought to stay in control as faces of her loved ones swept beneath them.

Reaching the end of the corridor, Malkia had counted twenty bodies, but only nine of them had been her people. *Nine too many*, she thought, disgusted that it had to come to this in the first place.

Leading the way, once more, Thora rushed down the corridor, avoiding the ones with too much smoke and broken walls. She finally skidded to a halt in front of gaping hole and pointed inside, pressing her back against the metal.

"Dasco and his servants dragged Hope and the others this way," she whispered, drawing her bow and arrow in front of her. "It's possible they escaped to another floor, but this area is where the statis pods are located."

Malkia stepped around the angel and peered inside the smoky room. One of the explosions had come from here. She examined the visible area, but the room was large and seemed to stretch far beyond her sight. Creeping through the hole, she noticed the floor was made of iron grates and just within her view was a railing. Another few steps forward and she peered into a vast warehouse, filled with pods from floor to ceiling. Knowing the ship wasn't that large and they were only in the middle of the vessel, she knew it couldn't extend too far. But the fact that the Elvens in which she placed her trust, were flying around with these pods made her shiver with sudden indignation. What was Hope planning?

"Maybe Hope didn't know this was here." Thora curled her hand around Malkia's elbow.

She glanced down at the Angel and shook her head. "I doubt that. But I'm not going to hang her yet. I'll give her a chance to explain."

A loud clang echoed from her right and Malkia whipped around to find the source of the noise. Rashuta stumbled into sight, clutching his swollen and charred side of his face. Rushing forward, Malkia held the Artemisian upright, before slowly lowering him to the floor.

Her eyes widened as she made sense of what she saw. Below, five Elvens had cornered Chantum, while several Artemisians and Angels were crouched farther down the length of the stasis chamber, hiding from the arrows and lasers of Dasco's warriors. Jayde and Kelsey stood back to back, circled by at least eight hovering Elvens. Both sides had their daggers and swords drawn, pointed at one another.

Malkia's gaze swept to Thora who was watching the events unfold beneath them. The Angel's eyes were narrowed and her bronze cheeks had a tint of crimson rising in them. "Where did all these Elvens come from?" Thora asked, turning to face Malkia and Rashuta.

"Many of Hope's followers turned on her," Rashuta managed to choke out. "She's—" He coughed, covering his mouth with his fist as he doubled over in pain. After a moment, he pointed. "Dasco dragged her down that way, with a small army covering him. If there are any

Elvens alive who still follow her, they would have escaped by now."

"I have to go help Jayde and Kelsey," Malkia said, gripping Thora's wrist. "Will you help Chantum and those Artemisians? I'll meet you down in that area after we're done."

Thora didn't reply, but bounded over the railing, landing on the metal floor below like a ravenous panther stalking her prey. She leapt through the air and sank her daggers into the first Elven in the crowd that surrounded Chantum.

Malkia lowered herself into the battle below and snatched the Artemisian laser weapon from her belt, aiming it at the nearest Elven. Her target fell with a thud, followed by the next two, just as she reached Jayde and Kelsey. Yanking her daggers free, she sliced through the next two Elvens, kicking one of them away as he fell toward her.

"Kill them all," she hissed at the women, gritting her teeth as an arrow narrowly missed her arm. She held out her palm and shot a wave of light at three Elvens with their bows. It sent them flying into a cluster of pods, shattering both bodies and glass.

Flipping backward through the air, she landed on the other side of the Elvens and drew out her daggers once again, deflecting an arrow before it found its mark in her chest. Malkia flicked her wrist, sending her dagger through the air and pierced the heart of a female Elven. The female winced and stumbled backward, locking eyes with Malkia, before tipping to the side and striking her head against the hard floor.

Another Elven flung himself at Malkia, knocking her off her feet. Her knees crunched beneath her and she cursed out loud, just as an arm curled around her neck and squeezed her esophagus. She sputtered, reaching back and striking her captor in the jaw with her fist. It barely fazed him as he grunted and tightened his hold on her. Rolling to the side, she tossed herself and the Elven, smashing his head against the ground. He loosened his hold on her and she flipped over on her stomach, rolling across the floor to escape him.

Yanking out her Artemisian weapon again, she aimed it at his forehead and ended his life in one shot. She sagged against the railing behind her, catching her breath as she examined the fiasco before her.

Thora had slaughtered all the Elvens who had cornered Chantum and they were off battling the ones down the aisle, along with the Artemisians. She caught sight of Maltese, taking two of the Elven's lives with a swoop of his sword. Her head tilted upward and caught sight of Rashuta's arm dangling over the railing.

"*Damn it*," she exclaimed, bounding up from her position and taking flight.

Landing next to him, she knelt and rolled him onto his back. His breath was raspy and his olive green skin had paled to a soft gray. She groaned, pressing down on his chest with her palms, and filtering her light into his body, pleading with the spirits of Theia to heal him.

"Stop," he whispered, gripping her hand. "I'll survive, but if you don't prevent Dasco's escape, we'll just be flying off to another battle." He lifted his head slightly, giving her a pointed stare with his crimson reptilian eyes. "You've given me enough. Go find that barbarian."

She nodded and jumped to her feet, the line between her eyes deepening. Finding Thora or anyone in the smoke-wreathed melee below was nearly impossible. Leaping over the railing, she floated just above the ground as she examined the chaos in every direction. Landing, she sprinted down the aisle between the rows of pods. Thora must have seen her, because she and Chantum flanked her within seconds.

A wall and another door came into view, and she skidded to a halt. This end of the stasis chamber was eerily silent.

"It's an escape vessel," Chantum breathed, whirling around and tilting his head to examine the area for any weaknesses.

"Where?" Malkia asked. She scratched her neck, irritation and frustration clouding her judgement.

"On the other side of that door," Thora told her, pointing as she sauntered toward it. "But they haven't departed."

Chantum's head snapped back to eye level. "How do you know?"

"Because I can see it through the glass," she replied, not taking her eyes off whatever she saw on the other side of the door.

Malkia and Chantum raced forward, just as Maltese and several Artemisians joined them. Peering through the glass, they could see a smaller luxurious vessel, large enough to fit a dozen or so comfortably. The door was jammed, and two Elvens crouched beside it working furiously on the damage.

"What are we waiting for?" Maltese barked, raising his weapon.

Malkia shoved Thora out of the way, praying Chantum moved as well, just as she heard and felt the explosion. Growling under her breath, she jumped up and whipped around to confront the imbecile. But, he had already stepped through the gaping breech, with his comrades at his heels.

Thora shot her an exasperated look and shook her head as Chantum asked if she was hurt. Two more Angels, along with Kelsey and Jayde came bursting through the thinning smoke, stopping when they saw the three of them standing in front of the destroyed door.

Malkia released an exaggerated sigh. Shaking her head in frustration, she beckoned for the others to follow her through the charred doorway.

The two Elvens were already dead and the door to the vessel had been pried open the rest of the way. The Artemisians were nowhere to be seen, which meant Hope could be in danger. Maltese didn't seem to have any sympathy, nor would he stop the onslaught until Dasco was executed.

A scream echoed within the small craft and Malkia sprinted across the threshold. As she entered into the main cabin, she raised her hands above her head and froze. Hope's feet dangled above the ground, with a large dagger pressed against her throat, and her wide eyes pleading for help.

FORTY-SEVEN

Elisa's Moment

DASCO HOVERED BEHIND Hope, with Maltese only a few feet away and his comrades slowly circling around them.

"I'll kill you both," Maltese muttered under his breath.

Malkia's head swiveled to look at the Artemisian. His face was bright red, and he gripped his weapon with such intensity that his knuckles were turning gray. He had officially become a liability.

Her feet moved her forward without thinking, and she slid her hand along Maltese's forearm. He flinched, but his stare remained firmly set on Dasco. "We're going to end this without taking Hope's life," she whispered, her breath hot on his skin. "Trust me, please."

His jaw muscles twitched and he peered down at her from the corner of his eye. "He's slaughtered dozens of my warriors tonight and sacrificed his own people, just for his selfish need to gain eternal life."

"Maltese, the Creators don't have eternal life." Her gaze shifted over to Dasco, smirking at the cowering Elven. "The Elven leader is mistaken and now he's the only fool in this ship."

"You lie," Dasco hissed, peering from behind the snow-white wisps of Hope's locks. "The scrolls foretell of their long lives."

"Exactly." She clapped her hands, startling the ones closest to her and making Dasco jump. Reaching out for Hope, she yanked the female

Elven from Dasco's grasp and cradled her in her arms as she led her away.

Maltese rushed forward and pressed his weapon against Dasco's skull. The Artemisian had the Elven's arm clasped tightly behind his back and a sudden memory of her abduction on Enyo galloped through her mind. The way Maltese was holding Dasco, along with the sneer plastered across his face, made her stomach swim with nausea.

He's not that creature. Similar, but not him. Malkia shook her head as Hope clung to her.

"Thank you," she whispered in Malkia's ear. "You're bravery will not be forgotten."

"What about Velem?" Malkia asked, stepping back and sweeping the area for her friend.

Hope's face fell. "Dasco executed him."

Malkia's lips drew back into a snarl as she whirled around to face the evil brute. "Take him outside. He deserves everything that he's about to receive."

Maltese dragged him from the ship and the others filed out behind him, following him back to the main exit. Backtracking through the cluster of pods, the nausea in Malkia's gut increased as she shifted around the dead and dying. She flew Hope over the massacre, finally ascending to the next floor and through the hole in the wall.

The stars twinkling greeted Malkia as she stepped from the ship and she gazed up into the sky. The moons had shifted while she'd been busy surviving and only two remained above as hues of fuchsia splintered along the mountain peaks, announcing morning was near. It had been a long night and just like her entire crew, she was exhausted.

Dasco was thrown to the ground. The Artemisians bound his hands and feet and the group surrounded him, spewing hateful comments at him. Pushing through the crowd, Malkia paused when she caught the eyes of the Elven, sorrow gripping her heart for all the ones who had perished during this journey. His death would mark a new beginning.

"What did you mean, the Creators don't possess eternal life?" Dasco asked, his eyes never leaving hers.

"Our Creators are just people," Malkia answered, walking along the edge of the crowd with her hands clasped behind her back. "You were deceived by my father, just like so many others. We, as the combined forces of Theia's Moons civilizations, stand here today and judge you for your undertakings." She gestured toward her team. "My mother." She grimaced from the memory of her mother's frostbitten hands. "Misty. Skye. Adelina. Tantiana." Her voice quivered. "Nearly the entire civilization of Artemis. Velem. Asha." Again her voice quivered and she twisted away from Dasco, staring into Ustarum's amber irises. "Where are Koleton and Damon?" She rose on her toes, searching the growing crowd.

"I thought they were with you," he said, gripping Malkia's shoulder. His eyes bored into hers. "You don't have to do this."

She took a sudden step back, heat rising in neck and staining her cheeks. "Do what? Kill him?" Her pulse quickened and she inhaled an unsteady breath. "Yes, I do. He's the reason so many have perished. Our lives will never be the same after this journey, but we'll be safer. Calmer." She whispered the last word, a deep sadness crushing her heart.

She whirled around and faced Dasco, a sudden fury exploding inside her. "All the awful things that have happened were because of you and my father. Everything. The deaths of so many innocents. The division between our civilizations. The war on Esaki that murdered my family and multiple others." With a large step forward, she rammed her finger into his chest. "My children," she growled. "You wanted to abduct my children. For what? Eternal life?" The laugh that rushed from her mouth was sinister, and almost evil, surprising even her. Drowning out the thought of her darkness, she drew back her arm, slamming her fist into the side of his jaw. "You egotistical, scheming coward." He crashed into the ground a few feet away, forcing the crowd behind him to skitter backward.

Unable to move his arms, he smacked the back of his skull on the dirt, driving a groan from his lips. "I'm just another one of your father's pawns," he muttered, rolling to his side and peering up at Malkia. "Don't you see that?"

She rolled her eyes. "It's too late for those manipulations," she spat at him. "You loved the control my father brought to your rule. Instead of doing what is right and just, you hoarded the power and allowed my father to murder and enslave innocents, whom you should've been protecting." Kicking dirt in his face, she leaned close. "Shame on you."

A hand circled her waist and she glanced over into Hope's rose irises. "It is done," the Elven whispered, a lavender aura surrounding her. "Now is the time for celebration and an opportunity to find our peace."

Malkia nodded and straightened, gripping Hope's hand. She nodded at Rashuta, as she walked through the crowd with the Elven, silently grateful he had survived. Without being asked, Chantum and Maltese hauled Dasco to his feet and with a magical binding cord, secured him to a nearby tree trunk.

The rest of the crowd spread out, indulging in the delicacies from the ship, along with the liquor that Dasco had specially stored for his journey.

Apollo and Cormac had returned from the forest, and Ustarum continued to heal the older man's injuries. While they were busy, Malkia sank to the dirt and closed her eyes. She dug her fingers into the soil and searched for the spirits of Theia. They greeted her with a bright warmth, radiating love and peace to every cell in her body and relinquishing the final piece of knowledge to her.

They whispered in her thoughts, showing her the truth of her existence. *The Illumanti know of your existence and their journey to meet you will not be halted. However, their mission is not one of destruction, as the Aletheians have claimed. Do not fear them, as they will deliver a message to you, revealing their true motives for their control over Theia and her moons.*

Malkia inhaled as the voice faded from her thoughts and the noise from the others tugged her from her reverie. "It is done," she repeated what Hope had said. "Finally, I will have peace."

Her eyes snapped open as screams filled the air. Jumping up, she searched the crowd for whatever had startled them, when her gaze fell on Dasco. Embedded in his chest was an Elven arrow and a crimson tint staining his tattered shirt. His jaw clenched as his wide eyes blinked several times. All around her chaos exploded, but she stood in place as she watched Dasco release his final breath, his mouth opening as his jaw relaxed. Exhaling slowly, Malkia took a step forward watching his head tilt forward and his body pull at the bindings that held him to the tree trunk. He was gone.

Twisting her head to follow the path of the arrow, her eyes swept along the tree line, settling on a lone Elven standing on a cliff above them. Her bow was at her side, and one hand rested over her heart as she stared at the man who'd enslaved her for over a year. Elisa stood proud, her snow-white hair tugged by the breeze.

Malkia raised her palm toward her friend. The others around her paused and lifted their heads, searching for whatever had caught Malkia's eye. Smiles and tears broke out as they lifted their palms toward the female Elven, saluting her for finishing the final deed of their mission.

FORTY-EIGHT

Shattered Heart

BEFORE SHE COULD focus on the search for Tantiana and the two men, Malkia returned to the ship and brought Zoe out of her stasis. It took more time than she had anticipated, but she was able to heal the child's head injury. Alexa and Ustarum assisted. It gave Zoe's mother the chance to learn the healing incantation and, because of their blood connection, the energy flowed easily.

"Thank you, Malkia," Alexa breathed, embracing her daughter.

Malkia patted her hand and raced from the room, eager to join the search.

"We haven't found Tantiana's body, and Damon and Koleton have vanished into thin air," Apollo told her, shaking his head, frustration crinkling his forehead. "It doesn't make sense. She would have connected with you if she was alive, right?"

Malkia nodded as she paced the floor on the bridge of her ship. "We need to return to that city and see if that man has abducted Damon and Koleton," she muttered, glancing over at Cormac who was piloting their vessel. The completion of their mission continued to invade her thoughts, and she struggled to believe the three who were missing would never be found.

The others had returned to their original meadow, alongside the beach, waiting for Malkia and her team to arrive. They'd agreed to discuss a diplomatic ending, where all species were equally granted rights to the moons and to the lands of Theia. The oceans belonged to the Whalians, Jarians, and Merpeople and no one felt the need to create contention with their cultures. The only one Malkia was still not entirely sure about were the Fenrir. Cormac had mentioned they were the wolfpeople, but she'd never had the time to ask him to elaborate.

The ship navigated around a lone boulder that rose from the edges of the ocean and pierced the clouds above. It was one of many that lined that shores as well as the depths of the oceans and Malkia's eyes examined this one as they circled it. Vegetation speckled its sides, appearing as lavender or crimson freckles, but for the most part it was a lone white rock.

Shaking her head, she focused on the terrain ahead, waiting to land near Dasco's buried body. The Elvens refused to give him a dignified releasing ritual, insisting that his remains should be used to seed new growth and life into Theia's vegetation. It was the least he could do.

Cormac settled the ship in the same field the Elven's vessel had rested earlier that morning. Racing down the cargo door, Malkia's eyes surveyed the meadow and the city beyond it, agitated by the thought of confronting the strange warlock again. She knew he was powerful enough to obliterate everyone, but skilled enough to hold back, even when they wreaked havoc on his peaceful retirement. Would he be as forgiving if she interrupted him again?

Trudging through the grass, a movement in her peripheral vision made her pause mid-stride. Pivoting to face the forested mountainside, she could see a pale hand gripping a rock as if whoever was connected to it was attempting to raise themselves. She glanced back at Cormac and Apollo, jabbing her finger at the person hidden by the grass. Their eyes followed her gesture.

She rose a few feet off the ground and caught a glimpse of red hair. "Koleton," she yelled. Darting over the grass, she landed next to the gasping man.

Blood was smeared across his face and as Malkia rolled him on his back, a gush of crimson seeped from his side, near his ribs. A stab wound was barely discernable, covered with the bloody mess. Pressing her hands into his chest, she channeled her light. She could hear Apollo and Cormac whispering a few feet away and her eyes fluttered open to look at them.

"Search the vegetation for Damon," she breathed. She squeezed her eyes shut. "They were together when they left the Elven ship."

"Ar-arrow," Koleton mumbled.

Malkia's eyes flew open as Koleton's hand wiped away a trickle of blood from his lips. "What did you say?"

He coughed, releasing another stream of blood from his mouth. The back of his hand was covered in the crimson liquid as it fell to the side of his face. Shaking her head, she poured more of her healing light into his body, refocusing on his injuries. The others would have to search for Damon on their own.

After several minutes she finally sensed the healing of his inner wounds. The warmth of her light twirled around her fingertips. She opened her eyes once more and stared down at the blinking eyes of her friend.

"How do you feel?" she asked, running her hand over his forehead.

"Like I was stabbed a few times," he grumbled, pressing his elbows into the soil and rising to a seated position. "But I do feel better."

"Where have you been?" Her gaze darted toward the trees, searching for Apollo and Cormac.

"Long story," he said, rising to his feet and pulling her up alongside him. "I know where Damon is."

Malkia followed him into the forest, running into Apollo and Cormac as they ventured farther into the darker area of the trees. Continuing through the thicket of the vegetation, a small cave came into view and Koleton ducked inside, waving for her to follow.

She knew it was useless the moment she entered the dark nook. Shining her light to the back of the cave, her eyes fell on her lover. An arrow had pierced deep within his chest, and his life had already drained from his body. Sinking to the ground, her entire body trembled as she choked on a rising sob. She gritted her teeth, fighting the desire to scream. Instead, she rested her cheek onto his chest and allowed the tears to come without restraint.

Reaching for his hand, she entwined her fingers with his stiff and cool ones, weeping even harder, and realizing she would never hear his voice again. She would never feel his gentle touch on her skin and would never possess a love as deep as the one she had for him.

Her entire soul shattered in that moment. She squeezed her eyes shut, drowning out the grief that was shredding her insides and hollowing her heart to a dark void.

She twirled her fingertips on the palm his hand, breathing in his lingering scent and burning his touch into her memory. It was all she could focus on—his skin pressed against her own and his warm lips devouring hers.

A hand curled around her shoulder and she snapped her eyes open to see Koleton kneeling next to her. Runnels of tears had cleansed his cheeks of the blood. Another sob shook her and she averted her face, burying it in Damon's chest.

She didn't know when Koleton left or when Mataya and her mother arrived, but when her mother's arms wrapped around her waist and drew her in, she didn't resist. Mataya settled next to her and ran her fingers through Malkia's hair, humming their mother's bedtime song. The sound soothed her and she clung to her mother, allowing the tune to rock her into a slumber.

FORTY-NINE

His Final Good-Bye

THE SECOND SUN was setting on the horizon, casting its final glow across the valley. Malkia quietly sat on the cliff above their ship. Her legs dangled over the edge and her gaze swept across the landscape, drawing in deep breaths and blinking back fresh tears.

Apollo had carried Damon's body back to the ship, where she had helped prepare it to be released to the stars. They had finished early and she had snuck away from the others, hoping to connect with Damon's spirit before the ceremony. But, she had felt nothing as she rested her palms against the soil of Theia. The spark of her energy seemed to have died right alongside the love of her life.

A hawk swooped down from the cliff above her and landed on a rock a few feet to her left. It twisted its head to the side, staring at her with unblinking obsidian eyes. She knew Jayde was watching her. It was the first time one of the hawks had been so close to her without Jayde nearby, and seeing it up close gave her a glimmer of hope. Its wings twitched, and she swore it winked at her, just like Damon had done so many times before. She swallowed hard and leaned closer.

Her breath caught in her throat as a familiar scent swept below her nose. The hawk spread its wings and launched into the air, leaving her wrapped in Damon's energy and light.

He was saying good-bye, and she pleaded silently for him to stay with her. Something unseen pressed against her cheeks and she held her breath for a moment, relishing in the softness of his lips. Her pulse slowed and she closed her eyes, inhaling his smell as if he was sitting right next to her.

When she opened her eyes several breaths later, he was gone. Kneading her achy shoulders with her fingers, she quietly vowed to keep going. Their children needed her to be strong and whole, able to guide their own grief as they dealt with the loss of their father.

The suns' light flickered and then disappeared entirely, leaving only the awe-striking hues of amethyst and fuchsia staining the farthest reaches of the western sky. She rose to stand on shaky legs and gave the valley one last look, before leaping off the cliff, just as the hawk had done. Landing in the field, she trudged through the grass toward the pyre and the newly built bier where Damon's body had been laid.

Koleton was standing next to it, his hand resting on the bier, with his eyes closed. As she drew closer, she could see the shimmer of tears streaming down his cheeks. Her hand slipped around the large man's waist and she leaned against him, staring at the shrouded corpse in front of her. He encircled her within his large arm and pulled her in close.

They stood in silence until the rest of their group circled Damon, and Mataya handed Zeke to Malkia. He needed to be fed. Settling on a boulder, a few feet away from the others, she nursed her baby, watching him snuggle in close to her. Damon had given her the best of himself and now she would continue for him and the other two children.

Her weary eyes looked over at her friends and family, staring at each face as they prepared the death ritual. They were all tired and grief-stricken, especially Landon, who had just had his father returned to him. As her gaze shifted across the crowd, a warmth of love filled her heart. They hadn't deserted her. In her weakest moments, they had held her up, refusing to let her quit. The battle with her father was over, and the Elvens who remained were now allies. The Creators were still on their way, but the worry of their reasons no longer created turmoil within her.

The lives that had been lost were more than she had feared, and her life would never be the same. However, she would live on. It was time to stop running and fighting, which was exactly what Damon had desired for his family.

She shifted Zeke over to the other breast. A flash of light caught her eye as she did so, and she focused on the buildings that stood across the meadow. A man in a robe emerged from the shadows and strolled toward them. However, this time the light that permeated the air around him was purple, just like her own.

A laugh bubbled from her mouth and she pressed her fingers against her lips, but Mataya heard her and turned to see what she had found amusing. Malkia nodded toward the man. Her sister swiveled around and took a step back as her eyes fell on the advancing stranger.

"He's coming," she yelled at the others. She pointed at the man and backed away even farther, pulling Esta and Landon with her.

The rest of the group whirled around and Cormac's arms flew out as he shielded Alyssa and Zoe from whatever the man would throw at them. The man chuckled and shook his head at their fear.

Malkia rose from her seat and handed Zeke to Alexa, who was guarding Branston from the stranger. "Don't worry," she whispered, clutching her friend's arm. "He's arrived to deliver a message. That's all." She waved at her people and strolled toward the man, meeting him a few yards away from the others.

"You didn't listen very well," he grumbled.

"Have we returned to your city?" she asked, settling her hands on her hips and squaring her shoulders at him.

He chuckled. "I consider this area a part of my city." He reached up and pulled the hood off his head, revealing the sagging skin of an elderly man. The webs of lines were etched across his face, deepening when he smiled. "I hear our people are on their way to meet you."

She nodded, pressing her lips together and waiting for him to continue.

"I can't say that I'm thrilled about their journey to our planet, but I believe when they arrive, you'll be able to reassure them of our worth as a civilization?" His purple eyes questioned her, clearly dubious of her abilities.

She cleared her throat, raising her eyebrows in question. "I don't believe you have anything to worry about. What's your message that you've been instructed to give me?"

"Who said I had a message?" he asked, a frown melting on his lips.

"The spirits of Theia," she replied, crossing her arms over her chest. "Are they incorrect?"

He stood silent, peering off to the side as if he was listening to someone. After a few minutes, he refocused on her, rubbing his palms together. "Yes, they're correct." He paused, studying her face. "I can see you have a soul to set free." He waved his hand toward the bier. "So, I'll stop delaying. The blood of the Illumanti flows through your veins, just like it does in mine. Because of this, your life will surpass many of your loved ones, however your three children are either half or pure and will have the chance to live just as long. But, our long lives aren't to be taken for granted. As you have seen with your partner, we can have our lives ripped away without notice."

"Where are you going with this?" she interrupted, annoyed by his disrespectful mention of Damon.

"Your partner was struck by the arrow of someone you have trusted in the past. A female," he whispered, his gaze falling to the ground.

Malkia's eyes narrowed and she took a step toward him as her hands balled up into fists. "Who was it?"

"All I can say is that she wasn't of Elven descent." He tilted his head to peer up at her. "But that isn't the only message I have been asked to bring you."

She gritted her teeth, a fury storming through her mind. "What is it?" she hissed.

"Let me be clear," he warned between clenched teeth. "I'm here to deliver these messages and that is all. Do not confuse my presence as a friendship that you can kick in the face because of your anger. Either you give me the respect I deserve, or I'll leave without finishing."

Closing her eyes, she drew in a few quick breaths, forcing away the bitterness that was swirling in her gut. Refocusing on him, she nodded. "I apologize. Please continue."

"Thank you," he retorted, tugging his hood back over his head. "The energy of this planet knows of your abilities. If there is conflict that needs to be eradicated, you'll be called to serve it. That is the curse of our lineage. Your advantages come with great responsibility, as Theia's spirit doesn't believe in giving without taking. I give this message to you as a warning, to be prepared. You might have hundreds of years of peace, but when that day arrives, you'll be expected to step up and do the bidding of this planet." She noticed his nearly hidden lips rise into a smile. "For this, I hand you the torch. You did well during your first journey, and it's been a pleasure to oversee your progress. Now I can see you're ready to be on your own."

Malkia opened her mouth, but nothing came out as she struggled to find the words. He didn't give her any chance to finish as he snapped his fingers and disappeared.

Shaking her head, she pivoted to see her friends and family watching with gaping jaws. She stepped over to them, a sudden realization rushing over her. He was the one who was with her in Domesca, when they discovered the deaths of the townspeople. His energy had been familiar, and she recognized it from when she was a small child. Searching her memory, she recalled several times over her lifetime when she sensed his presence, but believed it was just the energy of the atmosphere. And the drawings in the pyramid on Hemera had been his work. Which meant, he had his own pyramid, and someday, she would be called to do the same for another.

The group around her didn't ask any questions, and she silently thanked them for giving her time to think. Mataya handed her the torch and she held it over Damon's body, touching the spot in between his eyes with her fingertips. Sliding her fingers down to his heart, she pressed them into his chest and quietly whispered farewell.

The fire grew quickly and she stepped back, holding onto Landon's and Esta's hands. The group was quiet as the watched the flames engulf the entire bier. Malkia allowed the children to stay for the blessing upon his soul, and the incantation to hasten the process. Alexa tugged them indoors after that was complete, leaving Malkia, Apollo, Mataya, and Koleton.

The embers slowly died down and Malkia watched as the wind blew

Damon's ashes across the meadow and into the forest. Nothing would ever fill the void she could sense within her heart, but at least she knew he was at peace and flying with the Gods and Angels above. Maybe someday the Aletheians would return and allow her to see him again.

She still had so many questions for those Light Beings.

FIFTY

Peace

MALKIA'S TOES SKIMMED lightly across the ocean surf. Shivering from the water splashing across her legs, she leaned back on her hands, pressing them against the rocky path she had found not far from their new home.

She watched as a Whalian dove into the sea and resurfaced a few moments later. The first sun had just risen, scattering its auburn light across the glistening, aqua ocean, and streaming brightly upon her newly built town.

It had been twenty days since Damon's death ritual. Almost everyone had departed from the planet, returning to their homes or searching for new ones. Many of the Artemisians had remained, as had Elisa and her family. Their town grew alongside the old city that had contained the pyramid. In the first few days they had reconstructed some of the old buildings, while tearing down many others. It was disappointing that the small vessels Malkia had wanted to break into were all useless, but their parts were being used to build new ones, and a lingering excitement at seeing the finished result was a tightness in her belly.

Somehow, they had managed to unite and rebuild their lives.

Kelsey had disappeared, stealing one of the Elven fighter ships. It was obvious that she was the one who had murdered Damon and Malkia believed it was her revenge for Dario's death. Despite Malkia's desire to avenge Damon's death, the toxicity from her hatred for the woman wasn't gaining her any ground on finding peace. She was working on forgiveness instead.

She wanted to explore their new world and had met a few of the Whalians, while the Merpeople kept their distance. The Jarians didn't exist on this planet or at least nowhere near their new home.

And Tantiana. They had found her lying in the ocean, her head cradled in a deep groove of sand. She had survived. Although Malkia spent hours giving her the healing light she required. Tantiana remained weak for several days, and Malkia had needed a few more days to recover after the healing session. All three dragons had decided to remain on Theia, but they wanted more of their kind to eventually be allowed to migrate from Hemera.

At the sound of unsteady footsteps drawing near, she turned and peered at Cormac. He was stepping down the row of rocks, holding his hand over his brow to shield his eyes from the morning sunlight. He paused right behind her, drawing a deep breath.

"Your habit of wandering off, is beyond me," he grumbled, shaking his head. He leaned over and sank down next to her, gripping the wet rock so he wouldn't tumble into the water. "What has brought you down here again?"

"Just thinking," she replied, wrapping her arm around his and holding him steady. "It's a great spot to meditate and stay connected with the elements."

"You know I worry about you." His face twisted toward her, his smoky gray eyes locking with her own. He reached a hand over and cupped her chin within it. "You've been so quiet lately. It's difficult to deal with the passing of a loved one, as you know all too well. But, I hope you realize we'll remain with you for as long as we can."

She patted his knee and smiled. "I don't expect anyone to stay just to keep me company. If the warlock is correct, I could be called off at any moment. Then what?"

"We would stay with your children," he said, reminding her of their delicate ages. "And I'm sure many of us would choose to journey with you. We won't desert you."

"I appreciate that," she murmured, gazing back out into the vast ocean. The sky was now peppered with white clouds, spreading out in both directions.

He sat quietly next to her for several minutes. As the second sun rose over the horizon, Malkia floated from her seated position and settled on her feet. Clutching the man's arm, she pulled him up next to her and helped him climb over the rocks, guiding him to more sturdy footing.

"Will you tell me about the Fenrir species?" she asked, linking arms with him.

He nodded as he glanced down at her. "As you know, they're a breed of humans that have several characteristics of the wolf." His other hand moved across his body and patted the top of her hand. "How they acquired the combined traits remains a mystery, and might be something we look into at some point. The ones that were members of Damon's team back on Esaki were from a clan called the Forsaken. Their mother was a tyrant and murdered their father, which was when she made alliances with Thane."

"How did you learn all of this?" she asked, flicking away an insect from her hand.

"Back on Esaki, one of the other clans visited Domesca after you left for Thalia the first time," he answered, kicking a stone from the middle of their path. Malkia watched as it struck another larger stone and broke in two pieces, landing on the soil below with a soft thud. "We told them about the four from Damon's crew and they knew who we were talking about. Their mother had a history of violence amongst the clans and had nearly eliminated every member of the Forsaken, before she was banished from Esaki."

"Were her four boys left alone on Esaki?" Her brows furrowed as she peered up at Cormac.

He nodded. "Their mother left them for many years, only returning when she'd made an agreement with your father. Those four Fenrirs didn't find Damon by accident."

"I figured as much. We were pawns in my father's ruthless game. He was moving around pieces, without following any rules." She sighed and leaned her cheek against Cormac's arm. "We've come so far and lost so many. I look forward to the day when tragedy is no longer on my radar."

"Me too, my darling. Me too." A wide smile crinkled his cheeks, and he pointed. "Look who found us."

Malkia laughed at the blonde girl skipping down the pathway, her own light blossoming around her. Esta had been learning how to control her powers and was growing in her telepathy every day. However, teaching her restraint from invading others unwilling thoughts, was a continued struggle that frustrated both parties. But despite all of that, Malkia hoped her daughter would never have to use her telepathy for anything but fun.

Out of nowhere, a red-bearded man hurdled onto the path right behind Esta and the child screamed, sprinting away from him and throwing herself into Malkia's arms. Koleton threw his head back and howled like a wolf. Rolling her eyes, Malkia kissed the top of Esta's head and set her back onto her feet.

"It appears as if you thought you had Koleton fooled, once again." Malkia chuckled at Esta's wide eyes and Koleton's mischievous grin.

"I thought I'd lost him," she muttered, glaring up at the man. "How did you find me?"

"That's for me to know and you to maybe find out," he teased, dancing around the path like a chicken and swooping Esta up into his arms. Setting her on his shoulders, he skipped back up the path, leaving Cormac and Malkia behind. Esta shrieked with delight as she held on for dear life.

They reached their town not long after Koleton and Esta had returned. Malkia waved good-bye to Cormac and stepped into her small home. Wrapping her arms around Landon, she planted a kiss on top of his head, before picking up Zeke from his carrier.

"You lost Esta," she told the young boy, winking at him.

"She's impossible," he grumbled, shaking his head. He sank onto a wood stump and picked up a container filled with water. Gulping down a mouthful, he watched Malkia tidy up their cramped kitchen.

"Yes, she is," Malkia spoke from behind one of the walls. "Let's clean up and meet everyone at the meal house for breakfast. How does that sound?"

"Yippee!" Landon exclaimed, bouncing up from his perch. "I haven't seen Branston in two days."

A few minutes later, they were leaving the house and Malkia smiled as Landon raced toward the large building. She inhaled the sweet scent of freshly baked bread and her grin widened, knowing her mother and a few of her Artemisian friends were baking. They had been scouring the land, searching for new items to include in the recipes and continued to delight everyone with warm meals.

Malkia made her way up the steps, pausing just inside the doorframe and smiling at all her friends and family. Esta was sandwiched between Zoe and Koleton, and Landon had already found Branston as they raced to the food line. Her mother was in the cooking area, laughing with Ustarum and Rashuta, while Mataya spoke quietly with Elisa on a table nearby their mother. The eating hall was bustling with laughter and talk, sending a warmth of affection rushing over skin.

She peered down at Zeke, whose sapphire irises were curiously watching her every move. His light had not returned after Damon's death, but Malkia could sense it within him, waiting for that moment he would need to protect his loved ones. Holding him up in the air, she cooed at him, and he gave her a crooked smile of delight. She planted a kiss on his button nose and held him up to her shoulder. Strolling into the room, she smiled at her people, delighted with the happiness they had finally found.

Epilogue

MALKIA'S EYES FLUTTERED open. The wall across from her bed danced with the shadows of the outside vegetation, drawing a similar, but distant memory from her mind. Her life on Esaki seemed like another lifetime. But it was where the beginning of her new life began, tossing her into a conflict that united her with Damon, and returned Esta to her arms.

She shifted under her warm covers, turning to her side and inhaling deeply. It was the anniversary of Damon's death. Two years had passed since she said good-bye. The days had flown by, but not one had come to an end without her thoughts turning to him. She missed him more today than the day she'd lost him.

Closing her weary eyes for a moment, she opened them again just as a bright beam of light illuminated in her window and then quickly disappeared. Bounding out of bed, her heart rammed against her chest as she slid over to the window and peeked outdoors. She knew who it was and why they were here. It was time to meet them in the meadow at the edge of the warlock's city.

She yanked on a pair of black pants, followed with a long-sleeve black shirt. Pulling her belt with the sheaths and daggers off a top shelf in her room, she secured it around her waist, followed with the laser weapon that Apollo insisted she never leave without. Her hair was matted to one side of her head and she chuckled at her reflection in the mirror. A few minutes of brushing out the knots of her waist long hair, followed with a quick braid, and she was ready to go.

Tiptoeing down the first flight of stairs, she knocked softly on Mataya's door. She heard a grunt slide out from underneath the door and took that as an invitation to enter. Crossing over the floor, she sank down to her sister's bed and patted her on the shoulder. Mataya's half opened eyes greeted her as she twisted around.

"Where are you going?" she mumbled, propping herself up on her elbows. "It's the middle of the night." Her gaze shifted to the twilight glistening from the view outside her window.

"They're here," Malkia whispered. She sighed and squeezed Mataya's wrist. "I don't think I'll be long, but I'm still not positive about their motives. I need you to protect the children at all costs. Will you please have Ustarum, Mom, and any others help you ward this area from all outsiders while I'm away?"

"Of course." Mataya was now sitting up straight, her eyes wide as a yawn interrupted her speech. She held up a hand as Malkia rose from the bed. "How will I know you're okay?"

"I'll channel you as soon as I can." She knew this day would arrive, but having two years of peace made it difficult to face a possible new conflict. "I love you. Please do whatever it takes to keep my babies safe."

"I will. You know I would die for them." Her sister jumped out of bed and wrapped her arms around Malkia. "May Theia's light shine within you today and keep you protected within her arms," Mataya whispered in Malkia's ear.

"Thank you," Malkia murmured, squeezing her sister tightly. "I'll see you soon."

Without another word, she rushed from the room, flying down two more flights of stairs. Outside she drew in a deep breath of the clean, crisp night air. Her eyes rolled to the heavens and focused on the Esaki moon shining high in the sky, gifting her with renewed strength.

Her thoughts turned to the Aletheians as she strolled through her small city. They hadn't appeared in over two years and although her connection with the energy of the planet had only expanded, she sensed a withdrawal within herself that she didn't understand. It seemed as if the Beings had created a void within her, only they could fill. But despite her best efforts to communicate with them, they eluded her, leaving her to navigate through the end of her father's war on her own.

The warlock, who'd given her the warning, had also disappeared without a trace. She often wondered how long he'd been alone, waiting for the one to take his place. Now she was left to protect the moons of Theia and every day she questioned her ability to keep all the people of their system united and at peace.

She bounded into the air and flew to the shore. The first cylindrical stone structure rose into view and she headed toward it. On the lower edge, she could see the entry, and she glided inside, landing on the balls of her feet and stepping inward. A Whalian guard shifted and waved at her. She nodded in recognition, moving into the open space of the core and rushing up the stairs to the leader of the local Whalian population.

The door swept open, revealing the illumination of the flutter flies and a slightly sloped floor that was filled with the ocean water. A large body rose with a splash and Nikor twisted to face her.

"They've arrived," Malkia announced, stepping in only a foot, avoiding the water from Nikor's sleeping quarters.

"Are you positive?" the female Whalian asked, swimming into the light of the flies as she peered over at Malkia.

Malkia nodded, tapping her foot in the inch deep water below her. "I agreed to warn you of their presence. Do whatever you need to keep your people safe, but I don't believe you have anything to worry about. If they wanted to end our existence, I don't think they would take the time to stop and have a discussion."

"Agreed," Nikor replied. The Whalian yawned wide, rolling over on her back and setting her folded arms behind her head. "I wish you the best, pale human. Hopefully, they don't find you as unpleasant looking as we do."

Malkia rolled her eyes as Nikor burst into laughter, followed by a light snoring. *What a peculiar species.* Sprinting down the stairs, she burst outside and a few minutes later was back in the air, gliding a few feet above the shore and aiming for the mountain terrain off on the horizon.

The top of a silver vessel caught her eye and as she drew closer to the meadow, the massive ship loomed above her, double the size of the Elven craft. Her heart fell into her stomach as her eyes swept over to the forest. The memory of Damon inside the cave flashed through her mind. This place was a graveyard to her.

She landed in the field, her palms brushing up against the dew dropped blossoms waving ever so slightly with the breeze. Examining the area near the ship, she realized she was all alone.

Taking a few steps toward the ship, the cargo door suddenly groaned and cracked open, slowly sliding wider to reveal its occupants.

Malkia watched with her arms crossed over her chest, ignoring the fear dancing through her chest.

At first, only darkness greeted her, but as her eyes adjusted she noticed movement inside the ship. Seconds later, several personages stepped down the ramp. Her pulse quickened as they shifted into the light, revealing three females and two males, and all appeared human. Smiles were plastered across their faces and they quickly advanced on her position.

Glancing up at the vessel, Malkia wondered how many more people were hidden away behind its walls. She licked her lips, allowing her gaze to return to the individuals strolling toward her. Their features were smooth and flawless, with wide eyes that seemed familiar. Their confidence was unnerving.

A woman with long, white hair was leading the delegation. Her sapphire eyes sparkled in the moonlight and her red lips were as dark as the blood running through Malkia's veins. As she neared Malkia's position, she slowed her walk and held out her hand.

"Hello, Malkia," she spoke, her tone warm and inviting, reminding Malkia of her mother. "My name is Taryn." Her snow-white hair hung over her shoulders, curling as it flowed across her chest and shoulders.

Malkia reached forward and gripped Taryn's wrist, but was taken back when the woman shook her head and slid her hand down, clutching Malkia's hand. Taryn grinned and winked, slightly shaking Malkia's hand up and down, before releasing it.

The others flanked Taryn's sides, halting a half step behind her. "Do you know why we are here?" Taryn asked, entwining her fingers and resting her hands against her abdomen.

"You're here to ensure your experiments are not destroyed," Malkia replied, a new strength rising within her gut, although her hands continued to shake.

Taryn chuckled, glancing over at the two men, who smiled in return. "Yes. We like to keep tabs on the worlds we have populated, especially when they evolve to possess the abilities that you have. Each new Chosen Heir that is born seems to be more powerful than the last, and it pleases our Commander when she learns of our success."

"I was told you didn't want our species to evolve," Malkia said, swiveling her foot in the soil below. "The Aletheians didn't want you to return and my grandparents feared that you would slaughter everyone on the moons of Theia if you did." She shook her head, a blush rising in her cheeks. "The stories I've heard have contradicted one another, and I would love to hear the truth from your own lips. Are you here to hurt or eradicate us?"

The tall brunette standing next to Taryn cleared her throat. Taryn held up her hand and halted anything the woman was about to say. "We are only here to observe," Taryn replied, her eyes narrowing slightly. "But we do have a request. One that is directly from our Commander."

"And what is that?" Malkia asked.

"Will you accompany us back to Earth?" Taryn stepped forward, gripping Malkia's wrist fervently. "Our need for Illumanti with advance powers on our planet has doubled in the past decade. What do you say?"

Malkia shook her head, shaking her wrist to release herself from Taryn's grasp, but her fingers only tightened. "But my children—."

"You may bring the infant, as his pureblood will be accepted within our society. The other two must remain here," Taryn insisted, tugging Malkia closer to her. "We won't harm anyone on your moons, or this planet. However, we insist on your agreement to our request."

"*No*," Malkia snapped, yanking her arm back.

Taryn released her, but moved in closer, only leaving a few inches of space between the two women. "An unwise move," Taryn hissed.

"Why?" Malkia barked, squaring her shoulders at the woman. "Are you telling me it wasn't a request, but an order?"

"Malkia, these moons have an interesting history, and the evolution that has taken place won't be erased. If you want to keep everyone safe, while learning about these moons, I recommend you don't turn down our offer," Taryn replied. She stepped back, once more aligned with the others. "We aren't your enemy."

Shaking her head, Malkia swept a few wisps of hair out of her face, scowling at the unblemished and perfect face of the woman in front of her. The two men suddenly sprang forward, each of them gripping one of her arms. Malkia's light erupted from her body, fizzling out as the other two women muttered intangible words under their breath.

"*I'm not leaving my people,*" Malkia screamed, as the men dragged her toward the ship. She hissed between bared teeth. "*Let me go.*"

The men chuckled. Malkia kicked one of them in the side of his leg, but his iron grip only tightened. The three women followed closely behind, whispering under their breath and suppressing her powers as they neared the cargo ramp to the vessel.

Their direct surroundings suddenly shone with an intense light, and the men released her to shield their eyes with their arms. She sprinted away, seeing the Aletheians. Rushing into the mix of them, she peered up at their dazzling faces and smiled.

"*The Chosen Heir is never be removed from this planet, unless there is another to take her place,*" a male Aletheian bellowed over the cowering Illumanti. "Why did you believe you could break the rules and we wouldn't intervene?"

Taryn rose into a standing position and approached, her eyes flitting over to Malkia and back up to the Aletheian. "You have the infant. We would allow him to remain here for your use."

"*No*," the Aletheian snapped. "We are *not* fools. Why are you removing her from Theia?"

One of the men stepped forward, shoving Taryn back and surprising the woman with his sudden movement. "Malkia has inherited a unique blend of powers that none of our kind has ever witnessed. If we're able to duplicate her genetic sequence, we hope to press forward in our stagnated evolution."

The Aletheian twisted to peer down at Malkia. "Do you wish to accompany these people to become their lab rodent?"

She suppressed a laugh at his reference. Instead she shook her head. "I want them to leave and never return."

"There's your answer, and you'll respect it," the Aletheian ordered, twisting back to face him. "This is our star system to protect and that includes all the life that flourishes within it. Your Commander agreed to leave it alone."

"That was before you broke the agreement and brought Malkia to Earth without permission," the brunette woman spoke up, shifting around Taryn and standing next to the man. "You should never have crossed the boundaries."

"We eliminated the threat to your society and your Commander, once more, agreed to call it even," the same Aletheian's voice roared over them. "I won't tolerate your manipulations. Return to your ship and depart from this star system completely. If Malkia decides to reach out to you that will be her choice, but you are to never threaten her or her people again."

The man and woman nodded, stumbling backward a few feet. The third woman rose the ground, her smile spreading across her face as she dodged the others and glided up to the Aletheian. "Hello, my friend." She bowed toward the Aletheian, revealing a black streak of hair running through her snow-white locks. "We mean your star system no harm." Her gaze landed on Malkia and she beckoned for her to draw near. "This was only a test and nothing else. I apologize for our brash ways, but we required your full loyalty to the species of Theia. Both the Aletheians and yours." She curled her hand over Malkia's shoulder. "Do you know who I am?"

"The Illumanti Commander?" Malkia whispered, uncertain of her perception.

"Such a senseless title," the woman replied, her sapphire irises sparkling with amusement. "No need for formalities as you, my dear friend, are part of my family."

"What do you mean?" Malkia asked, glancing over Taryn's shoulder and noticing the other four had returned to a lined formation several feet behind the woman.

"Your grandparents are my mother and father, making you my niece," the woman replied, sweeping her hair behind her shoulders.

Malkia's brow furrowed as her muscles tensed. "They would've told me this. You're lying."

"No, I'm not. And my parents are not aware of all my travels." She pursed her lips and glanced up at the receding Aletheians. "My name is Alenka. When I learned of your heritage, I began my journey to your home, immediately, as you're the first from our family who has been chosen. The Aletheians warned you of my coming, but what they didn't tell you was that I was already on my way. Just like so many others, they manipulated the situation for their own cause."

"And are you doing the same thing, in this very moment?" Malkia questioned, eyeing the woman with freezing contempt.

"I can understand your mistrust," Alenka acknowledged, holding her hands against her chest. "We've manipulated you, forced you into a battle that you didn't want anything to do with, and giving you nothing but heartache along the journey. You've lost more than you've gained, and I recognize the pain in your eyes." Her expression softened. "We won't hurt you. And our motives were only to discover how loyal you truly were to your people."

Malkia exhaled loudly, finally relaxing just enough to notice the first sun was beginning to rise. "Why the test? You could've just asked." Her eyes darted over to the vessel and back to Alenka.

"Devotion and a love for a one's people requires more than a word," Alenka explained, holding her palm up between them. "Your light is their protection." A white spark burst from the woman's hand, dancing between the two of them.

"Everything you've endured, has occurred to allow your growth, so you're capable of leading with an open heart. I can see you are still guarded, but I believe in time you will instantly recognize an enemy. Your daughter already has this ability, but you do possess it as well. Honor that gift, as its not to be abused. Whatever you take from others must be returned tenfold to the energy of the universe." She paused, reaching forward and running her thumb across Malkia's cheek. "My advice to you, learn how to utilize all your abilities, even the ones that lie dormant within you."

Malkia recognized the glimmer of affection in Alenka's eyes. It was the same that her mother had possessed. She pressed her fingers to her lips and nodded.

Alenka handed her a bracelet with a stone in its central setting. "When the time is right, I would like you to join me in the travels of our universe, even if it's hundreds of years from now. But only once you know your duty to this planet and her moons has been fulfilled. Twist the top of the stone until it opens. Inside lies a button. Press it and I'll return for you." She smiled warmly. "This stone will also protect your light from being extinguished. Serums, nor magic will be able to take it as long as you wear it."

Malkia wrapped her fingers tightly around the bracelet. "What do I do now?" she asked, suddenly not wanting Alenka to leave her.

"Lead your people. Be their beacon of hope and guide them into the next step of your evolution." Alenka wrapped her arms around Malkia's shoulders, tugging her into a warm embrace. She kissed her niece's cheek and pressed her forehead against Malkia's. "Until we meet again."

Alenka stepped away, waving for the others to follow. They boarded their ship and closed the door. Sunlight suddenly poured into the valley, illuminating a brilliant lilac and pink against the jagged rocks and broken buildings. Kissing the vessel, colors burst across the shiny metal, greeting the morning with a radiant glow.

Malkia shielded her eyes and sprinted away from the ship, surrounding herself with her light to watch it ascend. As it disappeared from sight, it left a trail of smoke in its wake. With breath paused in her lungs, she looked down at the bracelet and secured it to her wrist.

Exhaling slowly, she rose into the air and flew to the ocean shore, settling ankle deep into the sparkling water and sitting in the wet sand. Her gaze darted across the horizon, releasing a deep sigh of relief as she watched her dragons swoop down from the sky, skimming just above the waves.

It's over, she thought. A soft smile rose on her lips and she threw her arms into the air, laughing as she fell backward, landing with a splash against the water and soft sand. She breathed in her newfound freedom and peace, finally releasing the fear that had consumed her mind and heart for far too long.